MY FAVORITE HOLIDATE

LAUREN BLAKELY

COPYRIGHT

ABOUT THE BOOK

Wanted: one hot billionaire to pose as my Christmas boyfriend. Must be willing to make my cheating ex jealous when you kiss me under the mistletoe at all the holiday parties. Bonus points if you make him cry.

To my surprise my billionaire boss is more than up for the challenge of coming down the chimney as my holiday boyfriend. The sexy single dad desperately needs a plus one at a Christmas Eve wedding, where he's the best man and I'm the maid of honor.

And since my ex is in the wedding party too, my boss and I team up as a pair of insta-lovebirds for the holiday season, including during the annual week-long Christmas competition leading up to the snowy destination wedding.

. . .

But soon staying up late to string the best popcorn balls ever turns into a scorching night in his arms where the chestnuts aren't the only thing roasting on the open fire.

Can all these winter wonderland nights seeking revenge turn into the real thing when we return to the office? Or are we destined to go the way of a Christmas tree on New Year's?

DID YOU KNOW?

To be the first to find out when all of my upcoming books go live click here!

PRO TIP: Add lauren@laurenblakely.com to your contacts before signing up to make sure the emails go to your inbox!

Did you know this book is also available in audio and paperback on all major retailers? Go to my website for links!

MY FAVORITE HOLIDATE

By Lauren Blakely

A Standalone Holiday Romance

This book is dedicated to anyone who ever wanted to bang under a Christmas tree.

1

EGGNOG SEASON

Fable

The thing about big Thanksgiving dinners is you can never be certain who's playing with your foot under the table.

Sure, I'm hoping my boyfriend Brady's the one dragging a foot against my fuzzy sock. That'd be better than Uncle Rick or my broody cousin Troy. But Brady's never played footsie with me before. Fine by me. Footsie is not my jam. Didn't think it was his either.

You learn something new every day, especially when you've only been dating for four months. Four mostly good months that have seen us spend lots of time with each other, each other's families and each other's friends.

I don't want to encourage foot play, though, so I just give my guy a faint smile. Then I nod to the head of the table, a reminder for him to pay attention since my boss, the host of this motley crew feast, is clearing his throat.

Brady just wiggles his blond brows like he didn't notice my silent admonition.

The footsie stops when Wilder lifts his tumbler of single-malt scotch, the glass catching the twinkling reflection of the blue-and-white string of lights flashing on the Christmas tree standing tall and proud in the open living room. "I want to thank you all for coming to this annual Thanksgiving dinner my dear aunt Bibi and I like to throw," Wilder says, then gestures affectionately to a faux leather chair in the living room where Bibi is conked out, tortoiseshell glasses in her hand, snoring loudly in front of the roaring fireplace. "And for participating in her new tradition this year—the Turkey Escape Room," Wilder says with an amused grin.

There's a collective groan at the table. Bibi's Turkey Escape Room in the basement was, admittedly, a little macabre.

"And now that we're heading into the Christmas season, provided you have no prior commitments and want to join us, I'd like to personally invite everyone to the Evergreen Falls Annual Best in Snow Winter Games Competition for a few fun-filled days before Christmas."

Iris, the perky blonde caterer sitting next to me, gasps in excitement. "Wow! That sounds amazing!"

It's cute that she's so into the festivities, especially since she only sat at the table a minute ago at Brady's invitation. He insisted she join us for the toast, having done such a great job with the meal.

"Let's do it," Brady calls out with a loud whoop before he looks at me, fire in his eyes. "And we are going to dominate, babe."

No surprise there. Brady and I are board game aficionados, and he has an intensely competitive streak.

But I'm not sure we ought to be throwing down in front of the host. Wilder, a cool, confident, thoroughly unflappable football team owner and real estate magnate, might know a thing or two about winning. Also, I don't even know if it works in my calendar to go to Evergreen Falls for Christmas. Or if I want to spend Christmas with my boss.

"I'm sure we'd have a great time at Wilder and Bibi's event," I say. That's diplomatic yet still fun—but also hypothetical.

"Love a good contest," Wilder says to Brady, his tone welcoming, except...

Is that Wilder's media smile? Like he's humoring Brady? I linger for a second on Wilder's expression. Seems like he's studying Brady, actually, trying to figure something out.

"As I was saying," Wilder continues, his voice like rich brandy, "Bibi and I would love to host all of you for the games at my cabins outside of Tahoe."

I smile at the euphemism. Calling his luxury resort just outside the fanciest area of Lake Tahoe a cabin is like calling a yacht a rowboat. Wilder has one of those too—a yacht—and the hundred-footer is definitely no dinghy.

Wilder must pick up on my amusement since he gives a no-big-deal shrug. "Technically, it *is* a cabin, Fable."

Brady laughs boisterously. "Dude, I can't wait to see your *technical cabin.*"

I cringe a little inside. Did he seriously call my boss *dude*? Wilder's not a dude or a bro.

I had doubts about bringing Brady along to this friendsgiving. He can be a bit of a Golden Retriever, sometimes—eagerly dropping the slobbery tennis ball into people's laps whether it's time for fetch or not. But the table is full of friends and family, mine and his, and at least he hasn't pitched my boss on the idea of being his stockbroker. So far, so good.

Wilder raises his glass in his snoozing aunt's direction. "Bibi tells me the Christmas Committee at Evergreen Falls has planned some extra-fun events this year, so I hope you'll all be there, full of holiday cheer and competitive spirit." He takes a wry pause. "Though, I believe her words were, ahem, *find the best snowball throwers and Christmas tree decorators in the bunch. Or else.*"

His obvious affection for his aunt is endearing.

Iris must think so. She raises her wineglass high. "You're all going to have such a great time. I love all things Christmas. I'm just a girl who's ready for eggnog season."

Brady sighs dreamily, as if picturing all things eggnog too. When...gross.

"Not me," I say. "Eggnog should be abolished."

Brady tilts his head my way. "You don't like eggnog?"

"Nope."

He strokes his chin. "Huh. I had no idea."

"And candy canes should only come in peppermint," Wilder puts in dryly. "No exceptions."

"No one wants a watermelon candy cane," I agree. Brady squints at me as if I'm some kind of enigma, but how often does the subject of eggnog or the chance to extoll mint's praises come up in conversation naturally? It's not like I handed him a list of secrets, detestations, and other fun facts about me when we got together. That's not my style.

The Thanksgiving table descends into a debate about the merits of candy canes, eggnog, and Christmas cookies. My sister Charlotte and her boyfriend, Leo, vote for gingerbread (also gross). Wilder's sister declares Yule logs underrated (true, but they need a brand makeover because...*that name).* And Cousin Troy says in a dead voice that he likes to lick candy canes into a sharp point (and, note to self, avoid that teenager after dark).

Eventually, the younger children ask if they can play video games before dessert, and at Wilder's, "Of course," a herd of kids thunders off to the game room.

The rest of us push away from the table, and I glance at the remains of the holiday meal—a polished-off bowl of rosemary green beans, a dish of homemade cranberry sauce, a to-die-for side of sauteed brussels sprouts, and the carcass of a big bird who definitely didn't escape any rooms.

Iris gets to her feet and smooths her hands down her chef's jacket. "I better return to dish duty. Thank you for letting me be included in the toast. That was so generous of you, Mr. Blaine," Iris says to Wilder, all cheery and bright, sounding like the spirit of Christmas herself.

"Call me Wilder," he says. "And your food was fantastic. I'll help with the dishes."

"Oh, please. You should relax," she tells him.

Since I have the spirit of a hard-working elf, I offer to pitch in. There's an art to stacking a dishwasher, and as an art girl, I've mastered it. "I'll join you, Iris. My dishwasher-stacking skills are unparalleled."

Wilder strides around the table, a challenging look in his clever green eyes. "But you haven't seen mine."

The boss wants to have a dishwasher-stacking competition? Bring it on. "Let the winter games begin early."

"Well, who am I to say no?" Iris says generously. "I appreciate the extra hands so much." She heads to the kitchen with a bounce in her step, and I follow, balancing an armful of teetering plates.

Brady swoops in next with the turkey platter, dropping a quick kiss on my cheek once I set the dishes on the counter. "I need to go wrap a gift for Bibi, babe. An early Christmas present to say thanks for tonight."

"That was thoughtful of you," I say. "She has a wrapping room down on the garden level. Wilder mentioned it earlier. Last room on the right."

"I know," Brady says, then whispers, "See? And you were worried I'd embarrass you."

"I was not," I protest mildly. Fine, maybe I was a little. But I never said that to him.

"You were," he goads, poking my ribs a bit too hard. "You think I'm too friendly. Too outgoing. But I did good. Right, babe?"

"Of course." I don't want Brady to think otherwise. He was pretty well-behaved.

He lets go of me, then flashes his salesman grin at Wilder. "And I'd love to talk to you sometime soon about your portfolio."

Ugh. He did pitch him, after all.

Wilder shoots him a curious look, arching a brow, before he says, "Noted."

And *I* note *that*. *Noted*, as in *heard it, not going to agree, but not being a dick about it because I'm classy.*

Brady nods, then scurries off.

Wilder and I set to work on dishes as the other guests clear the table. He rinses, and I stack. "Prepare to be dazzled," I say, showing off my extraordinary plate placement. "Look at how they line up just so. Be amazed at the perfect space ratio between the dinner plates and the salad bowls."

From his spot at the sink, with the cuffs on his tailored

custom-made dress shirt rolled up, he surveys my handiwork. "I'd expect nothing less from my top designer."

I preen a little. I landed the plum job a couple years ago, designing merch—like T-shirts and jewelry—for his big-game-winning football team, and I love it. "Exactly. I told you—unparalleled."

His eyes say *not so fast*. "Except...the bowls are traditionally the most challenging."

"Please. I am an architect of bowls."

He turns off the faucet, joins me at the machine, and proceeds to adjust a bowl here and a bowl there, creating room for two more. "Damn," I say with a whistle. "I guess there's a reason you're a successful business owner."

He laughs. "Yes, exactly."

We spend some more time straightening up the kitchen. I shoo my sister and Leo—who's also Wilder's best friend—out to the living room so they can relax before the dessert course.

Hmm. Not sure what happened to Iris. She was quite keen on dish duty before we got started. Come to think of it, I haven't seen her in the kitchen post-dinner at all.

She's probably cleaning up the table.

Soon, we're finished. I glance at the clock, then around the kitchen, then into the dining room. "Where's Brady? Seems to be taking a while to wrap the gift."

Before Wilder can answer, Bibi barks, "Who's ready for dessert? I had a terrible dream that someone ate all the pies without me, so we'd better get to it. Dreams can come true, you know."

"I guess someone woke up hungry," I whisper.

"Sugar plum fairies were probably dancing in her head," Wilder says, then checks his watch like he's keeping time in a sporting event. "I need to go help Leo... with a thing."

A thing? What thing?

He sounds a little evasive. But my sister's beau is a venture capitalist, and Wilder's a billionaire. Maybe the two friends need to count commas on their bank statements.

"Good luck with your *thing*," I tease. "I'll track down Brady."

Wilder nods to the living room. "Thanks again. Leo will want Brady here."

I'm not quite sure why it's so vital that Brady be around for the pies, but I'll be a good girlfriend and fetch him anyway.

I head down the steps to the garden level, past the floor-to-ceiling glass windows overlooking Richardson Bay and the twinkling lights of San Francisco beyond, and finally along the hall to the last room.

But the door is shut.

Odd, but if the present is a secret, maybe Brady wanted to keep it that way.

I reach for the knob and yank it open.

Well.

Iris the caterer is definitely not on dish duty.

She's helpfully wrapping Brady's package though.

With her mouth.

Brady's hand curls around her sleek blonde hair, tangling his fingers in the strands as he pumps with his eyes closed. "Mmm. Yes. That's right. Take that eggnog, baby. Take it all."

I freeze, trying to process what's in front of me. To make something of it that's not what it seems. Like, they're secretly practicing for a porn career to supplement the bills. Or they run a lucrative OnlyFans account to raise money for orphans.

Because why else would my boyfriend be fucking the caterer's mouth? I blink, then look again. And this time, when I peer down at Iris, I see red—in the form of fuzzy socks.

She's wearing Christmas-themed fuzzy socks as she jingles his bells.

I point at Brady, outraged. "You were playing footsie with her! That's why you wanted her at the table?"

Brady's eyes fly open right as they glaze over. He lets out a long cow-like grunt like he's mooing. "Coming."

Then Iris, on her knees, starts to swallow with an audible gurgle before she turns to me, freezing, a guilty look in her big, blue eyes.

"Babe, I can explain!" Brady blurts.

Iris's mouth is still full as she mumbles something that might be, "Me too!"

I raise a rigid, stop-right-there finger. "This does not require an explanation. Everything is quite clear."

As clear as eggnog.

2

READY OR NOT

Wilder

Leo's been planning this moment for months. He even learned to bake a pecan pie in preparation. Hell, he's been vision-boarding this proposal for the last year. My best friend is as romantic as they come.

He met Charlotte when he hired her as an interior designer for his penthouse in Cow Hollow and then his corner office in the Financial District—I've been expecting this moment ever since. Doesn't make me a fortune teller though. Leo called me that fateful day and said, *"I've met my future wife."*

Now, I'm ready to help the guy I grew up with in Las Vegas, far, far from the glitz and glamor of the Strip.

Once Charlotte sets the table with red and green dessert plates—where the hell did Iris go?—I tug Leo aside into the kitchen. "All set?"

He pats his pocket, then nods to the pecan pie he

baked for the proposal setup. Talk about commitment. "I am."

"As soon as I say *the pecan pie is a cherished family recipe,* you'll cut me off." I'm echoing his instructions, not wanting him to worry about a thing.

Leo breathes out, and I get a rare glimpse of nerves in his eyes. "And then I'll say..." He recites his speech, volume low. When he's done, I clap his shoulder and reassure him, "You've got this."

"I do." He nods a few times and then flashes an excited grin. "And I kind of can't wait."

Briefly, a wistful pang lodges in my chest. What would that be like? How would it feel to have that intense enthusiasm about a woman? A romance? A future?

But I don't linger on those thoughts too long. I've got my daughter, and she deserves all my attention. I'm just glad my friend is so enchanted.

The kids rush back from playing video games a few minutes later, including my eleven-year-old, who marches over to me.

"Is it time for that pecan pie, Dad?" Mac gives an exaggerated wink.

I wink right back. "Sure is. And why don't you take the whipped cream to the table?"

She delivers a crisp nod. "Diversion tactic. No one will know why I'm claiming the best seat in the house."

Leo shakes his head in amusement. "Chip off the old block."

"She sure is." I squeeze Mac's shoulder rather than patting her head. She'd be annoyed—rightfully so—if I messed up her perfect French braid.

I open Bibi's fridge and hand her a can of whipped cream. "Here you go."

"This is the best," Mac says, then whispers, "my camera's in my back pocket."

"Good job," Leo whispers back.

"You can thank me when you see the pics," Mac warns and then spins around, her long braid swinging as she goes. She sets the can on the table, then claims the chair closest to Leo's, and calls out, "Who wants pecan pie?"

Time to assemble the stragglers.

Like Brady *and* Fable, who's missing now as well.

Brady is not only Fable's boyfriend but also Leo's cousin. I hardly knew Brady growing up. He's several years younger than Leo and me, and I know my friend will want him here for the big moment. Leo's always looked out for his family. He'll also want Fable at the table since she's Charlotte's older sister.

And what Leo wants, Leo gets.

I turn to head down the hall in search of them, only to find Brady walking toward me, head down like a naughty dog retreating to his crate.

Right behind him is...the caterer? She's wiping the back of her hand across her mouth.

My brow creases. Where did these two go? "Did you find the wrapping room?" I ask Brady skeptically.

Something about this guy rubs me the wrong way. Hell, something about him has bugged me each time I've seen him. I can't say that to Leo, of course. I haven't said that to anyone. Not even Bibi.

Brady jerks his gaze up, his expression chastened. But he quickly rearranges his features. "Yup. Wrapped the gift too. It's here in my pocket." He pats his pocket, which looks suspiciously empty.

Iris says nothing, she just purses her lips as she passes me, a guilty look in her eyes.

Something is definitely up. But before I can do more than frown, the guest bathroom swings open, and Fable emerges. Her auburn hair is damp by her ears like she just splashed water on her pale, freckled face.

She looks far prettier than is good for me, and this isn't the first time I've thought that about my employee.

3

MY FASHION ACCESSORY

Fable

I'm fine. I'm totally fine. A little water, a little lip gloss. No one will know I'm angry.

Make that livid.

But I'm also not completely surprised about the 'nog job. Not because Brady's a hanger-on, not because Brady wears out all his welcomes, and not because he's a scheming, two-timing jerk apparently—though he is absolutely all those things.

But because...relationships always break down.

Like my last one. And the one before. And, oh say, my mom and dad's. Which broke down over and over and, yup, say it one more time, over again.

Romance and I aren't vodka and tonic. We're orange juice and toothpaste. But no one needs to know that.

I step into the hall, plaster on a smile, and run right into...the man who signs my paychecks.

Great. Now I have to fake it for him too. I smile wider, brighter. "Hey there, boss man."

Wilder cocks his head, studying me like he has X-ray vision and can see inside my soul. Nope. No one can. I zip up my soul suit so it's impervious to his perceptive eyes.

"Everything okay?" he asks.

"Everything is great!" Was that too cheery? Maybe.

"Are you ready for dessert?"

"Ready to skip it," I say, patting my belly, like I'm too full to stomach pie, especially pie made by Iris. Maybe I *can* skip dessert. Skip out of this meal and go grab a pint of Molly Moon's ice cream and binge a comedy on Webflix while knitting the blanket I will probably still be curled up in alone when I'm fifty.

But Wilder gives a professional smile—the same one he flashes when he wants someone to attend a meeting. The smile that says it's not optional.

"Just sit with us then for a minute," he says, and this feels like a clear order. A kind one, but an order, nonetheless. There will be no skipping out.

"Sure," I say, then he walks with me down the hall, peering at me again with some concern.

Wilder stops before we reach the living room. "Are you sure you're okay?"

I force out a bubbly laugh. "Why wouldn't I be?" I'm not about to tell him Brady was coming down the caterer's chimney at *his* Thanksgiving.

"Just checking," Wilder says, then sets a hand on the small of my back ever so briefly, sending a very unexpected shiver down my spine before we return to the table.

Everyone's set up again, with plates, forks, and all varieties of pie from pecan to apple to pumpkin. The well-appointed Christmas tree presides over us, its twinkling lights heralding holiday cheer. It's all so much happiness that I nearly run off. But something in Wilder's tone—*just sit with us*—has me pulling out a chair and sitting my ass down.

I've just picked up a fork when Wilder clears his throat and says, "*The pecan pie is a cherished family recipe...*"

Oh. There's a pie toast? Fabulous. I'll have to fake *I'm fine* for even longer.

Then Leo interrupts his friend, taking over the toast. "Speaking of cherished family things..."

Then, my sister's boyfriend pushes back in his chair, rises, and comes around to my little sister. The hair on the back of my neck prickles. My heart skitters.

Leo drops to one knee.

Charlotte gasps. I gasp.

"Charlotte Calloway," Leo begins, reaching into his pocket, "you are the love of my life."

Oh. My. God.

He's proposing to my sister, who's madly in love with him and has been since the day she walked into his home. My eyes well with tears as he tells Charlotte how much he loves her, adores her, and admires her. He pops open a box with a stunning vintage ring inside, then says, "This was my grandmother's cherished ring, and I would be so honored if you'd wear it and be my wife."

My heart climbs into my throat.

"Leo, you had me at *will you decorate my home*," Charlotte says, her voice breaking with happiness. She wraps her arms around him in the most romantic embrace I've ever seen.

Tears stream down my cheeks—mostly for her, but some for me. My baby sister is getting married. It's almost enough to wipe away the images of Brady getting his dick sucked just moments ago.

"Kiss the bride!" someone calls out.

Someone very familiar. Someone who just uttered *coming* in the wrapping room.

My chest burns. Are you kidding me? Brady's hooting for his cousin already? He doesn't even have the decency to shut the fuck up?

I can't believe I dated him. Of course I don't blame my sister—though she introduced me to him at a dinner party she and Leo hosted four months ago, saying she wanted me to meet Leo's cousin, who's *so friendly*.

She didn't force me to go out with him. I made that dumb choice on my own.

I refuse to look his way, staring instead at Wilder's daughter, who's taking pictures with a real camera. Is that a little pocket Nikon? I had no idea his daughter was into photography. Most kids—most people—can't handle a regular camera in our cell phone world. But the kid is a natural, positioned in just the right place, snapping the proposal photos like a pro. It's kind of adorable that Wilder's kid is taking the pics.

Once the photos are done, Leo whispers something in Charlotte's ear, and she beams, then nods enthusiastically.

They turn to the table, and my big-hearted, kind, talented sister says to me, "Will you be my maid of honor, Fable? It would mean the world."

I never knew it was possible to be elated and angry all at once—but I suppose you just take one heartfelt moment and add a dash of a dickhead ex. Voila. Instant cocktail of emotions. "Like I'd let you have anyone else," I say, my heart swelling with love for her even as my blood boils over Brady.

Then sweet, devoted Leo turns to Wilder. "And you've been like a brother to me my whole life. Will you be the best man?"

"I'm there," Wilder says, cool and steady.

Under the table, I cross my fingers.

Please let them have just a best man and maid of honor. Let the madness stop there. Pretty please.

But Leo turns to Brady next and says to his cousin, "And you have to be a groomsman, Brady."

"You know it, dude," Brady says, giving him some sort of bro-knock.

Kill me now.

When Brady puts his hand down, he waggles his eyebrows at Wilder. "We'll have to move up *that little stock talk.*"

Wilder, to his credit, gives Brady a professional smile but says nothing, too classy to turn him down here in front of everyone.

After more congratulations, Charlotte hugs me and then gazes at her new ring proudly. "I can't quite believe it," she murmurs.

"I can, and I'm so happy for you." I steal a glance at the door. Maybe I'll slip out after this hug.

But Charlotte squeezes me harder, then steps back, holding my arms. Her big, brown eyes sparkle as she looks me up and down. "You and Brady are going to be in the wedding together. Maybe you'll be next!"

I wither inside but put on a smile. I can't tell her what Brady did tonight. I don't want to ruin her special day. Instead, I strip any hurt away, like I've learned to do since I was younger. It's second nature. But I mean it completely when I squeal and wrap my arms around my sister again.

As I pull away, I catch Brady's eye as I say to Charlotte, "I'm so happy for you!"

I don't have to fake this happiness because I love my sister so much. I channel that joy into a wide smile I wear like it's my number one fashion accessory because *fuck you, Brady. You don't deserve to see me sad.*

Moments later, Charlotte rejoins Leo at the head of the table, and this time, she whispers something to him. His smile is pure delight. He clinks a fork against a glass to get everyone's attention, and then Charlotte clasps her hands. "We don't want to wait to get married," the bride declares. "We want to have a Christmas Eve wedding at Wilder's cabins. And we want all of you to be there. It'll be a big destination wedding, and in the days leading up to it, we can bring our families together for the annual Christmas games."

Out of the corner of my eye, I catch Brady catching Iris's gaze and mouthing, *Want to be my date?*

And if I'd thought this day couldn't get any worse, I was wrong.

4

SUIT NUMBER ONE

Wilder

"Do you have everything?"

Mac cuts me a *did you really ask me that* look in the sleek foyer as she hoists her backpack onto her shoulders. "Dad, I think the question is—do *you* have everything?"

I gaze up at the minimalist chandelier hanging from the ceiling of my home in Cow Hollow. It's hardly minimalist anymore. Mac insisted on decorating it with icicle lights. "The sass. Dear god, the sass from you, Mackenzie Elizabeth Blaine."

"Well. Do you?" my daughter asks again, her hands parked on her hips. "You have a meeting this morning with your designer. Did you remember to review the five tips for talking to creatives that I sent you the other night?"

A cackle echoes from the nearby kitchen. It carries, reverberating across the sunken living room, to where we're standing. "I wonder where she gets it from," Bibi calls out.

"You, Bibi. You," I say to her, then return my focus to Mac. She has her holiday recital rehearsal with her mom, so I need to get her to the Abernathy School even earlier than usual. "Bibi's driver is waiting."

I nod to the door. But my daughter is undeterred from her goal. "Dad. Did you read it? It's *really* important that you interact with all your employees with an open mind about what they do. That's why I sent it to you. But you can read it in the car too," she says, then nibbles on her lip as she taps on her phone, presumably hunting for the list of tips.

Before I can even tell her that I read it mere seconds after she sent it, she brightens. "Oh, here it is!" She swivels her screen my way.

There's a list on it so I read it out loud. "One: new instant camera. Two: that Pegasus series with the sprayed edges. Three: a secret door?"

Oh, I know what this is. And when I look up with an arched brow, Mac oh-so innocently says, "My bad. That's my Christmas list. But I'll send it to you so you can review it later anyway."

"I'll give it my full attention. What kind of secret door do you have in mind, Mac?"

She waves a hand airily. "Oh, any kind, really. Something that's a portal to another dimension or leads to a secret room. I'm not picky in the secret door department," she says, like the variety of secret doors is akin to picking Cosmic Crisp or Gala apples at the grocery store. "Anyway, did you read the list for your meeting?"

"Of course. It was helpful," I say. I would never *not* read something my daughter sent to me. Also, I am familiar with how to run a damn corporation. I've done it for nearly two decades and have the track record to prove I'm good at it. No, make that excellent, especially these last couple years as I've expanded Blaine Enterprises into new business areas. And yet, my own daughter is not convinced.

"Good. Because the world is changing, Dad. You have to make sure you meet people where they are." Mac is intensely serious as she doles out advice. "Don't point out mistakes. Welcome...*opportunities.* Don't laugh at them. Laugh *with* them."

"Someone has *Future Director of HR* written all over her." Bibi emerges from the pristine kitchen, her low heels clicking across the tiled floor. She has a dark red Santa hat with silver snowflakes perched atop her head and her travel mug in her hand.

"More like future boss of me," I mutter.

Bibi smiles at Mac and hands her a small pencil bag shaped like a long cat. "But as someone reminding her dad to take things to work, it seems you forgot your colored pens."

"Oops," Mac says, a little chagrined as she takes them and stuffs them into her backpack.

"Do you have everything you need for this morning's dress rehearsal?" I'm pretty sure she missed something when I asked her the same question earlier.

Mac smacks her forehead. "What is wrong with me?" She whirls and races up the floating stairs strewn with garlands, past the floor-to-ceiling windows with the stunning view of the Golden Gate Bridge, to her bedroom on the third floor.

"Apparently, managing you is a full-time job for her,"

Bibi says, then pats my cheek since she'll never stop patting my cheek.

"Eleven going on forty," I muse as Mac's boots echo through the house.

"I'm surprised you let her go upstairs with shoes on," Bibi says, glancing around.

I know what she means. Nothing is out of order in my home. The coffee table is neatly covered with a tasteful array of pinecones, and a mini Christmas tree perches next to the gleaming baby grand piano in the corner. The holiday decor is classy, courtesy of my daughter. She has an eye for it. I don't. Chess pieces I can visualize—not furniture pieces.

"She didn't give me much choice." And it wasn't a battle I wanted to fight. When she's older, I don't want my kid's main memory of me to be as the dad who never let her wear shoes in the house.

Mac flies down the steps, and the three of us head out, piling into the sleek black limo that carries Bibi everywhere she goes. "Thank you, Reagan," Bibi says to the woman who's been driving her since I first moved to San Francisco. "You are the absolute best."

"Thank you, Barbara. I have Playlist Number Three all queued up and ready to go," the driver says.

"Nope. I'm wrong. You're not the best. You're an official goddess. In fact, I had a dream in which I gave you a bigger-than-ever Christmas bonus this year, and that dream will come true later today."

Reagan beams. "Thank you, Barbara."

"You deserve it." Bibi turns to me. "And will you be giving out bonuses, too, this year?"

I give her a *seriously?* look. "Is the sky blue? Is my daughter sassy? Is my aunt relentless?"

Bibi pats my cheek. "That's the right answer."

"They'll be in the stockings we pass out before the holiday break."

Reagan gets behind the wheel and pulls into Monday morning traffic as Elvis's "Blue Christmas" fills the ride. Bibi likes to pick us up on her way into the office. It's a chance to spend time with Mac every day, which she's been doing more often since my mother—her sister—moved to London a few years ago to earn her bachelor's degree. Then, Mom stayed because she fell in love—*with school*. Now, she's working toward her master's in fine arts, and I couldn't be prouder.

Bibi fishes in her vegan leather bag, digs out a pair of tortoiseshell reading glasses, then swipes open her phone. If she's looking at her calendar, I'd better get out my shield. Tapping her regal chin, she says, "What's your schedule like this week, Wilder? It's December, so it's time for my favorite holiday activity—proving I'm better than a dating app. And lucky you! You continue to qualify as my favorite project."

Mac snort-laughs. "I wonder who she got this time," she says to me under her breath.

"Your guess is as good as mine," I whisper back.

Bibi looks at me. "I heard you, and I do know how to pick 'em, thank you very much. I was a matchmaker in a past life."

Maybe so, but my answer's the same as usual. "Thanks, but no thanks."

She's not the only one I'll say that to. I'll say it when my sister, Caroline, and her wife plot my romantic future and when my assistant tries to write a dating profile for me. There's not a man or woman I'm close to in a fifty-mile radius who isn't trying to set me up, especially around the holidays.

It'll be fun, they say.

Fun is a game of golf with my friends, a round of pickleball with my daughter, or a good book. Fun is *not* a string of bad dates leading nowhere, which is precisely where my aunt's past setups have always gone.

Bibi gestures to the car's tinted windows as it cruises through the city on a foggy morning in the first week of December. San Francisco is decked out for Christmas, with twinkling lights hanging from streetlamps and nutcrackers standing tall in store windows.

"And that means what?" I ask as Elvis croons.

"Wilder, it's the holidays," Bibi presses, like that'll change my mind. "What's wrong with a little romance?"

"Nothing," I reply, and Mac joins in as I say, "I just don't have time right now."

I wince, meeting Mac's gaze. "Do I say it that often?"

She nods with all the authority of an eleven-year-old. "Yes. Along with *eat all your kale* and *no YouTube after six on a school night.*"

"Sage advice." Bibi turns to me, shifting from dreams analysis and past life regression to boss mode. "But you know I was very happy with my husband for forty fantastic years before he died. It was the real thing, and it was wonderful—especially having him by my side during the holidays. We used to dance to 'Blue Christmas' every Christmas Eve as the lights on the tree flickered and the fireplace crackled." She sighs contentedly, and the picture she paints might be enough to make a weaker man second-guess himself. But not me.

"That's a lovely memory," I say. "And I'm glad you have it."

"So..." she begins, "maybe you don't think anything is 'right' with love because you haven't met the right person yet."

Because they don't exist in my book. Fine, Bibi had a happy romance, but my mother did not. She thought she'd found Mister Right, and look how that turned out. I shudder at unwelcome thoughts of my father, then dismiss them just as quickly as they came.

"Bibi, I know you believe in the Pisces dream for love—"

"That's not an insult!"

"Of course it's not," I say, placating her. "I'm simply saying you do. But you're also the exception to the rule. By that same logic, you could say Mom hasn't met the right person, but look at her." I'm thinking of the texts I exchanged with her over the weekend and her FaceTime call with Mac on Thanksgiving morning. "Mom's single, but name one person happier than she is. She's living her best life in London."

"He has a point, Bibi," Mac puts in. Dear god, I raised this child right.

Bibi tosses her hands in the air. "You've turned her into a mini-me."

I laugh.

Mac scoffs. "I have my own opinions!"

"Exactly. That's what makes you his mini-me." Bibi smiles like the sap she is for her great-niece. "And it's also why I love you like crazy."

"Love you too," Mac says.

We arrive at the school. I get out with Mac, smoothing the crisp front of my tailored shirt. "Your mom has you tonight," I remind my daughter.

"I know. She's right there." Mac points to the woman

with wavy blonde hair, bright red lips, and a Bohemian skirt floating over lavender Uggs. A burly security guard stalks a few paces behind her as San Francisco schoolkids stream past the wrought-iron gates and into the school's main entrance, with its pristine white limestone walls.

"Hey, love." Felicity greets Mac with her bright English accent and gives her a big hug. "You look smashing this morning."

"Thanks, Mom."

When they let go, Felicity flashes me a smile, pointing to my Tom Ford suit. "And you look...very CEO this morning," she teases. "Was it tough choosing between suit number one, suit number two, and suit number three?"

Mac chuckles. "He has more than three suits."

"And no, it wasn't hard." I don't tell her why it was easy, the fashion choice for this meeting.

"How's everything going? The Thanksgiving pics you sent were adorable. Sorry I missed it. I've loved that holiday ever since your dad introduced me to it."

"Hmm, letting down ten people at Dad's Thanksgiving or disappointing fifty thousand fans?" Mac pretends to weigh the options for her pop star mother. "Tough call."

"Ten of my favorite people." Felicity smiles. "But you're right. I had committed to the concerts first. I can't wait for the New Year's Day one, though, since I'll be here, and you can come."

Mac pumps a fist. "I love the VIP suite. It has the best snacks."

"That's all I could want. Good snack reviews," Felicity says.

"Your tour is getting rave reviews too," I point out.

Felicity gives a grateful smile. "That's always lovely to hear. I hope it goes without saying, but I'll say it anyway—

you're welcome to come to the New Year's Day show too, Wilder, if you don't have a hot date."

Mac snorts with laughter.

"What'd I say?" Felicity asks.

"Bibi is trying to set Dad up. *Again*." Mac rolls her eyes.

I roll mine too. "She does this every year. You'd think the law of diminishing returns would dampen her enthusiasm."

"The enthusiasm of a woman with more Santa hats than I have costume changes during a show?" Felicity says with fondness. But shifting to slight concern, she asks me, "But is it the worst idea? Maybe you could meet that perfect sparring partner at last."

Great. First my aunt. Now my ex-girlfriend. But at least I can laugh at her too-correct acknowledgment that she was never the right sparring partner for me.

We met in the city more than a dozen years ago. She's from London but has called California home for a long time now. We've always had an easy relationship. Felicity and I don't argue—not about Mac, not about custody, not about anything. We share our daughter, and we get along. We have since we got together and since we've been apart. It's...nice. I can't complain.

I'm lucky in that regard. I'm lucky in a lot of regards.

And I know what it's like to be raised by a father who doesn't show up. I won't be that kind of dad. Mac deserves all my spare time, even if my life is a little lonely when Mac goes to bed and the house is quiet. Or when she's with her mom.

But I don't need a partner to break the silence in my house. I can listen to music. Track down antique maps. Listen to a new episode of *The Best Damn Heist*.

No one wants to hear that the billionaire is lonely. I have plenty of things to fill my time.

"Mac, show your mom the costume for the holiday recital," I say, and Mac unzips her backpack and tugs out the fabric—a red sweater with snowflakes on it. The recital isn't until next week, but the school wanted to get ahead of any potential costume issues, hence the early dress rehearsal. I can't fault them for being prepared.

"It's fantastic," Felicity says breezily. "And I can't wait to see the rehearsal. I know it's going to be brilliant."

It's such a Felicity thing to say. No one wears rose-colored glasses twenty-four seven quite like my ex.

"All right, Mom. Let's go," Mac says, stuffing the sweater back into her bag. "But listen, I really want to know if I sound good. You have to tell me if I don't."

"I will," Felicity says.

We both know she won't. She'll tell Mac she sounds fantastic.

I kiss Mac on the cheek goodbye and return to the sleek limo, parked among other sleek limos, and slide inside. This time, as Frank Sinatra reminds me, Santa Claus is coming to town.

Bibi speaks into the phone pressed to her ear. "You don't say? Georgie broke up with the lawyer she was seeing?" There's a pause as Reagan pulls back into traffic. "Well, I never liked him. He defended that oil company." Bibi shudders dramatically. "So Georgie's seeing a matchmaker? Do I ever have a match for her. I had a vision about this, in fact."

Shaking my head vigorously, I pop in my earbuds and listen to a podcast about a one-hundred-million-dollar diamond heist at an airport in Morocco while, on the phone, Bibi tries to engineer a date for me.

One I don't want. If I were to imagine a romance—down the road, of course—none of Bibi's prospects are women I could picture myself with. I'd want someone funny and kind who wasn't afraid to keep me on my toes.

But that's not in the cards *now*.

At the stadium, Bibi and I go our separate ways—she handles our charitable contributions, and I handle, well, the whole damn business.

When I reach the C-suite, I stop short at the sight of my executive assistant. Shay is about my age—late thirties, though his pale complexion and devotion to sunscreen make him look even younger. His desk is covered with photos of his wife and cats, but those aren't felines on his sweater. Is that a fleet of Santas riding unicorns?

"Good morning, Mr. Blaine. I've emailed your agenda for the day to you. No printouts, just the way you want. Is there anything else I can do for you?" he chirps, then pops up from his desk, and whoa. Not just unicorns. *3-D* unicorns.

I've been trained not to comment on employees' clothes—thank you, Mac—but this time, it's a struggle to pretend I don't notice the golden horns sticking out from his sweater.

"Thank you, Shay. And I'm all good right now. How are Tater Tot and French Fry?"

I give myself points for my poker face and for name-dropping his cats.

But Shay just smirks. "Nice try, boss. But that means this sweater isn't just ugly. It's super ugly, right?"

"Excuse me?"

"Your reaction." He points at me. "The whole 'blank face' and focus on the kids thing." His grin widens. "I'm field-testing options for the ugly sweater contest. My mom sent this from the homeland, so it's one hundred percent Norwegian ugly sweater. How is it on the ugly scale?"

Eye-wateringly horrifying. "It's nice," I manage since it's not my place.

But he sees through me, pumping a fist. "Ten out of ten levels of hideousness. Yes! I can't wait to tell Lucia that Mom nailed it this year."

Lucia's his wife, who works in building ops.

Then, he's poised and professional again as he says, "Don't forget your ten a.m. with Fable Calloway from design."

"I won't," I say with an even stonier expression.

How could I? I've only been looking forward to that meeting since I woke up. Once inside my office, which overlooks the field and the best damn football team in the world, I check the time on my watch. One hour till my meeting with my lead designer. I check my reflection in the window. This suit does look sharp. I run a hand over the midnight blue jacket.

I did pick it for a reason. This is my best suit, and I like to look nice. The fact that the meeting is with Fable has nothing to do with my selection.

Fine.

Maybe it has a little something to do with it. But it's nothing I can't handle. Or hide.

Just like I've been doing for the last year or so.

5

FONDLE WITH CARE

Fable

Where is the new sparkly T-shirt? The one that will look amazing in all the employees' holiday stockings?

I swore I left it on my secondhand brushed metal table. The one held up by two whimsical metal frogs because frogs should only ever be whimsical. I set the shirt here last night to show the boss man. I shove aside the crimping pliers and a few half-finished earrings, then peer under the mason jar holding the wind chimes I'm making Mom for Christmas.

My pulse pounds with worry. We're meeting to discuss numbers, trends, and growth, but I really need to locate this special-edition shirt. It's not only a gift to go with the staff's bonuses, it's a tangible example of my vision for our merch in the new year. It's made from recycled textiles, and it's still gorgeous.

Wilder likes to give the shirts to employees first as a special holiday gift before we roll them out to the team merch shops. But I can only show it to him if I can find the dang thing. I scan the couch in case it's stuck between some cushions—like I was last night when I conked out after staying up too late making glitter dick shirts that say *Fondle with Care* on the front for Charlotte's Christmas-themed bachelorette party.

As I send the search party of one to my bedroom, Charlotte's ringtone trills from the back pocket of my black pants.

My chest squeezes uncomfortably, but I've put this moment off long enough. As in all of Black Friday, Black Saturday, and Black Sunday. I have to tell her that Brady and I are no longer together. That I picked a guy who cheats, just like our mom did. But unlike Mom, I won't let him keep walking all over me.

I swipe open the phone as I round the corner into my cubicle-size bedroom. "Hey, beautiful blushing bride," I say, all merry and bright.

Dammit, I am merry and bright.

I've had three days, a box of Trader Joe's wine, a football game (on TV since I was not in the mood to go to the stadium and cheer from the stands), and far too much time alone. My good friends, like Rachel and Elodie, and my besties Josie, Maeve, and Everly, were busy during the holiday weekend. They would have all made time for me if I'd asked, but I didn't want to be a downer. Now, there's no more procrastinating.

"How was San Diego?" I yank open the creaky closet door. Maybe I left the shirt hanging up here after I designed it?

"It was amazing," she says, singing that last word. "Leo took me to La Jolla, and we stayed at a gorgeous hotel with a view of the ocean, and I felt like I was living in a storybook romance. But now there's so much to do in such a short amount of time."

As I flick through hangers of shirts, she rattles off a wedding checklist of details like the photographer, the cake, the dress, the flowers, the tuxes, the string quartet and even something about snowmen and ice sculptures, which doesn't quite compute but I'll figure it out later.

"So, just a few little things," I say dryly, spinning around and heading for the bureau, where I shove aside the mood boards I made for the jewelry shop I want to open someday in the distant future when it doesn't cost me a couple of organs on the black market.

"Just a couple," she singsongs while I search the dresser. "But worth it. I have some new clients, too, who want the world from me over the next few weeks. Holiday rush and all. I crunched my free time in a spreadsheet, and I'm positive I can get all the wedding things done in the evenings. The next twenty-two evenings," she says, then gulps in worry. Christmas Eve is coming up fast.

"Do you need a wedding planner? I can find one for you." It shouldn't be hard to hire someone eager and hungry.

"That's *with* a wedding planner. Leo insisted on hiring *the best*, but I want to be involved. I want my dream wedding." She takes a beat, and I can picture her twisting her fingers uncertainly. "I've always wanted to get married on Christmas Eve."

I smile. "You say that like I don't know it already."

"You know all my teenage dreams," she says. Like how she wanted to excel in school, become a wildly sought-after interior designer, and fall madly in love with a cinnamon roll of a man. Check, check, check. The only thing left? The dream wedding. "Is that selfish?"

Big sister mode is activated. "Nope. It's not selfish, and I'll help you in any way." It's my job and my pleasure. "You know that."

"Really?" She sounds so relieved.

"Of course. I would love to."

"What did I do to deserve you?"

"You were born second," I say as I jerk open another drawer.

"True, true."

There it is! Safe and sound, though I've no idea why I left it in the drawer. Maybe I was just that tired last night. I grab the white shirt with the team logo printed in red and silver bling that I'm sure will be a hit with the female fans the team has been courting this season.

Now that I've got the bounty, I bite the bullet. "So, listen," I say to Charlotte, "This is no big deal, and it's all totally fine, but I'm not seeing Brady anymore."

Dead silence.

A few seconds later, there's a worried gasp. "What happened? Did he hurt you? Because if he did something to my sister a month—no, less than a month—before my wedding, I'll...I'll...put composted cow manure in his slice of wedding cake."

"First, love your attention to detail when it comes to revenge, but..." I pause, wincing. I can't tell her what he did. Not after she rattled off her DEFCON-5 levels of pre-wedding stress. "It was mutual," I assure her as I grab my oversized purple bag from the kitchen counter in my little Mission District apartment. "We just realized we weren't right for each other. But it's fine. I swear it's fine. It happens."

"Fable," she says sympathetically. "Do you need me to

come over later with a pin-the-tail-on-the-dickhead? We can throw darts at an image of his face."

As appealing as that may be—I love a good game of darts—she needs to focus on putting together a wedding in just over three weeks. "I'm great, Char. I swear. We weren't a good match. It was so mutual—it was, like, beyond mutual."

"Is it going to be weird to see him at the wedding?"

"No," I lie, trying not to picture Brady pumping a fist and bro-knocking guests at every opportunity. "It'll be fine. No problem."

"Are you sure?"

"Positive," I say, grabbing a jacket.

"I'll find someone to be on your team, then," she says.

I stop in my tracks at the kitchen counter. Wait. What fresh hell did she just utter? "What...do you mean?"

"Leo and I thought it'd be fun if everyone teams up. For the Evergreen Falls Christmas competition Wilder mentioned. The one in the town. The events are so fun—there's a snowball fight and a gingerbread house-making competition and more. We're thinking the bride and groom can be on one team," she says, then rattles off Leo's parents, our mom and stepdad, our dad and his third or fourth wife—who can keep track?—and then the cousins. My head is spinning with the inevitable when she says, "Oh. Hang on—Leo's just texted me. Brady's RSVP'd with—"

I knew this was coming since Brady, with the subtlety of an elephant, invited the eggnog drinker in front of me. Still, I groan inside, close my eyes, and stuff the shirt into my work bag. I mutter *Iris* right as Charlotte says it out loud. Or rather, she asks, "Iris, the caterer?"

AKA, Iris, who sucked the stripes off Brady's candy

cane. I can't believe he's already put her name on the guest list. But then, I can.

"That's so great he's found someone," I say, so bright, so bubbly I must sound like I'm on helium when, in fact, I've drunk a cup of pure dread. The last thing I want is to see them together at the wedding. Correction: the last thing I want is to see them together at all.

But I definitely can't tell my sister the truth now. I'll wait till the new year. Once Charlotte returns from her dream honeymoon, we'll grab brunch and laugh over my terrible ex and what went down.

Well, what went down Iris's throat.

After watching my father selfishly toy with my mother's emotions, after he promised to change after every affair, after he vowed to stay faithful *this time* then dramatically stole the limelight, I won't do that with Charlotte.

Besides, opening up isn't my favorite thing to do.

It's your least favorite thing, and you know it.

I tell that little, knowing voice to shut the F up. There's nothing wrong with keeping your feelings to yourself. It's safer than sharing. And frankly, kinder. This way, I can focus on Charlotte during her special time.

Brady's the past, and the past is behind me. I say goodbye to my sister and gallop out the door to catch a bus to the stadium.

* * *

At two minutes past ten, I vault off the bus and race to the employee entrance, where I wag my lanyard with my Renegades ID at the security guard at the door. He has no mercy for my labored breaths or the strands of hair falling from my clip on one side of my head—because, of course, it falls only on one side—or the sweat I'm sweating under my short-sleeve blouse. Running that far made me as hot as Hades, and now the blast of heating from the stadium raises my body temperature about a million degrees.

But once inside the halls, I hustle to text Wilder, tapping away on my phone.

Fable: Mind if I pump you late?

Seconds later, he replies.

Wilder: Excuse me?

I reread my text, and my cheeks flame with embarrassment. Thumbs flying to type a reply, I click-clack along the concrete corridor.

Fable: Join you late! I meant join you late! Sorry!

Wilder: Sure. I'm here whenever you get here. For the joining.

He's being good-natured, but he has to think I'm lazy and messy. Not a great look for a designer. I dash to my little office and snag the box of Christmas stockings, dictating another reply.

Fable: Sorry again! I really look forward to sleeping with you.

I dart to the elevator, then step into it with the box and my bags, and I try to catch my breath. The doors shut, and there's no reply from him. That's good. That has to be good.

But then, as the lift chugs up, I reread my text to be sure it went out.

"Are you *kidding* me?"

Thank god I'm alone in the elevator, with no one to see me shout into my phone like it's the ultimate dictation villain. "Speaking with you! I look forward to speaking with you! I should not be allowed to text or use words at all!"

I hit send as the elevator arrives on the executive level. I'm about to jog down the garland-decorated hall, but I think better of it and beeline for the ladies' room instead.

I can't meet with the team owner looking like this—like a hot mess. Literally.

I pop inside, march to the sink, and grab a starchy paper towel. After I wet it, I unbutton the top button on my blouse, then strategically maneuver an arm into my shirt to pat at my sweaty armpits, hoping I don't ruin my pretty peach top.

A few seconds later, I exhale, toss out the towel, and reclip my hair. After I wash my hands and dry them, I exit.

All put together again.

I may be a sweaty mess, and I may have sent an accidental sext, but I've absolutely got this now. I am an awesome designer. I can do this.

I started designing jewelry, working my way up as an assistant manager at a shop on Fillmore Street, and then snagging a job with one of the most prestigious businesses in the city. No, the whole damn world. In the last two years alone, our merch department has soared, setting records in the league with the coolest, freshest, most imaginative designs. Plus, I'm a few months away from *finally* paying off my college loans, and I've finally started putting something away. I'm seriously hoping the money I've been saving and the experience I've been gaining can help me achieve my dream someday—opening a boutique with my own line of eco-friendly jewelry. *Someday.*

I turn into the executive suite where a wreath hangs on the big wooden door that's ajar. Pushing it open, I step in as Shay's sitting tall and typing while wearing...wow. And that's one way to get into the holiday spirit.

"Unicorns are boring, said no one ever," I say, admiring his sweater.

"My thoughts exactly," Shay says with a smile, closing out of what looks like a photo collage on his screen of a couple long-haired calico cats sitting in a photoshopped sleigh, then says, "For my wife. The pic. It's one of her Christmas gifts. Also, Mr. Blaine is definitely expecting you." His helpful tone does nothing to underscore the meaning of his words—*you're late.*

"Thank you," I say, lowering my face.

"Go, go," he says gently but firmly shooing me into the suite overlooking the field.

When I enter, Wilder's sitting at his desk, relaxed, confident, looking like he's never once sweated in his entire life. There isn't a strand of thick, dark hair out of place on his head. His eyes crinkle at the corners in amusement. "Glad you could make it to the joining, Fable."

I fight off a smile, then stand tall, saluting him. "Renegades Christmas elf reporting for duty." That's my role in making the holiday gifts for the staff—I'm the elf to his Santa. "And I think you're going to love this stocking stuffer."

Grabbing the shirt, I set my bag on the chair. "Ta-da!"

I unfurl the fabric and release a cloud of colorful themed confetti that flies out in a ticker tape parade of red and green glitter dicks. They go everywhere and stick to everything—his desk, the carpet, and his *GQ* face.

6

GLITTER DONGS AND SHINY SCHLONGS

Fable

I've always rolled my eyes at those scenes in the movies when the heroine spills coffee in the hero's lap, then grabs a wad of napkins hastily in apology and dabs at him till she realizes she's touching the outline of his dick and... *awkward.*

Like, who would actually do that in real life? Pat a dude's lap and risk feeling up the crown jewels?

But I get it now—how it might happen. Because the instinct to clean up my own mess is as strong as my desire to hug the pair of Dachshund puppies I saw in a woman's cart at T.J. Maxx last weekend as she stocked up on dog beds.

Intense.

I'm digging into my purse, furiously hunting for something, *anything*, to clean the glitter Christmas dicks off Wilder's handsome face, his fancy tie, his expensive dress shirt as he removes his jacket quickly, assessing the damage. I mean, why make regular glitter dicks, when I can make holiday ones for Charlotte's holiday bachelorette party?

"Here," I say, stretching across his desk to shove a pack of tissues at him while I desperately try to find the file folder in my brain that stores information about glitter removal.

Think fast.

Got it! "Do you have any coconut oil? I read this article the other night when I was making the shirt. You dip two fingers in the oil, gently rub circles across your face, and..." Oh my god, what am I saying? No one has coconut oil in their office. "It, um, removes sparkly makeup."

The end of my sentence dies like a kite without wind as Wilder swipes at his cheek. He hasn't flinched since the glittering. He's wearing the most blank expression ever. I bet he kills it at poker. "I'm fresh out of coconut oil," he deadpans.

"I'm guessing no makeup remover then?"

"I don't have that either," he says.

But most of the red and green flecks landed on that crisp shirt he's wearing. I bet he's one of those executives who keeps a change of clothes at work. I swivel around, but a quick scan of his office doesn't reveal a garment bag or a handy-dandy costume change. Don't billionaires always have tuxedos at the ready? Must be another lie of the rom-com flicks.

I've got to be able to do something. I made this mess. I need to clean it up. Then, an image flashes before me. Or, more specifically, a collage.

"Lint rollers can remove glitter from clothes!" I shout, like I've unearthed the answer in a vicious game of charades.

I sprint across the plush carpet, yank open the door, and bound over to Shay's desk, powered by hope and a prayer. I slam down my palms, rattling the purple picture frame of a cat that sits in prime position by his computer. "Please tell me you carry lint rollers with you because you have long-hair cats?"

He's an Avenger called to assemble. "Of course. Would you like sticky, super-sticky, or extra-sticky?"

I lift a finger, ready to debate the difference between super and extra, before I shut myself up. Now's not the time for semantics. "Extra sounds fab."

"Always travel with rollers," he says, then snags one from his backpack—his holiday backpack, decorated with a Grinch face and the words *Cheer up, dude, it's Christmas.* "Here you go."

"You're the best," I say as I return to Wilder's office, swinging the door shut behind me. As I peel off the adhesive strip on the roller, he strides around the mahogany desk, and I practically slam into him. But I stop in time. A small miracle for me today. "Let me help," I say, then roll his chest. Up and down his pecs. Until it hits me—I *am* that girl in the movie.

The only difference is I'm not rolling his lap.

Also, when do bosses have time to get pecs of steel? Who cares? I'm just glad he does because I approve. Except he's my boss, and I should not even think about what's under that shirt. I swallow roughly, jamming the lint roller his way then backing off. "Um, you can do it."

"Thank you," he says, taking over the glitter-removal duty and methodically rolling, quadrant by quadrant.

"You're as good at that as you are at stacking a dishwasher," I say. Maybe the compliment will deflect from the terrible T-shirt mix-up.

"That's always been a goal."

Soon, he's sparkle free. Except...

I gingerly point at his face. At one of his carved cheekbones to be exact. "There's a little bit still there."

He swipes at the stubborn stripe of sparkly red sausages, but they don't come off.

"I think I have lotion in my purse. I could use that," I suggest, since it's the least I can do.

"That would be great."

I grab my purse and locate a small tube of hand cream. "It's Dark Kiss," I say, reading the label.

He gives a casual shrug, like *why not use Dark Kiss*. "Sounds perfect."

It does? Is that how he likes to kiss? Dark and dreamy too? I blink away the surprisingly tempting thoughts invading my brain.

"Here you go." I offer the tube to him. Probably safer than me squeezing it. I'd get it all over the shirt that covers his titanium abs, which go with his granite pecs.

He squeezes a little bit on his finger and rubs it on his cheek but misses the path of festive sparkles.

"Still there," I say with a guilty wince. He doesn't move. He barely even lets out a sigh. I really can't read him. But he has to be annoyed. My stomach twists. "Can I help?"

"Okay," he grits out like it costs him something.

"I'll be gentle," I say, trying to keep the mood light as I take the tube again, then step closer to him than I've ever been. Closer than when I rolled him. He's inches away now. Wilder Blaine is taller than I am, but not by an absurd amount. More like...a *just right* amount. With my fingertip, I pat along his cheekbone, and I'm close enough to notice he smells like falling snow and midnight—something calm and powerful all at once.

Something alluring.

I'm a scent girl. If a man takes the time to smell good, it says he cares. It says he tries. It says he doesn't take things for granted.

He'll make the effort.

To brush his teeth before he kisses you in the morning.

To dress in a fresh, clean shirt, rather than sniff-test his dirty laundry.

To pat on just the right amount of cologne for a date—the amount that makes your pulse speed up.

But a few seconds later, he's glitter-free, and I jerk my hand away. I can't spend the morning thinking about how good the man who signs my checks smells. That's a recipe for trouble. For losing a job I both love *and* need. For making more mistakes. For messing up this tremendous opportunity.

I have to rein in this momentary bout of lust since that's all it is.

Wilder gestures to the dove gray couch in his office. I sit, and he takes the navy blue chair across from it then adjusts his tie. It's slate gray and has whimsical illustrations of skiers on it. He's clearly ready for our meeting to finally begin and frankly, so am I. But it's time for me to apologize. "I'm so sorry. I was rushing and I grabbed the wrong shirt and I feel terrible. I'm pretty sure I have the actual shirt for the employees' stockings in my purse. I swear I'm an industrious elf. I can get it and show it to you," I say, then I lunge for my purse, ready to right this ship.

"Let's take five on that," he says, then rolls up the cuffs

on his shirt. "But don't think twice about it. I'm more interested in something else."

I tense and stop searching for the actual shirt. "What is it?"

His expression is intense, borderline severe. "Should we start a line of shirts with sparkly Christmas penises on them?"

He says it with such a straight face that I'm so tempted to pick up the gauntlet he's throwing. To toss out names for a line like that. Snazzy Schlongs? Twinkling Twigs? Or better yet—Glitter Dongs and Shiny Schlongs.

But I realize he's graciously letting me know he's not pissed. I grab the lifeline he's thrown and hoist myself back into the meeting. "No, but I *am* suggesting we start a line of sparkly shirts. Everything is better with a little bling."

I reach for my tablet inside my purse and unlock it, then show him my presentation on the growth of our merch and the bennies of sparkles, flicking through studies on human behavior that show how we're naturally attracted to shiny objects.

I stop momentarily when Shay knocks on the door and brings us two cups of coffee. Wilder and I thank him, and when he leaves, I return to the presentation. "It's the peacock effect. We're all drawn to that iridescent plumage. But here's the issue with glitter."

"It sticks to everything?" he asks wryly.

I smile and nod, taking that on the chin. "Yes, but it's also a microplastic," I explain.

He nods in immediate understanding, then adds, "Which means it gets swept down drains and blown by the wind."

"Exactly. But this glitter—on both the *Fondle with Care*

shirts and the one I'm about to show you—is sustainable. It's made from mango skins and coffee grinds."

His lips twitch in amusement, then delight. "I do love mango. Much more than...eggnog. But not as much as mint."

I grin. That eggnog conversation with Wilder before we stacked dishes was the best part of Thanksgiving. "After we give these out as a holiday gift, we can continue to produce merch in the new year that's eco-friendly and seriously cool. Would you like to see the shirt?"

He scoots the chair back a few inches, then smirks. "I'm ready now."

I did it! I've steered this meeting plane out of a tail-spin. Problem averted. I reach for my purse to retrieve the shirt I meant to show him, but as I stretch, something scratches me from inside my own top. I don't want to scratch myself in front of him—I'm not a monkey—so I subtly sort of wriggle around to relieve the itch—when a wad of leftover paper towel falls from inside my shirt-sleeve. Down to the floor. Landing on his plush blue carpet, like a stain, and making my point for me—I can't win today.

For a brief second, or fifty, I'm hoping he didn't see me shed, but he's actively trying to avert his eyes.

The gentlemanliness of the gesture makes my chest ache. It reminds me of my terrible weekend and my dread of seeing my ex at my sister's wedding. With shame coursing through me, I pick up the used paper towel, stuff it into my pocket, then lift my chin and try to play it down. "I'd like to ask Santa for a do-over on this meeting, please," I say with a too-bright smile. Never let someone see you sweat.

But Wilder doesn't bite on my low-key attempt at

humor. His insightful eyes search my face as he asks, "What's going on, Fable?"

It's said with such genuine care that words rush to my throat. I don't usually share the more emotional parts of myself, but the injustice of the Thanksgiving incident fires me up. "It's just...when I went to find Brady at Thanksgiving?" I prompt, reminding him of that moment.

"Right. When he went to the wrapping room and returned with the caterer, he looked a little chagrined," Wilder supplies. I shouldn't be surprised he remembers every detail, but I'm surprisingly touched.

"They were enjoying some pre-dessert dessert—"

Wilder growls. He actually growls. I haven't even said what Brady was doing, but the man is feral. "While he was with *you?*" He says it like Brady's committed the crime of the century by cheating on me.

"Yes. In my defense, I ended it with him right then and there...Well, she swallowed first," I add. I try to make light of the awfulness of what they were doing in the wrapping room. I don't want to relive that mortification. I'm not missing Brady—he's no loss. But I feel like his doormat, and I hate that. When I was in high school, I vowed to never let someone walk over me, like my father did to my mother. I don't want Wilder to think of me that way.

But he's on my side, clearly, and he's breathing fumes. "He's a prick, and he never deserved you. *Ever.*"

Well, sir. His outrage is kind of hot. "But that's not even half of it," I say, fueled by his ire and my own.

"What is it?" Wilder asks, his jaw ticking. "What's the other half?"

I bite my lip. Should I tell him this? He is the boss.

But he seems keenly interested. He's leaning forward in his chair, rolling up the cuffs of his shirt again like he's ready to go into battle for me, a warrior CEO. I pause, momentarily distracted by his inked forearms. Abstract black artwork travels up his muscular wrists. His complexion is fair but a shade darker than my very pale self, since I'm allergic to sunlight. Suddenly, I don't want to stop staring at those arms, but once he finishes adjusting the cuffs, I tear my gaze away.

Then, since he seems like he's on the edge of his seat, I let it all out. "He's bringing her to the wedding. They're teaming up for the Evergreen Falls winter games. And I'm going—"

I snap my mouth shut before I utter *solo*. I don't want to sound like I'm angling for a teammate for the contest or even a plus one for the wedding.

But Wilder seems to easily read between the lines.

"You want Brady to be jealous?" Wilder asks, and his hands have knuckled into fists against his thighs. The muscles carving his forearms flex, and I try not to notice because *don't think inappropriate thoughts about your boss.*

Correction: don't think any *more* inappropriate thoughts about your boss.

"No. That's not it," I say truthfully. I think of Mom once more. She took my dad back again and again until she finally kicked him out for good. I was sixteen then, though, and watching the door swing open for him more times than he deserved has stayed with me. Especially since he went on to do the same thing to his next wife and the next one. There's a lesson there, for sure.

Deciding that it's not the worst thing for Wilder to know I'm still a little fiery, a little salty even, about how the eggnog went down, I square my shoulders and say, "It's because people treat you the way you let them, and I want to show Brady how I deserve to be treated."

Wilder nods slowly. "You deserve to be treated with respect. With adoration. With real affection."

From someone else, the lines could sound trite—but Wilder doesn't bullshit. He's genuine. I know that from working with him. He's not the cold-hearted, unapproachable boss. He's, well, he's real. And the compliments feel like they fit.

But I also like the way he looks right now. Fierce and protective. Like it's against his very nature to do anything *but* protect me from my awful ex.

This is why he owns a winning football team in this city. Why he runs luxury hotels and a green business. Why he commands a boardroom. The man does not suffer fools.

If this were a movie and Brady worked for him in it, he'd call the philanderer into his office and find a way to fire him on the spot.

To make a point. *You don't treat my top designer like that.*

Instead, there's a knock on the door, and a warm, husky voice calls out, "Wild child, I come bearing Christmas joy."

It's my turn to fight off a grin since my first thought is that Aunt Bibi has an adorable nickname for Wilder.

But when he sighs heavily, my second thought is—why is he so perturbed that she's interrupting us?

7

MY WILD CHILD

Wilder

Bibi isn't a fan of waiting. Or of subtlety. The second she sets foot in my office, with another Santa hat on, she scans the situation like an AI robot examining its surroundings. When her shrewd eyes lock on Fable, they gleam with triumph.

A plan is hatching in those gray irises as she marches to my chief designer. I lift a hand in warning, trying to call her off. "Bibi."

But my aunt is faster, sweeping over to the couch, perching next to Fable, then smiling her way. "Just the woman I wanted to see."

I groan, and I'm about to cut in when Fable flashes Bibi a warm smile and says, "If you're looking for someone to dress you for the holiday season, I'm your gal."

Damn, she's fast to the draw.

Bibi's a gunslinger, too, flicking the pom-pom of her emerald-green Santa hat away from her forehead. "We should discuss my fabulous plans for holiday parties and the inevitable 'what to wear' question soon."

I interject, "No glitter for my aunt, please."

Fable chuckles, her hazel eyes that lean toward the honey shade meeting mine. I've often wondered if they're hazel or honey. But that's not a question you ask an employee. Right now, they're flickering, perhaps with...a secret. Our Christmas glitter dick secret.

Get over yourself, man. The glitter dick incident is not a special secret.

"I promise to keep her glitter-free," Fable says to me with a borderline flirty grin. But nope. I can't start reading flirtation into her smiles or her almost wink. Not when she just got out of a terrible relationship with a flaming fuckface.

Bibi clears her throat, taking back the stage. "But this raises another interesting point." She smiles, Machiavellian. She's in full Bibi business mode now. "As you know, Wilder, I love to give gifts throughout the season, so I have one for you today." Bibi takes a pause, but it's strategically short, so I can't stop her from where I'm pretty sure she's going. She snaps her gaze to my designer. "Fable, don't you think it'd be a great idea if my Wilder went on a date with CJ O'Leary? The new executive director of the San Francisco Art Museum is, wait for it...single. And it's the *holidays.*"

Yep. Called it. I knew she'd be upping the ante, enlisting Fable as a wingwoman to sell the idea of her next match for me. I have to hand it to my aunt. She's tenacious. Bibi has worked her way up in business and life, and she's fearless.

But is Fable...irked? Her festive smile has burned off.

Bibi holds up a hand like she's picturing a marquee. "I

can see it now. The single dad and the art connoisseur," Bibi waxes on.

As if that's how anyone would bill such a romance—the single dad is *not* how I'm known in social circles. Or in any circle, even though it's true.

"Maybe we should take an early lunch and discuss this elsewhere," I say to Bibi, hoping my tone brooks no argument. Then I try deflecting. "Also, why do you have a different Santa hat on?"

She flicks the pom-pom again. "This is my office hat. Or perhaps it's better to call it my thinking cap. Because this idea came to me mere moments ago, fully formed. Your sister and her wife love the match too," she continues, and of course, Bibi's already lined up Caroline and Hannah in her matchmaking camp. Bibi tilts her head Fable's way once again. "Wouldn't it be great to see my wild child find love?"

Fable snickers, likely at the nickname, but Bibi doesn't wait for her to answer.

"I even spoke with CJ's aunt, and she says she thinks CJ would be open to it as well."

I maintain a straight face. I know things my aunt doesn't, like CJ's true feelings on this matter. We're friendly enough. We run in the same social circles. And when she called me recently to ask about a fundraising contribution, she also gave me a heads-up that her aunt had been stirring the matchmaking pot. We had a good laugh over our meddling relatives and their quest to set us up. Something that won't happen since we're better off as friends.

"I'm not sure CJ and I—"

But I cut myself off before I finish the sentence. If I tell Bibi that CJ and I aren't compatible, she'll simply continue the hunt. She'll suggest someone else tomorrow, then the next day, then the next, like when she arranged a lunch with an investment banker who was thirty minutes late, never apologized, and asked if I had gold toilets. Or the ad agency owner who spent the whole dinner texting and scrolling.

Dating is exhausting, and what's even the point? Romance doesn't work out, and that's fine.

"She could come to the wedding as your plus one and compete in the Evergreen Falls games with you. Can't you picture them, Fable?" Bibi coos, not even trying to hide that she's using my designer to sway me.

My gutsy designer who's got the chutzpah of a Broadway star. Who else could wield a glitter Christmas dick shirt with that much panache?

My bold designer who found a way out of the snafu like a queen. The way Fable flew out of here to grab a lint roller was one of the sexiest things I've ever seen.

My gorgeous designer, with waves of shiny auburn hair, a constellation of freckles across her nose, and honey-hazel eyes that radiate warmth and humor. Fable, who opened her heart to me and whose outrage couldn't disguise the hurt I spotted underneath.

But it doesn't look like my designer wants to be a conspirator in Bibi's matchmaking game. Maybe she wants to be...another player? I try to read Fable as closely as I can. To understand what's happening in her clever mind when her gaze shifts subtly to me. It's like her eyes say *do it*, then her mouth says, "I can't really picture Wilder with her."

Is she testing the waters? Letting me know it's nice in here and to feel free to jump in?

If I had been attracted to Fable before, that attraction has ballooned now with her savvy.

But this is my building. My stadium. My playground. I need to bring this deal home. You don't get to the top in business without taking a few calculated risks. Fable wants a date for her sister's Christmas Eve wedding. I want to get Bibi off my back during the holiday season. And I'd like to show that Brady guy how a woman should be treated. More so, I'd like to show Fable.

I turn to my aunt. "I can't picture going to the wedding with CJ, either, but I need a moment with Fable..." A smile tugs my lips as I roll the dice big time.

Like I did years ago in Vegas when I found a way to pay for school after my father gambled away the money I'd saved for college. I was the first in my family to go—that had been my mother's dream for me and, later, for herself. I taught myself the markets. I took what little funds I had left and invested it. Learned the value of compound interest. Made it grow fast and furiously. Paid my way, built my own business, and created the life I wanted for my mother, her family, and me.

I'll ask Bibi to leave, then ask Fable if she'd want to be my fake date for the holidays.

But before I can make another move, the bold, brave woman in my office says, "He can't take her since I'm his date for the wedding."

8

MY CHRISTMAS GIRLFRIEND

Wilder

Sometimes, when you play cards, you get lucky. When that happens, you need to bluff so you don't show just how good your hand is.

I don't grin too big at Fable. I don't reach for her. And I definitely don't make Fable wait for an answer from me. I simply flash her a good boyfriend smile and go all in. "You are, little elf."

Her eyes flicker briefly with relief, then amusement, no doubt at the nickname, as she says, "And I can't wait, sugar plum."

I fight off a laugh. This woman wastes no time.

Bibi's brow creases. "Sugar plum?"

I smile even wider, feeling a little fizzy. "That's what Fable calls me. What can I say? The woman loves Christmas."

Fable and I are sitting across from each other with plenty of space between us, but she leans my way with obvious affection. "And he calls me little elf since I help with the stockings. But also," she says, like she's sharing a secret just with Bibi, "I have the cutest elf costume."

I can picture it now—a short skirt with faux fur trim. I can picture it all too well. "Yeah, it's great," I say, my voice a scrape.

"I should get you a sugar plum tie," she adds, looking my way with doting affection before covering her mouth with her fingers as if silently screaming in excitement. "That would be the best," she says when she lets go.

Bibi studies Fable with some skepticism. Possibly confusion. "But I thought you were dating that Brady character? The one who practically had 'secret fraternity handshake' written all over him."

Fable winces, like *ouch*.

I hate seeing her hurt, even by the reminder. "He was the wrong man for her," I say, and there's nothing fake about that sentiment.

Fable gives me an adoring look. "I tried to distract myself with him. But only because it was always Wilder I crushed on."

I nearly blink.

That word—*crush*.

It sounds too good on her pretty pink lips. Too tempting coming from her lovely mouth. It makes my pulse speed faster than it should.

"Really?" Bibi eyes Fable like she doesn't quite believe her, but her voice seems to say she desperately wants to.

Fable shrugs a little hopelessly. "I've always been a sucker for a man with abstract ink. Something that makes you think and feel. Something that's not hitting you over the head, but instead inviting you to...wonder."

Fuck me. She didn't simply notice the tattoos on my

forearms—not that they're hard to miss. They're on my knuckles too. But she has a goddamn opinion on them, and it's an opinion that sounds like poetry. The back of my neck goes warm.

Settle down, man. She's just playing along.

I try to cool my desire.

Time to sell this holiday romance like I'm making a pitch in a takeover bid. "You know we've worked closely together for a long while. Especially lately on the company's holiday gift. And I've always admired..." I pause, careful not to cross any lines—or any more lines. "Her mind. Her quick thinking. Her passion for football."

That's all true. Her obsession with the game I love is hot. There's not an opposing defense in the league that she hasn't studied, a starting lineup that she doesn't know, or a player on which she doesn't have an opinion. Come to think of it, I'd better revise that hot to a white-*hot.* Then I flash a smile and go for the close. "And her dishwasher-stacking skills."

Her hand flies to her chest. "Oh, stop. You know that's how you won me over, sugar plum."

"And I thought I won you over when I took you out for your favorite mint ice cream," I say, leaning into the flirty vibe to sell this fake romance to the judge and jury.

"Wait," Bibi says, skeptical as she raises a polished wine-red fingernail. "How long have you two been together?"

Bibi's not an executive at my corporation for nothing. For all her talk of dreams, visions, and past lives, she's incredibly grounded. She can spot a flaw in a nanosecond.

"It happened quickly," I say, also quickly. "The dishwasher stacking at Thanksgiving dinner was my undoing." My self-deprecating laugh covers any hitches in my on-the-fly fib. "You know how much I like everything neat, clean, and organized. When I found out Fable was single, I texted her the next day to ask her out for last night."

There. I've established the timeframe for this fake romance. Now, I'm locking it down in my mind. It's easy to get tangled up in your story if you don't keep track of the details, and I won't let that happen to us.

"It was so good," Fable says as she jumps in for the save. "The Mint-nificent flavor at The Best Ice Cream Shop in the City is top-notch." I'm impressed. They say the best lies have a grain of truth, and that shop does indeed have a mouthwatering mint ice cream.

"Last night?" Bibi asks. I see the cogs turning and know where she's headed. How could I have been out if Mac was home?

"Mac was at photography class," I explain.

"Oh." Bibi seems a bit flummoxed. "I didn't realize she was taking a class."

Fable and I obviously didn't go out, but my daughter is a gamer. She'll roll with this plan when I tell her to go along.

It occurs to me that Mac and Fable would be a formidable team. They're both sharp, smart, quick on their feet. I can picture them pulling off...well, anything.

"I had to seize the chance when I could," I told Bibi. "And we were just having a secret coffee date here," I add, gesturing to the two cups Shay brought in.

My aunt is not ready to give up her interrogation. "And you didn't say anything in the car this morning because...?"

Bibi's shrewd logic is making this much harder than I'd anticipated. Because it's a good question. Why *wouldn't* I have offered this dating info hours ago?

I'm scrabbling for a plausible answer when Fable smiles at me, hearts in her eyes. "Because a gentleman doesn't kiss and tell," she says, sounding like she's rushing to grab a rescue lint roller all over again.

I could kiss her for that save. Instead, I offer a smile—a romantic one. "That's right," I say, holding her gaze for a beat or two. *Her eyes.*

This whole time, Bibi's been shifting her gaze from Fable to me and then back like a spectator at a tennis match. She narrows her eyes one more moment, then lets out a victorious, "Finally! I've been waiting for *so long*."

Waiting? Please. More like moving chess pieces. But I give her this win. Then, she's all business, snapping her gaze to the woman next to her. "Fable, are you good at Christmas tree decorating?"

"I know my way around a string of lights," Fable says.

"You do like shiny things, my little elf," I add.

"What can I say? The peacock effect is strong in me," she tosses back.

"Good," Bibi says, squeezing Fable's arm. "Then I hope you beat that Brady character in the competition."

"You and me both," Fable says with a confidence that impresses me.

My aunt nods with decisive satisfaction. "And frankly, all the other competitors in town. The planning committee will vote on a winner, and we need to beat everyone who dares to enter."

Fable looks to me with amusement. "I guess it runs in the family—this competitive streak?"

"Seems it does," I say.

Bibi smiles at Fable, then shifts her focus to me. "Make sure you sort everything out with the cabins at your property there. And your mom can meet Fable when she joins us at Christmas. I'm so glad Elizabeth'll be done with coursework in time to come back from London."

I wince inside. Enlisting Mac will be easy enough. But enlisting my mother? I'm not sure how to play that, or how to fake it for her. She sees through everything. But I'll leave that decision to another day. "Yes, that'll be great," I say.

Bibi stands to leave, but before she goes, she turns back to me, her brow pinched. "Have you told HR?"

That nearly leaves me at a standstill. But only for a few seconds. I look to Fable once more just to make sure she wants this—this fake romance. This story we're peddling wouldn't work as some forbidden office romance where we'd sneak around. Since I own the team, I ought to set a good example. Follow the rules and all. While we are working on the stockings together, I'm not her direct supervisor. She reports to Sandra Clements, the VP of marketing. The employee handbook allows relationships so long as there's no direct report line. "I was going to do that today. I can let Sandra know as well. If that works for you, Fable?"

The ball is in her court, and she slams it back with a ferocious swing and a smile. "Definitely."

"Good. Disclosure is important, especially when you own the company. And it's a good thing Fable is not your direct report." With that, Bibi sails toward the outer office. But she stops short in the doorway, spins back around, and taps her emerald cap. "Told you this was my idea hat. Why don't the two of you team up in the office door-decorating contest too? Such a cute thing for a couple to do this season."

"I'm in," Fable pipes up. "Fair warning though. It's

going to be the best-decorated door here at Blaine Enterprises."

Bibi beams. "Can't wait to see it." She snicks the door shut.

We stare at it a moment, then Fable turns back to me, dropping her voice to a whisper as if afraid to break a spell. "Are you really okay with this?"

"The door decorating?" I ask, then shrug. "I don't usually decorate it myself, but it's fine. I can manage."

She laughs, shaking her head. "Not that. Also, I'll handle the decorating. If I leave it to you, everything will be black, navy, or steel."

"Not true," I protest.

But she arches a brow, looking me up and down like she's busting me. I guess my suit is blue and the tie is gray. "Fine, you're right."

She nods like *I told you so*, and then her smile burns off, replaced by concern. "But what I meant was—are you okay with the whole thing? You're not mad at me for saying I'm your date?"

For a moment, she sounds so vulnerable, a dramatic contrast to her fire and chaos, and I don't make her wait for an answer. "No," I hasten to say. I don't want her to think for a second that I'm not absolutely okay with this. "I was actually about to ask if you wanted to be my plus one. That's what I wanted to talk to you about when I said I need*ed a moment*."

Her eyes pop. "Really?"

"Yes. I didn't want to put you on the spot by suggesting it without checking with you."

Her hand flies to her chest. "Did I make you uncomfortable?"

"No. You read my mind, Fable. Don't you get it?"

"I wanted to make sure," she says.

"I'm very sure." I put that conviction in my voice and see her shoulders relax a fraction. "And I'd very much like your ex to see how a man should treat a woman."

Fable snorts. "Bonus points if you make him cry."

The thought that he'd done that to her—caused her to shed tears when she shouldn't have ever had to—sends fire rushing through my veins.

"I've never missed a bonus round before," I tease, only half-joking.

"Let's show him, then, sugar plum." I wince at the nickname, and she laughs. "Hey, it was either that or Santa. And as a nickname, Santa was giving me a little ick."

I chuckle but then turn serious again. I meant what I said—I'm ready for this charade, but Fable is my employee, and I need to give her an out. Not a subtle one, either, but a big red fire exit with flashing arrows and a neon sign flashing THIS WAY OUT. "But if you don't want to, we can simply move on. There's no pressure, and it won't affect your job—"

"Oh stop! I'm *not* the HR department. More like the head of matchmaking deflection."

"And when we beat Brady in the Christmas games, you'll have reached the department of revenge." I saw how her eyes lit up at Bibi's go-get-em words. Not only is this fake romance an opportunity to show her and her ex how a woman should be treated, it's a chance to beat that jackass in the games.

"Looks like I just ordered myself a Christmas boyfriend," she says, shimmying a little at the prospect of revenge. "I'll take twenty-five days of this gift, thank you very much."

I wish I could unwrap the gift of her. Undo a silky ribbon, let it fall to the floor, then...

I steer away from the almost filthy thoughts and do a mental one-eighty, reverting to my default gear—work. "I'd like to see the holiday shirt you made, after all."

Following my focus shift, Fable shows me a pretty design with a cut-out neck and "Renegades" emblazoned in a retro font, filled in with silver and red bling. It's festive and stylish. At least, I think that's what Mac would tell me.

"What do you think? My projections say it's on trend," Fable says.

"I approve," I say.

The next style she shows me has a more masculine cut and neck, with no glitter. I approve that one too.

Carefully, she folds the shirts, then under her breath, she says, "Thanks...wild child."

But no. That won't do. That's Bibi's term. "Don't call me that."

"I'm sorry."

"I meant—I like sugar plum better from you."

"You do?"

"Does that surprise you?" I ask, wishing I didn't enjoy getting to know these little details of her so much.

"A little."

I need to shut up. I need to stop enjoying this. This thing between us is all a ruse—a ruse meant to help both of us. That's it.

I focus on the plan for the stockings. We'll fill the stockings with the shirts, a box of holiday chocolates from Elodie's, a gift card, and the employees' Christmas bonuses.

When we're done, Fable's gaze strays to the windows

overlooking the field, empty now since it's an off day. "Did you see Hendrix's fourth-quarter diving catch yesterday?"

The team played Phoenix in the early afternoon. Mac and I watched from the owner's suite before she went to her photography class. "I swear he was parallel to the ground and still caught it," I say, proud of my players and their skills.

"What a game," she says with a happy sigh. "I watched it at home. Took my mind off things."

A pang lodges in my chest, chased by anger. Brady's why she needed a distraction. I really can't stand that asshole for hurting Fable. "I'm glad you had something to distract you." But then I replay what she just said. Hold the hell on. "Why didn't you come to the game? You usually do." She's told me she likes to watch from the stands with her sister or her friends so she can cheer the loudest.

She shrugs. "Everyone was busy," she says with a smile. A forced smile.

I burn inside again. I'm not sure I believe her excuse. I suspect she didn't go because of that fuckwit. "Then you should come to the next home game."

I'm about to offer her coveted fifty-yard line seats when she says, "I'm sure I will. I have tickets." She shifts gears immediately. "And we have a lot to do before then with all this holiday gift planning. I love giving out gifts. Do I get to help you hand them out before the break like a good little elf?"

I go with her change-up. "Will you wear that cute little elf costume?" I ask before I can think the better of it.

Her lips curve in a grin. "Of course I will."

I stare at her for a long moment. Damn, she's beautiful. But I've thought that about her before, and I won't let errant distractions stir me from my plans. In fact, I *really* ought to return to the fake dating plans rather than worrying about where she'll watch the next game from. "We should work out some details. If we need to be seen together publicly before the wedding."

"Good point. We probably will."

"I'll give it some thought. And then, at the cabins, you can stay in another room and—"

A buzz from my desk interrupts me as Shay speaks through the intercom. "Your father is on line three."

"We can talk details later." Fable waves me off, and I don't know if I should hug her or shake her hand. As if she senses my unease, she lets herself out quickly, and I don't have to choose.

Shame though. Especially since I'd have preferred the former.

Chin up, I head to my desk, take a fortifying breath, then steel myself. "Hello."

"Hi, son," my father says, and I hate that he calls me that. For so long, I've felt like the adult in the relationship, parenting him. It sounds so wrong to be called his kid. "Great game this past weekend," he adds. "I told you Hendrix was the best receiver money could buy."

I clench my jaw. He never told me that. I made that call. I spotted the receiver's talent and made sure my GM got him. "The whole team is the best in the league," I say, *and I have the rings to show for it.*

But I don't say that part. Or much else. Instead, I listen as Dad chats about life in Vegas, how his friend Victor is doing as he nears retirement, then clucks his tongue. It's his tell—he's about to ask for something. "So listen, son. Can I borrow ten grand from you? I went underwater on a game last week."

A poker game he shouldn't have played in. A poker game that means he's back to earning his one-day chip again, if he's even going to meetings. He's earned many years' worth of one-day chips. It's pointless to even want him to change and more pointless to think he might.

I can't trust him. Never have been able to, really.

I shouldn't do this. Truly, I shouldn't. But I do it anyway. It's just easier this way. "I'll wire it to the usual account."

"I owe you one," he says, and he probably believes he'll pay me back.

When I finish the transaction, I make a large donation to the art museum, one well over its holiday fundraising goals. Still needing distance from him, I reach out to Mom to check in on her studies and studio work.

Mom: I'm winning an award for best portraiture in my class! And get this—it's of a dog!

Wilder: Can't think of a better thing to paint.

Mom: It's a booming market, I'm told. Maybe you should expand into dog portraiture studios.

Wilder: Honestly, it's not a bad idea.

Mom: I'm helpful like that. I'll send you a photo of it later.

Wilder: I can't wait.

And I mean that. For a while, she didn't like to show her paintings to anyone. It took her long enough to admit that was what she wanted—to go to school. When she won a place in her first-choice program, I happily wrote the check and bought her a flat in London where she studies. But she'll be here for the holidays soon...

Which reminds me. I'd better text my Christmas girlfriend.

Wilder: We should probably have a dinner to hammer out any other details.

Fable: Yes, we need a good hammering.

I chuckle. This woman is going to test all my resolve. And the thing is, I'm pretty sure I'm here for it. So I click over to my calendar to see what Mac and I have planned for the week. A photography class. A mini-golf game. I write back.

Wilder: How does sex sound on Saturday?

I hover my thumb over the send button, but whoa, that's some typo. I correct the errant word to 'six' and head to the window, looking at the field, picturing it filled with fans for the next game as they cheer on one of the most successful teams in the league.

But all the while, my mind keeps slipping in a different direction.

I've got to stop thinking about sex on Saturday.

* * *

The next night, I read another chapter in *The Inheritance Games* to Mac, review her Christmas list, discuss her wild ideas about secret doors, and then tuck her in. After that, I head to the kitchen to make sure we cleaned up completely after dinner. Then, I'm reviewing a report from my CFO when an idea strikes me. A quick check of the time tells me it's not too late.

I have Fable's home address, so I hop over to another browser window and send her a small holiday gift slated to arrive tomorrow evening, ordering a red bow to go with it.

Well, it's not only the season—it's also just the right way to treat your fake girlfriend, and she did drop an enormous hint.

9

FAKE REAL ICE CREAM

Fable

This will be easier over text. At least, I hope so.

On Wednesday evening, I'm settling into the bus, heading to meet Charlotte at the florist. But first, I fire off a text to her. Best to tell my sister the news first when she can't see my face.

> Fable: So, I'll be going to the wedding with the best man.

But I don't send it. Is that too random? Too selfish? I don't know. My stomach churns with worry as the bus trundles through the city to Kiss My Tulips.

I try again.

Fable: Leo's buddy asked me on a date...

That's a little better. Maybe? I drop my head in my hand. Why didn't I think through the logistics of lying to my sister and...EVERYONE ELSE? I wince, then stare out the window at the city rolling by. Early evening shoppers lug red and white bags from department stores. Busy humans dart in and out of shops, no doubt hunting for the perfect gift.

This is the season when everyone tries their hardest for the people they love. I love my sister, and I've always wanted her to be happy. When we were growing up and our parents were arguing, when Mom was hurting, when Dad was trying to win her back, I made it my mission to look out for my younger sister—to make sure she was happy even if Mom and Dad weren't. Really, is this *that* different?

I handled the situation with our parents when we were kids. Now, I can't think of this fake romance with Wilder as lying. It's simply...*handling a complicated situation*. Yes, that's it. And handling a complicated situation is an act of love.

On that note, I delete the text and try again.

Fable: Funny thing. I'm going out to dinner this weekend with Wilder Blaine. And we're going to your wedding together too.

Then I hit send, hoping she's too frenzied with flower ideas to think much about it.

No such luck. A few minutes later, I get off the bus and walk to the shop, where I spot Charlotte waving me down on the sidewalk, bursting with excitement. "You're dating your billionaire boss?"

It's a shriek. More like a shriek heard 'round the world.

"Yes. I am," I say, but I lower my hands, the gesture saying *let's keep this quiet.*

"Details!"

"He asked me to dinner this weekend." That part's true.

She grabs my hands, her smile wider than the city block. "And to the wedding? Like, you're going to the wedding together too? The best man and the maid of honor. Oh my god, Fabes," she says.

She's too excited, and I'm too big of a jerk.

But I tell myself all of this is true. Wilder and I *are* having dinner this weekend. We *will* go to her wedding together. "Well, we have to do that competition. Someone, cough-cough, is kind of obsessed with games," I say, deflecting a bit, then I stage whisper, "You and Leo."

"We are! And this is so cool. I'm so excited," she says, hooking her arm through the crook of my elbow as we head to the shop to check out succulents for a Christmas Eve wedding bouquet. "But it's early days," I caution. "So, we're taking it slow."

"Of course, of course. You'd better keep me posted." We reach the shop. "And I'm happy for you."

"Thanks, Charlotte," I say as a kernel of guilt wedges into my heart. I don't want to be a liar like my snake of a father. But this is absolutely not the same kind of lie he whispered in my mother's ears, telling her he was working late again, telling her he was out of town, then telling her he knew it was a mistake and he'd never do it again.

Everything I said to my sister was true. When Wilder and I inevitably split up after Christmas, that will be totally true too.

No need to add my drama to everything she's worrying about while planning a last-minute wedding. If I tell her we're fake dating, I'll need to tell her why—that the caterer she recommended for Thanksgiving was enjoying Brady's eggnog special—then Leo would insist on kicking Brady, his own cousin, out of the wedding party.

That's not fair to them. It's not their circus or their monkeys.

Brady's my monkey and Wilder's the new ringmaster.

Or something like that.

We head inside, and I spend the next twenty minutes oohing and aahing over green succulents. We choose an unconventional but low-maintenance flower style for her bouquets. There's a sister shop of Kiss My Tulips in Evergreen Falls, so we can look at their options here and pick up the final arrangement in the cute little Christmas-obsessed town where my sister will get married.

When we're done I say goodbye, then head home, nearing a bell-ringing Santa on the next corner. I reach into my purse for some bills, then drop them into his shiny red bucket.

"Ho, ho, ho, and Merry Christmas. May all your Christmas wishes come true," the jolly man says.

"And yours as well," I say to the guy in the red suit and long white beard. Once I pass him, I wonder though—what are my holiday wishes? Simply to survive the wedding without feeling like a doormat? Sure, that's definitely one. To make a point that I won't let people think they can walk all over me? Yes, definitely. But Wilder also said the other day in his office that he'd like to show my ex how a man should treat a woman. And I'd like him to show me as well. I suppose maybe that's a secret wish of mine now too.

To know what that's like.

No.

It's my wish to know how Wilder Blaine treats a woman.

Even if we have to keep it a secret from my sister, I want this wish to come true. I need to tell someone. This secret is clawing at my heart, nagging at my brain. Then, like a cartoon anvil landing on my head, I know who to tell. My friends Josie and Maeve, and of course Everly too. Josie's a librarian, Maeve's a painter, and Everly is the publicist for the Sea Dogs, one of the city's hockey teams. They aren't connected to Wilder's world, and we've spent a lot of time together since Josie moved to San Francisco last fall. Plus, Maeve has been insisting she had a feeling about him ever since we ran into him in the lobby of his hotel one time and he offered to comp us a room. We didn't need one, but when he left, Maeve promptly declared, *Someone has a crush on you*.

That's Maeve for you. A little wild. But also wrong. I denied it then, I've denied it every time she's brought it up since, and I'm denying it now. Still, I know they'll be the perfect audience. I text them and since they're all around, we hop on a video call the second I walk into my apartment.

And tell them I do—every single detail of my holiday romance, true and fake.

Maeve chuckles. "I told you so, I told you so, I told you so."

"He does not have a crush on me," I say.

"Mark my words, friend," Maeve says, emphatic. "I saw it in his eyes."

"Maeve, you think everyone has a crush on everyone," I say.

Josie laughs, her head tipping back. "Can confirm. She does."

"I can't help it if my crush radar is finely calibrated and picks up the tiniest details."

"Or maybe you want everything to be a crush," Everly suggests to Maeve. "You are a bit of a hopeless romantic."

Maeve's aghast, her jaw down near her black shirt. "A bit? Only a bit?"

"Fine. You're *a lot*."

Josie laughs. "We're all *a lot*." But then she adds in a stage whisper, "But I hope Maeve's right."

"Shut up. She's not." She has to be because I can't go there.

I stuff the idea of his crush in a far corner of the closet. I won't entertain the notion at all.

When I end the call, I find there's been a delivery to my building, and it's so thoughtful, it makes my chest flip.

See? That's real. I don't feel like such a liar as I dig into the ice cream Wilder sent. The very real ice cream.

* * *

On Saturday evening, the banging on my door is so loud it's like her calling card.

"Coming, Josie," I call, hurrying over to look through the peephole. Waves of chestnut hair are piled on top of her head in an effortless bun I know isn't effortless at all. Black-and-white cat-eye glasses frame her heart-shaped face, and her fair skin is flawless—well, my girl rocks the skin-care routine.

I swing open the door. "You have the most recognizable knock in the universe. It sounds like an elephant stampede."

"Nice to see you too," she says, then steps inside, lugging a couple of red-and-white-striped canvas shopping bags stuffed with gifts—books from An Open Book, toys for her little nephews, and records, it looks like.

"Hello, Mrs. Shopping Claus. Let me guess. The albums are for Wesley."

She smiles, her eyes twinkling. "Yes. Wesley's on his way home from a road trip, so I'd better wrap them tonight. I have a feeling he's the type to look for his presents in advance."

That's her hockey-playing boyfriend, who she's been with for almost a year—but only after a twisty, turny romance. They were roomies first, and Josie's brother is the captain of Wesley's hockey team. Talk about *forbidden.*

"But right now, I'm at your service. I'm all for picking just the right outfits." Her knowing grin is a nod to the outfit she didn't plan to wear the night she met Wesley—an oversized T-shirt and pink fuzzy slippers.

"Thank you for putting your dating trauma to my good use," I say.

"It is for a worthwhile cause." She sets the bags on the floor and backs up, getting right to business, roaming her eyes up and down my outfit. As a designer, I have an eye for clothes, patterns, and pairings. But as a woman going on a fake date with a billionaire, I need some backup from a friend.

"The sweater is cute," she says, pointing at the cranberry-red V-neck sweater that slopes just so off one shoulder. "The little white cami under it is great. The hair is gorgeous." She nods to the soft waves on my shoulders—the result of an afternoon of toil with the flat iron. "But..." Josie continues, drawing out the word and the inspection.

My heart sinks. "What's wrong?"

"It's the skirt." She points to my knee-length black skirt, which I've paired with simple black heels. "I would go with something else."

I smooth the fabric unnecessarily. "The man wears custom suits to work. I need something nice." Especially after the paper towel incident, I want to look classy for Wilder. He's a classy man who sent me a delicious gift the other night, complete with a red satin bow that had my mind wandering to other uses for bows.

"What he wears to work is not the point," Josie says.

Oh. I get it. "You're saying he might not wear a suit tonight," I say quickly, then bite my lip. "Right, right." I picture him at Thanksgiving in his crisp dress shirt and slacks. "He'll probably wear—"

Josie curls her hand around my forearm. "This isn't about him. It's about you. Wear what you're comfortable in."

That sounds too easy. "Are you sure?"

"Trust me. I *know*," she says kindly. "On our first date, Wes didn't care about the baggy T-shirt and slippers or that I looked like I'd just gotten out of the shower."

That was a fair point, especially how things had worked out for them.

"I hate that you're sort of right," I grumble.

She cups her ear. "Did you say you love that I'm right?"

"You're a little right." That's all I'll admit. I get what she's saying, but our situations are different. "But I *have* to look like I'm trying. That's the point—this is for show."

She smiles softly. "I'd think, especially when you're fake-dating, you wouldn't want to try on too many different personalities. It's best if you be you."

I part my lips to highlight the flaw in her logic, but dammit, I can't.

"Okay, you're *really* right," I admit as my stomach swoops with nerves. "What the hell am I getting myself into, Josie? I date bikers and stockbrokers. I date bartenders and project managers for an app that takes a picture of your cat when it uses your computer to tell you that you weren't hacked. I don't fake date or real date *billionaires*." I slow my roll, breathe, then add, "Especially billionaires who send me Mint-nificent ice cream."

Her big eyes pop. "So Maeve was right?"

"No," I say, scoffing. "He's just generous."

She clears her throat. "He looked at you like he thinks you're gorgeous last fall at The Resort and now he's sent you your favorite ice cream?"

"He did." I briefly savor the tasty memory and the card too. ***Happy holidays to my favorite elf***. Then I'm back to the current convo. "Anyway, my point is—"

Josie waggles a finger, cutting me off. "Nope. Tell me more about the ice cream he sent."

"It was sweet. It was creamy. It melted in my mouth."

Her eyebrows shoot higher. "And he sent your favorite flavor, you say?"

Oh no. Oh, hell no. I can see where she's going, but I won't follow. "It's not a sign, Josie," I say, trying to head her off before she gets to Romance Lane. "It was just ice cream, nothing else. Besides, everyone likes mint. Mint is not a sign."

She smirks. "Oh, it's for sure not a sign if it needs a triple denial."

I give her a serious look. "I mentioned my favorite ice cream shop when we were in his office, creating a whole backstory of how we supposedly started dating. That's all." But I did like the card. It's stashed in my bedside table.

"And then he sent it to you for real." She is a dog refusing to let go of a bone.

"Yes, Josie. It was real ice cream," I say firmly. I stare her down, and she gives it right back to me, staring hard like she's waiting for some reaction. Like I'll connect the dots then be over the moon with glee.

She'll be waiting a long time. I'm a realist.

"Wilder is a strategic man," I say. "He knows how to get things done. Yes, the ice cream was amazing, but he also knows how to play the game."

"The fake dating game?"

"*Any game*," I emphasize. Then I shrug, lightening my tone. "Besides, his assistant probably sent it. It was nice, but it doesn't mean anything."

"It means he listened to you," she points out thoughtfully.

As her observation sinks in, there's a tiny flutter in my chest. A warm and lovely feeling that only lasts a second, maybe three or four. But I don't linger on it. This fauxmance isn't about flutters and feelings. It's about faking it and faking it well.

"As I was saying," I say, grabbing control of the conversation. "I need to look like I belong on a date with him."

She laughs, but it's with me, not at me. It's reassuring as she says, "He asked *you* to be his wedding date."

"His *fake* wedding date," I remind her.

"Yes, but out of all the women in San Francisco, he asked you. Because he likes you."

I bark out a laugh, then shake my head fiercely. "He asked me because he feels sorry for me. He has a hero complex, and he needs a shield."

She gives me a look with those soft blue eyes. "He might need a shield, but he also likes you."

The last thing I need is for that idea to take root in my head. "This is a *you scratch my back, I'll scratch yours* situationship."

Although, it's not really an even trade. Does Wilder... feel sorry for me? Is that why he offered to be my fake date for the Christmas Eve wedding? Maybe I can subtly determine an answer to that question tonight.

"Besides, I have loans to pay off, a dream I'm saving up for, and a job I like. I'm not interested in dating my boss," I finish, back on the topic. "I'm not really even interested in dating, given how my last relationship ended."

"All that may be true but he wouldn't want to spend all this time with you if he didn't enjoy your company."

I hold out my hands, confused. "What does that have to do with what to wear?"

She cups her mouth and raises her voice. "Get out of the fancy business-lady skirt and put on a short skirt and some cute boots. Dress like you. Be you."

And...she's really, truly, absolutely right. I'm faking being a girlfriend. I don't want to fake being me.

Taking her advice, I hustle to my bedroom and grab a short white skirt and a pair of cute, lace-up ankle boots. "By the way," Josie calls out, "I finally got us into that paint-and-sip class."

"Ooh! The one with the teacher who can supposedly teach us talent-less painters to paint *anything*?" I've been dying to take one of Rana's classes. Maeve loves her.

"Yes. I had to sell both kidneys, but it's worth it. Her

classes are booked for months. Rana had just enough room for the four of us."

"Perfect. Your kidneys will go to a good cause," I say.

I grab a necklace I designed from my jewelry case—silver, with a pair of bells on it. I return to the living room and hold my arms out wide.

"Yes," she says, clapping like she's in the audience at a Broadway musical. "You look like you. A fun, bold, confident designer. Now go."

I leave, but I don't let myself think Wilder asked me out for any other reason than I was in the right place at the right time.

But the ice cream was really good.

10

THIS STUPID ATTRACTION

Fable

I'm early this time. I don't want a repeat of the other day where I fly in late and, I dunno, my bra detaches itself from my boobs and flings itself at my boss. I mean, that could happen. Sentient bras could be a thing and then an eye could get poked out.

The Lyft drops me off ten minutes before we've planned to meet, and I hope that gives me time to settle in and, well, not trip and fall face-first into his lap.

This girl learns from her mistakes.

With my chin up and confidence on, I walk to the white door with the holiday garland hanging around it, warm white lights softly twinkling overhead. Wilder picked a place called Dahlia's in Presidio Heights, and it looks like a bistro in Florence. When I walk inside, a confident woman with an ivory complexion and diamond Christmas tree earrings greets me before I can even say hello.

"You must be Fable," she says.

I laugh nervously. "Yes. I am."

"Perfect. I'm Dahlia. We're expecting you."

"Um, okay," I say, and I'm not normally speechless but I'm not normally greeted like a special guest at a restaurant or even recognized before I've given my name. And I'm definitely never greeted by the owner herself, especially for a Michelin-starred restaurant.

"We have the best table in the house for you," she says as she guides me through the packed place past a dozen or so tables with small vases filled with white roses and holly berries, surrounded by white votive candles flickering in the dim lighting. The brick walls are lined with art, some abstract, some landscapes of Italy, I think. Maybe Tuscany. I'm not sure, but chefs in the open kitchen plate dishes of steaming pastas and herbed chicken next to mouthwatering bread. As we pass the kitchen, I say, "The decorations are amazing. Classy but cozy."

"Ooh, that's a vibe I like," she says, "And are you having a good weekend so far?"

"Yes. It's great," I say, mostly because I don't know what else to reply with. It's a standard question, but at the same time, I wasn't expecting this sort of star treatment.

"We have you out here on the patio. I hope you love it and if you need anything at all, let me know. Any of my staff is happy to assist," she says, then opens the door to a star-lit patio with heaters set up under an outside tent. It's like...a Christmas garden in the middle of the city. Poinsettias hang from brick columns. Short evergreens stand in terracotta pots in the corners, with red bows and twinkling lights on the branches. Above us, strings of blue and white lights form a makeshift ceiling. Music plays quietly on a speaker, the soft notes of Nat King Cole making me warm all over.

Yes, it's good I arrived first so I can catch my breath in this most unexpectedly romantic restaurant.

When Wilder sent me the name of the venue this afternoon, I only looked up the menu. I didn't poke around and check out the photos. But now that I'm here, it's clear this is definitely a place where you bring a date. It's warm and intimate and an escape from the city.

Dahlia guides me toward a corner table, and I guess I won't beat a man like Wilder to the punch. He's early. Of course he's early. That makes all the sense in the world. He's not a man who arrives late.

He's not looking at me though. His head's bent over a book, a few lines in his forehead creasing as he reads. I can't quite tell what it is, but it's a small paperback, almost like the kind of thing you'd buy at a garage sale.

It's jarring. Maybe because I figured he'd be summoning a private jet for a quick flight to Madrid to meet a new business partner or reading some book with a ridiculous name like *Pears Never Ripen* when it's really all about *101 Tips on How to Convince People to Do What You Want*.

Instead, his nose is in a paperback.

I step closer and he stops, closes it, and takes his time letting a smile form. When Dahlia and I arrive, he stands.

My breath catches.

Here, in the soft light of the patio, Wilder doesn't look like my boss. He looks like...a man on a date. He's wearing dark slacks and a cashmere V-neck sweater with the hint of a white T-shirt under it. The cuffs are rolled up twice, revealing those corded forearms and the artwork on them.

His green eyes sparkle. He's not wearing his big game rings.

"Here you go," Dahlia says, but her words are faint. I can barely focus on her and she drifts out of sight, out of mind.

I swallow roughly. Try to get my bearings.

"Good to see you, Fable," he says, then leans in, cups my arms, and almost, *almost* kisses my cheek. But his lips don't quite touch me. It's like an air kiss and it takes a surprising amount of willpower not to lean closer. When he lets go, I'm left with the scent of falling snow in a forest and a fresh new ache in my chest.

"You look lovely," he says, like a declaration.

I open my mouth to speak, but once again, I come up empty. I'm at a loss. I feel a little wobbly. Like my breath is coming faster than I'd expected. Like my skin's a little tingly. Like...holy shit.

I'm stupidly attracted to my boss. This is bad. This is so bad.

"Hiiiii," I say, then gulp and then sit, patting the cushion tied to the wooden chair. "Nice...chair. It's a nice chair. Good for sitting."

What even are words?

"Yes, it is," Wilder says with a hint of amusement as he takes his seat.

I glance around but can barely focus on the other diners or anything but this out-of-sync beating in my heart. "This place is...nice. For, um, eating."

"Yes, restaurants can be good for food, I've heard," he says.

Get it together, girl.

"The owner is nice. That's nice for..."

"Owning?" he asks with a warm smile.

Oh god. I set a hand on my sternum and take a deep breath. "I'm sorry. I just...I don't know...Do you feel sorry for me?"

What the hell is it about Wilder Blaine that makes me say things I normally wouldn't?

"No," he says with kindness, certainty, and crystal clarity.

"I hate when people feel sorry for me," I admit. I can't seem to stop with him.

"Then you have nothing to worry about." He tilts his head. "Do you feel sorry for me?"

I scoff. "God no. Why would I?"

"Exactly," he says, cool and in control. "I could say the same about you."

He's quiet for a beat, while his words sink in. He doesn't see me differently. He sees me...as an equal. We may be boss and employee, we might be a billionaire and just a woman who's barely paying off her college loans, but here tonight, in the context of our pretend Christmas romance, we're on even footing.

He nods to the empty wineglass on the table. "Do you want wine? Champagne? Water? A stiff drink?"

I laugh, full of relief and gratitude. Then, because we are on even footing, I find mine once again. "Are you saying you think I need one?"

"Perhaps." He smiles, the corner of his lips lifting in an electric grin that makes my chest squeeze. With his chiseled jaw, light dusting of dark stubble, and emerald eyes, Wilder Blaine is obviously good-looking. Of course I've always known that. But I've known it in a distant way. An inaccessible way. In the way you admire the ocean, or the Golden Gate Bridge, or a photograph in an art gallery.

He's been out of reach.

He's not distant now. He's the man sitting across from me on a December night as holiday lights twinkle on the heated patio. He's the man who wants this fake romance as much as I do. Which seems wild, because this time two weeks ago I was dating someone else. Someone who turned out to be a lying, cheating jerk. Funny, how seeing someone's true colors can help you get over them real fast.

I lift the wineglass, considering it as I meet Wilder's gaze. "I probably could use a very stiff drink, but I'm pretty sure it's a sin to order anything but red wine at an Italian bistro," I say.

There. I've got my groove back. I've got my words back. I can do this.

"I wouldn't want you to be guilty of that," he says, then gives a chin nod, presumably to a server.

When she appears seconds later—seriously, did she teleport?—he says, "We'll have the Italo Cescon Pinot Noir." He adds the year, and I'm seriously impressed.

"As you wish," the server says, then returns shortly with a bottle. After she makes a show of presenting it to him, she pours a glass for us both and he thanks her. When she leaves, he raises his glass to me. I expect him to say, "To getting to know my fake girlfriend" or "to destroying Brady."

Something playful. Something that picks up on our reasons for being here.

But he says, "To being the best fake daters ever."

Once again, the man has surprised me. But he's also delivered an excellent reminder. This is fake.

I shove these nascent, fizzy feelings far away, then lift my glass.

"No one will know this isn't real." Then I take a beat and add, "Except us."

His smile falters for a second, then he echoes, "Except us."

11

CHESTNUTS ROASTING

Wilder

It's like an icy dose of reality but that's for the best. What was I thinking, picking this restaurant? Treating this necessary component of a temporary partnership like a romantic date?

I could very well have scheduled a meeting at the office to prep. Or a lunch appointment, for fuck's sake. Instead, I picked a Saturday night at a cozy bistro, with fine wine, soft lighting, and romantic holiday music.

Real smart.

But I can't let this vibe get to me. I may not read romance novels, but I know plenty of fake dates turn into something more, and I won't let that happen. No matter how easy Fable is to talk to, how beautiful she is with her lush copper waves, her honey-hazel eyes, and her glossy lips, nothing more will ever come of this—because you can't trust love. I learned that growing up.

Saw that in front of me with my father. He promised

us so much—lavish Christmas trips with the family, New Year's celebrations along the California coast, most of all, time spent together, one-on-one—but it ended up being a lie. He gambled everything we had thanks to his addiction.

Nothing good can come from a lie.

Best to focus on the purpose of this *meeting*. Getting to know Fable over a meal so we can pull off this holiday faux-mance.

We review the menu and when she's done, I ask politely, "Did you find something you like?"

"The mushroom bolognese made with zucchini noodles," she says, then stage whispers, "Mostly, I want to see how the zucchini holds up."

"Against wheat?"

"Exactly. Is it a pale imitation or a brand-new taste sensation?" she asks, like she wants to get to the bottom of a great mystery, and I should not think it's adorable that she's adventuresome in ordering. So I won't. I just won't.

"And you?" she asks.

"The eggplant parmigiano with asiago and goat cheese. But I'll get two. Mac just entered her leftover phase."

"I've never left mine."

"I haven't either. Leftovers are the unsung heroes of the food world."

"Because the flavors have had time to hang out together," she adds, and I've got to keep things in check. I'm not going to let this tidbit work its way into my heart. It's just an agreement over leftovers.

When the server arrives, I'm grateful for the interruption. After we order, it's time to get down to business. "For us to be the best fake daters, we should be sure we know a few key things about each other," I say, and her ex's name is bitter on my tongue, but it's a necessary reminder of what this arrangement with Fable is about, and what it's *not* about. It's not about romance. It's about mutually beneficial help.

She lifts her glass, giving me a thoughtful look. "You don't know me after working with me for the last couple years?"

Fair question. I give her an honest answer. "I know you're a hard worker. You're talented. I know your favorite flavor of ice cream, that you beat everyone in the office's fantasy football league last year, and that there's no sequin shape you can't master," I say with a smile. "But I don't know the personal stuff."

"Like which side of the bed do I sleep on?"

The side with me.

And I shouldn't go there. *Focus, man.*

"Let's stick to food. Any allergies or likes and dislikes?"

Fable shoots me a *c'mon* look. "You want to talk about allergies? Should we discuss favorite mutual funds too?"

"Don't threaten me with a good time," I fire back.

"Fine, fine," she says, then puts a little purr in her voice as she adds, "ROI, net revenue, exponential growth."

"Now you're talking," I say, then take a beat. "But seriously. I don't want us to make a rookie mistake at the wedding or in the Christmas games leading up to it. Everyone will know our relationship is new, but for them to buy that it's serious and not a ruse, frankly, we need to show we know each other."

She nods crisply in understanding. "We're on the same page."

And since we are, I do something I rarely do in business—speak first in a negotiation. "Here you go. I don't have any food allergies, but you should know I can't stand mayonnaise. I love spicy food, ideally as hot as inhumanly possible. I drink coffee, a lot of it, probably too much. But my dirty little secret is I prefer hot chocolate, only I never order it when I'm out. I make my daughter do chores and clean up after herself, but admittedly I do spoil her at the holidays, and I justify it because she's such a good kid and I'm so damn lucky she is. Also, she wants a secret door for Christmas, but I think that's mostly because she's been reading books with secret doors in them. Speaking of reading, I often stay up late reading, and I wake up early every day to exercise since cardio's not only good for the body but for the brain too. I speak Mandarin and learned it in college. I think ice cream is proof of the existence of a higher being, I never sleep with socks on, I don't walk around in my house with shoes on, and I'm an Aries."

She smiles. The endless kind. "I can't quite believe it."

"That I told you all that?" I suppose I can't quite believe it either. I don't usually share so much info.

"That you dropped your zodiac sign into casual convo," she says, then adds, "and of course you're an Aries."

"My mother's into signs. She has *strong Libra energy,* she's always said. I learned it from her."

"And you have strong Aries energy," she says, with an approving look and tone, and it feels a lot like a compliment I shouldn't let myself like too much. "Also, mayonnaise solidarity. It's disgusting. But I disagree about morning. Mornings should be annexed onto the night, and days should start in the afternoon. I often stay up late to work on new jewelry designs, reading with my earholes. I listen to audiobooks," she adds, but I'd guessed that was what she meant. "I'm allergic to shellfish, but that's okay because I don't eat fish or anything with a face for that matter. Mac sounds like a very lucky girl, and I, too, would enjoy a secret door. I sleep with very fuzzy socks on because I love fuzzy socks, and all socks *should* be fuzzy. Also, I wear shoes everywhere in my apartment, because shoes are proof of the existence of a higher being." She pauses, her lips curving before she says, "But ice cream, especially mint, is a close second on the proof scale. Also, I intend to destroy the office this year, too, in the fantasy football league, partly because my mid-season trades were absolutely elite," she says, and yep, it's white hot, her confidence about all things grid-iron. "I don't know any other languages, unfortunately, but I can say one very useful thing in French." Then she rolls her lips together, pops them, and adds, "And I'm a Leo."

"Yes, you definitely are," I say. No sign has ever suited someone more. I file away those details in the Fable file without lingering on them like I want to. "What can you say in French?"

I expect the same French line everyone knows, courtesy of "Lady Marmalade." But instead, she says, "Je voudrais pomme frites s'il vous plait." A request for fries.

Chuckling, I shake my head at my assumption. "I stand corrected."

"Were you expecting voulez vous couchez avec moi ce soir?"

Do you want to sleep with me tonight?

Expecting it. Wanting it.

That's a dangerous place to linger, so I admit that was, indeed, my assumption. "Though, for the sake of accuracy, I should point out that you know two French phrases, Fable."

She concedes with a laugh. "You got me there. I guess it *is* a good thing you like mutual funds more than I do."

"I don't actually like them," I correct. "I like hedge funds."

She rolls her eyes playfully, happy to take me down a peg. "Yes, yes. Of course. But what I'm most interested in is this food convo. Why don't you order hot chocolate when you're out?"

My nose wrinkles. "It would look..."

"Weak? Silly? Childish?"

I hesitate, not sure I want to admit how important pretenses can be in my world. But she's nailed it. "All of the above," I say, answering honestly.

"I figured as much. But don't worry—I'll keep your hot cocoa secret," she says, then lifts a finger. "If..."

One eyebrow raises in question. "*If*? This is a secret-keeping negotiation?"

"Obviously." She tilts her chin like she's staking her ground. "A secret for a secret."

"You'll tell me one of your secrets in exchange for me confessing my hot chocolate love?" I grin. "That's an interesting bargaining strategy, Fable."

"No." Her chin climbs higher. "I'll keep this secret in exchange for another."

A laugh bursts from me. "You just basically want me to give up more secrets?"

"It's not that hard for you to serve them, evidently," she counters. "I already know what you sleep in."

I sip my wine, set it down, and meet her curious gaze. "But do you, Fable?"

"Yes, I do," she says, digging her heels in.

"I only said no socks," I remind her.

She taps her temple. "I put two and two together."

I'm playing with fire. I know that. But I toss some more kindling onto the flames. "Go on. Tell me what I wear to bed."

Like she's the clever detective assembling clues as she paces through a well-appointed drawing room, she says, "If you don't like having socks on in bed, it means you get hot in bed. Which means you don't wear much. Which would usually mean boxer briefs."

Damn. She is very, *very* good.

But so am I.

I don't move a muscle. I don't let on that she's heading down the right path using her own smarts. I wait patiently.

"Except, you have a kid, so propriety dictates you probably don't just wear boxer briefs," she adds, then taps her chin. "You probably wear gym shorts to bed. And you do it every night even when Mac's not there, since you like routine," she says, and my lips threaten to twitch in a dead giveaway, but I tamp down the impulse. "So I say workout shorts. And when you get up—first, before anyone else in the house—you pull on a T-shirt." Her eyebrows dance. Her irises twinkle. "Am I right or am I right?"

Try as I might to stay all business, she makes it impossible. I drop the stony face, letting a smile form. "Almost, Fable. Almost."

She huffs, all over-the-top playful. "Fine. What did I get wrong?"

I lean forward, elbows on the table. "I don't like routine." I take a beat, reading her body language, the way she shifts subtly closer, her head tilted, then I add, "I love it."

Fable doesn't have a comeback for several seconds.

Then she says in a softer voice, almost a little husky, "That tracks."

I don't know if that's good or bad. I'm not sure I want to know, so I leave it alone.

She sits up straighter. "My turn."

"But that seemed like your turn," I say.

She points at me. "You started this whole thing with asking me about food allergies. So I can either take my turn, or you can ask me, I don't know, something about health insurance. Or my favorite columns in a spreadsheet."

"That last one's easy. It's always ROI," I toss back.

"You and your ROI." Then she leans closer and taps the minimalist vine tattoo knuckle on my right forefinger. A current rushes through me. "That ought to be your next tattoo."

No one, not a single soul, has ever kept me on my toes like this woman. We may have only shared monthly meetings in the past, but now I'm cursing myself for not making them biweekly. No, weekly. "*Me and my ROI*, or just *ROI*?"

"ROI, Wilder. ROI."

"I think that's the first time you've called me by my name." *Or touched my hand, but who's counting?*

She hums, like she's rolling the tape, checking the files of our conversations. "I guess it is...*sugar plum*." Then her brow knits, and a flash of worry crosses her eyes. "Is that okay? Calling you Wilder?"

"Yes." I nearly add *hardly anyone does and I like it when you do.*

I'm grateful—*mostly*—when the server swings by with our entrees, setting them down, then offering pepper and grated cheese. We say yes to both and when he leaves,

Fable lifts a fork, then says, "Okay, then, *Wilder*. It's definitely my turn. And I am going to threaten you with a good time," she says, then takes a bite of her zucchini noodles as the music shifts to the upbeat "Sleigh Ride."

"Have at it," I say, then dig in as well.

After she chews, she tips her forehead to the speaker, perched near a trellis with garlands snaking up it, curling around white icicle lights. "And this is really important for your Christmas girlfriend to know," she says, and my skin warms hearing those words. "What is your favorite Christmas song?"

"'Let It Snow.'"

"You just threw that down with zero hesitation," she says.

I hold her gaze, not looking away for a few risky seconds before I say, "I know what I like."

Her cheeks pinken, and she swallows. It's hard to look away from her neck. Long, pale, elegant, and adorned with a simple chain and two delicate silver bells over the hollow of her throat. But perhaps I stare a little too long, giving away the corollary to my last statement.

I tear my gaze back to my meal, take another bite, at a loss for words for the first time tonight.

She takes a bite too, and when she's done, she asks, "And why do you like it? The song?"

"Because I like snow. It's soft, it's quiet, it's peaceful. Snow makes everything beautiful. You can have the busiest day, a million things going on, but when the snow falls, it calms the whole world down."

Snow is also thoroughly romantic, so I keep that to myself. But then again, maybe I shouldn't. This is a make-believe romance for the next few weeks. It can't hurt to lean into that. "And it's romantic," I add. "When you look out the window and you see the flakes falling and everything goes hush, it makes you want to spend the day, and the night, with...that special someone."

"It hardly snows in San Francisco." She sounds wistful, but I can solve that.

"It usually snows at my cabins in Evergreen Falls," I offer as the tune ends and "Have Yourself a Merry Little Christmas" begins.

"They're hardly cabins," she says, teasing me once again on that front.

"The snow doesn't care about that."

She's quiet for a beat, clearly thinking. "Are we sharing one? You mentioned the other day that I'd have my own room, but I know your *cabins*"—she stops to sketch air quotes—"usually have living rooms and a couple bedrooms."

Reasonable question. "We'll have to for appearance's sake. I'll make sure we're in a two-bedroom one. You'll have your own space. I don't want you to be uncomfortable."

"I won't be."

"I'll make sure you get the bedroom with the best view of the mountains. And the snow," I say.

She looks away from me for a few seconds, toward the windows that give a view to the inside of the bistro, maybe even to the reflection in the glass of the lights. She turns back to me. "I hope it snows then."

"Do you like snow? Or are you a summer girl?"

"I like all seasons." Faintly, almost imperceptibly, she lifts her face, like she's drawing an inhale, then says, "But I find I'm liking winter."

For a breath-held moment, neither of us says another word. In those seconds, the ions between us seem to spark. Dangerous thoughts. I snuff them. "And you? Your favorite Christmas song?"

She pauses for a second, perhaps reorienting to the shift. "I like so many. 'The Christmas Song,' 'Winter Wonderland,' this one..." she says, as Judy Garland sings in a tune that's full of longing, and honestly, a little sad. "But not this version. Nothing against Judy."

"Which version?" I ask, intrigued. I'm not that up to speed on Christmas covers, but she'll probably say Sinatra. That's a reasonable guess at least.

"Have you heard the cover by Tinashe?"

I shake my head. I haven't even heard of the artist, but I don't admit that. "No."

"She's a pop singer. Kind of R&B," Fable adds, seeing right through me, but not pointing it out, which I appreciate. "She did a cover that sounds a little like—"

She cuts herself off, like she's gone too far. But I have to know. "Like what?" I ask, more desperate than I want to let on.

There's a beat. An internal debate behind those warm eyes. Then a decision as she says softly, "Like a seduction."

And I'm no longer warm. I'm roasting. "I'll have to listen to it then."

"Wilder," she says a few seconds later, "does this end after Christmas?"

It's like someone's opened the front door during a snowstorm—a blast of cold swirls around me. But of course it ends after Christmas. It's designed to end. That's the nature of a fake romance. And fake romances can't hurt you, so I shake off this *chill* as I say, "That seems ideal. Do you agree?"

With a sad smile, or maybe even a frown, she nods. "Yes. After the wedding, I suppose."

I hate this discussion, but I didn't get to where I am today by backing down from difficult conversations. "Late December or even right after the new year would be most believable, and everyone will be busy then anyway, so hopefully they won't even notice."

"Exactly! We can figure out the specifics later though?" She asks that question as if planning a breakup is the last thing she wants to do.

Same here. "That sounds like a good plan. Especially since we have doors to decorate and snowballs to throw before then."

"We do," she says, then smooths her hands across her lap and exhales. "Now, enough of that. Let's talk about something fun."

"Like what?"

"What were you reading when I arrived?"

Ah, this is a much better conversation topic. "A detective novel," I admit.

"Something juicy and pulpy?" she asks, like she's eating that up.

"Yes." I pause. "I don't usually admit that's what I read for pleasure."

She gives me a conspiratorial smile. "I'll keep your secrets."

She knows more than most people already. All the more reason to keep the secret of this crush that's growing stronger by the hour. A crush that'll be snuffed out after the holidays.

* * *

That night, as I'm sliding under the covers in just shorts and trying not to replay that dinner over and over, my phone buzzes. I swipe it open to a message from Fable. She's sent me...a song. The cover for "Have Yourself a Merry Little Christmas." I listen and she's right.

Wilder: It does sound like a seduction.

I need to stop. Truly, I do. I should leave this alone. But then she replies, and it's impossible to put my phone down.

Fable: I'm listening to it now too.

Wilder: In your fuzzy socks?

Fable: Of course. They have snowmen on them. Would snowflakes on socks get you to wear socks in bed?

Wilder: Only if this song were playing.

Fable: So I guess you can break your routine.

Wilder: Every now and then it's been known to happen.

Fable: Even though you love it?

Wilder: Even then.

Fable: So, would it be breaking your routine to go to a co-ed wedding shower? With me?

. . .

It's just a text. There's no tone of voice. But in my mind, I can hear her warm voice pitch up in hope that I'll say yes. Like this is a date. Before I reply, she writes again.

Fable: My sister just texted me. She has a client who owns a cute café, and she can get a private room there next Sunday for it. Should we go together? To practice our routine?

Wilder: I'd love to.

Then I set my phone down so I'm not tempted to keep up the volley since it feels too good. Everything does with her. I squeeze my eyes shut.

It's not a date, man. It's practice for the town's winter games and the wedding.

Still, I listen to the song again as I search online for fuzzy socks. With gingerbread men on them. With candy canes. With mistletoe. Then I send her several pairs to arrive tomorrow morning. With another note. ***Happy holidays to my Leo elf.***

There. Just another layer of Fable detail. After all, I'm not simply showing Brady how a woman should be treated. I'm showing her, and she deserves to know how it feels when a man pays attention.

Besides, the more we practice at being a couple, the better we'll do when the games begin.

That's what I tell myself as I open my old paperback

and try to get lost in the story. But something nags at me and I'm not sure what. Did I forget something? It feels like it, but I'm drawing a blank. I return to the book, but then, as the hero can't keep his eyes off his heroine as she leaves, it's obvious.

I was having such a good time, I forgot to cover one very key issue on our date. I put a note on my calendar to handle it at the office first thing.

That's when I see what's on the agenda for late Monday morning—Shay's scheduled time for me to decorate the door. I'm sure he did this per Bibi's orders, since she wants me participating in all things holiday at the office. I drag a hand through my hair. I like to do things I'm good at. The last thing I want to do is decorate a door.

But then again, it's an excuse to spend more time with Fable.

Maybe I can learn to like decorating.

12

SANTA'S BUTT

Fable

Women can't survive shower planning solo. It's a special kind of task that requires not one, not two, but three girlfriends for support. The next night I call on Josie, Maeve, and Everly, assembling them in our favorite bookstore. An Open Book on Fillmore Street officially wins all the Christmas competitions in the world because its window display is made of—wait for it—a stack of books, forming a tree, and covered in lights.

The tree topper is none other than my friend Hazel Valentine's newest romance novel. I'm so proud of her, even though I really wanted her to name it *Christmas is Coming*. She said retailers *might* find that a tad too racy, so she opted for *The Twelve Hate Dates of the Holidays*, which works since it's an enemies-to-lovers romance, obviously.

I push open the door, and the bell jingles. The store is warm and cozy, with an electric fireplace crackling and stockings hung from the mantel, each stuffed with books. I walk past the displays to the café, where I find my three friends poring over a coffee table book about Paris.

"I want to go there. And get lost in a library," Josie says, with a happy sigh as she points to a full-page image of a cobblestone street in front of, naturally, a bibliothèque.

"You know Wesley will take you. And when the hockey season's over, maybe I can convince Max to take me there too," Everly seconds. She started seeing the goalie for one of the city's hockey teams, and he worships the ground she walks on.

"I just want to go there and paint," Maeve says, wistful in her own way.

My heart squeezes with happiness for my two paired-up friends and their happily ever afters. But that feeling is chased by a tiny bit of jealousy. What would it be like to feel the way they do? Wildly content. Joyful, even, with their partners.

I've always wanted a big love—even in spite of what I saw in front of me growing up. Each time I went on a date with someone from an app, from a setup, from anywhere, I believed in the possibility of big love. Hoped for it.

Do I still believe in a happily ever after? Hard to say given my track record, and certainly a fake romance won't help my cause.

But a smile tugs at my lips as I think about last night. It was the best date I've had in ages. Too bad it wasn't real.

I head to the table. "Should we hold the shower in Paris? It's not a bad idea," I announce cheerily, shoving my romantic woes into a corner.

Josie looks up, her eyes alight with approval. "I'm not saying no to that."

Maeve nods vigorously. "Maybe Charlotte could have

her wedding there. Yes, convince your sister to get hitched in Paris on Christmas Eve."

"Oh, sure. No problem. She's only wanted a small town, snowy wedding her whole life, but I'll see what I can do." I sit, unwinding my scarf.

"Does that mean we need to order a snow machine if it doesn't snow in Evergreen Falls?" Everly asks dryly.

"You know what? I think we do," I say.

Josie chuckles. "From what you've told us, I bet Leo would be all over that for Charlotte."

My heart goes soft once again. That's another happily ever after too. "He'd do anything for her."

And I try not to feel an ounce of envy for his over-the-top love of my sister. I'm happy for them. Truly, I am.

Besides, it's not like I'm even on the romance market right now anyway. I'm on the sidelines this holiday season for all intents and purposes and that's fine. Just fine. I had a taste of a great date, and that's enough.

I get down to business. "So, she wants a brunch next weekend. Co-ed of course. And casual. She has a restaurant already booked, so all we have to do is plan some fun games."

Josie nods sagely. "Planning games is my middle name."

"Planning anything is," Everly says, correcting Josie.

Maeve holds up one finger, stop-the-clock style. "But, more important, have you all gotten your sequin shorts for the bachelorette party?"

"Does Santa wear a suit?" I ask in faux indignation. "But of course I did."

We get to work planning all the things. When we're done, Maeve bats her hazel eyes at me. "So, how is it dating Wilder Blaine?"

I give her a look, then hiss out in a low voice, "It's fake, Maeve. And you know it."

She gives an over-the-top nod. "Right. Of course."

"Maeve," I warn her.

"But really, I mean it. How is it fake dating the man?"

I flash back to dinner last night, and how I felt when I walked into Dahlia's and saw Wilder at the table waiting, his emerald eyes locked on me as I walked to the table. The way my chest flipped. How I felt a little fizzy.

"Perfectly fake," I say, and I hate lying to my friends.

They're my people. I trust them with my life. They'd bury bodies for me. But this is merely attraction for him, and nothing—not a damn thing—will come of it.

* * *

But there's a problem. A big problem. And it's not the stuffed Santa butt that's sticking out of the box I'm lugging down the corridor of the Renegades stadium late on Monday morning.

It's the wedding shower this coming weekend.

"The café fell through and every place I called is booked!"

Charlotte is freaking out as we talk on the phone while I make my way to the flagship team store, lugging a canvas bag of decorating supplies and a box full of pink shirts I designed before the start of the season—shirts we can barely keep in stock, but I just got a new shipment, so I'm hustling my way to unload them before I go to this meeting with Wilder.

I hoist the box higher and focus on Charlotte. "Why are you doing this?" My sister's not the one who should be taking all this on. As the maid of honor, I should be organizing the venue. "I'll make some calls. I'll try Happy Cow, Morning Glow, Green Pantry..." Any of these brunch places would be perfect for a shower.

"I tried them already! Booked! All of those. With Christmas brunches. Hanukkah lunches. Holiday coffees," she says, and I'm pretty sure the players on the practice field can hear her desperation. "And I would do it at our place but—"

"But you're having the guest bathroom redone," I finish. It's been vexing her for some time. The prior owners of Charlotte and Leo's new townhouse had inexplicably covered the bathroom in wallpaper featuring illustrations of couples on sex swings. Charlotte's replacing it with a tasteful, yet cheeky, flamingo print.

"But they can just use our bathroom, I suppose," she says, talking herself down. She's nothing if not rational, even when she's careening toward an official bride freak-out. "It's fine," she says. "No big deal. There's no reason guests can't use the en suite."

I frown as I near a hallway that leads to the practice field. "First of all, weird. No one wants to walk through your bedroom to use your bathroom, and you don't want that either. Two, you're not going to host your own wedding shower." I catch a familiar figure coming toward me down the hall, dressed for practice, helmet in hand. It's a short week, and Carter, my friend Rachel's husband, is heading to the field for a light practice. I wave at him with my free hand while I reassure Charlotte, "I'll find a place, so stop. Just stop. I can handle this."

Carter pauses beside me, eavesdropping. Pointing to the phone, he mouths, *"Need a place for something? You can use our house."*

I tell Charlotte to hold on a sec. "You're sweet to offer..."

Before he can answer—before I've finished my sentence—a familiar voice cuts in.

"I've got this."

Deep, rich, warm...I spin around, and my heart flutters to see Wilder walking up behind me. Maybe he came down the other hallway.

I look away to hurriedly finish the call. "I'll call you back, Charlotte. And I will find a place. I promise."

"Thank you," she says fervently. "You're the best."

Hanging up, I look at the two men. I'm a little confused, but I'm grateful. "That's nice of both of you," I say.

"Yes, thank you, Carter," Wilder says to his star player. "But if this is about the wedding shower, I have it under control."

"No problem, Mr. Blaine," Carter says. The man is technically his boss too.

Wilder chuckles, shaking his head. "It's Wilder," he says, clearly not for the first time.

Carter nods and turns toward the exit. "Right, Mr. Blaine."

As he heads to the field, I look at the team owner in a three-piece suit. No jacket though. He's just wearing charcoal slacks, a butter yellow dress shirt, and—holy shit—a vest.

My chest heats up. Why are vests so hot? I don't even know. It could be the way they hug a man's waist. Or how they accentuate his pecs. Or maybe it's just the promise of buttons.

Of undoing them, nice and slow.

"Is this for the shower this Sunday?" Wilder repeats.

Right. Yes. The shower. Not the great unbuttoning. "Yes."

"Leo texted me," Wilder explains. "He asked if I knew a place."

"Wait. Let me guess. You own some brunch spots too," I tease, adjusting the box under my arm. "On top of your *cabins,* the golf course, your clean energy businesses, and all your Vegas hotels."

He smirks. "You forgot I have a hotel here in San Francisco too."

"I didn't forget." The Resort is where I ran into him that fateful night over a year ago with my friends. "I hear that place is supposed to be real swanky. Someone keeps telling me to stay there."

He gives a hint of a smile. "You should try it for yourself sometime. See if you agree."

"If you insist," I say, then focus on practical matters. "So, is that where the shower would be?"

Wilder takes a beat, those green eyes glinting. "Actually, I thought...I could host it at my home."

My breath catches. His home. "That's so nice of you." The words aren't rote or empty. It is remarkably kind of him to offer his house, which must be amazing.

"Thank you." He steps a little closer, his snow and forest scent tickling my nose. He lowers his voice like we're keeping a secret, and I suppose we are. "But as the best man and maid of honor, wouldn't it make the most sense if *we* host it together?"

I hadn't even thought of that. But for appearances, that makes sense. "Sure. Yes. Of course."

I'm gobsmacked already, and I haven't even seen his house. Is pre-gobsmacked a thing? If so, I'm feeling it.

"It'll be like practice for the Christmas competition,

and why not give ourselves the home-field advantage?" Damn, his strategic mind is hot.

"Yes. That's so wonderful of you."

"Of *us*, Fable," he corrects. His warmth makes it clear that this offer should seem like our idea as a couple. His gaze lingers on me, and I feel unmoored. "Would you like to let her know?"

My heart is beating faster than usual. "Yes. I will."

"And maybe you could come over in advance?"

"To help you get ready?"

He laughs, but not at me. More *with me* as he shakes his head. "No. Because it wouldn't make sense if you're seeing my home for the first time when everyone else is. You should know where things are, like the library. The movie room. The bathroom..."

"The bedroom," I say on a breath, and the word seems to linger between us. What is Wilder's bedroom like? I picture a huge bed, soft covers, elegance, and masculinity. And I'm desperate to see it.

"Right. Exactly. All the rooms." Wilder nods, businesslike—just like I should be. "I'll text you, and we'll find a time before the party that works for both of us."

There's silence for a few seconds. It's clear this conversation is over, but he doesn't make a move to go. I don't want to end the interlude, either, so I think of something to say. "Also, thank you again for the socks."

I texted him my thanks yesterday, but it's worth saying them again in person.

"Are you enjoying them?"

"I slept in them last night," I say.

He blinks, then he reaches for the box in my arms. "I'll carry that for you." He takes the carton of shirts, glancing inside, and his brows climb skyward. He peers at the stuffed rear end of jolly old St. Nick in confusion then turns to me. "Are we selling Santa's ass at the team store?"

I smile like the Mona Lisa. "Don't you worry about Santa's butt, sugar plum."

As he walks with me to the team store, a smile of dawning realization spreads, slow and steady, across his handsome face. "I see where this is going, Fable."

"Of course you do."

Placing the box of pink shirts on the counter, Wilder moves one hand to brush my shoulder, like a boyfriend saying goodbye. My shoulder likes his hand very much. So much that I don't move. I just...savor the touch.

When he lets go, my shoulder misses him.

"I'll see you at my office in fifteen minutes," Wilder says. "With Santa's butt."

He leaves, and I reach into the box, grab the stuffed butt, and drop it into my canvas bag without looking.

Because I'm not thinking of Santa's rear end. I'm checking out my fake boyfriend's ass...the whole time he's walking away.

13

THE FINEST

Wilder

Shay is on an early lunch break, so this door-decorating session at my office seems as good a place as any to tackle the topic I forgot at dinner. I was having too good a time getting to know her and I didn't address a key issue that should have been covered in a fake girlfriend debrief.

I can't put off the inevitable any longer.

As soon as Fable enters the admin area, I shut the outer door and get right to business. "Let's chat."

She sets down a bag of decorations outside my office, her eyes flickering with worry. "What's wrong? You hate Santa's butt that much?"

Ah hell. I shake my head. "No. I'm sure it's fine. I'm sure everything you picked out for the door is."

She's quiet for a beat. "I was aiming a little higher than fine," she says, clearly hurt. "But fair enough."

Shit. I've insulted her by making her think I don't care about decorating. Well, I don't care, really. But she does and that's what matters. My heart squeezes. All my instincts tell me to tuck a strand of hair behind her ear. Reassure her. But I fight them off. "I didn't mean it like that," I say, trying to cover up the way she's got me a little flustered with this desire to comfort her. "I'm no good at decorating," I admit. "So I trust your taste."

She smiles, a sign I'm forgiven. "Good. Because I planned something fabulous for the door. Just for you."

That shouldn't make my pulse spike, but it does. Especially the *just for you.* "I'm sure I'll love it," I say, as businesslike as I can be with her.

After a pause, she says with a playful pout, "You'd better, mister."

I roll up my cuffs, and her eyes stray briefly to my forearms. "Put me to use."

"Green ribbon with gold piping. Let's hang it around the doorframe. It's in the bag."

I riffle around for it, find it quickly, then I get to work. Since we have privacy here, I clear my throat. I'm all professional, like I'm having a conversation with a board member. "I neglected to cover this fake romance agenda item at dinner the other night," I begin.

"Oh no. You forgot an agenda item," she deadpans as she works on covering the front of the door in shiny red paper.

I don't take the teasing bait. If I do, I'll keep flirting endlessly with her, and we'll never hammer out the expectations. Deals fall apart when parties don't communicate their goals. "I thought it would be helpful if we address some of the ground rules, if you will, of this arrangement."

"Yes, sir. Let's address them, stat."

I give her a pointed look but stifle a laugh. "The mocking. Dear god, the mocking," I say as I align the ribbon around the frame.

"Oh, is that against the rules too? I'd better write these down then."

"Don't worry. I'll send you a meeting recap later."

"Oh, thank god. Whatever would I do without that?"

I'm about to volley back when I remind myself—*no more flirting.* In fact, it's best if I stick to rules to protect myself—no more fuzzy socks and ice cream gifts. No more texts about seductive Christmas cover songs.

"We already know the story of our first date—the ice cream shop. Saturday at Dahlia's would have been our second one, so we're covered there if it comes up. We know the key details about each other. But we probably need a checklist for things like the shower. And any other events leading up to the wedding," I say, then bite off the rest of the bullet. "The dos and don'ts."

She stops her work, knitting her brow in question. "The dos and don'ts of how to fake date?"

I grit my teeth, then just say it. "Public displays of affection."

"Aah," she says, understanding dawning. But then, she sighs. A little heavily. "We should."

But I rewind to her sigh. "What's wrong?"

"It just reminds me—I feel sort of bad lying to my sister."

I hadn't thought of that before. But it makes sense. "Do you want to tell her the truth?"

She shakes her head adamantly as she tapes down another swath of wrapping paper, making sure to position a pre-cut hole in the middle of the paper about five feet high on the door. "No. She has too much going on, and I didn't tell her what happened with Brady at Thanksgiving. I don't want to stress her out."

The Fable picture becomes clearer. She doesn't like to be the center of attention. She likes to focus on others. She adores her sister. "But if you want to tell her, that's perfectly fine," I say, since that's all I can really offer her. Though I suppose there's one more thing I can do. "Or if you want to call it quits, I will understand that too."

Her eyes flash with *hell no*. "I'm no quitter," she says as she stops her work briefly to look me in the eyes. "Do you want to?"

I'm dead serious as I say, "No."

The last thing I want is for this make-believe Christmas match to end.

"Does Leo know the truth?" she asks as she finishes fixing the wrapping paper in place.

I shake my head, but it doesn't bother me that he's not in on it. He doesn't need to be, and I'm not wired to share those details with a friend. "He doesn't, and I don't need to tell him. The only one who knows is Mac."

A smile forms on her face, slow and easy. "You told her."

"I wanted her to know the truth. And I didn't want to disappoint her," I say. Then swallow. "When it ends."

"Of course," Fable says with a frown. "That's thoughtful. I admire that." She sighs, but it's one of acceptance. "Let's get to it then. Rules. Guidelines. Dos and Don'ts."

I glance at my watch since I have a call in fifteen minutes. "I don't want to make you uncomfortable. What's acceptable to you? A kiss on the cheek in public? Holding hands?"

She takes a beat, seeming to give it some thought as she

digs into the bag and retrieves a red ribbon. "We need to be believable but not like we're constantly selling it. People get busted when they try too hard and sell something too much."

She's not wrong.

Memories of my father overcompensating flash in my mind. Moments when Mom would ask if he was okay and he'd say everything was fine, fine, fine, selling it almost like he was in a Broadway musical, one step away from using jazz hands and spirit fingers.

When you try too hard, you eventually get caught. And he did—caught losing everything. A dark cloud passes over me. That's why I give him money. I worry what he'd do if he was in that situation again. What would he turn to? Would he hurt himself? Steal from someone? Disappear? I have no idea, and sometimes—no, most of the time—it's easier *and* safer to help him out of a hole. Still, I've learned one lesson from watching him. *Don't oversell.* "I agree. So we can't be all over each other. Not to mention it would be inappropriate for a fake romance."

"You're right. It can't be excessive," she says as she nudges me aside to twine the red ribbon around the green ribbon I hung.

"I touched your shoulder earlier today. Was that okay?" I ask.

Her cheeks pinken. I've never known Fable to blush, but then we've never talked about affection before.

"Yes, that was okay," she says, then swallows. Noticeably. My gaze stays there on her throat too long, and I force myself to stop thinking about how much I want to run a finger over the hollow of it.

"Holding hands?" But I picture doing that at the shower this coming weekend and it seems off. I shake my head, dismissing the thought as quickly as it came. "That feels performative."

She laughs. *At me.* Of course she laughs at me. That seems to be her favorite pastime.

I arch a brow, asking, "What's so funny?"

"The use of the word *performative* in the context of fake dating."

This woman will never not knock me down a peg. I stifle a smile as she stretches to reach the top of the door. I step in and help her, my shoulder brushing against hers as I say, "It's good to be prepared."

"Yes, it is, Mister Agenda," she says, still chuckling.

"Fable," I warn her, but it's playful too.

"Wilder," she says, taunting me right back. "I say holding hands is fine if we're sitting next to each other on a couch, for instance. But I don't think we should walk around holding hands. Like, *tra-la-la. Aren't we cute, holding hands, look at us.*"

"Exactly," I say, grateful she gets my point even as she pokes fun at me. "What about other shows of affection?" I picture her in my home, in the kitchen, entertaining guests, and it feels natural that I'd set a hand on her back. Enticing too. Obviously. I stop my work for a few seconds. What the fuck have I gotten myself into? Still, I ask evenly, "A hand on your back?"

"Have at it," she says as she twists the ribbons together on the other side.

"A playful shoulder bump?"

"Yes, but not too many. Too many touches would be" —she stops, takes her time, lets a smile spread— "performative."

I give her a stern stare. "You're never going to let me live that down, are you?"

"Probably not," she says, shooting me a *gotcha* look right back.

"Fine. I probably deserve that," I say, then ask her what else I can do for the door decorating. She tells me to grab the door wreath hook from the bag. As I root around in the bag, I find a silver metal knocker with an elf perched on it. I hold it up. "Are you sending me a message, Fable?"

"Yes. That I'm watching over your office next to this Santa's butt wreath that I made," she says, then grabs the elf hook and positions it on the nail on the door—the one that's accessible through the cut-out hole. Then, she grabs the wreath from the bag and hangs it on the hook. It's made with burlap and colorful ribbons. She adjusts it so Santa's ass, stuck in a chimney, is sticking out of my door.

But I'm still stuck on the last thing she said. "You made *this?* For the contest?"

She gives me a soft smile. "Yes. Well, it's really for you," she says, a flash of nervousness in her eyes, but hope too. "I wanted your office to look the best. And you've been so generous with your gifts. The least I could do was make you something from scratch."

I stare at the wreath, even more astonished. "This is incredible."

"You think so?" she asks, beaming.

"I do." I roam my eyes up and down the door, then turn my gaze to my designer. The woman who enjoys making homemade items. The woman who went all out for me. The woman I can't stop thinking about. Decorating might not be my thing, but I could decorate all day with her. "It's not fine," I say, correcting my earlier statement. "It's the finest."

"Thank you." Her smile is its own reward. It's wide and

joyful, and I want to swipe my thumb along her bottom lip, kiss the corner of her mouth, taste her.

Which brings me to a vital topic in the dos and don'ts. I've been tiptoeing around the main attraction. Avoiding it. But I can't any longer. Since this topic is best addressed behind closed doors, I motion to my office. "Let's finish in here," I say.

"Perfect. Because I brought lights for your desk."

I stare at her, a little amazed. She goes above and beyond in her creativity. "You did?"

"Yes. But will it cramp your style if some corporate bigwig comes into a meeting and sees the flashing lights on your desk? I don't want to ruin the big bad wolf vibe you've got going on."

I lift a brow. "Is that how you see me?"

Her lips curve up the slightest bit. "I don't know, Wilder. Do big bad wolves send mint ice cream?"

Two can play at her game. "Perhaps they send them to Little Red Riding Hood," I say as we head into my office.

"Well then, Little Red Riding Hood approves."

"So does the wolf," I say, and I am so fucked. Five minutes after telling myself to follow some rules for self-protection, I already know that I won't stop sending her gifts. I won't stop texting. This has been the most fun I've had in a while and I'm...addicted—and I'm allowed to be. Nothing can come of this ruse, of course. How could anything come of a romance that started as a lie? But I'll enjoy it while I can.

I shut the door behind us.

She beelines for my desk, fishing around in her bag of tricks for lights, presumably. In no time, she gets to work on stringing them around my desk. Yes, this is the moment. She's occupied with a task, so I say as coolly as I can, "And what about a kiss?"

She spins around, a string of lights in her hand, question marks in her eyes. "Now?"

What? Now? Before I can even answer—and I'm too stunned to answer—she adds, "Sure. A practice kiss couldn't hurt."

I can't think. I can't breathe. She keeps surprising me left and right, and I barely know what to do. I'm a man who prides himself on control, on strategy, on knowing what cards to play at all times. With her, I'm knocked senseless, especially as she sets the lights down on the desk, then closes the distance to me a few feet away.

I still haven't said a word. I really need to say something. *Anything.* She tips her chin up offering her pretty lips to me. Questions rattle in my head. Should I do this? Is this crossing a line? Is this wrong?

Finally, I manage to ask, "Are you sure?" It comes out like it scrapes my throat.

A tilt of her head. A curve of her lips. "You don't bite, do you? Like the big bad wolf?"

A bolt of lust shoots down my spine. I try to ignore it, to resist it when all I can think is *the better to eat you with.* "Only if you want me to."

Her eyes flicker with something that looks a lot like lust. "I'll take a rain check on the biting. But it's a yes on the practice," she says, then parts her lips the slightest bit.

I didn't plan this meeting as a dress rehearsal for a kiss. But I also know how to spot an opportunity and how to seize one. I step closer, run a finger along some silky strands of auburn hair, taking my time to sweep them across her face and tuck them behind her ear. Her breath hitches. I let go of those strands of hair, then brush the back of my fingers along her jaw. Her chest rises and falls. Her eyes track me the whole time, watching my face, then my hand. I'm drawing out this moment, stretching it like elastic till my fingers reach her chin, holding her.

I lean in then drop my lips to hers. It's a barely-there kiss. Just a brush of our lips. But it makes my bones crackle and my mind buzz. Her mouth is sweet, her breath minty. It lasts one, two, maybe three seconds. But I'm dangerously close to getting lost in the kiss, so I jerk back, try to clear off the fog, then ask clinically, "Was that fine?"

She blinks, looking a little hazy, a little happy. Then, she must collect her thoughts, since she says, "No."

What the fuck? What the hell was wrong with that? I can still feel the kiss rattling my body everywhere. But I shouldn't let on that I'm disappointed in myself. I try to treat her critique as part of our fake romance planning. "Why don't you tell me the issue so I can fix it for the next time?"

"Wilder...it wasn't fine. It was the finest."

Oh. *Oh, fuck.* I'm going to play those four words on repeat for the rest of the day—*it was the finest*. I try to clear away the fog of that kiss. "So a kiss like that is acceptable PDA," I say, as if I need to confirm that's why I kissed her.

"Yes. Or a cheek kiss," she says, then pats my chest. "I trust your instincts."

My instincts are to cancel this meeting and haul you into my arms. Kiss you deeply till you melt, grab my collar, and tug me against you.

I'm fighting a losing battle with her. I have to wrest control of this situation, and I have to do it now. I grab her hand from my chest before she can pull it away, clasp it tight then bring it to my mouth. I press another kiss to the top of her hand.

"Oh," she gasps quietly as a flush spreads across her cheeks.

I've gained the upper hand at last. "Hope that wasn't too performative for you."

"Not in the least," she says when my phone buzzes in my pocket. Both grateful and annoyed over the distraction, I say, "That could be Mac."

School's not out yet, but you never know when your kid might call.

Fable gestures for me to answer as she resumes stringing the lights. "Of course."

But when I pick it up it's a text from my father. ***Thanks, son! You helped your old man a lot. Appreciate the dough so much.***

I sigh heavily as I set the phone down on my desk unanswered. At least he's not...robbing a convenience store. Not that he's done that. I'm not even sure why that came to mind. But then, maybe I am—he's stolen from Peter to pay Paul.

"Is everything okay?"

I fix on a smile. "Mac's fine. It's my father."

As she aligns the lights, she's quiet for a beat, then asks, "And is everything okay with him?"

No. Things are never okay with him. My chest tightens, but I don't like this feeling. "Family," I say, admitting that much as I move next to her, helping once again. "You know how it goes."

"I told you about my terrible ex the last time I was in your office. It's the inner sanctum. Don't you hold out on me."

I'm not used to being called out like that, but I'm getting used to it with her and I'm liking it. "He's complicated. We don't have...the best relationship." It can't hurt for my fake girlfriend to know that.

"Same. With my dad. I don't like how he treated my mom when they were together."

I flash back to what she said about Brady in my office last week. How people treat you how you let them. How I feel like I understand her more now from that simple admission. "Same here. My dad took advantage of my mom. Of everyone. I have to be on my guard."

"I get that," she says, her warm eyes filling with sympathy as she finishes adorning my desk. "You have to look out for yourself."

"And your family," I add.

"Absolutely."

Darkness flashes in her eyes, and solidarity too. In this moment, in my office, I suddenly feel far closer to my fake girlfriend than I've felt to a woman in a while.

Maybe even closer than I felt to her in the bistro the other night. So close, I almost invite her to Mac's recital in the early evening. She made me a wreath, and she tasted like heaven.

The words are forming on my tongue. *Would you like to come with me*? But we just practiced a kiss and laid down the rules of our fake romance—and attending a recital my daughter's performing in wasn't among them.

I thank Fable for decorating the door instead, for the gift of the homemade wreath, and most of all, for her time. Then, before I say anything more and before she can tease me in the way that's my undoing, I show her to the door and dial into my meeting.

* * *

I leave work at five to attend the recital with Felicity and Bibi, where I do my very best to shove thoughts of Fable aside. When Mac sings a new arrangement of "Let It Snow" with the rest of her class, it's easy to focus just on my kid. Singing's not her thing. I doubt she'll sign up for a Christmas concert again. But Mac wanted to this year, probably to make her mom happy.

I admire that about her. Even though she's wise beyond her years, and more strategic than most people I know, she also has a soft heart, my daughter. I record a short video so I can send it to my mother. When the song ends, I turn to Bibi and whisper proudly, "She did great."

"She sure did," Bibi says, then nods to the video. "You should send that video to Fable."

"It's for Mom," I point out.

"But I'm sure Fable would love to see it too."

"I'll do it later," I say, then turn my focus back on the concert. But I'm thinking once again about Fable. Maybe I will send her the video after all.

14

WHEN THE FAKE BOYFRIEND FAKE BOYFRIENDS

Fable

This evening after work I head to Elodie's Chocolates in Hayes Valley to meet my sister for the best part of planning her wedding. We're picking out gifts of chocolate as favors for the guests.

But a funny thing is happening to me as I walk down the block to my friend's chocolate shop. My brain keeps replaying that three-second kiss in Wilder's office earlier today.

I can still feel the confident brush of his fingertips across my cheeks, the way he held my chin, how he coasted his lips across mine. My skin tingles from the memory of an innocent kiss that didn't feel innocent at all. It felt more like a hint of an after-dark kiss.

When I reach the store, I square my shoulders, determined to leave that kiss behind as I go inside. Charlotte's already here at the counter chatting with Elodie, who's decked out for the holidays in a rockabilly dress in red, white, and green stripes.

"Elodie has Christmas truffles for us," Charlotte calls.

"And you can taste test as many as you want," Elodie says from behind the counter.

"Perfect," I say as I reach them. "I'll take one of those and one of those and one of those and one of those and one of those." I point to pretty much every chocolate in the store.

Elodie gives me a double-dog stare. "Don't challenge me. You know I'll let you try everything."

Instead she hands us a tray with five truffles. My sister and I head to a table to sample them.

"This one is amazing," Charlotte says of a hot cocoa-themed bonbon.

And here I go again. Thinking of Wilder and his hot cocoa secret, and now this kiss secret. But is the kiss a secret? I don't even know, so I stuff a piece of chocolate in my mouth instead. "Mmm. This is good," I say, trying to focus on the taste of the chocolate rather than the flavor of my boss's kiss.

"So good," Charlotte echoes.

"Do you want to have some at your shower this weekend?" I ask.

She winces. "I need to talk to you about that. Since it's co-ed, Brady's coming. We had to invite him."

My smile vanishes. But I'm not entirely surprised he'll be there. "It's no big deal."

But in the back of my mind I'm picturing Brady sauntering around Wilder's home with Iris. The last time I saw the caterer, her mouth was opened wide. It's going to be so hard to unsee that image every time I offer her a canape.

"Really, it's fine," I say, since my sister is looking at me like *for real?* And besides I have a fake boyfriend for this very purpose—so it looks like I've moved the fuck on.

"But Iris isn't coming," Charlotte quickly adds. "Why should I invite Brady's new girlfriend anyway? She's coming to the wedding. I don't need to invite everyone to the shower," Charlotte says, all badass and supportive at the same time, like she is.

Still, I don't want to be treated with kid gloves. I definitely don't want her to think I can't handle my emotions. I've got those fuckers mastered and have for a long time.

"I can handle seeing Brady, no problem," I say breezily.

Charlotte flashes me a big smile. "Especially since you'll be with your new guy. I'm so excited you're hosting it together. And so, so grateful. Tell Wilder thank you!"

My gut churns with guilt. She's totally on my side, and I haven't even told her that this thing with the best man isn't real.

"I will," I say, then I redirect her attention to the chocolates. As we sample some more, she tells me about an idea for the shower, then we order the hot cocoa truffles as favors. When we're done, we say goodbye to Elodie, then Charlotte asks if I want to join her for some Christmas shopping.

"Is that a trick question?" I ask, arching a brow. She knows shopping and I are tight.

"Oh good! I told Leo I'd be home kind of late because I had a feeling I could twist your arm."

"You know me so well. And I'll do some of my shopping too," I say.

"To Fillmore Street," she says, naming my favorite place to exercise my credit card.

I stick out my arm. "Go ahead. Twist it twice."

We take off for my personal shopping heaven. The block is home to a cute card, puzzle, and tchotchke shop called Effing Stuff, my friend Rachel's jewelry store where I used to work, some cute boutiques, and my favorite vintage clothing shop in the city. I can snag Christmas gifts for all my friends as well as for family there.

Ten minutes later, I head into Effing Stuff to track down an I Hate Everything mug for Cousin Troy while Charlotte finds some irreverent coasters for our mom, so we head to the counter together. As I'm swiping my phone screen so I can tap pay, the woman at the counter says, "You're both all set."

Confused, I turn to Charlotte. "Did you sneak attack pay?"

But my sister looks just as confused as I am. "I didn't."

The clerk offers a smile. "Everything's covered. Wilder Blaine called and said you can get whatever you want."

What? How? When? I can't even speak as questions ping-pong in my head. Finally, several seconds later, I form words. "He did?"

I can't believe it.

The clerk nods. "He said you'd be Christmas shopping and that it would all be covered. And everything for your sister too."

Charlotte spins around, delight in her eyes. "That's some plus one."

I'm too shocked to say anything but, "yes, it is." Because this is nicer than anything a real boyfriend has ever done for me.

And it doesn't stop. When we head into Better With Pockets so I can pick up something for Everly, the man at the register says the same thing.

When I go to An Open Book to buy some books for Josie, everything has been covered there too.

When we pop into Bling and Baubles, Rachel grins and says, "You can have anything you want. Plus, free gift wrap."

For some reason, that last part makes me laugh the hardest. Maybe because Wilder even included gift-wrapping in his sneak attack shopping spree.

When I stop in the vintage shop to pick up a jacket that Maeve has been eyeing, the same song plays over again at the register.

As we leave, I ask, "How did he even know where we were going?"

But then I realize what must have happened right as Charlotte says, "Leo."

Charlotte told Leo, then he must have mentioned it to Wilder, and then Wilder went ahead and covered our entire Christmas shopping trip.

Talk about thoughtful.

When we're done, and laden with gold and silver bags, stuffed with beautifully wrapped gifts, I feel a little bit like I'm in another world. Shocked by what the man did. But also, I feel...frothy.

And special.

Something I've never really felt before either.

Charlotte's Lyft pulls up outside the last shop. She stops before opening the door to the black sedan.

"Want to share? I can add a stop."

We live in opposite directions, so I wave her off. "Mine will be here any minute."

She blows me a kiss. "Love you. You're the best. Sorry I freaked out this morning about the shower, sorry about

Brady, sorry about everything. But I'm not sorry you have a hot new man who loves to spoil you!"

She waves and disappears into the car. As it peels off, I whisper, *I don't have a hot new man.*

A pang of longing for what I don't have digs into my chest, but I do my best to ignore it. It's selfish to feel any sort of loss right now as I carry bags of gifts my fake boyfriend surprised me by paying for.

Besides, I need to thank Wilder for this wildly unexpected gift. Then focus on making it through seeing my awful ex nonstop the week of the wedding, showing that jerk how a woman should be treated, and in the meantime—all the time—saving for my new business.

Funny though, how Wilder already showed me tonight how a man should treat a woman.

My smile won't disappear. I stare down at the bags once more. This was just so...wonderfully extra. I take out my phone to thank him as I head to the bus stop a block away. I didn't really order a Lyft. I don't need to spend extra money on cars.

When I reach the stop, I open my texts.

Fable: YOU DID NOT JUST DO THAT!!!

He replies a minute later.

Wilder: I trust you had a good evening.

Fable: Seriously! THANK YOU! I can't believe you did that! That was above and beyond the brief.

Wilder: Disagree. It's exactly what a fake boyfriend should do.

Right. He's fake boyfriending. Of course that's what he's doing. And while it is above and beyond, it's also for show. I need to remember that. Still, I thank him one more time. Because that's what a good fake girlfriend should do.

Fable: And it was so thoughtful and I'm so very grateful. I truly appreciate it. How can I thank you?

Wilder: You just did. 

Ha. Is that an emoticon? I guess that's my thank-you since I'm pretty sure the man has never used one in his life. And I suppose I'll have to take him at face value—that my thank-you was enough.

Fable: I hope I'm as good a fake girlfriend as you are a fake boyfriend.

Wilder: You're wonderful, Fable.

I sigh contentedly, enjoying the compliment so very much. Those were rare with Brady too. And he never really treated me to anything. But I don't want to get too lost in the Cinderella fantasy. I return to *agenda items*, as Wilder likes to call them.

He'll definitely want to know that Brady's coming to the shower, especially after his PDA review at work today. He clearly wants to make sure we don't miss a beat. I don't want Brady to catch on either. No way am I giving that rat bastard the satisfaction of thinking he's hurt me.

Before I can even tap out the details, there's a new text from Wilder and the words ***Thought you might enjoy this***. It's a snippet of his daughter performing at her school concert and it's absolutely delightful.

Fable: I love it! It's your favorite song. Did she pick it for you?

Wilder: I think so. She also sang because her mom sings. So, I think it was a gift for both of us.

Fable: That is too much! My heart is full! You two get along? Her mom and you?

Wilder: Yes. We're friends. We stayed friends. I'm lucky like that.

Fable: It's not luck. It's work and effort, and this kiddo is worth it.

Wilder: She is. She's pretty amazing. But enough about me. How was the shower planning?

Fable: Yes! And Charlotte wants to do something kind of fun for the shower.

Wilder: More fun than a co-ed shower with the maid of honor? I'm on pins and needles.

Fable: I see what you just did.

Wilder: What did I do?

Fable: Co-ed. Shower. Like save water, shower with a friend.

Wilder: I didn't realize my Christmas girlfriend had such a naughty mind.

Heat spreads across my cheeks. I shouldn't flirt with him. But he's the one who mentioned a naughty mind. I hop onto the bus and reply once I sit down.

Fable: Maybe I do have one.

Wilder: That is very good to know.

And he's flirting right back. My stomach flips again, and I tap out a reply—***Do you?*** But then I backpedal, erasing it. Just because we practiced kissing doesn't mean we need to practice sexting. I return to the shower.

Fable: Anyway, her idea is that we're all going to dress as characters from Christmas movies.

He's silent. For several minutes, my phone doesn't buzz or beep as the bus chugs through the city toward my little apartment where I'll work on some of my own jewelry designs tonight.

I check my phone again. There aren't even three dots dancing. I can hear the dread loud and clear, though, in his eventual reply.

Wilder: We are?

Fable: We are!

Then there's the sigh of resignation.

Wilder: We are.

Fable: It'll be fun!

Wilder: If you say so.

A good girlfriend, fake or real, would make things easier for her guy. I hop off the bus and head to my apartment, replying as I go.

Fable: I can help you come up with an idea for your costume if you want. Maybe this is how I can thank you! I'm pretty creative.

Wilder: If you insist on thanking me by picking a costume, have at it. But I'm not going as Santa Claus.

Fable: Please. Santa's not hot. Of course you aren't going as Santa.

Wilder: You want me to go as someone hot?

Fable: You're my fake boyfriend. You'll look hot.

Wilder: Then, you should pick. Also, thank you.

Fable: I could tell you didn't want to pick. And I like costumes.

Wilder: I had a feeling.

Fable: Why?

Wilder: You seem like the type who can always have fun.

Fable: Do you ever have fun?

Wilder: I'm having fun right now.

I shut the door to my place and quickly change, then write back.

Fable: Me too. I'm wearing my fuzzy snowflake socks…

I pause, considering my next words. Then, what the hell?

Fable: They look hot.

Wilder: Of course they do. They're on you.

I gasp. And once more I replay the kiss. Then I tell him what his costume is.

* * *

The fake boyfriending doesn't stop at shopping. The next day while I'm working, an email lands on my computer from Shay.

Dear Fable,

Wilder has arranged for a private suite for you at this Thursday's game. He said you can invite as many friends as you'd like. Hors d'oeuvres included of course. Can you let me know by end of day if you can make it?

Thanks so much! We paw-sitively hope you can!

Shay

Once more, my jaw drops. Is he for real?

No, he's fake, girl. But seriously. This is elite-level fake boyfriending. I write back in all caps with extra exclamation points and a thousand thank yous.

And on Thursday night, I roll up to the stadium in my Renegades gear with Maeve, Josie, Everly, Charlotte and Leo, and also Rachel and Elodie. Josie brings Wesley, and Everly brings Max. Elodie brings her husband while Rachel brings her sister, Juliet, since her husband—Carter—is on the field prepping to play the game.

I've been to private suites before at the Renegades. I've stopped by the owner's suite. But I've never—naturally—had my own private one.

I'm giddy as I head up the elevator to the suite level, bouncing as I walk down the hall, and more excited than I think I've ever been when an attendant opens the door, and says, "Enjoy the game, Ms. Calloway."

But then, when I look at the spread, I'm simply touched. It's all my favorite foods, from olives and cheeses and nuts to mushroom bruschetta, to corn flautas, to zucchini fritters.

And there's no mayonnaise or shellfish in sight.

My heart pounds. I don't deserve this level of fake boyfriending, but holy fuck. I am going to enjoy the hell out of it.

"Go Renegades!" I shout.

"Damn, this is nice," Wesley says, then strides over to the tables full of appetizers. "Can we come to every game?"

"Yeah, it'd be great if you could get a private suite for every home game, Fable," Max calls out as he follows Wesley.

"Athletes," Everly says, smiling affectionately. "Food is a tractor beam for them."

"Um, me too," Josie says, then follows the guys.

Everly squeezes my shoulder, then says in a soft voice, "Maeve was right."

"Oh stop," I say, but I'm blushing.

By the end of the third quarter my voice is hoarse from cheering on the Renegades and shouting *you were wrong* at the refs when the door swings open. Wilder's dressed in a suit, no tie. He strides in during a commercial break and comes up to me as I refill my water.

"Are you enjoying the game?"

"Yes! Thank you, boss—"

I'm about to say *boss man*, when I stop myself. He's supposed to be my boyfriend. Would I really call him boss man here in front of everyone? "Thank you so much, sugar plum," I say, then...fuck it. I plant a quick kiss on his cheek.

His breath catches for a second, but he clears his throat and says, "I told you that you should come to the next home game."

That's what he said that day in his office when we made this arrangement. When he seemed bothered that I'd watched the Thanksgiving weekend game at home alone instead of with friends. So he made it possible for me to watch this one with them. All of them.

I look around at Everly and Max, checking out the

popcorn offerings. At Josie and Wesley, her head on his shoulder in the front row, at Rachel chatting with Juliet and Elodie. This is so...generous. I don't even know how to properly thank Wilder. "You really did this to make sure I could see the game in person?"

His smile is wry as he looks toward the glass overlooking the field with a confident nod. "It's better in person than on TV, isn't it?"

That's all he says. Then he turns to leave. But I stop him, grabbing his arm, then dropping another kiss on his cheek.

"That wasn't for practice. That was for real. Thank you."

There's a pause as something unreadable passes in his eyes. "You're welcome," he says, and I watch him go.

But then, maybe it wasn't unreadable. Maybe it was actually that he enjoyed watching me...have fun.

15

HIS OTHER TUXEDO

Fable

On Sunday morning, my eyes are bigger than moons when the car pulls up outside a three-story, slate-gray home on a cul-de-sac in Cow Hollow. I didn't even know there were cul-de-sacs in the city anywhere. But then, I've never had a reason to cruise down a street populated by nine-figure homes before.

I haven't been able to stop gawking at this whole block as the black town car Wilder sent for me rolled through his neighborhood at the top of the city. It's not like I'm dying to live in one of these mansions. But I am human and these homes are just so...gawk-worthy.

I step out of the car, feeling a little like a princess as the driver, in his livery cap, holds the door for me. "Thank you."

"But of course," he says, then sweeps out his arm toward the gated entryway. "Mr. Blaine is expecting you so the gate should be unlocked."

Gates. Drivers. Palaces. This is all so much. The wrought-iron door groans open easily then clangs shut behind me. The front lawn boasts low hedges, neatly trimmed and decorated with white icicle lights for the season. I stride along a stone path, up the front steps, and to the doorway. On a looming black door hangs a huge wreath, the pine scent from it tickling my nose.

I lift a hand to knock when the door swings open.

It's not Wilder. It's his daughter, with her hair perfectly combed back into a French braid. "Oh, hi. My dad told me you were coming. I was hoping we could finish that jigsaw puzzle we started the other night." It's said with that trademark Blaine confidence as she waves me in.

It's seriously adorable that Wilder enlisted his daughter to help us with our fake dating plan. And it's seriously fun to play along with her. "Right. When I came by on Tuesday after work?"

"Like our new routine," she adds, and she is the spitting image—well, personality wise—of her father.

Smooth. Cool. Quick on her feet.

"Yes. Our new routine," I echo.

I'm about to step into the home when I remember something Wilder said at our dinner last weekend as he rattled off his personal details. I toe off my flats, leaving them in the entryway. Mac takes my coat.

"He sent me to get you. He had to finish a phone call with my grandma," she says, and I was admittedly expecting her to say *his CFO* or *the New York office*, but it's delightful Wilder's talking to his mom in London right now. "I can show you around a little bit."

"I would love that," I say.

Mac ushers me into the house. "My dad and I did most

of the Christmas decorating. Because...Confession: I love Christmas decorating."

"Double confession: me too. And you did an amazing job."

"Well, I didn't do *everything*. He hired a party planner to add some extra touches for today because I can't do it all. Even at my age. But I did those a couple weeks ago." She points to the garlands lining a floating staircase on the opposite side of the home and the tasteful sprigs of evergreens arranged around red and white candles on side tables.

"You've got mad skills," I say.

"Thanks," she says with a proud lift of her chin as she escorts me into the sunken living room. I tell her I enjoyed her Christmas recital, and she sighs. "I'm just glad it's over."

"You don't like performing?"

"It's fine," she says with an easy shrug. "But it's not my thing."

In the corner of the room stands a tall fir tree, neatly decorated with silver and red bows. But it's the ornaments that catch my attention. "Your ornaments don't match." I can't hide my delight. I'd figured Wilder's tree would be decorated with understated silver, gold, and red orbs, like a tree in a fancy department store window.

Nope.

On the branches hang paper cutout snowflakes, pink yarn stars, and homemade snowmen glued to popsicle sticks. "I made those," Mac says. "They *could* be better. But want to see the rest?"

"I'd love to," I say. "I love homemade ornaments."

"Me too." She guides me down the step, onto a plush carpet that feels like walking on a fluffy cloud, then past a glass coffee table, and finally to the tree. She shows me a red cardboard picture frame with a photo of her and Wilder sledding on a toboggan. "That's from Evergreen Falls a couple years ago. There's this one hill there where you can go super-fast."

I stare, smiling stupidly at the two of them in their snow gear, flying down a hill. "Is there sledding in the Christmas games at Evergreen Falls?"

Mac pauses, then her eyes twinkle. "Yes! There is."

"I'll have to do some recon. Get in some practice runs."

"But it's only for kids. Still, sledding is always a good idea."

"It is."

She points to an ornament made out of a walnut and decorated like Rudolph, with lopsided googly eyes and a red puffy ball for a nose. "I made this last year. That was my walnut phase. But I should have used a better...nose thingy."

"No." I immediately cut off that notion.

"No what?"

"It's perfect the way it is. It has so much personality."

"Really?" She sounds so doubtful, a contrast to the girl who opened the door.

"You're talented, and it looks like you had fun making it," I say. That's what matters. I point to a matching one a few branches up, this one missing an eye. "Especially since there are two."

"Oh, my dad made that one." She drops her voice. "He's terrible at crafts. Don't tell him I said that."

I bring my finger to my lips. "I won't say a word." Even though I find this intel as delicious as the sledding tidbit.

"He tries, but it's just not his thing," she says with a *what can you do* shrug. "But he's good at other stuff."

Understatement of the year. "He is. And you're good at photography. I saw my sister's proposal pics. They're so good, Mac."

"Thanks," she says, and now there's real pride in her voice. Photography must be important to her. "I'm taking a class, but I also just learned by doing it. Over and over."

"Best way to learn."

"I like it better than singing," she says as she shows me more ornaments. "I bet you can make great ones. My dad says you're really talented."

"He does?"

"He said *she's the best designer in the business. Still can't believe we were lucky enough to snap her up, but the sales don't lie.*"

"Thank you for sharing that." I might be floating.

The sound of footsteps pulls me back to Earth, then his voice. "Good to see you, Fable."

I turn around, and my pulse surges wildly, beating in my throat.

I've seen Wilder in suits before. But this time feels different. Because we're in his house? Because he's barefoot and that just makes him seem a little vulnerable for the first time? Because of that test kiss? Because of all his extravagant gifts?

But no. I dismiss all those reasons.

Today's different because he asked me to pick his costume. Like a real girlfriend would do. Because he sent me photos of the suits in his closet so I could choose for him. I picked black slacks, a white shirt, a black jacket, and no tie. Like the iconic scene at the end of *Love Actually* when Hugh Grant appears at the children's Christmas show at the school in the dodgy part of town.

A smile takes over my face.

"You look just like the prime minister," I say, a little mesmerized, "when he's caught kissing his Natalie behind the curtain on stage."

"You really do," Mac seconds.

Wilder swivels to her. "I asked you not to watch it. The movie is rated R."

She rolls her eyes. "I didn't, Dad. I googled the pics, okay?"

"Okay," he acquiesces, then runs a hand gently over her hair, careful not to mess up her braid.

Then we're both quiet as he looks me up and down.

Red sweater. Black pants. Gold belt. Like the prime minister's love interest in the oft-debated Christmas flick everyone loves to hate and hates to love. And a delicate necklace that's all mine. Something I made myself in the jewelry-making class I teach once a week—to show the students what's possible.

"And Fable looks perf," Mac says. Then she eyes the neckline of my red sweater critically. "Except, hold on."

She runs off, racing up the floating stairs.

It's just Wilder and me, standing in front of the tree, looking like a Christmas movie couple. The weight of this moment hits me. We're doing this—faking it. Not just for ourselves. But for others. I'm faking it for my sister, her fiancé, and all their friends, as well as our own families.

And also for Brady—that asshole who thought he could hurt me. But he'll see I've moved on when he arrives in a few hours.

Thoughts of Brady fall from my head when Wilder says, "You look...lovely."

Impulsively, I say, "So do you." But just so he doesn't think I'm hitting on him, I quickly add, "You look just like the character. In the movie. Except for one thing..."

He tilts his head. "What's that?"

"Your hair's not quite as messy."

His lips quirk up. "That so?"

I don't think. *I do.* I step closer and run my hands through his perfectly combed, wavy brown hair.

It's soft.

His hair feels so good.

And his breath seems to hiss out when I'm close like this. When I touch him. When I slide my hands through his soft strands.

"Your hair is…" I swallow the word but then find it again, meeting his gaze. "Nice."

"Thanks," he says, his voice raspier than usual. A little gritty too.

Mac's footsteps rattle on the floor. We step apart, the moment breaking.

Seconds later, Mac flies down the stairs to stop in front of me, a paper snowflake in her hand. "She had a snowflake on her neckline. In the movie pics," Mac explains.

Right. Of course. I looked them up, too, but I'd figured a red sweater would be sufficient for the costume. Maybe not for an eleven-year-old though.

"Then it's a good thing you made one," I say, then I bend so she can pin this makeshift addition to my costume to the neckline. Her tongue's poking at the corner of her lips as she concentrates. Once she gets it just right, she says, "There." She steps back, sizes me up, and says, "It's perfect now. Right, Dad?"

He curls his hand around her shoulder and looks me over. "Beautiful," he says.

Does he mean the snowflake or me?

Duh. The snowflake. He's complimenting his kid's

handiwork. "Yes, thank you, Mac. It's a beautiful snowflake," I say.

"Thanks. I'm going to make sure we have popcorn," she says. "So we can watch anything but *Love Actually* during the shower."

"Good plan," Wilder says, and when Mac disappears, presumably into the kitchen, Wilder says to me, "I'll show you around so it seems like you know the place."

It's make-believe, this holiday romance, but it's not hard to pretend I'm in a fairy tale as he takes me through this castle of a home.

First, there's the library on this level, which has a few detective novels scattered on a table near a plush green couch. A ladder rests against some mis-shelved middle-grade books, adventure stories, and time travel tales.

"A girl could get lost in here," I say, admiring the wooden bookcases, then running my fingers across some of the spines.

"Yes, it's been known to happen with a certain eleven-year-old," he says wryly.

"Takes after you," I say.

Stopping at the ladder, he smiles, proud and deservedly so. "She does. But she has an artistic side, too, like her mother."

"I noticed. Her ornaments are top tier," I say, then add in a conspiratorial whisper, "can't help but love her crafty side."

"You have one as well," he says. "Our door is going to win."

I wave a hand. "We'll see."

Resting a forearm on the ladder, he nods to my neck. "Your necklace. Did you make it?"

I lift my hand to touch the simple, delicate chain. It's

rose gold, with a tiny bow at the throat. "I did. Recycled metal for the chain. And the bow comes from some vintage pieces I sourced at a cool flea market in Darling Springs."

He lifts a brow, clearly curious. "You do that?"

"Go to flea markets around the state to source materials?"

"Yes."

"Nearly everything I make comes from recycled materials."

"Like in the shirt design you're working on for us," he says, putting clues together like in one of his detective novels.

"Yes," I say. "It's my thing too."

He seems almost...taken with this intel. "So, it's our thing—looking after the planet," he adds. It's as if we've just discovered we both dog-eared the same scenes in the same book as a kid or want to visit the same Aztec ruins.

"Seems it is," I say.

He doesn't look away, just studies the chain from a slight distance, then raises his gaze to mine again. "Would you ever want to do that full-time? Make your own jewelry? Or really, do more of that?"

Yes, god, yes. But should I say that to my boss? I'm not sure I should let on that my dream is to one day open a shop, or two or three. Bosses want to believe you'll stay with the company forever. They don't want to know you have other goals and aspirations. Loyalty, I'm sure, is important to him. "Maybe on the side," I say, hedging my bets.

"Like an Etsy shop? I could see that," he says.

The fact that he can picture it and not be threatened

by it makes my heart glow. "Yes. Like that," I say, taking a small step in sharing my dreams with him.

"You should. They're too beautiful to keep to yourself."

But there's a nagging feeling in my stomach. I don't want to lie to him. "Actually, I have one already," I confess.

He lifts a brow. "An Etsy shop?"

"I just dabble for now. Sell a few things here and there," I say.

"What's the name?"

"Made by Fable," I say, then roll my eyes. "It's not that original."

"You have the perfect name for a designer. It's artistic and creative. It's a good name for a shop, Fable," he says, and there's no faint praise in his tone. I can tell he means it.

"Thank you."

He lets go of the ladder, steps closer to me, and reaches toward the necklace. Briefly, he runs a finger across the little bow. My skin buzzes from his seconds-long touch, then his words, "So pretty." Then, he heads to the door. "Should we continue on our tour?"

I take a moment to get my bearings before I say yes, then follow him downstairs to a gym, and also a home theater where Mac and some of the kids will hang out during the luncheon party. He gestures to an empty red bowl that says *popcorn* on it, sitting on the sideboard.

"That's from last night," he says, swooping it up and dropping it in the kitchen with Mac as she sorts out popcorn spices. Then, he guides me up the stairs, and I drink in the view for miles as we go, the Golden Gate Bridge and the endless ocean spilling over the horizon. We reach the bedroom level, and he shows me Mac's room with its unmade bed that he clearly didn't insist she make this morning. There's also a huge, messy desk covered with cameras and lenses. Photoshop is open on the computer screen.

His home office is next on the tour. Antique maps cover the walls. "Do you collect?"

"I do," he says.

"Why?"

"I like knowing what the world was."

"To know what it can be?"

"Yes. Exactly."

"That's very you," I say. "Especially with your new businesses, like the energy ones."

"You think so?"

"Yes. You like to understand the future. To help shape it."

"I hope so. And I hope to shape it for the best."

"And you like to understand people," I say.

He holds my gaze for a beat. "I do."

That warmth I felt earlier spreads. He understood how frazzled and hurt I was that time in his office when I spilled glitter Christmas dicks on him. He understood me the next time when I felt guilty over *not* telling my sister the full truth. He understood me at dinner when we talked about snow and winter and songs.

And he's trying so damn hard to make sure we pull off this fake romance. Brady hardly tried at all with our real relationship. My own father barely tried to fix things with my mother after cheating on her over and over, and she still gave him chance after chance. And sure, some of my past boyfriends tried, but not to the extent of this man.

Wilder? He shows up every single time for every single thing. It's admirable. It's attractive. My throat tightens briefly with emotions, but I swallow them down as we leave.

I face a new battle when we reach his room next. The suite is three times the size of my tiny place and fifty million times nicer, with warm cream walls, soft carpeting, and floor-to-ceiling windows. I swear I try not to *ooh* and *aah* the whole time. The bed, low to the ground on a blond wood platform, looks like it's made of sweet dreams, with soft gray, blue, and white pillows. The windows show off the whole city and the ocean beyond. His bed is neatly made, and this feels entirely him too.

I'm about to say that when a loud thud echoes from the corner of the room. I spin around, alarmed. "What was that?"

Wilder drags a hand through his hair. "Penguin," he says.

"Penguin?"

A second later, a large tuxedo cat saunters out of the closet, stretches luxuriously, then sashays over to Wilder. The cat has white gloves, a black body, and a half-face, mostly black, but with a white mouth. "You have a cat," I say, stunned.

"The rumors are true."

I spin around, swatting his arm. "Stop it! You never even dropped a hint that you had a cat. You didn't mention it at dinner or in your office dos and don'ts."

"I guess there was so much else we covered, it slipped my mind," he says, but there's something else in his eyes—the hint of an excuse? A cover-up? I'm not sure.

"Well, you ordered me to come early so we could pull this off." I park my hands on my hips. "Now I learn you've been hiding a cat?" A cat who's...a little in love with

Wilder. The feline is rubbing against his leg. Purring. "Is your cat marking you?"

With amused resignation, he bends to pick up the critter. "She was supposed to be Mac's. A few years ago, she wanted to adopt a cat, so I took her to Little Friends, and she picked this cat. Then, once we returned home, the cat...well, she picked me."

As if on cue, Penguin rubs her head against his chest. A laugh bursts from me. "Your cat is obsessed with you."

A smile teases his lips like he can't quite believe he's enchanted this feline. But judging from the rumble of her purr, he definitely has. He scratches her head. "Yes. She is. So there you go. I have a cat. Mac named her," he says, then sets the fluffball on the bed. She flops down, sticking a leg up in the air and bathing for all the world to see.

"She matches you, tuxedo cat and all. She's the perfect feline for you."

He glances down at his suit. "I'm not wearing a tuxedo right now."

"No, but I bet there's one in your closet."

He steps closer and holds my gaze, his eyes gleaming. "Two, Fable. Two."

He doesn't look away. I roll my lips together, liking his stare more than I should. I shake off this feeling blooming in my chest—whatever it is—and sweep my arm around the space, indicating his home.

Yes, it's luxurious, out of nearly everyone's league. But it's also lived in and loved. "I like your house. It looks like home," I say.

Tilting his head, he studies me, his eyes soft, vulnerable. "Thanks. Hardly anyone says that." A pause. "Actually, no one."

"Then they're missing the obvious."

"Yeah?"

"Yes."

For a few seconds, the air feels charged. Like we've crossed some line, more than we did with our practice kiss. Or maybe the crackle and pop comes from being, well, seen.

Before we leave his room, though, he sets a hand on my arm. His expression serious, he says, "Let's be the best best man and maid of honor there is. And let's show Brady that he's the one who lost."

He takes my hand, and we walk down the stairs like that—even though no one's looking.

But I'm looking. And I'm liking this. "You're holding my hand," I whisper.

He starts to let go. "I was...practicing."

"We're getting good at that. Practicing."

There's a slight hitch in his breath, then he grits out, "We are."

I grab hold tighter on his hand so he can't stop. "Keep practicing."

He blinks, and for a few dangerous seconds, I swear I see something real flash in his eyes.

But that can't be. He's just very, very good at everything he does, including this game. And soon, it's showtime.

16

HAVE YOURSELF A MERRY LITTLE PAYBACK

Wilder

The number of men here in undershirts with smudge on their faces is...well, there are too many. At least that's better than adults in bunny jammies.

"Grown men in jammies," I say to Leo. Leaning against the kitchen counter, we watch the guests drink mimosas and discuss their costumes. "Things that should not be allowed in public."

"Even for a Christmas costume party, jammies are too much. Also, I don't like the word jammies."

I laugh. "So don't use it."

"That's it. Done. Never saying it again."

"I'll hold you to that." Besides, Ralphie detested the pink bunny pajamas made famous in *A Christmas Story*. Memorializing the kid's humiliation, even a fictional kid...?

"That's just wrong," I say, nodding to the not one but two guys dressed in pink flannel.

Leo tips his chin toward a man in a Scrooge costume —a nightshirt and a robe. "Another costume that's an excuse to wear pjs to a party. Wrong too." He turns to me. "Does that make us scrooges?"

"If we are, I'll die on Scrooge Hill. You shouldn't wear slippers, bathrobes, or pajamas out of the house. Or *to* someone else's house. It defeats the basic premise and promise of pajamas," I say, then eye Leo's getup—John McClane, AKA Bruce Willis's character from *Die Hard,* in the classic tank top. "But you're okay."

Leo gestures to his action hero attire. "It was either this or *Elf*."

"And you picked McClane because you don't look good in tights?" I ask, with a straight face.

He laughs. "Man, I'm not sure anyone does," he says as my gaze strays again to the door. It's been doing that often as I await the inevitable.

The arrival of the jackass ex.

As if the alarm system read my mind, the panel by the door buzzes. Leo and I head to the foyer and check the screen. I grit my teeth at the sight of Brady, but I let him in, anyway. He strides inside and—*that's* his costume?

Of course that's his costume, glasses and all. It's so fitting.

"Leo, my man!" he says. I think I detect a British accent. Or really, Brady's attempt at a British accent? Guess he's committed to his character. "Are you counting down the last days of bachelorhood?"

Leo laughs, shaking his head. "More like counting down to the most wonderful day of all."

"Right, right," Brady says, all jovial and cousin-y.

It takes every ounce of restraint not to give him a piece

of my mind. I know what he did. And he's scum. He hurt Fable.

There's also part of me that's keenly aware that if she hadn't walked in on him, we might not be faking it. And so far, this fake romance is the most fun I've had in a long time.

Leo tips his forehead toward the living room. "Better join my sexy *Mean Girl*," he says and makes his way toward Charlotte. She's wearing a short red dress and a Santa cap like, I brilliantly deduce, a character in that movie wore. Or *characters*, since Josie and Maeve are dressed the same, which would never happen by accident. Everly's here too, but she's in a red cape over a black-and-white dress. I don't recognize her costume either.

Brady turns to me, slugging my biceps, and goes back to his normal accent. "So I hear you and I both have good taste."

I stare at him blankly. "What do you mean?" To be clear, I know what he means. I just can't believe he's going there, and my feigned confusion keeps me from throttling him. But, oh, how I want to.

"Dude. I hear you picked up my former girlfriend." He wiggles his brow as he elbows me. "Good on you."

If he weren't my best friend's cousin, I'd go to jail tonight for pummeling the smirk from his face.

Or not. That's only an impulse and not how I do business. I play chess all day. No one can devise a sharper strategy. This asshole does not know who he's dealing with.

I open by moving a pawn, remembering his offer the last time I saw him. "So, back at Thanksgiving, you wanted to see if you could manage my funds."

The look on his face is Christmas morning joy. "Yes.

You gave me that *noted,* and I've been jonesing to talk to you more about it."

While the other guests discuss dresses and bouquets, string quartets and deejays, Brady blathers on about how I should invest in tech. *Really? Tell me more.* I try to give him the same courtesy I'd give anyone who came to my office.

Focus.

Well, I don't give audiences to men who cross the woman I'm a little obsessed with.

When he's done, I nod, soberly absorbing all that keen insight while I move my final piece toward checkmate.

I didn't invite his insight or actually say I wanted to hear more. I just needed to let him run on until I was ready to close the conversation, which I do now with finality.

"Thanks for all that insight. And I didn't have a chance to tell you then because Leo had just proposed to Charlotte." I pause, clap his shoulder like a good old sport, and relish this moment. "But I'm all set on the portfolio front. Such a shame we can't work together."

Then I leave him, and I head to join my fake girlfriend in the living room.

A small victory is still a victory.

"*No* is just the first stop on the road to yes!" Brady calls after me with a *good one, pal* chuckle. "I'll convince you over Christmas, Wilder. Mark my words."

This guy is relentless. For now, though, I ignore him.

When I reach Fable, I don't hesitate to wrap an arm around her waist, to lean closer, to sweep her hair away from her neck.

I don't check to see if the jackass is looking or worry that he'll see through the ruse. Because nothing's fake when she leans into me, her scent tickling my nose, her nearness frying my brain. Turning closer, she whispers, "You're good at that, sugar plum. No one can tell."

Yes, I am good at this, and I don't want to stop. Reluctantly, I break away from the private moment and focus on the party, on being a good host. All my attention goes to the guests.

Right until Fable heads to the kitchen and Brady follows her.

17

SO VERY FUCKABLE

Fable

Brady is Alan Rickman from *Love Actually* because only a person with zero self awareness would pick that character. The cheater. The Alan Rickman who broke all our hearts in his square glasses, a thin black scarf, and a black jacket. The Alan Rickman who got Emma Thompson a Joni Mitchell CD instead of the necklace she deserved. The most hated character in Christmas cinema.

I want to kick him in the knees and watch him fall to the floor. That guilt I felt when I first fibbed to Charlotte about being with Wilder? I don't feel an ounce of it now. Because of Brady.

Nope. I don't want him to feel sorry for me. Ever.

I'm in the kitchen, freshening up a charcuterie board like a good hostess, when he strides over, leaning an elbow on the counter. "Wow, Fabes," he says. "I didn't realize you'd moved on so quickly."

He's one to talk. "Quickly?" I whisper-seethe under my

breath. "Not any quicker than moving on to someone while still being with someone else."

The jackass smiles smugly. "I had a feeling it'd be hard for you to see me with Iris. That's why I didn't bring her."

I ignite. Flames roar in every cell in my body. "You didn't bring her," I bite out, "because she wasn't invited. We didn't invite everyone who's coming to the wedding."

He gives a chin nod as he reaches for an olive. "Sure. Right. That's the reason."

Why did I ever date him? Was he this odious when I was with him? *Please, universe, tell me he was a smidge less odious then.*

I draw a deep, centering breath, then move the fuck on. "I've always had a thing for Wilder," I say, arranging the final slice of Gouda as I gaze lovingly at the man across the room, chatting with guests but looking at me with eyes that promise—*say the word and I'll come for you.*

I give him a reassuring smile, telling him I'm okay.

A subtle nod comes from him.

Wilder does look seriously handsome as the prime minister—debonair and hot at the same time.

Smart, powerful, *and* fuckable.

And...where did that come from?

I've never thought of him, or anyone as smart, powerful, and fuckable, but now that I'm looking at Wilder, those adjectives go nicely together.

They make it genuinely easy to take my charcuterie board and walk away from Brady without a second thought. I want to sit next to the so very fuckable man who's my Christmas boyfriend.

* * *

Wilder and I sit on the couch with the twenty-or-so guests gathered around. There's Maeve and Josie, along with my sister. Everly's here too, her blonde hair in braids since she's dressed as Cindy-Lou Who. Her boyfriend, Max, is the Grinch. At least, I think he's the Grinch. A green fluffy collar is his only nod to the costume theme. But that fits—he had a reputation as the league's grumpiest goalie until Everly, as the team publicist, helped him rehab his image.

Mariah Carey belts out her holiday wishes on a state-of-the-art sound system while we play our wedding shower game—*He Said, She Said, Who Did*.

Wilder reads from a card. "Who made the first move?" With patient eyes, he looks to the guests.

Josie, Everly, and Maeve shout *Leo*.

The groom gives a *can you blame me* smile and then drops a kiss onto my sister's cheek.

Josie takes the next card and reads, "Who said I love you first?"

We all shout, "Leo."

Charlotte raises a finger, her candy-red polish shiny under the chandelier. "I said it a second later." She kisses her groom's forehead, and Leo smiles dopily.

Max goes next, clearing his throat and reading, "Who, after their first date, said, 'I met the person I'm going to marry?'"

Everly adds, "Awww. So sweet."

I snap my gaze toward Wilder, who grins as we shout in unison, "They both did."

His shoulder slides against mine as we laugh, and a spark shimmies across my neck. I peek at his face and catch a glimpse of his green eyes. They flicker with something playful but soulful too, and then he wraps an arm around me, tugging me close. A tingle slides down my spine then spreads through my whole body, warm and bright.

Across from me, Brady's chatting amiably with Leo and some of the other guys. Maybe the condescending *Sure you moved on* comments are finished and we can all have fun and celebrate our friends' happiness.

I hope so. It's nice right now with everyone getting along. It's nice, too, to play pretend with Wilder, like when he held my hand. Like how he's touching me now.

"We should refill drinks," I say.

"Good idea."

He stands, and I follow him, but a high-pitched squeak from my sister stops us before we leave the living room. It's followed by an excited, "Mistletoe alert!"

She points at us, standing under the archway into the kitchen.

Wilder and I crane our necks in sync.

Directly above us is a sprig of mistletoe. Who hung it? Did Wilder put this here when he and his daughter decorated? Or was this the party planner's doing?

Who cares? It's showtime.

The rest of the guests are cheering now, too, chanting, *Kiss her*. Including my ex.

I suppose it's a good thing we practiced that kiss in his office. But as I wait to be kissed once more by my smart, powerful, fuckable billionaire fake boyfriend, the run-through seems superfluous. Because my desire is no lie.

18

A FOOT POPPER

Fable

This kiss needs to seem like our twentieth or fiftieth—not our second. I don't want to mess this up.

But when Wilder meets my gaze, my worries disintegrate and something else takes over—an insistent need that climbs the stairs of my heart. The need to be kissed... by him.

There's not a second to choreograph this moment. This is a one-take situation. His eyes pin mine as he whispers, just for me, "Practice makes perfect."

My chest flutters. I answer him with a tilt of my chin, even as questions flicker through my head. Will he wrap an arm around my waist? Drop a peck on my lips? Cup a cheek? The answer comes a second later when he lifts his hands to hold my face in a firmer grasp than the one in his office, and I tremble at that first touch. Tender and caring. Possessive and in control.

Music floats by, and I faintly register "Have Yourself a

Merry Little Christmas." At the chorus, Wilder inches closer, and time slows. Anticipation wraps around me like a magic spell. Our audience fades into the distant background as Wilder's breath coasts over my jaw. A sound escapes my lips—a hungry murmur that surprises me.

That delights *him,* judging from the way his lips curve up. That little sign smooths out the last of my worries. I close my eyes, and his lips brush over mine. That scent of cedar is intoxicating. I melt like snow under the winter sun as Wilder kisses me under the mistletoe.

I don't know how it happens or when, but my foot pops up like in every iconic kissing photo, like in every movie smooch.

Now I'm having my own kissing moment, and my body takes over as he leads me through our first kiss for an audience. But it's not three seconds like the one in his office. It's longer—maybe ten, possibly fifteen. I don't even know. It's just soft and yet passionate all at once.

My chest tingles. My belly swoops. There's not even tongue, yet I'm dizzy everywhere. It's the best fifteen seconds I've spent in ages, and I want it to become five minutes. Five hours.

When he breaks the kiss, I miss his lips terribly.

My breath hitches, and I nearly whimper.

Wilder's eyes lock with mine. Heat flickers across those clever green irises. Something else too. Fondness? Affection? No, I'm not sure it's either of those. It's something I can't quite name. Desire mixed with longing, maybe.

I swallow. Try to center myself. Shake off the fog of lust.

The room comes back into focus. The song winds down to the end.

My sister claps. "Now that's a mistletoe kiss," she declares, then turns her face to Leo's and cups his cheek, tugging him close. "Makes me want one from you."

Awareness of the audience snaps me out of the haze. So does Brady's dude-bro chant as he eggs on his cousin. "Do it, do it, do it now, cuz."

I cringe. He's officially ruining my post-kiss bliss. I want to live in this bubble a little longer, especially now that the focus is on the bride and groom, as it should be.

Wilder and I back away from the mistletoe, heading into the kitchen, our staged kiss a mere party footnote.

But for me, it's the whole story. I'm still breathless when I stop at the kitchen counter and lean a hip against it. Fiddling with the sleeves of my sweater, returning to the mistletoe question.

"I didn't pick you as the mistletoe type," I say softly.

"I'm not," he replies, moving closer.

"So it was the decorator?" I ask. It feels vitally important, somehow, to know who hung the mistletoe. The office kiss was a practice one. But this was for an audience. Did he want it? "Mac said you hired a party planner."

"I did, but the planner didn't hang it up." He sounds a little dazed too. Come to think of it, he hasn't said much since we moved into the kitchen. His eyes even look a bit... hazy.

Wait.

Did he like the kiss as much as I did?

The thought lodges in my brain and won't let go.

He turns his gaze toward the staircase leading to the movie room. "But I think perhaps my daughter may be," he says. "A mistletoe person, that is."

Does Mac have a little Christmas matchmaker in her? I let my mind wander to thoughts of Christmas with him and his daughter. To the crackle of the fireplace, the scent of pine, the familiar music that feels like home. To baking cookies in this kitchen—though not gingerbread, of course—then making more ornaments with her. Whimsical animals like foxes wearing scarves, polar bears with argyle sweaters, and reindeer in boots. We three could hang them on the tree together, and then when Mac goes to bed, Wilder and I could kiss under the mistletoe again.

What is happening in my head? I'm fantasizing about ornament design with his daughter? About after-dark kisses with him?

This is foolish and dangerous.

I blink off the cozy and sexy thoughts, but when I meet Wilder's handsome, nearly inscrutable face, he doesn't seem so inscrutable anymore.

The haze in his eyes? It does look like longing, a little. Or, really, a lot.

But surely that's just the side effect of an unexpected sultry kiss. It's a byproduct of fake dating. Someone could even list it on a pill bottle—side effects of fake dating may vary and include, but are not limited to, swoons, stomach flips, and naughty thoughts. You may want to talk to your pharmacist about what to expect and watch out for. If symptoms persist, see your love doctor.

I smooth a hand over my sweater, sliding into hostess mode and returning to the reality of this shower we're hosting for my sister and Wilder's best friend. "I should see if...if anyone needs anything."

Wilder clears his throat, nodding a few times, almost like he's clearing away the fog too. "Same here."

My chest twinges with hope, with a dangerous ache. But I can't spend this party wondering if he liked his daughter's Christmas decorating touch. Or if he liked our kiss in the same way I did.

Besides, he let me know the score from the start.

My boss wants us to be the best fake daters there are to get his aunt off his back and to show my ex what he's lost. Wilder's a competitive man so of course he'd give me the best fake kiss in the history of Christmas. Even if I liked it, even if it felt real.

That mystery solved, I return to the party and box up the memory of his lips as I refill the pitcher of Christmas mojito mix.

Doesn't take long for my friends to join me.

"Just friendly?" Josie asks with a smirk.

"I mean, that was such a *just friendly* kiss," Maeve seconds while Everly grins.

I blush and say nothing, because they're right.

* * *

"We should have a costume contest!"

This brilliance is brought to us by Brady a little later as we finish a round of *What Would the Groom Say*. He's seated next to the bride and groom, on the couch across from Wilder and me.

I shake my head at Brady. "I don't think so."

He pouts. "C'mon. What's a Christmas movie costume party without a little contest?"

"A Christmas movie costume party," I say dryly, trying to hide my annoyance. He didn't plan this shower. I did. But I don't want to let on he's a pebble in my shoe because then he'll really think he hurt me. His *you moved on quickly* comment aside, he seems to believe the mere sight of him with Iris would destroy me. I can't let him think that, but anger would definitely tip him off. I take a quiet, calming breath, then say as sweetly as I can, "Also, it's not a costume party. It's a wedding shower."

He snort-huffs. "Yeah, but we all went to the effort to dress up. Per the host and hostess rules," he says, pointing to Wilder then to me, like he's uncovered the culprits. Wilder's body is tight. He's the picture of coiled restraint as Brady keeps talking. "And everything's more fun when there's a competition, right? Isn't that why we're having the Christmas competition before your wedding next week?" Brady whips his gaze to Leo, seeming to seek approval from the cooler, older cousin.

Leo shoots him a placating—I think—smile. "Well, sure. Somewhat. Charlotte and I do love games," he says, and there's a bit of *save me* in his voice. He's the peacemaker in the bunch, that's clear.

"And we love Christmas, so it made sense to make it an event," Charlotte adds, and the subtext in her words is crystal clear—*that doesn't mean we want this casual wedding shower to be a costume contest, you jackass.*

Though, I might have just added the *you jackass* in my head.

But Brady's not good with subtext. He rubs his palms together. "Let's do it then! A little impromptu *who wore it best*?" Puffing out his chest, he bleats out like the emcee of a boxing match, "Will it be the studly Alan Rickman in this corner, or every single man who dressed like John McClane in all the other corners?"

Jesus. He's already declaring himself the winner of the Christmas movie costume contest. He's also a sexist pig. "Or a woman could win," Everly says, reading my mind.

"Yes, exactly," I say, not so sweetly.

"So, you're in, Fabes? I knew it. I knew you'd get right

back into the swing of fun and games," Brady says, and I want to smack him.

Because he's saying the same thing he said before—*you moved on quickly*, even though he also thinks I'm crying in my salted caramel ice cream over all I've theoretically lost.

It's like he's trying to goad me into admitting I'm stuck on him.

I grit my teeth, hunting for an appropriate comeback to say in front of friends and family, when Wilder cuts in. His voice isn't the loudest in the room. He doesn't need to speak with volume, since he speaks with authority as he says, "No. There won't be a costume contest today because sometimes it's fun to just show up in costume. It doesn't have to be a sport." He pauses, and the only sound is Frank Sinatra crooning that he'll be home for Christmas. Then, once his words have sunk in, he adds, "Why don't we open gifts?"

It's said decisively. A man who's moving the agenda along without needing to pet any ruffled feathers.

"If you say so," Brady says under his breath.

Wilder turns to him, his eyes hard. "Yes. I do."

Cold, clear, crisp.

And I'm a little turned on at the way Wilder's putting Brady in his place.

Brady shrugs, then adjusts his cheater's glasses. "All right, boss man. Your house, your rules. But know this—the gloves will be off at Christmastime." He smiles at Leo. "Am I right or am I right?"

Leo laughs, possibly still placating him. "Sure. I know you'll play to win, Brady. You were always competitive."

Brady turns his attention to Wilder. "And that's a good thing. I'm going to win the competition and that'll prove to you that I'm the right man to manage your money."

"Is that so?" Wilder asks, sounding amused.

But I burn hotter, this time with irritation, frustration, and, fine, I'll admit it—*hurt*. This jerk hurt me at Thanksgiving. And for a while here earlier today, when Wilder kissed me under the mistletoe, I nearly forgot *why* I'm faking it with my boss.

Now it's all coming back to me.

I'm faking it because this asshat thinks it's okay to treat women like crap. I flash back to Wilder's words in his office the day we decided to do this.

You deserve to be treated with respect. With adoration. With real affection.

Then to Bibi's that same day.

I hope you beat that Brady character in the competition.

Cheating exes who think women are disposable don't get to win a damn thing. I lift my chin, fueled by Christmas revenge. "We'll be ready, and we'll win," I blurt out.

Wilder reads me like that. He loops an arm around my shoulder, squeezing me. "We will. And just to make it a little more fun, whoever wins, whether it's someone from town, or from the wedding party—I'll donate ten thousand dollars to the winner's charity of choice."

I jerk my gaze to him, a smile forming fast on my lips. I'm impressed. That was even hotter—the throwdown and the gesture.

Brady wolf whistles. "Damn, the boss man does not fuck around."

I clasp my fingers through Wilder's, like an adoring girlfriend. "No, he does not."

Round one goes to the best man and the maid of honor. Take that, Brady.

19

MY LITTLE SIDEKICK

Wilder

"I don't know why you think it was me," Mac says dryly —too dryly—after she spits out her toothpaste that night.

I lean against the bathroom door, arms crossed, shaking my head. I will get her to break. It'll just take a little more time. "I can't imagine."

As she sets her toothbrush in the holder, she shrugs nonchalantly. "I mean, do I look like the sneaky type?"

With her blonde hair in a braid, and her too-big eyes, she's the picture of innocence. "You? Not at all."

"Exactly," she says, then rinses her mouth with water and spits it out, setting the cup on the vanity like it's a gavel. "Case closed."

"Have you considered law?" I ask as she reaches for a towel and wipes her mouth.

"Actually, I have. Environmental law. I think I'd be a good attorney protecting the forest and polar bears." Her gaze drifts pointedly to her pajamas—they're covered with cartoon polar bears wearing Santa hats.

"I'd hire you," I say as we head down the hall to her room.

"I already have my first client, and I haven't even gone to law school yet."

"Let alone high school," I say as she turns into her room and flops down on the bed. Her desk is still a mess, but she helped with the party clean-up, so I table the request to tidy her desk till tomorrow. She grabs a book from the nightstand but doesn't thrust it at me. "So how *was* the party?"

She sounds too eager for a report.

I could tell her, but two can play at her game. "Good," I say evenly, giving nothing away since she gave nothing away when I asked if she'd hung the mistletoe.

"Just good?" Her little voice pitches up.

"Yes, just good."

She heaves a sigh. "Dad. How could it have been *just good*?"

I adopt an intensely curious expression. "Why would it have been more than just good? Any reason in particular?"

She rolls her eyes. "Dad!"

"Mac," I deadpan.

She drops her head into her hand, then mutters, "Fine. I hung the mistletoe." She lifts her face, scowling. "There. Are you happy?"

"Very much so."

"Now tell me. Was the party good? Did the mistletoe work?"

"Now you tell *me*. Why did you hang it?"

She pushes up on her elbows. "Because you're fake

dating," she says, so amusingly impatient that I nearly double over in laughter. "And you want it to be believable. Couples kiss under the mistletoe all the time. I know the drill. I've seen the movies. Now, did it work?"

Too well.

But I won't tell her that. I won't tell a soul that Fable's kiss is playing on an endless loop in my head and it will be for days. I won't utter a word that Fable's scent—strawberries and champagne—is branded in my mind, and the soft, sweet taste of her lips is intoxicating me hours later. That if our first practice kiss in my office did a number on me, this one will be my downfall.

"It worked to help sell the romance," I say since that's true, and since my kid is damn good at being a sidekick.

"Good." Then she pats my arm. "I know you didn't want Bibi to set you up. So I want this to work for you." She pauses, brow knitting, cogs turning. "And I just want you to be happy."

"I am happy," I say, trying to figure out if there's more to her sidekicking than meets the eye.

"You're happy with work and me," she says, then curls her hands tighter around the covers, "but maybe the mistletoe made you happy too?"

Ah, hell. I can't let her get ideas. Even if her mistletoe was strategic, I can hear the little bit of hope in her young voice. Mac is eleven. She's sharp as a tack and more clever than a book. I could see her engineering a romance even out of a fake one.

But that's not in the cards. Love is for other people. It's for people who don't have trust issues a mile long. And I could never trust a fake romance. For a romance to truly work, it needs a solid foundation—not one built on a game of trickery. This is a fun, intoxicating, wildly addictive game, but a game, nonetheless. Hell, I couldn't even make a romance work with the mother of my child. And she's a kind, warm, thoughtful person. Clearly, I'm not cut out for big love. Best to remind my daughter of the score. "It's a fake romance, Mac. That's all," I say, letting her down gently.

"Okay." For a second, she looks sad, but she seems to dismiss the emotion quickly as she hands me the book. "Let's read."

I read to her for a long time. Finally, she yawns. Her eyes flutter closed as she murmurs, "So the party was more than good."

She sounds as satisfied as Penguin rubbing against my leg. I ruffle her hair and say yes, but she's already asleep.

I head for my home office and do some work, stealing glances at my phone. The third time I do it, it hits me why —I'm hoping Fable texts.

But I don't even know what I want her to say. *I can't stop thinking about the kiss?*

Well, yeah.

I sigh in frustration—with myself. Then I stare out the window over the city, festive lights twinkling in red and white on the houses in Cow Hollow, the Presidio, and the Marina, up to the ocean and the Golden Gate Bridge. A pang digs into my chest. Too bad it's not snowing. It hardly ever snows here. But if it did, I'd bring Fable to my office and we'd gaze at the view, the flakes falling, making the whole world hush. Then, I'd tug her against me and kiss her until her fingers roped through my hair and she begged for more.

And on that note...I shake off the fantasy.

Annoyed that I let my mind wander that far, I dive

back into this report. A few minutes later, my phone buzzes. Maybe it's her.

Take it slow, man. Don't be all over it.

But I don't listen. I grab the device, hope jumping inside me until I click on my texts.

Dad: That recital video is the best! Did you show it to your mom?

My shoulders sink. *Yes, of course I sent it to Mom.* I sent it to him, too, just to be a good son. But I'm not irritated with him this time. I'm irritated with myself for wishing the text was from Fable.

Wilder: I did. She enjoyed it. Glad you did too.

Dad: So much! At least I did one thing right—raised you.

But did he? He was hardly around. He was always off at the tables, gambling, trying to win the big one. He was wandering into casinos, casing out private poker parties, hunting for a score. Mom was the parent who was around every morning, every evening. She was there for my sister and me. And the three of us were left to pick up the pieces he left behind. Broken, dirty pieces.

Wilder: Thanks. Appreciate that.

I send the text even though I don't entirely mean it. But my mom raised me to be polite, so there's that. Then, I pick up the phone and call my sister, chatting with her about her kids, her holiday plans, and what we can do for Mom for Christmas when she arrives in Evergreen Falls. "It'll be a fight to the death to see whose team she plays on," I say.

"Because she's your secret weapon. She's as cutthroat as you are," Caroline says.

"Ouch."

"The truth hurts," she teases, but it's not a joke. I am cutthroat. Am I that way with romance too?

I dismiss that thought because it's good to have standards.

"I'll survive your arrows," I say dryly.

"Of course you will. Nothing gets to you."

What the hell? Is it pile-on-Wilder night? "Do you think I'm a robot?"

She laughs. "I think you're a badass," she says, then shifts topics. "And how's your girlfriend?"

"She's great," I say, maybe too easily.

"Good. Because if she's not, she'll have me to answer to. Also, I seriously can't believe you started dating someone right when I was going to introduce you to my friend Claudia. She runs a horse therapy farm, and she loves football." So much for *not* introducing me. She's teeing me up for the next match when this one ends.

And it will. But I don't want to think about that yet.

"Believe it," I say, and at least it's true enough through Christmas.

* * *

"And now, I am ready to be fabulous," Bibi calls from the kitchen the next morning, having replenished her coffee in her travel mug.

"You're always fabulous, Bibi," Mac says as she holds the door open. The three of us leave my home, taking off for Bibi's limo.

Once in the car, my aunt sips her morning fuel and adjusts her hat. Today's installment of the twenty-five hats of Christmas is a red baseball cap with a pom-pom on top. "So, how was the shower?" she asks casually.

"It was fine." I can't get all hearts and fluttery and tell her that it was wonderful and that spending time with Fable is too good, too fun, too fantastic. Sure, it would help keep up the ruse, but I don't want to give Mac any ideas, and I've got a full day ahead. I can't walk into the office like a cartoon version of me. I don't want to linger in memories of kisses that felt all too real.

This is why nothing can come of this dangerous attraction. I can't even trust our fake real kisses. My head hurts just trying to untangle if they're authentic or not.

"Did you have a nice time with Fable?" Bibi asks.

"I did," I say, again keeping my answers simple, remembering the rules Fable and I set last week—*People get busted when they try too hard to sell something.*

Bibi smiles. "Good. It's good to see you dating."

Yes! Even if she's not responsible for the pairing, Bibi seems pleased I'm paired. That's a relief. I've succeeded in avoiding her holiday romance machinations so far.

Shay's and Caroline's too. I just need to keep it up a little longer.

"I'm glad you're enjoying my love life," I say dryly as the car weaves through Monday morning traffic en route to Abernathy School.

Bibi takes another drink and crosses her legs. "I am. Especially since you'll bring her to the team party this week, right?"

I sit up straighter. Blink. Wait. "What? We're not having one this year. The staff voted to donate the money we'd spend on a party to charity."

"Wild child," she chides. "I know *that*. I don't mean the staff party. I mean the fancy team holiday party—the one for all our sponsors and corporate partners. It's Thursday night at your own hotel. Did you forget?"

I did.

I fucking did. Because I've spent the last week thinking of that kiss, and that wedding shower, and showing up for Fable and being the best damn fake boyfriend I could be so Brady would know he was a stupid jackass to do wrong by the best woman ever. So, yeah. Maybe I nearly forgot the party.

Okay, correction: I couldn't possibly forget the annual holiday party for the football team I own—the one where we make the sponsors happy by giving them a chance to fanboy with the players. But yes, I *absolutely* forgot that, *of course*, I should bring my girlfriend to that fete.

There's only one problem—I haven't asked her yet. Is she even free? My chest tightens, and I'm about to improvise when Mac tilts her head and smiles Bibi's way. "Dad didn't forget. He just mentioned it this morning," Mac says about as subtly as a kick under the table. "Right?" she prompts. "We talked about it at breakfast."

"We did."

"And weren't you mentioning it to Fable yesterday? She said something about needing a new dress. I hope she has time to shop." Mac smiles serenely. She is the greatest sidekick ever.

"Yes. I hope she does too," I say.

"I'll make sure the party organizer knows you have a plus one then," Bibi says.

After we drop off Mac, I send Fable a text.

Wilder: Desperately need your help. Can you come to my office in thirty minutes? Avoid Bibi at all costs.

20

DO YOU WANT A LITTLE SNOWMAN

Fable

Well, that's foreboding. It's also impossible because when I look up from the message on my phone, I come face-to-face with said avoid-ee coming toward me in the corridor. One very determined woman with stylish tortoiseshell glasses, wide-leg slacks, and lasers for eyes stops in front of me, and the hair on my neck stands on end with worry.

"Fable," she says in a warm voice that tells me she's also up to something. "Just the person I wanted to see."

"Oh?" I ask, clutching both my phone and a little gift I made for Wilder last night after the party. I wish I could surreptitiously text the world's fastest SOS to my fake boyfriend. ***Why, Wilder, why? Why must I avoid her?***

"Yes," says Bibi. "I understand you need something to wear."

It's an answer, but I don't know the question. Something to wear for work? For the wedding? For a meeting? "Definitely," I say, stalling.

Her shrewd eyes size me up and down as she holds her tablet like a clipboard. "What's your favorite style?"

For binge-watching Christmas flicks by the fire? For a cocktail party? A caroling contest? Given that the Christmas competition at Evergreen Falls starts this weekend, she could be asking about any of those. But I might blow our cover if I'm clueless about something I should know.

"Oh, you know, something simple."

She narrows her eyes. "A little more info would be nice. Don't you think?"

No, Bibi. I don't think it would be nice. I have no idea what you're talking about. "Simple and stylish," I say with a smile that masks my confusion.

She taps her chin. "Red? Black? Green? Fur-lined?"

"Not fur," I say, aghast. "Does anyone wear fur? Never fur."

She stares at me like I've lost it. "*Fake fur,* Fable. *Fake fur.* Do I look like a murderer?"

"No. Of course not," I say, chastened. "Definitely not a murderer."

"So, fake fur then," she says. I still have no clue if she's asking about a fun new coat or a saucy Mrs. Claus dress. "Now, what about shoes?"

"Something fun but comfy. You know," I say breezily. But inside, I'm stewing about how Wilder might need some lessons on timely texting. Like, oh, say, providing relevant info before his aunt ambushes me.

"Well, isn't that always the goal?" Bibi pauses to look at her phone, I suspect to check her calendar. "Are you free tonight, then?"

I can't pretend I know what she's talking about anymore. "For what exactly?"

She flashes a soft smile. "For an appointment with my stylist of course. Arbor will make sure you have a fantastic dress for the team party Thursday night. Mac brought it up this morning on the way to the office. She said you'd mentioned you'd need something to wear."

Ah, that's it! The team party! And I must be going with my Christmas boyfriend. And his clever daughter covered for me this morning. Damn, that's impressive espionage for an eleven-year-old. But Thursday night is my paint-and-sip class with Josie, Everly, and Maeve. Josie finagled her way into that class with her double kidney sale. I'd hate for both of her kidneys to go to waste.

But telling Bibi I can't go to the event could topple this fake-dating plan like a flimsy house of cards.

Weighing my options, I decide I'll have to miss the class. "Of course. My bad. I had so much on my mind with the launch of the new merch I forgot it was coming up. And I definitely need a dress."

Well, I don't want to make a liar of Mac.

Bibi pats my arm sympathetically. "I'll send a car for you tonight. I'll make sure Arbor has a nice glass of Veuve Clicquot waiting. You deserve to relax as he styles you for such a big party."

Tension slams into me at those words—*big party*. It's one thing to pretend to be a billionaire's girlfriend at a bridal shower amongst a few dozen friends (and one terrible ex). But in three nights' time we'll be among million-dollar athletes and the glitterati of the city. That's who goes to the team holiday party—chairpersons of Fortune 500 companies who sponsor the team. Heads of charities that partner with them. Players and partners of players.

I don't know what to say. Except—"Thank you."

It comes out awkwardly. I feel a little awkward.

"I'll be there too," she adds in a reassuring whisper, perhaps sensing my nerves. "Don't you worry one bit."

It's kind that she offers me support for a party, but it also makes me wonder—am I a little *My Fair Lady* in Wilder's glittery world?

* * *

The second Shay shuts the door to Wilder's office behind me, I wheel on my fake boyfriend. I'm a little irked that he left me hanging. "You need lessons in texting," I whisper-hiss, shaking the gift I'm holding for him.

"Why?" he asks with genuine confusion as he comes around his big desk, walking toward me, looking like a million dollars in dark slacks, a crisp burgundy button-down, and a tie that's almost silvery in color. "Do I need to use lingo like HMU?" He sounds horrified at the thought of shortened lingo for *hit me up* as he gestures for me to take a seat on the dove gray couch.

"No, you need to use words and sentences and give me info," I say, and I'm pretty sure I'm still sweating from that encounter with Bibi as I grip his gift, sending all the tension in me into the bag containing a crocheted ornament. "Your aunt ambushed me about the team party!"

As he sits on the navy-blue chair, I relate what went down in the hall with the fake fur and the stylist and Mac saying I needed a dress.

He alternates between chuckling and wincing, before asking with an amused lift in his brow, "She actually said that? *Do I look like a murderer?*"

"Yes! She did. And I still had no clue it was the team party," I say, plucking at my blouse.

I slump farther onto the couch, wishing I could curl up and nap. That was exhausting.

"I'm sorry I didn't tell you sooner," he says with genuine remorse. "It truly slipped my mind."

"And she's sending me to her stylist. He'll probably hate my hair and tell me to do ten million crunches."

Wilder scoffs. "You don't need to do ten million crunches."

I flap a hand toward his obviously flat stomach. "You probably do one crunch and get instant abs. Is that your secret?"

His lips twitch in a smile. "How do you know I have abs?"

"Because the universe is unfair." *Also because your shirts fit nice and tight, and it's unmistakable.*

He rises, moving from his chair to sit next to me on the couch—closer but not too close. He draws a breath then, when I'm meeting his gaze, says, "One, you're gorgeous as you are, and you don't need to change a thing. And two, the universe *is* unfair."

I sit up, ears pricking. He called me gorgeous. I feel like Rudolph when he learns Clarice likes him. "I am?"

I should shut up. Really, I should. But I've never been that good at shutting up when I'm savoring an unexpected compliment.

And that was a tasty one.

Wilder's green irises blaze with intensity. "You are, Fable," he says, his tone so serious, so intense that my foot would pop again if I were standing. Instead, a million hummingbirds flutter inside me. "Thank you." I pause, wondering if I should bring up the next point. Maybe I shouldn't, but I do it anyway. "Am I your *My Fair Lady*?"

"Fable," he says, gentle but firm too. "Why would you say that?"

I frown, then look around his office, pointing to the window overlooking the stadium that he owns. "We don't live in the same world. Your aunt has a stylist named Arbor who serves Veuve Clicquot. She's sending a fancy car. And I made you a thank-you ornament from yarn," I blurt out, and his eyes widen at the last point, but I keep going. "And I spilled Christmas glitter dicks on you, and I live in a tiny apartment and—"

I swallow the words *I'm sweating*. I don't need him to know that whole encounter threw me off. But it threw me off because I don't want us to fail. I like this ruse with him. It started as a necessity, but it's also become fun.

Because of the kisses. Because you liked the kisses. Because you can't stop thinking about your boss's lips on you.

Oh my god, the voice in my head needs to shut up. I try my best to silence it as Wilder reaches for me and takes my hand, clasping it.

His touch is both reassuring and a turn-on. "You're not *My Fair Lady*. You're not a project. Bibi just likes...to do those things. To treat people to the good life, I suppose."

"It's not because she thinks I'm wrong for you? I mean, she was going to set you up with the executive director of the museum, not the director of team merch."

He smiles, confident and magnetic, and doesn't let go of my hand. "I like the team. And I like the merch."

There's an undercurrent to those words, but I don't dare let myself read into it. Instead, I breathe out calmly. My pulse settles. I'm being silly. I smile apologetically and squeeze back, maybe so he won't stop holding my hand. "Sorry. I just want to do the right thing. I don't want to mess this up for you."

His eyes pin me with intensity. "That would be impossible. For you to mess it up."

I furrow my brow. "Why do you say that?"

He doesn't answer. He tips his forehead toward my other hand. "Don't think I didn't notice the gift confession." A sly smile teases his lips. "You made me an ornament?"

I roll my eyes. "It's nothing," I say.

He drops my hand and raises a finger. "It's not nothing."

"You haven't even seen it yet."

"It's from you. It's not nothing."

The command in his voice sends a shiver down my chest, right to my core. I raise my hand, the one that's been clutching a tiny white paper bag with the gift inside. "Mac showed me the ornaments she made yesterday. And I wanted you to have one from me. It's just a thank you," I say.

His smile is no longer sly. It's like he's mesmerized. "You made this?" he asks, opening the bag. "For me?"

"Well, I made you the wreath for your office door too," I say, downplaying it, but I don't know why.

"And I love the wreath. But this is for my home," he says as he reaches into the bag eagerly. His reaction makes my heart stutter. He pulls out a crocheted snowman with a little ribbon hanger on it. "I love it."

"Because you like snow," I explain, but my breath is feathery. My chest is warm.

"I was thinking of snow last night," he says, his eyes darkening as his gaze returns to mine.

"You were?"

"Yes. You said you liked winter at the restaurant. At Dahlia's. But do you like snow?"

My pulse spikes. He was thinking of me when he was alone at his home. "I do like it."

He grips the ornament, his nostrils huffing. "Good to know." He pauses, his eyes never leaving my face. My stomach flips. I don't want him to look away. "I'll hang this tonight."

"Will you think of snow?" I ask, breathy. But what I'm really saying is *will you think of me again?*

The corner of his mouth twitches. "I will."

I want to lean into him, to catch his mouth with mine, to thread a hand through his hair and demand he kiss me hard on this couch, in his chair, on the...

A wicked thrill rushes through me, and I'm suddenly fixated on his desk.

He parts his lips like he's going to say something. Something like *get on my desk right now and spread your legs.*

I blink off that lusty thought.

He must erase whatever's on his mind, too, since he returns to our earlier topic. "Do you want me to cancel the stylist my aunt arranged? I can send you a dress instead."

My breath catches. This man loves to give gifts. The socks, the ice cream, the football suite, the shopping spree, and now a dress. "Do you like shopping, Wilder?"

He's quiet for a moment, like he's weighing what to say. "For you, I do."

That's not making me want him less. "So you'd shop for a dress for me?"

"If you wanted me to, yes."

I'm tempted to say yes to the dress. But I also kind of want to go to the stylist too. Maybe I do have a little *My Fair Lady* in me. "Would it make me greedy if I said both?"

He laughs, seeming a little delighted. "Considering I

sent you into the lion's den unprepared, you should have both." He thinks for a minute. "I'll send a dress to your office today. Why don't you pick shoes with the stylist?"

"You're too generous. You don't have to. I swear."

His smile is pleased, in control, a man who's getting what he wants. "I know. I want to." He pauses, then adds, "But you should pick your own necklace. One of your pieces. I like seeing the ones you make on your neck."

That sends a charge down my spine. The idea that he likes my creations on my throat makes me feel a little shimmery all over. "I will," I say.

"Good. I look forward to it," he says, holding my gaze like he's already picturing something pretty adorning my skin.

I let out a long breath. "Thank you. For reassuring me. I'm sorry I came in a little hot earlier."

"I like it when you come in hot," he says. The sound reminds me of how we talked yesterday after the kiss. It reminds me, too, of how he's been looking at me in the last few minutes. And it definitely reminds me of these unexpected fantasies of mine.

"Wilder?"

"Yes?"

I shake my head. "It's nothing." I'm not certain what I was going to say, even though I'm sure my tone was breathy, feathery even.

He grabs my hand again, linking his fingers through mine. I gasp from the touch, the desperation in it. "Are you sure it's nothing?"

"Yes," I say, but I don't sound convincing.

He doesn't let it go. "Is this about the kiss yesterday?"

And the way I'm thinking of you now too. "Maybe. Okay. Yes," I admit.

"What about it?" he asks, seeming impatient.

"Was it believable?"

"Yes," he says, wasting no time. "It was believable to me."

There goes my stomach once more, cartwheeling this time. "Me too."

He's quiet again for a beat, then says, "We'll probably have to be affectionate again at the party on Thursday."

I wish it were Thursday now.

This fluttering in my chest isn't going away. This pull in my belly isn't disappearing. And this ache between my thighs is only intensifying. Feeling bold, I throw caution out the window. "Should we...practice again?"

The answer flies out of his mouth. "Yes."

In no time, he's up and striding across the plush carpet to the door and flicking the lock closed. I stand, my pulse skyrocketing. Then, because I can't stop thinking of his desk, I move toward it, and he's right behind me. When I reach it, he crowds me, his arm stretching along my side to grab the phone on the smooth wooden surface.

Why is he grabbing his phone? "Do you have a call—"

But the question dies when he hits play on Spotify. The sultry sounds of the Tinashe Christmas cover float past my ears as his actions register fully. He's turned on a song to drown out the sounds of our kissing practice.

With my heart speeding wildly, I spin around, and Wilder's looming over me. "Just in case," he says, answering my unfinished question.

"In case...I'm loud?"

His jaw ticks. He presses his lips together. Squeezes his eyes shut like he's at war with himself, then he opens them. "Yes. But I need to know for sure. Are you okay with this?" He gestures from him to me, then all around us.

Yes, I'm keenly aware of the situation. He owns the company I work for, and direct report or not, this fake romance could be messy. But he disclosed this romance from day one. HR knows, and if we were to break up, he's the kind of normal human who wouldn't fire me for a made-up sin. For all intents and purposes, we're having a relationship. Besides, this job isn't my end game. I've got a side hustle, one I want to make into my future.

Right now, though, I'm only thinking about the present.

I grab the collar of his burgundy shirt. "Shut up and practice kissing me."

21

ONCE UPON A DESK

Fable

As the music pulses, he drops the snowman ornament onto the desk, then covers my mouth with his with zero hesitation. This isn't a three-second practice run. This is not a mistletoe moment. This is a stolen office kiss. I clutch the fabric of his expensive shirt, clinging for dear life as his lips crush mine. I back up against the edge of the wood, my ass barely above the lights I strung last week.

It's a hard, deep kiss from my billionaire boss. I grip his shirt harder, tugging him closer. My blood rushes to the beat of the sultry song.

It's a full-body kiss, and I can't get close enough to him. I yank him nearer, and he grunts—a carnal noise against my mouth. A low, dirty groan. His right hand grasps one hip, then his left hand comes down on the other. He's bending over me, my back bowing on his desk.

Wicked images flash before my eyes.

Me scooting up on the mahogany then lying back, tugging him on top of me.

Him hiking up my leg.

Him grinding against me.

"Oh god," I gasp into his mouth.

I didn't plan to say that out loud.

He breaks the kiss, eyes wild, mouth lush, and—I steal a furtive glance down—cock hard. It's tenting his tailored suit pants. Wilder Blaine is outrageously aroused by me.

This is like waking up to learn I now speak French. I have a whole new way of understanding the world—a world I want to take a delicious bite of. I wind my fingers tighter around the collar. "I'm ruining your shirt."

I say it with zero guilt.

"Don't care," he mutters with even less concern then scoops me up, lifting me onto the desk, making sure I don't knock the lights around it as he sets my ass on the wood.

I tremble, then glance around the office. It's huge, with windows overlooking the field. With a massive desk for the owner. With me on that desk. Have I had boss fantasies before? I don't think so but right now, all I want is to be taken in the morning by this powerful man.

I lean back farther, making my intentions clear. The Christmas music is my wingwoman, the song turning sexier.

"Fable," he says as a warning.

"Yes, Wilder?"

His eyes squeeze shut. There's that battle again. But only I can assuage it.

"Practice," I urge. "Practice with me."

He opens his eyes and shakes his head, but it's not a no. It's resignation to this lust. "You," he mutters.

That's all. Just *you*.

In one fell swoop, he pushes a folder of papers off to the side. My skin tingles from the thrill of watching them fly.

He roams a hand along the outside of my thigh. I've never been more grateful to be wearing a skirt. His strong palm travels down my leg, and I whimper. I actually whimper. It just feels so good. His touch is nothing like the caresses I've received from other men I've dated. Wilder is strong, determined, and focused completely on me. When he reaches the hem of my skirt, he plays with it then murmurs, "What am I going to do with you?"

Touch me.

But I'm afraid to say that out loud. Afraid to voice how potent this lust has become. I'm not sure I need to speak though. I use my body instead, letting go of his shirt collar and grabbing his tie. Then I find words.

"Kiss me again," I say as I tug his mouth back to mine. His stubble whisks across my face, and I'm sure I'll have whisker burn when I leave.

He kisses me deeply but with tenderness too. With a sigh. And a groan. With one hand on my skirt. His mouth coasts down my jaw, then to my throat, and he's kissing the hollow of it. Has anyone ever kissed me there, like this? Like I'm precious and sexy all at once? No. No one has. I feel like I will die from desire. I'm clutching his tie, and he's kissing my throat, and his hand...

I gasp.

His hand is inching up and under my skirt.

Yes, yes, yes.

The word beats in my veins. It thrums in my body. I need this so badly. And I don't want to take a chance he might stop. So I let go of the tie, reach for his wandering hand, then guide him up higher and higher still. A clear *all systems go.*

"Fuck," he mutters in a strangled gasp.

I meet his gaze. "Fuck yes," I say, desperately.

He smiles, like he can't believe his luck.

Then, his smile burns off as I let go of his hand, and he takes over. He slides his fingers up the inside of my thigh, closer, closer, so close.

I arch my back, curling my hand around his neck, my breath coming fast. He hasn't even touched my wet panties yet, and I'm aching for him. He inches higher, teasing with those talented fingers that skim across my flesh. Then, with his whole hand, he cups me where I absolutely ache for him. My mouth falls open. "Ohhh," I moan.

I feel him smile wickedly against my face. "So fucking perfect," he praises. "I want to make you feel so fucking good."

"News flash: you kind of already are," I gasp, lifting my hips, seeking more.

"I know," he says, and that's borderline cocky, yet it makes me wetter. "What I mean is...I desperately need to make you come. Right here. On my desk. Right now. Can I?"

My mouth falls open. My breath staggers out. I blink. "Is that even a question?"

Another wicked smile. Then a taunt. "I don't know, Fable. Is it a question?"

"Yes. The answer is yes. Whatever you're asking. Yes."

He drops his mouth to my throat again, then skims his fingers under the damp panel of my panties. He pushes it aside then glides his fingers along my wet pussy.

I shudder in pleasure.

He groans like an animal.

This is a line. And we're not just crossing it. We're obliterating it on a Monday morning on his desk as his fingers trace a dizzying circle against my clit, then move down my center, where I'm soaked for him.

While bent over me, he strokes my slick heat, then drops his mouth to mine. He kisses me ferociously as he plays with me, rubbing faster, following my cues, swallowing my needy sighs as the music covers up for us too. Pleasure winds tighter in me, curling in my belly as he plays with my clit, then pinches it. I gasp into his mouth. Loud, maybe too loud. He breaks the kiss. "Quiet, little elf, while I make you come."

I nod, eager to try, eager to please.

I watch his face. I don't know who's enjoying this more —him or me. His eyes are dark, etched with wicked determination as he brushes dizzying circles along my clit expertly, confidently. This is a man who isn't worried whether I'll come. This is a man who intends to give me a screaming orgasm.

The realization tips me over. I shudder everywhere. My thighs clench.

"Wilder," I whisper a warning.

"Shh," he says, then covers my mouth once more, kissing me as he hits me just so, just right, just perfectly till I tremble and shake as an orgasm slams mercilessly into me. I'm moaning, murmuring, panting his name, but he's shutting up every noise with passionate, hot, deep kisses as he coaxes the orgasm out of me. But he doesn't stop. Instead, as I'm still coming down from that high, he slides two fingers inside me.

My breath halts. "Are you...?"

"Do you want me to stop?" He eases out his fingers.

I grab his wrist, halting him, shaking my head. "Don't say such a terrible thing."

A grin takes over his handsome face, and he thrusts back into me, then fucks me harder with his fingers, deeper, urging me with his body to keep going.

I've never had multiple orgasms before.

My head falls back. I hold on to him for dear life as he crooks his fingers inside me.

My head is hazy. My body hot. My heartbeat chaotic. And soon, as he fucks me harder, my brain goes offline till I'm frantic with the need to come. "Yes," I moan, and then an orgasm crashes into me, and he sends me over the edge again.

I collapse onto his desk, but he catches me, looping an arm around my back as he gently eases out his fingers. With me spread out on his desk, he presses the gentlest kiss to my lips, then straightens his spine, adjusts his tie, and brings his fingers to his lips.

My eyes pop wide, and I push up on my elbows and watch him lick the taste of me off his fingers. His eyes are fiery. His hair is sticking up in all directions. His lips look bruised. He's a man who's just fucked a woman well. And he licks every last drop of me, sighing contentedly as he finishes. "So fucking delicious."

And the world remakes itself yet again with a fresh new realization—my boss wants to eat me.

"Excuse me," he says, then strides across the room to a

door. Must be the executive washroom. He heads in, closes the door, then turns on the faucet.

I push up, looking down at the mess of my clothes. My skirt is twisted. My panties are useless. My hair is probably a nest.

I hop off the desk, adjust my underwear, then smooth down my skirt. When he emerges, he holds the door open for me. I keep my head down as I walk toward him.

I don't know how to look my boss-fake-boyfriend in the eye after he's made me come twice in his office. But when I reach the door, he grabs my wrist and jerks me against him, my breasts to his chest. His eyes locked on mine.

"Don't hide your face. You were gorgeous when you walked into my office, and you were stunning when you came," he says, and he's without guile, without agenda.

The compliment sounds beautiful on his lips but it's terrifying too. I don't know where we go from here. To bed? To my knees? To the couch? "What happens next?"

He swallows roughly. Winces, then says, "We go to the party and we should be even more..." He pauses, like the words strangle him. "Believable now."

The subtext is clear—we can't do *that* again.

"Right. That was just..." My gaze drifts to the desk.

He studies me for a beat, reading me perhaps. "A one-time thing?" he asks, like he's testing that concept.

For my sake? Probably. Yes, he's probably making sure of the rules of the road. Like he did last week. He's wanting to make sure this tryst changes nothing between us.

I don't want him to think I expect sex and a fake boyfriend. I mean, that would be an amazing gift waiting for me under the tree, but I'm not sure Santa thinks I've been good enough to deserve that.

"A momentary lapse of reason?" I continue, giving him an out.

It's like a dance of denial, one we both seem to need to play for some reason.

"Yes. Just a practice...a very thorough practice," he adds.

"And now we're done with practicing. We got that practice out of our systems."

He says nothing for a few seconds. His handsome face is unreadable. Then he nods. "We did." A pause. "It doesn't have to happen again."

The words are almost open-ended, like maybe he'd be okay if it did. But I don't want to read anything into this situation. It's already veered in directions I never saw coming.

"You're right. It doesn't." I head into the bathroom and straighten up, and when I exit, Wilder's at his desk, organizing the papers. His hair is smoothed down, his tie is neat. The evidence has been erased.

When he sees me, he comes around to the desk and picks up the snowman. "Thank you again," he says, like I'm an employee who gave him a Christmas gift.

Well, I did.

"You're welcome," I say, then head to the door.

"Fable," he calls out.

I turn back, and he's closing the distance between us. "The party. Are you able to go?"

Oh, right. The reason I'm here in his office in the first place. Except, I frown, remembering the class I was going to take with Josie, Everly, and Maeve. "Yes, but I have to cancel a class with my friends."

"That's the only way you can attend?" he asks with concern.

"It is," I say, telling him about the paint-and-sip class and the coveted spot with the instructor. But I wave it off. "It's fine. My friends will understand. The party's important, and I roped you into this whole fake-dating thing anyway."

His brow furrows. "One, you didn't rope me into anything. I went willingly. Two, I don't want you to miss the class. Especially since one of your friends worked hard to get you all in."

But it's not like he can move the lesson, so I simply smile and exonerate him. "We'll take it another time."

Later that day, a courier brings a box to my office. It's silver and wrapped in a bright red bow. My heart skitters as I open it and peek inside. Gasping, I gingerly touch the soft material of the satin-y red dress with the swingy skirt that I suspect hits right at the knees.

It's so Christmas cocktail-y, it's perfect. I'm not even sure what I like better—the double orgasms or the dress. I decide I like both.

That evening, as I'm drinking champagne and trying on the dress at the stylist's, I peer in the scalloped full-length mirror, amazed it fits perfectly.

"Someone knows your size," Arbor coos, standing behind me.

I never told Wilder my size, and yet he knew exactly what to get me. Just like he knew how to play my body.

"He's good at shopping," I say, since I can't get caught up in this gift-giving. It's part of the fake romance. It's the magic of make-believe—that's all. It's Wilder fake boyfriending like no man has fake boyfriended before.

Arbor chuckles, rolling his playful brown eyes. "Hun, if a man sent me something in my size, it wouldn't mean he had a knack for shopping. It'd mean he had a knack for *me*. And your boyfriend has a very big knack for you."

I fight off the flutters. There's no point in denying Arbor's assessment. A boyfriend is supposed to have a thing for his girlfriend. It's fake though. That's all. Today's tryst in his office was simply a momentary lapse of reason into lust.

And we got that lust out of our systems. That's all. "We'll see," I say evasively, fighting off a smile.

"Oh, yes, hun. We absolutely shall see." After Arbor selects a pair of sparkly, silver shoes, he blows me an air kiss. "Can't wait to be right."

I try once again to stop grinning as he sends me on my way.

I take out my phone to text Josie, Everly, and Maeve to tell them the bad news about the class. But there's a new text from Wilder on my phone that stops me in my tracks.

Wilder: Rana is free tomorrow night. She'll be doing a private class for you and your friends if they're available since you can't make the one on Thursday. I hope you, Maeve, Everly, and Josie enjoy it. It's a gift. And a thank you for being my date for the party.

I'm fizzy all over, and I don't think it's from the champagne or the orgasms.

No, when he sends the next note, it's clear that it's definitely not from either of those.

Wilder: Also, I made a dinner reservation for the four of you at Gabriel's, a restaurant next to the class, and arranged for a penthouse suite at The Resort if you want to make it into a full-on girls' night out.

I squeal. I fucking squeal. The man has been offering to comp me a room at his five-star hotel for more than a year. He didn't wait for me to take him up on his offer. He just did it. And I just love the way he takes control sometimes.

Like a boss.

Fable: Have I told you I owe you the biggest thank you in the world?

Wilder: You owe me nothing. It's my pleasure to treat you the way you deserve. Whether that means in private suites, on shopping sprees, or...desks.

A hot wave of desire crashes over me.

Fable: I really like desks.

Wilder: Me too.

But still, I have an idea for how to thank him. That night when I'm home I get to work on it, breaking out all my tools.

* * *

The next night as Josie, Everly, Maeve, and I arrive at a studio near Japantown, where the paint-and-sip classes are held, my friends can't stop giving me *the look*.

"Stop," I mutter to them as we reach the door.

"Stop what?" Josie asks, faux innocent.

"Stop grinning like that."

"Like what?" Maeve chimes in.

"Like you all think you know something," I whisper.

Maeve's smile ripens. "Oh, I know *nothing*. Just that your fake date arranged not only a last-minute private paint-and-sip class with a very coveted teacher so you wouldn't miss it, but also dinner for the four of us at a fabulous new restaurant that's practically impossible to get into."

"And he's comping us a penthouse suite in his hotel," Everly adds, making the point too.

"It's nice. That's all. He's nice," I insist.

Josie snorts. "That's not nice, Fable. That's above and beyond."

So is giving me two orgasms on his desk. I roll my eyes,

mostly so it masks the way my stomach flips once again. "Hush. Let's go paint and sip."

We do and it's the best class I've ever taken.

Dinner at Gabriel's is the most mouthwatering meal I've ever eaten.

And the penthouse suite is the most decadent place I've ever stayed. I let myself enjoy every second of this night, especially since I know they're ending when the year ends.

Like we planned.

22

THE DATING HANDBOOK, PLEASE

Fable

Is there a handbook somewhere for fake dating? If so, I could use it right now as I slide on red-and-white-striped tights under my little green elf dress on Thursday afternoon. I'm in the ladies' room on my floor, getting ready to hand out the corporate Christmas gifts with Wilder.

It's the first time I'll have seen him since I learned exactly how good he is with his hands. A blast of heat rushes through me. I could barely get that first office kiss out of my head, not to mention the mistletoe kiss, and now the session on his desk has claimed a permanent spot in my brain.

But I've got a job to do before the Blaine Enterprises holiday break begins tomorrow. I cinch the black belt at my waist, smooth a hand over the flouncy green skirt, then adjust my elf hat. No elf ears for me though. A woman has her limits.

I fluff out my red strands of hair, slick on some lipstick, then take a deep, fueling breath. I'm ready to elf it.

I head to Wilder's office, where Shay is thrusting his arm in the air in a rocker salute behind his desk. "We won!"

I tilt my head, a tad concerned. "The door-decorating contest?" It seems kind of unfair for the CEO to win, even though Santa's butt is so cute.

"Yes, Lucia and I! We decorated the door in ops with cat drawings for a Meowy Christmas," he says, then shows me a picture.

Oh, that *we*—Shay and his wife, not Shay and the boss.

"And you deserve it," I say.

"We get three free nights at The Resort hotel in the honeymoon suite."

"Can confirm that hotel is amazing. And I hope you have a great cat-mas," I say, and I'm about to knock on Wilder's half-open door when I stop. *Just because his fingers were inside you doesn't mean you can walk in like you own the place. Check with his assistant.*

"Is Wilder here? We're doing the stockings," I explain, and oh…is my voice squeaking with nerves? Yes, yes, it is.

"I am," Wilder says in that rich, brandy voice, emerging from his suite in a charcoal black suit, with a cheap drugstore Santa hat atop his thick hair.

I huff. "Wilder, are you Scrooge?"

"How am I Scrooge?"

I flap a hand his way. "You're wearing a regular suit and a hat, and we're handing out gifts."

Shay rolls his eyes. "Total Scrooge."

Wilder lifts a challenging brow to me, then Shay.

"Does Scrooge deliver stockings full of gifts for every employee?"

I park my hands on my hips. "No, but Scrooge also does not have an elf. This elf works for Santa."

"Ah, but you look good in an elf costume," he says, and his gaze lingers on me for a good long time. So long that chills erupt along my skin.

"You two want me to just leave right now?" Shay jokes.

He doesn't know the half of it. But even so, I return to making my case. "Wilder, you're supposed to be Santa. You need the whole regalia—the beard, the red suit, the boots, and everything."

"No," he says.

"No?"

"No." It's a line in the sand.

Shay coughs under his breath, muttering, "Lovers' spat." Then he points to Wilder's office. "Go fight in there, kids."

"We're not fighting," Wilder says.

But we kind of are. So I grab his hand and drag him back into his office, shutting the door. "I thought you were going to dress up as Santa for us to deliver the stockings?"

He gives me a look like *that'll never happen*. "Do I need to remind you?"

What is he talking about? "Remind me of what?"

"What my Christmas girlfriend once said," he prompts then says, "I quote, *Santa's not hot. Of course you aren't going as Santa*."

Ohhhhh. That's what I said about the Christmas movie costume party. "That does ring a bell."

"You also said Santa as a nickname gave you the ick."

I gasp, all over the top. "What is wrong with me? Am I a Santa hater?"

He smiles smugly. "Maybe you are."

"No! I can't be."

He gives me an *I told you so* look. "Be that as it may, I'm wearing a suit instead."

It takes me a moment to fully register what he's saying. "Because I said Santa's not hot?"

He nods. "Yes. And because you also said *You're my boyfriend. You'll look hot*."

"And you want to look hot...for me?"

"Yes." His eyes pin me with a heated stare, like he did the other day on his desk. He looks like he wants to bend me over it. A spark slides down my spine at that wild thought. Then he nods to the door. "Now let's go deliver the presents, little elf. I have a busy day, and we have a busy night."

He leaves first, leaving me with the admission—he wants to look good for me. Because I'm his holidate? Or just because?

No idea, but I really could use that handbook.

Especially since he's all business as we deliver the gifts, stopping by Shay's desk first of course.

"I'm going to use the bonus on more hideous sweaters for next year," he declares.

"Excellent plan."

Then we stop by the marketing department, where T-shirts are admired, and chocolate is popped open, and bonuses make for sparkly eyes. We visit Sandra's office, where my direct supervisor *ooh*s and *aah*s over the gifts. "I knew you were working on this but it's even better than I imagined," she says of the shirt. "Can't wait to advertise it and sell it."

"A marketer after my own heart," Wilder says.

As we make the rounds in human resources, I keep

thinking of the picture we present—him in his sharp suit and Santa hat, me in the elf dress. Like we match. Like the couple they think we are. But do fake boyfriends want to look hot for their Christmas girlfriends? Do they want to bend them over desks? Do fake girlfriends want their pretend lover's fingers fucking them in the office?

My face flushes at the memory and I try to push it away, but the questions chase me as we visit the operations department.

I finally push them aside when we pop by Bibi's office. She's wearing a red-plaid Santa hat today, and she eagerly takes the stocking. "I wonder what could be in here," she says, like she means it.

"As if you don't know," Wilder teases.

"Hush. Let me have my fun," she chides him, then retrieves each item in the stocking one by one, delighting in all of them. "Well, this is a surprise. Thank you, Santa and his elf."

"You're welcome," I say.

"Enjoy," Wilder says.

"See you tonight at the team party," Bibi calls out.

When we're heading down the hall again, Wilder looks my way, then scans the hall, perhaps making sure it's just us as he lowers his voice. "How was your class? The paint-and-sip." He's no longer using his boss-in-the-office tone. He's thoughtful, interested, and entirely boyfriend-y.

I smile, thinking both of the class and how he made it happen so I could attend the party tonight. "It was amazing. Rana is so talented, and my friends had a blast," I say. *And Maeve and all my friends think you have a crush on me, and I'm beginning to wonder if maybe, possibly they're a little bit right?* I shake that out of my head. "And the dinner was incredible. And so was the suite."

His smile is of the closed-mouth variety, but pleased too. "Good. That's very good."

Something flickers in his eyes, almost...like a gleam. Like Tuesday night was all part of some grand plan. But that's a wild thought too. "I really appreciate it," I say, placing a hand on his arm and stopping him. "I mean it," I add, genuinely. "You said you wanted to show Brady how a man should treat a woman, but really you're showing me."

That smile of his? It gets a little bigger. That gleam in his irises? It sparks a little more. "Like I said, it's my pleasure."

I arch a skeptical brow. "Really? Is it?"

His smile burns off, and he stares at me with red-hot lust. "Yes. Really. Treating you is an absolute gift."

My breath catches once again. And I feel...like champagne. Everything is heady and lovely right now. "Thank you," I say, briefly wondering if he got my thank-you gift that I sent to his home with two-day delivery. Wondering, too, if it'll ever be enough. "I wish I could properly thank you."

He gives an easy smile. "You gave me a wreath. That was wonderful."

"A wreath?" I ask with a laugh.

"It was homemade," he says. "And the crocheted snowman too."

"Well, then, wait till you see what I can do with glitter and T-shirts," I tease.

He drops a kiss to my cheek, then pushes my hair off my ear to whisper, "I can't wait."

Chills erupt over my skin, and I want to tug him into a

closet, an empty cubicle, anywhere. But we're at work, and even if we're publicly dating, I can't publicly climb him in the hallway.

Shame.

I wrench away, saying, "I'd better behave in the office."

A smile shifts his lips. "Yes, or Santa will put you on the naughty list."

"Pretty sure I could find my own way there."

His eyes darken, and he grits out, "I have no doubt."

Then he gives a nod, like he's resetting. Me too. We continue on our way.

After we finish delivering the stockings full of special-edition T-shirts, Elodie's chocolate, and big holiday bonuses to every employee, he checks his watch and says, "I'll see you tonight. I'm sending a car for you at six."

"Not you yourself?" I try to quell the flicker of disappointment in my chest. It's fake—he doesn't need to knock on my door.

"I have to drop Mac at her mom's place on the way." His eyes darken as he steps a little closer to me outside his office. "But I can't wait to meet you there."

Same. It's the same for me. But I don't dare say that out loud. It's too scary a thought.

That evening, the grand ballroom at The Resort is bathed in a soft glow from the twinkling blue-and-white lights that adorn every corner. A towering Christmas tree stands proudly in the center, its branches heavy with red glittering ornaments and shimmering silver tinsel. Laughter and festive tunes about sleigh bells ringing bounce off the walls, mingling with the clinking of glasses and the rustling of guests—women in eye-popping dresses and big athletes in sharp suits.

High tables are draped in red linen, boasting centerpieces bursting with fresh poinsettias.

As I stand in the entryway, flanked by open French doors, hunting for my date, nerves flutter through me. Sure, I know all the football players since I work for the team, but they aren't *my* friends. I can't glom onto them at the party.

Well, except for Carter, since he's married to Rachel. Maybe I can find them. Latch onto my friend and never let go. It'll be better if I hang with Rachel anyway. Surely, Wilder will be busy the whole party. He'll need to shake hands, smile, and say hi to all the guests. Everyone will want a moment with the owner. I'm simply here to keep up the dating ruse. I channel my best, bold, sassy self as I smooth a hand down the fabric of my dress. *You've got this.*

And as I'm entering the party, chin up, I nearly walk into Sandra, the head of marketing and the woman I report directly to. "Hey," she says, furrowing her brow. "I didn't realize you'd—"

But she must cut herself off before she adds *be here*. Of course she's not used to seeing me at functions like this. I'm not usually senior enough to be invited to the fancy team party. I'm only here because I'm the owner's arm candy.

I smile and give a cheery "Happy holidays," since that's easier than talking about the elephant in the room—that I'm dating the guy (wink, wink) who signs everyone's paychecks. Including hers.

Ugh. I feel sick.

"But it's good to see you," she says, quickly recovering.

"You've been doing such great work this year. You deserve to be here."

Oh.

I didn't expect those kind words. "Thank you. I appreciate that."

"You really have. I never would have imagined merch would become so important, but you have your pulse on what people want."

I smile. No, I beam. "That means a lot to me."

"And you mean a lot to the team," she says, then sets a hand on my arm before she's called away by a group of well-dressed people as they walk through the door.

That was unexpected and a nice little ego boost. I turn around to hunt for my friends again when I hear a familiar voice.

"Wow."

As if I summoned her with my thoughts, Rachel appears by my side, dressed in a short, sexy, silver cocktail dress that hugs her curves and hips. She wears a necklace I made her—with a jumping reindeer on it. My necklace is from the same line, a shimmering snowflake on a pendant, made from old glass bottles.

"Wow to you too," I say, focusing on her since that's easier than taking the compliment. "You look amazing. Especially your bling."

"Thank you. But you really do, Fable," she says, apparently intent on laying the compliment on me. She reaches out her arm, gently touching the strap of my dress. "This is gorgeous."

"I guess I clean up okay," I joke.

But she's serious. Her amber eyes laser in on the red dress Wilder sent me. I love the way it feels. And looks. "Where did you get this?"

My cheeks pinken. Maybe from the lie I'm here to unspool, or maybe because it thrills me a little to say, "Wilder sent it to me."

Her jaw comes unhinged. "Girl!"

"He has good taste."

"Understatement. He picked it out and sent it to you. Like in the movies?"

Well, yeah. But I honestly think that's part of being the best fake daters there have ever been. It's easy to turn to fiction—TV, film, books—for examples of how to pull it off. Now that I think about it, that office tryst probably falls under the same heading—it's helping us pull off the act. There won't be any awkward moments now that his hands have been up my skirt. In fact, maybe *I* should write that handbook for fake dating. I'll include the recommendation for at least one consensual hands-on session to increase believability of affection. "Yes."

"So, this romance between you two is...?" She waits for me to explain more.

I gulp. What the hell do I say? I was wrong. I shouldn't *write* the handbook, I need to study it.

"It's early days and all." I feel terrible not telling the full truth. Rachel is a good friend and a mentor in a lot of ways. Her store was the first to carry my Treat Yourself line of necklaces.

"Looks like the early days have been good," she says, and guilt twists in me. Rachel lets out a low whistle of admiration. "That's a skill, Fable. Picking a dress like that."

"He's a smart guy," I say, trying not to read too much into it. Wilder's good at everything, plain and simple. He's amazing at gifting. This present isn't really about me anyway. Besides, I felt bad enough fibbing to my sister. I don't want to feel worse lying to my good friends too, like Elodie and Rachel.

"Anyway, how's the store been going for the last week? I know this is the busy time." I turn the focus on her. That's second nature to me, anyway. It's so much easier to focus on other people. Then I don't need to crack open my heart or my feelings. Pesky things.

Rachel catches me up to speed on her jewelry shop, which is busy, busy, busy for the holiday season, and that makes me very happy. I tell her more about how things are going as the team designer, how creative the students were at my jewelry-making class last night, and when I finish with the bling-y shirts for the new year, she says, "I always knew you'd do big things. And you're still working on opening your own shop someday?"

It feels so far off, but I suppose that's how dreams are. "Someday. I have no idea when. I've been working on new designs for it at night."

"I love that. You'd better let me carry some even when you compete with me," she says, and she's teasing. We both know that a rising tide can lift all ships.

Carter strides in next to her, wrapping an arm around Rachel but meeting my gaze. "Good to see you here, Fable."

That's a reminder that I'm not usually here. That I won't be here next year. Wilder and I will split up in late December or early January...and that's a sour thought. One I don't want to linger on. "You might be seeing a lot of me tonight. This is not my scene, so I plan on following the two of you around like a puppy. Cool? Cool."

Carter laughs. "Whatever you need."

Rachel smiles. "You can hang with us, but..." Her eyes

latch on something behind me, then she leans in, whispering, "Someone is coming for you."

Is the heat turned up in the room? I can't even make out the click of Wilder's wingtips amongst all these other expensive shoes and tailored suits, but from Rachel's words, I can feel his presence. He's coming closer, then goosebumps rise on my bare arms when he moves next to me.

"There you are, little elf," he says, meeting my gaze. He drops a kiss to my cheek. It feels too good, I have to work to regain my bearings.

"Hi," I say, and it comes out soft and maybe a little seductive. Was that intentional? Perhaps it was.

"Sorry I couldn't pick you up," he says, apologetic. "I wanted to though."

"I understand," I say. "Was Mac happy to see her mom?"

"Very much so. And Felicity was excited too. It was nice."

I love that he gets along with his ex. That they co-parent so well. I've never heard a bad word about Felicity from him, and it's refreshing.

Wilder turns to Carter and Rachel. "Good evening, Carter. Rachel, you look lovely. What do you two have planned for the holidays? Well, besides destroying the competition in the final games on the schedule."

"That's always at the top of my list, Mr. Blaine," Carter says, and we chat about football for a few minutes until they excuse themselves to mingle.

Wilder turns to me, and he's a little more relaxed than the Wilder of this afternoon when we delivered the gifts. He probably had a lot on his mind then, with him delivering the Christmas bonuses and shutting down the main office for the rest of the year. Now he seems like the man who kissed my cheek in the hallway and whispered that he *can't wait*. His green eyes are fiery as they travel up and down me. "I'd like to say I knew the dress would look this beautiful on you, but you have continued to stun me. The dress doesn't make the woman. The woman makes the dress," he says.

The thermostat shoots through the roof from the weight and heft of his compliment. It makes me feel heady, unlike any I've had before. "Thank you." It hardly feels like that's enough.

"But my favorite part?" he adds.

I'm giddy as I echo him eagerly with, "What's your favorite part?"

"Your necklace," he says, and a burst of pride swirls through me since I made it. I lift a hand to the snowflake, touching the smooth surface. "I picked it...for you."

He gives me a look that burns through me, sending sparks of flames licking higher in me. Casually, like this is a familiar gesture with us, he lifts his hand and runs his fingers across my pendant. He barely brushes my skin, and still, my knees go a little weak, my head a little fuzzy.

"So you understand the choice I made earlier today."

My mind snags, but then I connect the dots. He meant it when he said he wanted to look nice for me earlier, just like I wore a necklace for him tonight. "I do," I say, a little breathy, then it's my turn to compliment him, and it's easy because the man is the definition of sexy elegance in the tailored charcoal suit, white dress shirt, and...I gasp when he tugs up the sleeves of his jacket just far enough for me to see the Santa cufflinks. I reach for them on the cuffs of his crisp shirt, fingering the metal. "You got them. I didn't think you would wear them tonight."

"Of course I would," he says, like it was a fait accompli. "They're Made By Fable."

That's the name I engraved on the inside of the cufflinks that I made this week for him. I…glow. "Yes."

His lips quirk up in the most amused grin. "I saved the Santa for tonight."

"You really did," I say, still not quite believing he's wearing something I made to a team party.

"Like I said, I like your homemade gifts," he says.

The glow inside me burns even brighter. "Good. That's so good."

We say nothing for a beat—just hold each other's gazes. It's like everyone disappears. Everything feels heady, hazy, like we're the only ones in the whole ballroom.

But I have to remember—we're here for show.

For Bibi. For his sister, Caroline. For Shay. For all the people who want to match this man with someone when he doesn't want that. When he simply wants to be a businessman and a father.

I nod toward his aunt, chatting by the Christmas tree with a group of well-dressed people, then run a hand down his arm and whisper, "Let's make sure Bibi knows how very taken you are."

He showed up for me at the shower. It's my turn to show up for him.

"Stake your claim, Fable," he says, those lush lips crooking up in a slight grin.

We make our way through the crowd, and as Wilder says hi to players, advertisers, and business associates, he loops an arm tighter around me. Runs his fingers over my back. Brushes a strand of hair off my shoulder. I shiver with each touch while my mind burns with hot memories of the other day in his office. *Yes, that office kiss got all the tension out of my system.* And it made us so much more believable.

Finally when we get nearer to Bibi, Wilder looks almost drunk on me. I feel a little euphoric, too, from his touches. Even though they're for show, they feel so good.

When we reach her table, Wilder leans in and presses a kiss to my cheek, scratchy, warm, and all kinds of tingly. It sends sparks down my spine.

"You're so affectionate tonight," I say, loving each of his sweet nothings. He's really pulling out all the stops.

"You bring it out in me," he says, then meets his aunt's eyes. "Can I refill your drink?" There are servers for that, but she says yes anyway.

When he leaves for the bar, Bibi offers me a small smile. "He certainly seems quite taken."

It's the same thing Josie, Maeve, and Everly said but I'm not going to let it go to my head. Wilder's acting the part and, like in most things he does, he excels at it.

"The feeling is mutual," I say.

"Good," she says, and that's reassuring too—that we're pulling this off.

When Wilder returns, I slide up to him. If she thinks it's good that he's taken with me, I'll give her good. I'll give her the best. "Hi, sugar plum."

"Missed you, little elf," he says, using the nickname again, but this time with a little more...warmth, or maybe sexiness. Works for me.

Bibi tilts her head, watching us with those sharp gray eyes. We must look quite the couple. Arms wrapped around each other, hands on each other, dove eyes.

And...hell.

We're selling it too hard. We went over the top with the affection and the cutesy names.

He's staking his claim too much.

I'm doing the same. This is bad, and I didn't even realize I was careening down this rocky path.

I can only hope Bibi doesn't notice, but she locks eyes with him and says in a too-observant, too-inquisitive tone, "This is so interesting. I've never seen you like this before with a woman, wild child."

He straightens, not quite alarmed, but clearly a little concerned. "Like what?" For the first time, worry tremors his voice.

"So affectionate."

Uh-oh.

"Fable brings it out in me," he says, fast on his feet.

"I'll say," Bibi observes with a smile. But she studies us like she's trying to find the flaw in a reproduction of a painting. "It's fascinating. And so lovely to see."

But is it? Or is she onto us? I need that handbook now more than ever since I think we just violated a rule.

23

BIG EYES AND FUNNY BODIES

Wilder

That can't happen again.

A mistake like that will expose our game to my shrewd aunt. I can't risk Bibi's disappointment and that's reason enough to work on a new fake romance plan to ensure zero mistakes. The next morning, as I take an early phone call for a year-end meeting with the renewable energy division an idea hits me. A list for Fable and me to keep us on track during the Christmas week. And we can discuss it on the drive to Evergreen Falls later this morning.

* * *

An hour later, before I leave my home, I set out some kibble for Penguin in the kitchen and give her a scratch on the head. "The cat sitter will come by and bring you more food."

She rubs up against my leg, purring loudly. I take

some photos of her, like I usually do. Since she always likes seeing the cat, I send a couple to Mac who's in school today, then at her mom's till tomorrow morning. I pet the feline some more, Fable's words echoing in my mind. *Your cat is obsessed with you.*

Maybe I understand obsession a little these days.

But I'll do my damnedest to leave it behind in San Francisco. Bringing it with me to Evergreen Falls is entirely too risky—for my head and my heart. I head to the garage, calling Felicity on the way. We chat as I toss my suitcase in the trunk of my car—a matte black electric vehicle built from the ground up by a renowned pair of car builders in New York, Max Summers and his wife, Henley Rose.

As I close it, I answer Felicity's question about when Mac will join me. "I'll send Bibi's driver to pick up Mac and her cousins, along with her friends, tomorrow."

Felicity laughs softly. "Or should I just put her on a private jet?"

I laugh too. "Yes, it is ridiculous I suppose that a driver will escort our daughter and company. But she did request it. They like to watch movies in the limo."

"Of course Mac requested it. I would have requested limo rides when I was eleven too, if given the choice."

"Same here." I shift gears to Felicity. "Good luck at your New Year's Day show. Mac and I are excited to see it," I say, then wince at the reminder of the calendar. Fable and I will likely be "broken up" by then. I don't want to think about New Year's Day or breakups.

"Will you bring your new woman?" Felicity asks, her voice teasing and playful. "Mac's told me all about her."

I wish I could say yes. "We haven't talked about it," I

say decisively, hoping that ends the conversation I don't want to have.

"Let me know so I can get you extra VIP tickets. It would be lovely to meet her. Did you find the right sparring partner at last?"

Frankly, I'm not sure I'd be able to fit romance in my life if it came my way for real. But I have plenty of other good things going on, so that's just fine. And really, I have two more immediate issues occupying my mind—refining this fake romance routine so Bibi won't see through Fable and me, and then slaughtering that asshole ex of Fable's in the Christmas competition. "Let's not get ahead of things. We're just dating," I say, hoping to dodge the topic of the right person.

Felicity laughs. "Wilder Blaine. Someday you're going to fall head over heels for a woman and I'm going to write a song about the unbreakable man breaking."

I roll my eyes. That will never happen, but still I say, "I'll consider myself warned."

I end the call as an unexpected thought lands in my head—breaking. Me breaking. In the cabins, when it's snowing, and the world's gone quiet. I set my hand on the roof of the car, letting that image roll through me. It's tempting, like a siren, but dammit—I can't let it distract me. I shake it off then hop in the car, where a text flashes on the screen from my mother. I click on it.

> Mom: Are you heading to Evergreen Falls today? Can't wait to see my granddaughter soon. And you :) Also, I have a question about Mac's present. But I need to check on something first. More later! Xoxo

. . .

I send a quick reply, letting her know yes, I'm on my way, I'm glad I'm second best, and I'll help her with the present question anytime. I drive to Fable's place in the Mission District. As I turn onto her block, a zing shoots through my chest over the prospect of seeing her any second. I've been feeling those zings more and more lately.

But it's probably just the natural curiosity over checking out her building. I wouldn't be so successful if I didn't learn everything there was to know about all aspects of my business, from deals to contracts to employees to, apparently, fake girlfriends. After I park, I head up the steps and press the exterior buzzer for her place.

Her face appears on the screen, with a bright but apologetic grin. "I'm almost ready. I swear! I just had a minor toaster mishap, but I'll be down in five. Actually, do you want to come up?"

More than I should.

"Sure," I say, and the zing makes a liar of me.

So, that *wasn't* just natural curiosity. It was hope—the hope to learn more about her. Nothing to do but give in to it since seconds later, she's letting me in.

I head up the stairs to Fable's home, more thrilled than I should be to see an employee's apartment. I pause at the top of the steps, not to catch my breath, but to settle the pulse that's stupidly springing in excitement.

Get a grip, man. She's your fake girlfriend, and this is not a window into her world.

But when she swings open the door, I'm all wrong. It's a window into her life and I'm ravenous for the view.

Her red hair is piled in a bun, and she's wearing jeans

and a white sweatshirt that slopes off one shoulder, revealing a sliver of pale, kissable, freckled skin, and that silver snowflake necklace that I want to drag between my teeth only so I can lick what's under it. I stare a little too long at her collarbone, remembering how she tastes. Like strawberries and champagne. Remembering, too, how much she likes kisses on her collarbone, her shoulder, and especially at the hollow of her throat. The way she trembles when I touch her there...

But if I linger too long in this memory, I'll slip into other ones. More electric ones. Memories of the sounds she made when she came undone on my desk, of the way she shook when she fell apart underneath me, and most of all, how she tasted when I licked her off my fingers. Heat blasts through me like the door to a furnace has opened. All I got was just a taste and I want so much more.

I have to slam the door shut on that memory just like I close the door to her home.

"Come in. I'm almost ready. Make yourself comfortable," she says, and I try to blink off the lusty thoughts as she gestures to an emerald-green couch in the middle of the little living room. Across from the couch is a metal table, held up by two brushed nickel frogs that look like they were sculpted straight from a fairy tale. That's so very her. "Do you like frogs?" I ask, hungry for this intel too.

"Of course," she says breezily. "They have big eyes and funny bodies."

Another zing down my chest. Because she has a reason for liking frogs. Fucking frogs. What is happening to me?

"Let me just grab a couple things for the wedding and I should be good to go," she says.

"I presume you've packed extra glitter dicks, just in case?" I tease, remembering that fateful morning that led us here—when she glitter-dicked me with her sister's bachelorette party outfit.

Pretty pink flushes across Fable's cheeks, but she volleys right back. "I always have emergency penises on hand."

I resist the urge to offer my cock in case of emergency, but it's hard. Only that thought's not going to help me as we head toward a long car ride, so I quickly change course, pointing to the kitchen counter. "What happened to the toaster?" I ask.

"A battery fell in it from the smoke alarm."

My brow furrows. Something's missing there. "Is the smoke alarm not working then?"

She winces. "Yes. Maybe. I think so?"

"Did you use the toaster?"

"No. I tried to get the battery out but it was stuck, so I skipped breakfast."

I take a beat to process all that. "Go. Get ready. I'll take care of it."

"Really? Thank you. I was going to do it, but—"

"I've got it, Fable."

In the kitchen, I pick up the toaster, peer inside, then turn it upside down. Some crumbs fall out and the battery slips and slides. I wiggle the toaster a few times to no avail. After unplugging it, I find a pair of wooden chopsticks in a drawer, then use them like tweezers to remove the slim battery. When it's free, I grab a kitchen towel and wipe the counter clean.

A few minutes later I'm up on the stool, replacing the battery in the smoke detector till it's fixed firmly in place when she emerges with her suitcase.

She stops. Whistles. Then claps.

"What's that for?"

"I guess that joke is wrong."

"Which joke?"

"How many billionaires does it take to change a smoke detector battery? None. He hires someone to do it."

I shake my head, trying but failing to hide a smile. "The correct answer is—one, if he's handy."

"And you are. Thank you," she says, with genuine gratitude. But curiosity perhaps, too, as she asks, "How did you learn to change a smoke detector battery? Don't you have people for that?"

"No. I do it myself."

She seems flummoxed momentarily, but then she nods. "You're very capable."

"Did you think I was...what? Spoiled?"

"Actually, I don't know."

"I wasn't raised with money, Fable."

"Oh. I didn't know that," she says.

"I know how to change a flat tire. To cook a meal. To perform CPR. To fix a faucet and change a lightbulb," I say.

She dips her face, like she's hiding a smile. One I want to kiss off. When she raises her face, she says evenly, but like it takes some effort, "That's good."

I have to know. "Why? Why is that good?"

She presses her teeth into her lips, then says, "I like that you're normal too."

My heart pounds too fast, then too recklessly. I blame that damn organ for the next thing I say, "I like your apartment. It's very you."

"Thanks." She pauses. "That actually means a lot to me."

As we leave, I take the suitcase, then set a hand on her back despite the fact that no one's watching. But it feels right to touch her like this. It's not helping my intention to compartmentalize, but that's fine. I've got a plan, and a plan always helps.

When we reach the car, I load her suitcase into the trunk, shut it, then scan her block. "Now, let's get you breakfast."

Fifteen minutes later, she has a toasted bagel and a coffee in hand as she slides into the passenger seat.

Once I'm in the driver's seat, I push bagels and thank yous out of my mind, shoving them next to desk orgasms and hot mistletoe kisses. It's time to work on our fake romance plan—phase two.

"Now listen, we can't fuck up again like we did at the party."

"With Bibi? You felt that too?" Fable asks, and of course she noticed—she's the kind of woman who really seems to see people and understand nuance.

"I did. That arched brow of hers gives me nightmares. She can sniff out a lie like a bloodhound in a Santa hat. But I have an idea to keep us on track when we're in Evergreen Falls."

"I'm all ears."

I flick the turn signal as I near Divisadero Street, then toss her a playful smile. "It's a naughty and nice list."

24

BOARDROOM BOSS

Fable

Well, then. "Santa Blaine is in the car," I say.

His lips curve up the slightest bit—a tease of a smile. "It seemed...on brand for us," he says evenly, an explanation even though he doesn't need to justify his list. "A naughty and nice game."

But because I can't seem to resist teasing him, I add, "And if I'm a good girl, will I get an extra present?"

He flashes me a quick glance as we near the Golden Gate Bridge. Correction: a quick, stern glance. "Ah Fable, you'd have to be an extra good girl to get an extra present," he says, like a command.

I sit up straighter in the seat. "I can be very, very good," I say, obedient. Then I arch a brow his way. "I promise."

He breathes out roughly, like he's enjoyed those words from me—the promise of them. But maybe that's just part of this fake dating game, just like I'm into his naughty and nice list because I like a little competition. That's all.

"What do you want for Christmas then?" he asks, his tone genuine.

I wasn't expecting him to ask me that. My eyes slice to the rust-colored suspension bridge, a beautiful beast rising over the water. "The Golden Gate Bridge. In a snow globe," I say, just for fun. And just in case he really does get me something, and I bet he will, since that's so very him, a snow globe is an affordable gift.

"Then if you're a good girl, Santa will make sure you have it."

His voice is deep, hot, a little raspy. It sends a thrum through me. And I need a moment to get my bearings before I respond, "Then I'd better make sure I'm on the nice list."

"Yes. That's where you'll want to be."

My pulse beats a little faster. I take a long breath to calm down. Refocus. "So, this list. It's designed to keep us on track in the romance department?"

"Yes, because a close call is too risky," he says, and I want to tease him a little about the structured nature of his list, but the fact is, he's right. We're not simply dipping our toes into the fake dating kiddy pool at the Evergreen Falls Annual Best in Snow Winter Games Competition. After our two public appearances at parties already, we're definitely a "thing" now. We need to be that thing for the next five days until Christmas since we'll be in Evergreen Falls through then.

"I agree," I say.

"If Bibi sniffs us out, that'll be bad. She'll have my head. Plus, my mother is coming," he says.

"From London?" I squeak. I don't know why this surprises me. Of course it makes sense that his mother would return from London. I just hadn't thought about her. She has *strong Libra energy*, he told me at dinner. She's into the zodiac signs and art and her granddaughter. But that's all I really know.

"Yes. She'll be there on the twenty-third," he says, but his jaw ticks. Like he's a little uncomfortable. "She's...very astute."

My stomach churns. She's his mom, and moms always know what's up. Guilt stabs at me. "Wilder," I say, softly.

"Yes, little elf?" It's a silly name, but he says it without an ounce of sarcasm. I suspect he's using it to stay in character.

"Are we going too far? Lying to your mother?"

He seems to give that some thought for a minute. He's weighing it, I can tell. "It'll be fine," he assures me, but that's not the issue. The issue is I know how he cares about her. Of course he cares about Bibi too, but Bibi can be pushy. From what he's told me, his mother is not.

"We can tell her," I offer.

He snaps his gaze quickly to me. "Fable."

"I mean it. Mac knows. I don't want you to have to lie to your mother. Clearly you don't want to."

"She'll understand," he says.

He's ready to move on. But I can't leave it alone. "Understand that we're faking it? Or understand why we didn't tell her? I don't want you to have to do something you don't want to do."

I feel like I'm imploring him. But this whole fake dating scheme was my idea in the first place. Yes, he went along with it. Yes, it benefits him. But I know he adores his mother, and I don't want him to struggle with the guilt I feel over not telling Charlotte.

Briefly, he looks away from the road, his gaze softer, but determination still in his eyes. "I appreciate your concern. Truly, I do. But she knows what her sister is like. She knows what *my* sister is like. She understands the necessity." He takes a beat then moves on. "But I don't want to focus on me. I want to focus on the bigger issue—the man who's determined to beat us. The man who wants to show off his new girlfriend in front of *you*. The man who thinks he knows how to treat a woman," he bites out. "I won't let him hurt you. But if Brady finds out," he says, and the sound he makes is downright feral. It's a growl, low in his throat. I'm not at all sure what that's about, but it's sexy as hell. "He'd seize that opportunity and use it…to gloat."

Shame crashes into me as I think about the man I mistakenly thought cared about me. For the four months we dated, I believed we were going somewhere. I genuinely liked him. He seemed fun, friendly, eager to please. And, he *was* eager to please—another woman.

That massive fail in my romance picker is Reminder Number One why I need to be careful with my heart. Why my caution with emotions is a damn good idea. The more I let people in, the more they can hurt me. I shared my hopes and dreams with Brady. I told him about my friends, and how important Josie, Everly, and Maeve were to me. I told him about my desire to open a shop of my own someday. I told him, too, that I was scared.

A lot of good that did.

I grit my teeth, fighting off a wave of tightness in my throat, the threat of tears over my own foolishness.

But I don't linger too long in this emotion, since Wilder adds, "And I refuse to let him do that—gloat." It's said with steel as we wind past the craggy cliffs of the Marin Headlands. His hands grip the wheel tighter. His knuckles are almost white. His reaction to Brady is so intense. No man's ever reacted that way because of me. I'm not sure what to make of it, but it's oddly thrilling. Maybe even more so than the double dose of *O*s he gave me earlier in the week.

"Thank you," I say, kind of amazed he cares this much about my feelings. It's new and different.

"It's your sister's wedding. I don't want her or you to worry about a thing. I want you to be able to celebrate your sister like I know you want to."

My chest squeezes with brand-new emotions. Warm, soft ones. Tender ones. "That means a lot to me."

"Leo adores her. They're the real thing," he says almost solemnly, with heartfelt admiration for the two of them.

"They are."

"That's why we need to pull this off. If we make a mistake, and Brady finds out that our romance isn't real, he will be a dog with a bone. He will never let it go. I can't have that happen during this special time for your sister. And you. Is that clear?"

Boardroom Boss is absolutely in the car, and I am into it. I love that he wants this to go off without a hitch not simply for himself, but for me and for my sister. His passion is addictive.

"Yes. So how does the list work?"

As we cruise along the highway past Corte Madera, he goes into detail. "At the team party, we made a tactical error by being too over the top with our...affection."

Ironic, considering we crossed all kinds of affectionate lines already. But there's a difference between stolen touches behind closed doors and public displays of affection. "Now that the competition is beginning and we're all in close quarters, we need to come across as real and authentic. We need to sell it less and *be* it more. First, I suggest we dial back the nicknames, to 'honey' perhaps instead of 'little elf' all the time. To 'sweetheart' or 'sweetie' instead of 'sugar plum.'"

That makes sense. I can see his point. "Simpler names. More believable ones," I say, then get started right away with a purposeful, "sweetie."

"Thank you, honey." He flicks the turn signal and hops into the next lane before he adds, "Along those lines, here's how I see the game working. There will be plenty of activities in the common area for the cabins. So obviously, when we're with others and anytime there is some sort of over-the-top gesture from you or from me, we get to call the other one on it."

"It's like a game within a game? I am definitely here for that. So what do you have in mind? If I squeeze your ass too hard do I have to make you Christmas cookies?"

A laugh falls from his lips. "As a matter of fact that sounds like a perfect consequence. I might be rooting for us to fail then."

"Nah. You'd never root for that. Even if you like cookies and cheek squeezes."

He laughs. "True. Very true. Here's another. If you tell a ridiculous story about me that feels unbelievable, I get two hours to relax in front of the fireplace."

He deserves time to relax. I almost want to tell a silly story to give him that moment. But I wouldn't sabotage us. "Fair. And if you call me by a nickname that is certifiably sickeningly cutesy, I get a massage. I do love massages," I say, wiggling in the seat and saying deeply, in pre-appreciation for a massage, "I don't get nearly enough spa days. I wouldn't mind more of them."

"I should find a spot to send you to if that happens. In Evergreen Falls?" He takes his eyes off the road for a second, looking at me like maybe he'd rather not send me to a spa—that he'd rather touch me himself.

My breath catches unexpectedly from his gaze. "Unless you're offering," I say before I even have a chance to think about the temptation of those words. "You are good with your hands."

He growls, low and rumbly, deep in his throat. Perhaps that was too risqué, especially since we agreed what happened on his desk was a momentary lapse of reason. A one-time practice.

His voice lowers to a smokier tone. "And I like using them...on you."

My skin tingles. I might like this naughty or nice list too much. "Now I kind of want you to call me a nickname that's sickeningly cute," I say, a little tease in my tone, like a sexy invitation.

He's quiet. Focusing dead straight on the road. His hands grip the wheel tighter as if he's fighting off the urge to say *me too.*

Or maybe I'm imagining that's the battle he's waging.

For a few miles we're silent, perhaps both processing the list. What it means to be naughty and nice together. What it means to be over the top in a fake relationship and what it means to be real.

Perhaps, most of all, what it means to break the rules we've set for ourselves—a momentary lapse of reason.

Which raises a question. "What if we're just good at it? What if we're believable and authentic? Can I still make you a hot cocoa?" I ask.

He steals a glance my way as we pass the rolling green hills of Novato. "I would love that," he says, so earnestly it makes my heart go soft.

I give in to another impulse, this one to set a hand on

his arm. "You probably haven't had one since last Christmas."

"That's true."

"Then maybe that should be an addendum to our naughty and nice list. If we're believable—truly believable—we'll have hot cocoa together some night just like you wanted."

"That sounds nice too," he says, like he's fighting to keep the vulnerability out of his voice—fighting but failing. I hate that he feels he can't be vulnerable with me.

If we weren't driving, I might scoot closer, rest my head on his shoulder. Instead, I lift my hand and gently run it across the hair just above his ear. "Does that feel real?"

He shudders. Subtly, but still, it's there. "Yes," he admits.

I shouldn't do this while he's driving. I really shouldn't. I'm not even sure if it's the competition spurring me on or something else entirely. Something I'm just beginning to grapple with. But I do it anyway. I set my hand on his arm, giving a gentle rub of his shoulder. "How about that?"

"Real," he mutters, his jaw tight.

I move my hand on the denim of his jeans, just above his knee. Like a girlfriend would. "Authentic?"

He takes a beat for a quarter-mile stretch of the road. Then, he says in a barren whisper, "Perfect."

I'm tempted to leave my hand right here for the rest of the drive—for authenticity's sake and all—but when his phone rings and the name *Mom* flashes across the screen, I rip my hand off him.

25

ONE OF THOSE NEWFANGLED SITUATIONSHIPS

Wilder

I'm wavering. I don't usually waver.

But then again, my mom doesn't usually call when my fake girlfriend is in the car. My fake girlfriend who's feeling more real by the minute. My fake girlfriend who knows I don't want to lie to my mother.

Still, my finger hovers by the answer button on the car's dash.

Fable looks at me with concern, then says, "I can just be quiet. She doesn't have to know I'm here."

The thought sends my mind reeling. Reminds me of my father and his lies. The way he hid his whereabouts when he went out and gambled. How he'd call from quieter places to hide the fact that he was in a casino. My heart squeezes with a wave of emotion for Fable. For her willingness to make this easy for me. For her eagerness to help. But I won't ask her to double lie by pretending she's not even in the car.

I don't waver as I say, "No."

"Wilder," she says, like she can convince me otherwise. She could probably convince me of a lot of things. But in this case, I'm not bending.

The phone rings again.

"I won't pretend you're not here," I tell her, resolute, then hit answer.

"Hello, Mom," I say.

"Hi, kiddo," she says.

Fable whips her gaze to me, her warm eyes dancing with delight. *"Kiddo,"* she mouths.

"How's everything going? Also, we're not alone. Fable is in the car with me. She works for the team," I say, then with barely a pause, I add, "we're seeing each other. But she's not my direct report."

There. That last part will matter to my mother. Just like it mattered to Bibi and, well, to the employee handbook.

Fable waves to the dashboard screen though, of course, Mom can't see her. "Hi! I can't wait to meet you. Wilder has told me so much about you. How is London?"

Mom takes a second or two before she answers with, "London is lovely, but so is Evergreen Falls. And are you heading there too?"

"I am," Fable says. "We're in Wilder's car right now. Also, did you know he can change the battery in a smoke detector, Ms.—" Fable turns to me, asking with her eyes for Mom's last name.

"Hunter. Elizabeth Hunter," I supply.

"Ms. Hunter. He also fixed my toaster. He's a handyman! So thank you, since I can only assume this is your excellent work," she says.

"As a matter of fact, I'm pretty handy. I did teach him all those things, but credit to him too. He was dead set on knowing how to do everything. So glad he's put those skills to good use." And just like that, Fable is charming my mother.

"Well, he *is* an Aries. They're determined and independent," she says.

My heart should not be beating faster. It should not be surging simply because Fable remembers details about my mother, like her passion for the signs of the zodiac. But it is. It fucking is.

As I drive and they chat, I fight off a fresh wave of feelings for Fable. Must focus on the road. Only the road. Not on the ease with which the woman I'm supposedly seeing is winning my mother's heart.

When they're done chatting, my mom clears her throat. "Wilder, I have a question about Mac's gift. Can you send me a photo of Penguin's tail?"

I laugh. "You think I have a photo of the cat's tail?"

"Yes. I do," she says. "I bet it's on your camera roll. I bet you took one of her this morning."

Fable's jaw drops, like I've been busted. Then, more amused than she's ever been, she jumps in, saying, "He did, Ms. Hunter. He did. He loves taking pictures of the cat."

My mom sighs happily. "He takes them for Mac."

"It's so sweet," Fable says.

"Yes, I'll send you one when we stop," I say to my mom.

"Well, stop soon! I'm finishing her gift—Penguin's portrait—and I want to get the tail just right."

"Yes, Mom," I grumble.

Mom chuckles in response. "Now you can keep him in line, Fable."

I wince, guilt slicing through me. Fable was right when she said it'd be hard to lie to my mother. My mother's not like Bibi. She's not constantly trying to set me up. She understands why I'm relationship-free. She's the same. She knows romance isn't a thing that works out for some of us, and she's happy nonetheless.

She'd understand this fake-dating thing with Fable. Except, I don't want to ruin anything for my pretend girlfriend, who leans closer to the phone to hit the mute button. Her voice is serious as she says, "I want to tell her the truth. We can't lie to her. Please tell me you're okay with it."

The plea in her eyes. The vulnerability in her voice. The kindness of the gesture. Sometimes I wish she'd make it harder not to fall for her.

I hit the turn signal and say, "Yes."

It's easier than I thought it'd be, but that's how it goes with her.

Fable unmutes the phone. "Ms. Hunter, can you keep a secret?"

"Oh, this sounds interesting. And of course," my mom says as I turn onto the next exit ramp.

"Good. Because we're going to need your help to pull this off," she adds.

"Well, my day just got a lot more interesting."

"This is vault level. The kind of vault that only a compassionate, balanced Libra who can see all sides can handle," she adds.

"That's me," Mom says.

There's a pause, a deep breath, then Fable jumps.

"Wilder is not my real boyfriend." Fable almost sounds disappointed.

There's silence on my mother's end of the line as I pull into the parking lot at a roadside store. Then she says, "Ah, this is one of those newfangled situationships?"

I appreciate her attempt to understand this, but it's time to jump in. "Bibi is Bibi-ing, and Caroline is Caroline-ing, and you and I know it's not going to happen. I needed a plus one for the wedding to ward them off, and Fable graciously agreed," I say, quickly getting to brass tacks. "Her ex-boyfriend happens to be the world's biggest prick and he'll be at the wedding, so all the better that he sees she's moved on."

"To a better man," Fable adds with an emphatic nod.

There's a beat. Then, an "I see." It's like her Libra brain is weighing this new intel. "So it's fake, but you're actually going to the wedding together?"

"Yes," I say.

"And traveling together?"

"Yes."

"So the way I see it, it's not really a lie. She *is* your plus one," Mom says as I cut the engine.

"I am," Fable says, with obvious pride.

"Well, I'll keep your secret, but I can't imagine anyone will be suspicious. You two seem like you actually like each other."

She signs off, and I look at Fable with her gorgeous copper hair, her pretty pink lips, her creamy skin, her bold and bright attitude. Her spirit. Her energy. Her heart.

Little do they know it's becoming a lot more than like.

* * *

"Popcorn?" I ask as we walk down the aisle of snacks at this roadside gourmet-ish shop.

"Well, it *is* a road trip," she says.

"Three and a half to four hours. That makes it a road trip?"

She's emphatic as she nods. "Yes, it does. And road trips require snacks. What do you like? Oh, right. Chocolate." She stops in the sweets aisle. "Hold on—fancy chocolate."

"I can't help it if I have good taste," I say, then let my gaze linger on her a little longer.

Her hand seems to flutter over her chest as she grabs a bar of salted dark chocolate. "You do. Also, snacks are on me," she says, and she swings past me to head to the counter.

I dart out a hand and catch hers, tugging her toward me. Shaking my head, I say, "They're not."

"Wilder," she says on a plea.

"You already stepped up and told my mom. I am buying the snacks and that's just that."

"Bossy," she mutters.

I smirk. "Does this surprise you?"

"Not in the least." Then she murmurs under her breath, a little sensually, "*Sir.*"

Well, then. There's a whole lot of info delivered in that tone. I can't not ask, "So not only does it not surprise you, it sounds like you don't mind it either?"

She tips her chin up at me, challenging me with, "What do you think?"

I don't think. I *do*. I slide my thumb along her pretty chin. God, it feels so good to touch her again. "That you like to give me hell. That you like to keep me on my toes. And that you love to give me a hard time."

She leans into my touch, almost like she's saying with her body *don't stop.* "And I think you love all those things too," she says in a husky voice that gives a little hint of her desire.

My thumb travels up to her cheek. She moves with me, her breath gusting across those gorgeous lips. "You'd be right," I say, heat flaring inside me.

I could stay here all day like this, touching her face and trading quips. But we're in a convenience store on the side of a road. I force myself to let go of her.

I take the food, buy it, and return to my vehicle with her. I slide back behind the wheel and turn on the car as she rips open the popcorn.

"Wait. Is it okay to eat in here?" She gestures to the dust-free dashboard and the heated passenger seat.

"Yes, of course."

"Are you sure? It's a nice car and everything."

"And I can clean it if need be," I say.

"From handyman to cleaning man," she says, seeming amused, then she dips her hand into the bag and pops some in her mouth. She offers me the snack. I grab a couple kernels, then put the car in drive and head off, returning to the highway. Once we're cruising along the highway on our way to the small mountain town I turn on a Christmas station, then return to what she did earlier with my mother as Destiny's Child sings about Rudolph the Red-Nosed Reindeer. Fable took a big leap and trusted my mother with our secret—and she did it for me. "That was thoughtful of you, Fable. What you did with my mom," I say, with some vulnerability.

"It just made sense," she says, almost downplaying it.

But I won't let her think it was no big deal. It *was* a big deal. "No. It was more than that. It meant a lot to me. The fact that you wanted to. That it mattered to you to tell her. I was...touched."

She parts her lips, possibly to make light of it again, but she seems to stop herself. "Good. I'm glad. You've done so much for me already. I wanted to do something for you—something you wanted," she says, her patent honesty hooking into my heart, making it soften even more for her. I didn't think that was possible. And yet, it's happening.

"It makes things easier. And you were right—I didn't want to lie to her. Thanks for..." I pause, searching for the right words. "For making things easier for me."

Her smile is warm and kind. "I had a feeling," she says, then takes a beat. "Tell me more about her. I know she lives in London. She's going to school there? Getting her master's degree?"

"Yes, she finished her bachelor's there too. A few years ago."

"So she went back to study? Good for her. That's so cool," she says, as the highway narrows and we drive higher into the hills. The snow-capped peaks of Evergreen Falls aren't too far away now.

"It was her dream for the longest time. When she was married to my father, she wanted to go. She even told him as much a few times when I was maybe ten or eleven. But he said it was too expensive and there was no need," I say, my voice tight with simmering anger. "Of course the irony is he took what little college savings he'd had and gambled it away."

She winces. "I'm sorry to hear that. Is it...an addiction?"

This isn't how I'd planned to tell her. In fact, I'm not sure I'd planned to tell her at all. But she figured it out, and I don't want to lie. Temporary though as this is, trust is vital. After all, we're trusting each other with the secret of this fake romance. "Yes. He goes to meetings. But he relapses all the time. He's had more one-day chips than I can count. His good friend, Victor, often keeps me posted on how my dad's doing," I tell her. "Victor is a blackjack dealer at one of the casinos and he'll sometimes give me a heads-up since my dad doesn't always give me the details. But Victor will let me know if Dad lost a big game or something. He looks out for him, which I appreciate," I say, my shoulders slumping some, because I wish I didn't have to rely on Victor. "When he does call—my dad—he's almost always asking for money, and he's utterly unreliable. I invited him to Thanksgiving a couple years ago so he could spend time with Mac, and he said yes, but then canceled at the last minute."

Apparently, the valve has been opened and I can't shut it off. "I don't know if it was a poker game, or a woman, or he just couldn't get it together. But he didn't show, and I called Victor, and Victor didn't even know what was going on. Mac was such a trouper when she went to bed, and she said she missed seeing him." My jaw tightens at the memory. "The next time my father called a few days later, I told him that he'd let her down. He made up a song and dance about a last-minute shift and needing the money. Though maybe it was true. He loses most of what he has."

"Wilder," Fable says in a voice thick with emotions. "I'm sorry he's got those demons and that they're hurting you and Mac."

But that's not the full truth of it. "Sometimes he asks me for money," I admit. "Sometimes I give it to him." My eye twitches—a reminder that that's not the full truth. Briefly, I look at her straight on. "Actually, most of the time I give it to him, Fable."

Her voice is kind—a forgiveness. "I understand. Sometimes we aren't always ready to do the hard thing. So we have to do something easier first."

As we rush past a sign boasting that Evergreen Falls is twenty-five miles away, I steal a glance at my traveling companion. She's beautiful, funny, and wise beyond her years. And she's the first person I've confessed all that to. "I don't usually tell people about him," I say.

"I won't tell a soul," she says, then mimes zipping her lips and tossing the key.

That's not what I was getting at though. "No, Fable. That's not why I said that. It wasn't to ensure you'd keep the secret." I pause, so the weight of the words can sink in. "It's because I wanted you to know."

Perhaps it's an admission of sorts.

She doesn't say anything at first. The only sound in the car is the chorus on "Silver Bells" and the whooshing of the other cars on the highway.

Briefly, I wonder if I've said too much.

But my chest feels a little bit lighter. From having told her about my father, and about wanting her to know.

I don't regret it.

At last she speaks, soft but clear. "I like knowing you."

And it's like my chest is expanding, making room for the way my heart is growing for her.

Too bad it's only temporary.

As I slow at our exit, Fable points to a wooden sign painted red, with the words *Welcome to Evergreen Falls* in white on it. A red-and-green garland illustration coasts around the border of the sign, inviting us to enter this town that feels like it's in another world. "I have a feeling we're not in San Francisco anymore," she says in a quiet voice.

"We're not at all," I say, and the distance from our regular lives is making me let down my guard even more.

Trouble is I'm going to need some kind of distance from my fake girlfriend in Evergreen Falls or else I'll fall entirely in love with her before Christmas.

26

ONLY ONE ROOM

Fable

There's no snow in San Francisco, but that's not a problem here in Evergreen Falls, mere hours and mountains away. As we turn off the main road, a blanket of snow-covered trees welcomes us to the cabins, almost as if the town has conspired with Mother Nature herself to look its best for the Christmas competition.

My eyes widen at the sight before us. Elegant cabins dot the snowy hillside like an advertisement for rustic sophistication. "They're chalets," I say proudly, then look at the man driving the car. "You should be seriously proud of what you've built. I know I'm proud of you."

"Well, I didn't actually build them. I just own the resort."

I tilt my head. While I love his dry humor, I mean it. "You made this possible with hard work and focus," I say earnestly as he pulls into the gravel lot.

"Thank you. It was Bibi's idea first, but now I love it

too. I like to host everyone here during the holidays. Friends and family," he says, and that's generous—giving up the revenue from potential customers at this time of year to use the space for family and friends instead. "I hope you enjoy it."

He sounds so earnest, like it's truly important for me to have a good time. But I have been, and I will, even with my ex in the background. Wilder is the best company, I'm learning. He's attentive, interesting, and clever. He's always got my back. The more time I spend with him, the more I enjoy spending time with him.

And that's not even considering his talented hands. They really are magic.

But honestly, so was that mini road trip. It was like we were in our own little world, especially when he opened up about his father. He's normally so, well, bossy and precise. Clever and deliciously powerful. But in that moment he was vulnerable in a whole new way. I felt closer to him then than I ever have. That makes me think maybe we can even be friends after this ends.

I don't like the thought of this ending. At least not right now—not while we're in the thick of it. This is where I need to be on my game—the best fake girlfriend ever. I have to give the holiday performance of a lifetime, but it shouldn't be hard here in Evergreen Falls. This place is lovely.

It's serene and peaceful in exactly the way I'd imagined, with snow blanketing the grounds and evergreens rising tall and proud, flanking the cluster of cabins he owns.

The ones he reserved for us connect to a main dwelling with a living area the families can share if they want. But the couples have their own mini chalets. Ours is a two-bedroom so there's plenty of space and privacy. And bless him—he told his assistant to put Brady and Iris in a cabin off by itself. One that doesn't connect to the main house.

I could kiss him for that flex alone. I mean, kissing him is no hardship. The man's mouth is magic too.

He parks the car in the gravel lot and gets out, then comes around to my side to open the door. I step out and look around more. The cabins are nestled in the foothills, their roofs dusted with shimmering snow that glitters in the afternoon sun. Each building is a picture-perfect post-card from a Christmas village, with stone chimneys and colorful lights that will no doubt be twinkling in the windows when evening falls. The air is crisp and clean, carrying the scent of pine and wood smoke.

A few seconds later, the main door swings open and Bibi stands at the entrance, dressed in a fluffy white parka with a Santa hat I haven't seen before perched on her head—this one is the color of red wine, with gray strands in the faux white fur. She sweeps her arm out to the side. "Fable, you're going to love it here. I just know it," Bibi gushes, heading out in her snow boots to greet us.

"You're right. I already do," I say. I didn't know I was looking for a relaxing getaway from the city, but I'm getting one and I don't mind at all.

"Oh, good. It's going to be such a great week," she says, squeezing my arm. "For you and my wild child."

She pinches Wilder's cheek. "You haven't done that since I was ten," Wilder says, amused but surprised too.

"That was short-sighted of me. It's awfully fun."

Hmm. Someone is over the top right now and it's not Wilder and me. But I'm not sure what to make of Bibi's hostess enthusiasm. Except, Wilder did note at Thanksgiving how much she enjoyed the holidays. Bibi and her late husband used to host the whole family here, he told me. This must be her way of carrying on that tradition. My chest warms at the thought that she's including me in it.

Then chills when I remember the reason—we're faking it.

But I push those thoughts aside as she leads us through the snow-covered pathway toward the entrance. "I have something special just for the two of you. I can't wait," she says.

Intrigued, I arch a brow Wilder's way. He shrugs lightly, then carries our bags up the wooden porch. A wreath hangs on the door, adorned with bright red ribbons and pine cones. Bibi gestures for us to enter and... whoa.

We're not alone. My mom is here with her husband, Julio, but not my dad, which is good. The guests of honor are cuddly as can be on the love seat, with Leo's arm draped around Charlotte's shoulder. Wilder's sister, Caroline, is here with her wife, and Mom's brother Uncle Rick is here too, with his girlfriend and his kids. Wesley and Josie are here as well. So are Everly, Max, and Maeve. They're all lounging on the huge couch in front of the crackling fireplace.

Thankfully, Brady and Iris haven't been invited to this little living room get-together. As Wilder greets his best friend, Charlotte pulls me aside and tells me Brady had car trouble, so they caught a bus in and then made tracks straight for their cabin early this morning to *check out the sweet digs*, as my ex apparently called them in his best stockbroker bro voice.

"The best man and maid of honor finally made it," Leo teases after I introduce Wilder to my mom.

"We were placing bets on when you'd show up," Wesley teases, since the guys on the hockey team love to bet—or so I'm told by Josie and Everly.

"We weren't sure if you needed an engraved invitation or not," Max puts in.

"But we can make one for you if you need it," Maeve adds. "You can help since you're crafty."

It's not like we're late. But maybe everyone came up earlier than we did.

"I didn't realize everyone would be here already," Wilder says curiously, and that's odd for him to forget.

Bibi flings her hand to her chest. "I didn't tell you? The town switched up the schedule and moved some things around, and we don't want to miss a single event. We were all aiming for a morning arrival. And everyone made it," she says, and I'm pretty sure Wilder told me mid-afternoon was the plan, but I'm not going to point that out. "But you're here now, and I have good news."

"Okay," Wilder says, seeming wary of his aunt.

I am too. It feels like she's doing this on purpose. Like Wilder was right to be concerned about her...machinations. Maybe she wanted us to be the last ones to arrive.

Bibi gestures behind her toward a sliding glass door that leads to a deck that boasts a view of the hills and the next cabin. The one with—is that a heart on its door? "For some reason, I was given the honeymoon cabin. The one with the cozy bedroom with the fireplace and the sleigh bed. A hot tub too. But that's silly. You young lovers deserve it."

And I was right. She is up to something. But that knowledge doesn't change my reaction. My throat goes dry. My brain short-circuits. The honeymoon cabin can't possibly have two bedrooms, can it? It has to have one. Which means...*one bed.* Confused, I turn to Wilder. How is he going to handle this...proximity?

He's more stoic than I've ever seen him but a vein pulses in his neck. "The honeymoon cabin?" It's a question paved with gravel.

Bibi's grin is supersized. "Yes. Isn't that perfect? With its one cozy, intimate room."

"What about Leo and Charlotte?" I ask because I don't want to be rude to the bride and groom.

"Of course we have one too," my sister says, clearly enthused that I'll get a cabin just like hers.

One room. One bed. Five nights. And an admission hanging over us that the one time in his office can't happen again.

My stomach tips upside down. I'm not sure how we're going to handle the sleeping arrangements. But this honeymoon suite *mix-up* feels like an early test in the competition, and dammit, I'm not going to let us lose. I grab Wilder's strong arm and tug my Christmas boyfriend against me, his hard body snug against my side. No idea if I'm winning or losing our private naughty or nice contest, but in for a penny, in for a pound. "Sounds great. Right, hun?"

I tip my face upward, then dust a kiss to his cheek.

His breath catches, then he says, "Yes."

Like this is all he's wanted.

Take that, Bibi.

27

THE GOOD FIGHT

Wilder

It's not like I've visited every cabin here at this resort, but I'm sure we can make one of the honeymoon suites work. I don't entirely know how it's set up or decorated, but I'll find out any second, and I'll devise a plan for tonight right away.

A plan to deal with all this temptation pulsing between us.

With my jaw as tight as my muscles, I open the door. When Fable and I step inside, I take in every detail, like a robot scanning the landscape for intel. The king-size sleigh bed is adorned with plush pillows, a fluffy white duvet, and a red fleece blanket draped over the foot of the mattress. The room is L-shaped and in the little nook sits a cozy couch opposite a fireplace. Next to the fireplace is a Christmas tree, decorated simply with strands of lights, some tinsel, and several candy canes. The scent of pine and mint is faint but welcoming all the same.

It's a lovers' suite for sure. No two ways about it. But we said that time in my office was a once-only thing. A lapse. Something we needed to get out of our systems. We got it out and here we fucking are—sharing a bed.

My chest burns. My mind unhelpfully supplies a thousand filthy images. I fight the desire to look at the gorgeous woman next to me and toss her on that bed right now to test it out. I've got to get this lust under control. *Now.*

This is fine. This is totally fine. I can work with this suite.

Robot mode activated, I don't waste a second cleaning up the mess Bibi made of my plans. I grab the bags and set them inside. The second the door closes with a click, I gesture to the sofa. "I'll take the couch," I declare firmly. There are no two ways about it. This is not up for discussion.

But Fable swivels around and stares at me like I've lost all common sense. Well, I feel a little tossed around. I don't admit that often, and I'm sure as fuck not admitting it now to her. Fable's kiss on my cheek knocked the breath right out of me. If anything more happens, I'll be lost to her and she'll know what a fool I am for falling.

"Wilder," she says, arching one brow. "That's ridiculous."

My confidence stalls for a second, but then I remember Bibi's stunt in front of all our guests and decide to stand my ground. "It's fine."

"It's two-feet long."

"It's six," I correct her. To prove my point, I walk along the carpet next to the sofa, measuring the furniture with precise steps. I complete six steps and turn around, victorious. "Six. There you go."

She rolls her eyes. "And you're over six feet."

"Six one."

She nods like *I told you so*. "Exactly. And I'm, wait for it, not six feet. So I'll take it."

"This is not a logic problem. It's a manners issue," I say, sharply. "You're not taking it."

She snaps her gaze to me. "Did you just give me an order?"

I did. And I sounded like a dick. But I don't relent. "Yes. Because there is no way I'm letting you sleep on that couch."

She crosses her arms. "Is that so?"

"Yes, that's so," I reply. As Fable narrows her eyes at me, I can see the gears turning in her head. She's always been quick-witted and fiercely independent, and I know she won't back down without a fight. Something in me wants that fight. I'm not sure why, but I do.

"You can't just dictate where I sleep, Wilder," she retorts, her voice laced with defiance. "I'm perfectly capable of making my own decisions."

Of course she is. I don't doubt that for a second. But a flicker of challenge crosses her eyes, daring me to push back even harder. It's a turn-on.

"This is not about control, Fable," I say, keeping my voice steady despite the current inside me. "This is about chivalry. And as the gentleman here, I'm taking the couch."

"This is chivalrous?"

"What would you call it?"

She crosses her arms and stares right at me. "You're bossy."

"I am the boss."

"Yes, back at work. But right here," she says, pointing

to the floor, "we're in this situationship together. And this is a ridiculous solution." She takes a step closer to me, her voice low and intense. "You can't control every aspect of this fake relationship, Wilder."

She's so infuriatingly headstrong. Like a goddess whipping up a storm. I should stop this argument, but it's not in my nature to step down. "I'm not controlling it. It just makes sense."

"You can't decide for me, Wilder. We both deserve a comfortable place to sleep, and that bed looks plenty big enough for both of us."

The bed.

Dear god, the fucking bed.

That's the issue. That's why I can't back down. The thought of sharing a bed with her is too alluring. Actually doing it, though, would be my downfall. I would reach for her at night. I would press a kiss to her shoulder as I was dozing off. In the middle of the night, when the world went calm and still, I'd wrap her in my arms and whisper sweet nothings in her ear. Like *I'm so hung up on you.*

I pinch the bridge of my nose. This is the worst idea. How the hell did this whole situation go so wrong?

Because you're fake dating, you fuckwit!

And on that note, the voice inside my head has called me a fuckwit for the first time. I need to get a grip. I gave in to my desires in the office. I can't keep doing it, and I can't be dangerously close to her. I take a moment to gather my thoughts, breathing in hard, letting it fuel me. But I reach the same conclusion on the bed situation. I dig my heels in harder. "No, Fable. I won't budge on this."

Fable's eyes narrow. "And who are you to decide where I sleep?"

"I'm your fake boyfriend," I reply, my voice steady

despite the tension crackling between us. "And it's my responsibility to make sure you're comfortable and safe."

She huffs, her lips forming a stubborn line. "I can take care of myself, Wilder. I don't need you playing the hero."

The tension between us crackles like electricity, sending hot sparks down my spine. "It's not about playing hero," I explain, taking a step closer to her and ignoring her dangerous suggestions we share a bed. "And it's not right for you to sleep on that couch so I will."

She remains defiant. "What if I want to sleep on the couch?"

She probably thinks she has me in a corner. That she's caught me on a technicality. But watch this. "Then we'll both sleep on the couch," I declare, crossing my arms in solidarity.

She opens her mouth to argue, but then abruptly shuts it. Fable's eyes widen in surprise at my unexpected compromise. "Why are you so infuriating right now?"

Because you're spectacular. Because I can't stop thinking about the way your lips brushed my damn cheek out there in the living room and how much it excited me—a kiss on my fucking cheek. Because if a cheek kiss fires me up that much, what will I feel if I have you again? And I want you so fucking much. Because you're fighting with me, and no one fights with me. Because I want to push you away and pull you close at the same time.

I don't say any of those things. I'd give everything away. "Because you infuriate me," I huff out.

"Well, guess what? The feeling's mutual," she says, then she wheels around and marches to her suitcase to unpack.

That won't do. We're not done. I follow her across the soft carpet, grab her wrist, and spin her around. The unexpected force of it yanks her against me. Her chest to mine. Her face tipped up.

Like at the party at my house. Like the moment in my office. Like...now.

She gulps, surprise coasting across her red lips. Her eyes widen, beautiful hazel pools that have me intoxicated. Eyes that remind me, too, that I shouldn't push all her buttons. I need to get a grip. I take a breath and stand down. "I'm sorry I was so...infuriating."

She pauses, then nods, accepting it. "Couples do that. They infuriate each other."

It's said without the fire of a minute ago but with another kind of flame in her irises. A warm, hazy, inviting one.

"They do," I say, and I don't let her go. She doesn't make a move either.

"A fight...it makes this whole thing...more believable," she says softly, like a peace offering, but also an opportunity—for practice.

"Fighting *is* authentic," I admit. "It's a normal thing. Couples fight, and they make up."

"We should be able to...believably make up," she says, breathy, feathery. "Don't you think?"

But I can't think anymore. Not with those lips parted, not with her soft body in my arms, not with the snow outside.

And really, the person I should stop fighting with is myself. I'm a goddamn CEO. I'm an expert at concealing emotions. My poker face is unparalleled. I won't give away all my feelings because I won't let myself.

With that internal war waged, I move the fuck on.

"Yes, we should," I say at last, and then I stop arguing

and I drop the fierce hold on her wrist so I can cup her face instead.

Fable's breath hitches as my hand gently caresses her cheek, my thumb tracing the curve of her jawline. Her eyes flutter closed as she leans into my touch. Without another word, I lean in and capture her lips with mine.

There's no mistletoe this time to justify it. There's no audience to perform for. We don't need any more practice. This kiss is for us. This time, I kiss like we fight. I crush my lips to hers. I kiss her hard, a demand for more. Fable grabs the collar of my shirt, twisting her fingers around it.

That.

Right there.

Her hands on me.

Her hungry mouth.

This whole kiss undoes me with its urgency, with the way we're unleashing the fight into passion. I jerk her impossibly closer, my hand curling around the back of her head. I'm not gentle, though, and she doesn't seem to want me to be judging from the way she presses against me. Asks for more with her body. I give her a bruising kiss, and she moans into my mouth. I stop to nip the corner of her lips.

"Oh!" It's said with excitement—a thrill even.

I meet her gaze with a smirk, maybe to cover up the way my heart is pounding too fast. "It's...believable. This makeup kiss," I say dryly.

"It is," she deadpans.

Neither one of us lets go. I don't want to. And when her fingers twist tighter into the fabric of my shirt, I take that and run with it. "We should be sure, though," I suggest.

"Yes. Please. Be sure."

I take another kiss. I deepen it this time. Somehow, it's more urgent and hungry. I grip her hair more tightly, and she takes a step back, pulling me with her, then another till the back of her legs hit the couch. She tugs me down onto the sofa.

This is so damn risky. And yet I move with her, flopping next to her onto the cushion, then pulling her onto my lap, my arms wrapping around her. She straddles me, hands gripping my face. The kiss is electric, sending shockwaves through my body.

We could kiss all day. All night. All year.

This is hardly a kiss for believability's sake any longer. It feels all too real in the press of her palms on my stubble, in the heat of her skin, in the subtle grind of her hips. She's not quite sitting on my lap, but she's damn close, and she's rocking slightly.

And that feels all wrong too. All wrong to let her walk away unfulfilled. Good thing I know how to negotiate. I break the kiss, smooth a palm across her soft face. "I'm sorry I was such a dick."

"You were a dick."

"Let me show you how sorry I am."

Her irises flicker with questions and with excitement too. "What do you mean?"

My hand slides down her face to her neck, over her throat. She moves with me murmuring as I travel lower, over her breasts, along her belly, then to her jeans, teasing at the button.

"I want to apologize properly," I say in a low, smoky voice.

"Wilder," she says, like a warning, but an invitation too. She swallows, then asks, "How?"

She asks it like she can't resist.

I pin her with a hot, molten stare. "With my mouth."

"Oh god," she whimpers, then slumps forward, as if desire has melted away her bones. Maybe even her common sense, too, since it's obliterated mine.

In a second, she straightens, shimmies off me, and pops open the button on her jeans. I stand, head to the door, and flick the lock.

When I've returned to the couch, my eager fake girlfriend has pushed off her jeans.

"You do belong on the naughty list, Fable Calloway." I stalk closer.

With a filthy grin, she says, "Why don't you make sure of that?"

And as I sink to my knees on the soft carpet, I think of nothing but this white-hot need to taste her. She's wearing that white sweatshirt and pink panties. "I've no use for these," I say, hooking my thumbs into the waistband and skimming them down. She lifts up her hips, helping me along.

Her unchecked need matches my own. And when I slide them off her, the sight of her wet, pink pussy makes my cock thump. I groan in appreciation, then run my finger along her mouth, meeting her gaze. "Your pussy is fucking beautiful," I tell her.

She gasps, then shudders, then stretches a hand to touch my mouth too. "So's your mouth. The better to eat me with."

I grin, like a wolf, then lower my hands to her thighs, spreading them apart, giving me a beautiful view of all that glistening wetness. I run the pad of my thumb along her pulsing clit. She jumps, then moans.

"You really like fighting, Fable," I tease.

Her hands dart out and she grabs my head, gripping hard. "And you better really like apologizing."

"Oh, I do. I really do...when it comes to you." Then I show her how sorry I am. I kiss her pretty clit, flicking my tongue up and down as she gasps and groans. I suck on her, my eyes rolling back in my head from the heady taste of her desire. Her hands dig into my skull. I swear I can feel her nails, and that revs my engine. It amps up my own lust. I suck harder, kiss deeper, lap her up.

She hitches up a leg, gripping my head harder with her inner thigh. Lust ricochets through me, and determination too. I press my palm to her other leg, push her open wider, raise my face. "Part those pretty legs for me, baby. Nice and wide. Let me worship this sweet pussy."

Her eyes are glassy. Her breath is coming hard and fast. But she takes orders so damn well as she spreads her legs wide, making herself more vulnerable. "Like this? Does this help you say you're sorry?"

"I'm so fucking sorry," I growl, then dive back between her thighs, feasting on her arousal, tongue-fucking my Christmas girlfriend till she's rocking furiously against my face. Grabbing my skull. Cursing the most filthy *oh fucks* I've ever heard.

But I don't want anyone to hear her. No, those noises are mine and mine alone. As I eat her, I lift an arm and cover her mouth. Like that, I bury my face in her sweetness as she bucks against me, crying out into my palm and then coming on my face. She tastes fucking incredible, better than all my dirty dreams.

I lick her slowly, easing off.

And when she starts to come down, I stop, giving her a final soft, tender kiss before I straighten and meet her heady gaze.

"Like I said, I'm very, very sorry I was such a dick."

She swallows roughly, then leans forward, cupping my cheeks. "You were a total ass."

Then, she kisses me, and I think I might die of lust right now.

But there's a knock on the door and her sister's voice, like bells saying, "We're heading to town. The snowball competition is in an hour. Let's go!"

We wrench apart, and I'm breathless and dizzy. Her chest is heaving. My dick is a flagpole in my jeans. She shudders out a breath and says to Charlotte through the door, "Coming." Then she looks at me and smiles, too amused as she whispers, "That's what she said."

And I laugh. "She sure did."

She brushes her palms down her sweatshirt and fluffs out her hair. But her lips are bee-stung, and her cheeks are flushed. Good. I hope everyone knows what I did to her. She lifts a finger my way. "Don't think this means our argument is over."

I battle a smirk. "Yeah. I figured you liked fighting."

"I did."

Did.

But we can't keep doing it. Or it'll feel too real for me. "It's good practice. It makes everything more believable."

"It does."

"And now we've practiced," I say, crisply.

She's nodding too, adamant, on board with the plan. "We should be...good to go? Unless you want me to..." She doesn't finish—just lets her gaze drift down my body, landing on the outline of my hard-on.

I breathe out roughly. I want that more than nearly anything. But I'd be so fucked then. "We don't really have time now," I say in a non-answer.

"Right, but that's not what I meant."

"I know, honey," I say, facing her and her question head-on. "I do, but I don't want to get...addicted. To practice."

"Sure. Of course," she says, nodding. A ghost of a smile shifts her lips. "Just so you know, I haven't had orgasms like the ones you've given me in a long time."

My brow furrows. "Through oral?"

She shakes her head. "From another person."

Oh.

Oh.

I shouldn't ask the next thing, but I do it anyway. "How long?"

She shrugs. "Before the other day on your desk...it was more than a year."

I flash her a smug smile. "Good thing you threw all those glitter dicks at my face then," I say, "so you can truly experience how a man should treat a woman."

She laughs. "It really is."

I rise, look down at her. I should walk off, but I can't help myself. I need to crow about one more thing. "By the way, I was right."

"About what?" she asks, her eyes still a little foggy.

I take my time, lick the corner of my lips. "You taste fucking delicious."

Then, I turn away from her as she pops up and rushes for her suitcase. I head to the en suite bathroom, where I remind myself that once is all I'll allow.

I liked it far too much to let it happen again.

28

SNOWBALL-ISH

Fable

There's no rest for a fake dater.

I can't even come up for air. As I grab a scarf, beanie, and mittens, I can still feel his mouth on me. His lips. His *lips.* I can still feel the rush of heat in my body. My chest flips from the filthy memory of his wicked apology. But I can't keep losing my pants for him, no matter how talented his hands or his mouth are.

So fucking talented.

But the more we cross the line, the more complicated this holiday ruse becomes. And honestly, as much as I want to return the favor—and I do, oh hell do I ever—I don't need or want a complication. Or, like he said, an addiction. The *O*s he bestows are definitely of the addictive variety.

I want this wedding to go smoothly. I want to win the Christmas competition. He clearly doesn't want a distraction. If Wilder and I keep lunging at each other, we run the risk of becoming...real.

Even on a temporary basis.

And real couples hurt each other. With words, with deeds, with disappointment. If it feels all too real, he could back out or change his mind. Or we could get too caught up in the moment. It's best we keep this romance as fake as it can be.

We leave the suite and Charlotte ferries us from the cabins immediately, urging us through the main living room and out the door. "The snowball-fighting competition was moved to today. It starts in forty-five minutes," she explains, enthused. My sister sounds like she can't wait. Makes sense. She's always loved activities—the more the merrier for my outgoing sister.

"I thought that event was tomorrow," I say to Charlotte as I tug on snow boots by the cabin door.

"The snowball fight isn't usually for another day or so," Wilder adds.

Charlotte shoots us a look like we don't make sense to her. "Did either of you hear what Bibi said? The town tweaked the schedule a bit to fit in more events," she says, and yes, Bibi did say that, but with the 'welcome to One Bed Town, population you' talk it'd slipped from my mind. Must have done the same to Wilder, or perhaps that apology fried the schedule right out of his brain in an out-of-character moment for both of us.

A fresh new worry digs into my chest.

What if my sister sees through us? If she learns we're fake dating because of Brady—even though Wilder needs a plus one too—she'll worry about me. She'll feel responsible. She'll think it was her fault for introducing us, and then she'll feel like she should tell Leo, and I don't want her to carry that guilt. Ugh. Why does Brady need to be related to my sister's amazing groom? Family ties sometimes just suck.

I don't want to add more stress to her plate. Not when she's having so much fun. This is exactly what I want for Charlotte—her happiness. Her joy. She's in her element and I don't want to steal focus like my father did over and over, especially around the holidays.

It's her moment to be the star. It's my moment to blend in.

That means I need to pay attention. Not trip over little details. "It's a good time for a snowball fight," I say, trying to forget what just went down. *Him.*

"It's going to be great," Charlotte says as she bounds down the steps toward the driveway, clasping Leo's arm happily, like she can't get enough of her fiancé. "I guess the snow is particularly snowball-ish this afternoon."

With the grin of a wildly-in-love man, Leo presses a kiss to her hair, curling out from under a red beanie with a white pom-pom bobbing on top. "It just snowed the other night, and studies show the perfect snowball consistency is two days later," Leo says in an even tone, like he's evaluating hedge funds for his portfolio.

Or really, putting his friend on.

Wilder seems off his game, though, and arches a brow skeptically. "That's the ideal time for snowball consistency? That's why the competition was moved?"

Hmm. That's odd for Wilder not to quite pick up on the joke. Especially since Bibi's watching us like a hawk while opening the passenger door to Caroline's SUV.

With an amused scoff, Leo claps Wilder on the back. "Hell if I know. They moved it because they moved it.

What do you think? There's a snowball competition conspiracy?"

"Perhaps the whole town is in on the conspiracy," Bibi puts in, her eyes meeting Wilder's.

He seems to blink off his confusion. "Yes, the Evergreen Falls conspiracy," he says, smoothly once again.

We slip into the car and the second the door closes, I whisper, "Are you okay? You seemed off."

He grips the steering wheel but his expression is blank for a beat before he says, "Just...distracted. I'm fine now."

Yup, I can't fall back into bed with him because we'll both be distracted then. Distraction would be very bad the week before the wedding. "Anything I can help with?"

"I was thinking about..." He takes a long beat, like he's gathering his thoughts. "Just a deal I'm working on. It won't happen again." He starts the car.

"Wilder, I'm not worried about that. You just seemed..." *A little lost in time.*

But I don't say that. I should probably leave it well enough alone, but I want to help him. As he backs up the car out of the gravel drive, I shift to a related topic. "Do you think they know we're up to something? Because we were questioning the timing?"

"No. At least I hope not," he says as he heads down the mountain road.

But that doesn't really ease the tension between us. I'm not entirely sure it's post-sex tension now. It feels like some other variety. "Are you irritated that the town moved the event?"

"No. It's fine," he answers tightly, but then sighs, relenting somewhat as we wind down the curving road toward the town. "I was just expecting it to be in a day or two, and I thought maybe we'd..."

"Practice?" I offer, though that word feels charged now, even if I know he means it genuinely, as in snowball practice.

"Yes, to be honest." He sounds almost sheepish admitting that.

That's sweet. "You really do want to win?"

He slows to a stop at the first stoplight in downtown. "Isn't that the point?"

Yes, that was my goal—to beat Brady. But I already feel like we're on a ship that's drifted away from its destination. I'm not sure why, though, or which port we're headed to.

Maybe it's safest if I steer us back to where we started. We talked about the competition in the car on the way up —Wilder was downright issuing a call to arms against my ex. Wanting to protect me from any Brady gloating, and that was hot as hell. I'll steer us back to that. "Of course I want to win too. I suppose practice would have helped. But we're just going to have to wing it. I'm sure you're good at that."

The light changes and Wilder turns the car onto Main Street. But he doesn't say anything. He doesn't answer as to whether he's good at winging it. Have I found his Achilles' heel? "Wilder, are you not any good at throwing snowballs?"

He scoffs. "Of course I can throw a snowball. Just wanted to practice, as I was saying."

I can't resist. "You really like practice, don't you?"

His expression is stern again as he pulls over, parking the car along the curb next to a toy shop called Play All Day. He holds my gaze, those green eyes like emeralds, shining like jewels. "Certain types of practice more than others," he says, his hot gaze directed distinctly to my mouth, then moving down my body right to my thighs where his face was buried just moments ago. His gaze travels back up and my pulse skitters as he stares intensely at my lips with something like longing. Then, as if it costs him, he raises his eyes, meeting mine. "It's that I want to win...for you."

He swings open his door and comes around to my side, leaving me to mull on that. After he opens my door and we step out into the picturesque downtown of Evergreen Falls, I'm still hanging onto those two words.

For you.

They feel like they have weight to them.

Yes, of course he's doing this competition *with* me. Of course he has his own reasons for faking this romance. But there's something almost carnal, possessive even, in the way he said those two words. He wants to win...for me. Like winning for me means something more than revenge on my awful ex. It's almost...gallant.

But I'm not entirely sure what to make of his admission or if I'm even reading him right. Maybe I need more practice in understanding my inscrutable boss. In getting to know him better.

Yes, I think I'd like that.

Outside the toy shop I stop in my tracks, a few paces behind Wilder, as reality clobbers me with the obvious stick.

Am I *interested* in my boss?

Of course you are. He's gorgeous and brilliant, and he spoils the hell out of you. He's a clever, intelligent, attentive listener, a passionate thinker, and he's a little obsessed with taking care of all your needs.

My heart gallops thinking about the way he listened

on the drive up, the things he asked me, how we talked to each other. Wilder Blaine is caring, thoughtful, bossy, and driven and somehow he's putting all that energy into me.

Yes, I'm attracted to him in all the ways.

But that's a normal side effect of a fake romance. I can't get caught up in this temporary attraction. Especially since I have to make sure this pretend romance works for Wilder too. He needs this plus one. He needs it so badly he told his mother the truth about us.

Time to put whatever this bloom of feelings is all the way behind me. As I drink in the small-town holiday charm that envelops Main Street, something inside me loosens. I relax into the holiday ambiance as we check out the town. Charlotte and Leo lead the way, chatting with my mom, while Leo's talking to my mom's brother, Uncle Rick. Bibi's chatting with Caroline and Everly, while Max holds Everly's hand. Josie and Wesley are peering into storefronts along with Maeve, who's by their side, chatting with Cousin Troy, which is what everyone calls him, as if that's his full name. Christmas garlands and pretty lights adorn every shop, casting a warm and inviting glow over the cobblestone streets. The air is filled with the scent of pine trees and the aroma of gingerbread cookies from the bakery up the street.

I swing my gaze from storefront to storefront, checking out the cute little café with red-and-white-checked cloths on the tables inside on one side of the street, then a general store on the other side, peddling both stockings and sundries to stock up on.

"Do you like it?" Wilder asks the question like it's vitally important that I connect with Evergreen Falls. Like he's created the town just for me. That's a ridiculous thought, of course. This town existed long before he built those cabins. Yet a sense of pride of place rings in his voice.

I look at him, beaming as I answer, "I do. We have some time, so why don't you show me around a little bit more?" I gesture to the end of the block. Our group is already ahead of us. We've got a little space from them. "We can't practice throwing snowballs after all. Might as well just enjoy this town before we're thrown into the competition fire."

Then subtly, or maybe not that subtly, I raise my hand an inch or two toward him. An invitation. His gaze swings down to it immediately. The corner of his lips curves up. And in a heartbeat he takes my hand, threading his fingers through mine.

There's a soft, barely audible sigh of relief that seems to float past his lips.

I don't say anything. I just enjoy the feel-good moment as we make our way through the bustling crowds. The cobblestone sidewalks are dusted with a light layer of snow. Shop windows are decorated with wreaths and ribbons, and children laugh as they rush toward the snowball competition in the town square. They'll go first, with adults competing after.

Wilder points out all the little shops in Evergreen Falls from the Sugar Plum Bakery, to the toy store with model trains chugging around tiny tracks in the window, from the Holly Lane antique shop, to a Christmas decor shop that looks like it belongs in a Bavarian Christmas village —Mistletoe Emporium is the name. He tells me the town has an international flare to it, with residents hailing from France, Thailand, Lebanon, and Canada among others.

The mayor's mother moved here from Japan and met her husband in this town after he moved here from Vancouver, Wilder tells me. "You'll meet him soon. Dan Bumblefritz is the host of the competition," he says.

"Can't wait," I say.

Wilder tells me more about the townspeople—the sheriff's family all moved here from Mexico, after a stint in Texas, and the woman who runs the bakery is from Paris. Ooh la la, indeed. We stop outside A Likely Story, snapping pics of the store's window display of Hazel's *The Twelve Hate Dates of The Holidays.* At the end of the block, Wilder nods to an ice skate rental shop.

"That's Mac's favorite," he says, as he's said each time we've passed a new store, and I laugh.

"I'm getting the sense she likes everything Christmas," I say.

"She's passionate about it," he admits.

I sigh, mostly contentedly. "I like it too."

"Hmm." He sounds doubtful.

"What's that hmm for?"

"I hear some reticence," he says.

He's too observant and really there's no need to hold back now—not after the things he's shared and the way he let me into his world with his mother. "When I was younger, my parents fought a lot, but often around Christmas. Usually over whether Mom was going to take Dad back or not. He wasn't faithful to her," I say, painful memories rising up of the lies he told.

Wilder growls, like he wants to rip my father to pieces. "That's terrible. There's no excuse for that."

"I know," I say, my heart heavy. "He cheated over and over. I wish she'd left him sooner. But she usually took him back. Until she kicked him out for good when

I was sixteen," I say. "But the last few Christmases were always tense. Even when she took him back, there was this undercurrent that it wouldn't last. Pretty sure Charlotte and I always felt like we were walking on eggshells."

"Is it going to be awkward when he arrives? Seeing him here along with her?" Wilder asks.

"No." I shake my head. "I've gotten used to him being who he is. I just...sometimes I hurt for my mother, and for the Christmases that weren't as magical as they could have been for Charlotte and me."

"I'm sorry, honey," he says, with so much genuine concern that my heart squeezes.

He stops outside the Sugar Plum Bakery, searching my gaze, maybe checking to see if I'm okay. And I really am okay. Maybe even a little...amazed at this man and the words he just uttered. Or really, the way he said them. "You said *honey*."

He tilts his head, his brow furrowing. "Isn't that what we decided in the car? As part of our list?"

"Yes, but it felt so..."

I catch myself before I say *real.*

I stop talking. I need to stop reading too much into a pretend romance. That moment felt real because Wilder's good at pretending. Because he's good at everything. Because he's Wilder. But also because he's patently honest—the night we plotted this at dinner at Dahlia's, he vowed we'd be the best fake daters ever.

That's all any of this is and I'd be a fool, like my mother was, to believe in anything more. Even when he finishes for me, asking, "So real?"

Still, I swallow roughly.

He seems to do the same.

"It did feel real, but you're good at this," I say, chin up and cheery, so I don't get caught.

I can't.

He parts his lips, like he's about to say something, but then he rolls them together. He squeezes my hand... warmly. "Or maybe," he begins, running his thumb along the space between my thumb and forefinger, stroking it in the chilly air. "We're good at it."

His eyes lock with mine and something so vulnerable flashes in his irises that my chest aches all over again. My breath comes in a staggered gasp, and I look down at his thumb, grazing my skin in a mesmerizing half-arc over and over. Every sweep sends chills down my spine—the kind of chills that heat you up.

What are we doing? We smash into each other and then we rip apart. We come together and we back all the way off. It's whiplash. Sexy whiplash, but whiplash nonetheless.

"So," I say, returning to the naughty and nice list, "do we both get hot cocoa tonight? Because it seems real and authentic?"

He lets go of that spot on my hand and runs the back of his knuckles along my jawline, and I shudder on the street outside the Sugar Plum Bakery. He keeps touching me even when he says we need to stop. Like he did in the gourmet shop when we got popcorn. Like he did, of course, this afternoon. Like now. He must be suffering from the same whiplash I am. I don't tell him to slow down, though, because I feel soft and woozy everywhere. My head pops. My skin sizzles. And everything is hazy.

"We both win, I guess," he says, then leans in once more and drops a dizzying kiss to my forehead. I close my eyes, savoring the delicious attention.

I'm seeing stars. I grab onto the collar of his peacoat so I don't fall. When I open my eyes, I catch sight of Bibi down the block.

Is she staring at us approvingly?

We resume our pace. But when Wilder takes my hand once more, I can't help but wonder what's real and what is fake.

29

THE REINDEER GAMERS

Wilder

I'm no pro athlete.

I'm the man with the bankroll and the brilliant ideas. The guy who moves chess pieces around. The one who checkmates someone else.

But when it comes to snowballs?

I'm James Bond. I have a license to kill. As a kid I mastered how to peg a friend with a snowball. On winter days, I didn't stay inside and play with spreadsheets or stock sites. I flew outdoors whenever I could and learned how the real world worked.

And here's how it works in a snowball fight—you battle to the death.

It's what we did in the winters when we visited my father's relatives in Reno, one of the snowiest cities in Nevada. That's where I learned to slay the competition. I guess that's the best thing to have come out of my relationship with him.

We're deep into the fight as the sun dips low on the horizon, the streetlamps of the town park flickering on.

Fable and I have outlasted a lot of the other teams so far, including Caroline and her wife, Fable's mom and her husband, Fable's Uncle Rick and his girlfriend, Maeve and Cousin Troy—since she picked him as her teammate saying he seemed like a fierce competitor and he was—as well as plenty of townspeople, like the couple who owns the Mistletoe Emporium and the managers of Play All Day. We even bested Max and Everly, and Josie and Wesley, and those guys are pro athletes. I work with athletes all day long, and they're shockingly competitive. But then, so am I.

Bibi paired up with the town's sheriff, and there's never been a more Bibi moment than that—pure strategy.

But she's out of the running now, and I've got a job to do—finish this off. As I duck behind our snow fort—a picnic table flipped up—I steal a quick glance at my teammate. Her cheeks are the sexiest shade of winter pink from racing around and killing others too. Fable is fantastically ruthless as she packs a snowball nice and tight, then hands it to me, coolly whispering, "Leo's on the move. Kill him dead."

She's vicious, and it's such a turn-on. I pop out from behind the fortress, find the target, and cock my arm, take aim and fire at my best friend.

Bam!

Nailed him right in the shoulder.

Leo groans in defeat. "Are you kidding me, Blaine?"

I fire off a victory grin his way. "I am not. See you later, Whitlock."

I wave him goodbye, and he hangs his head, but he's not a sore loser. He's just having fun as he and Charlotte fold, heading off the field but still watching from the outskirts. Charlotte peers around, looking at Fable, I suspect. Come to think of it, she's been studying her sister more than usual since we arrived, but now's not the time to think on why. Now's the time to attack without mercy.

We're down to the final few players. Fable's father arrived in the nick of time for the competition and announced he was here with a booming, "The father of the bride has arrived! The fun can begin."

Asshole.

He's got a barrel chest and big arms. He has the strength you'd expect of a man with a sturdy build. But he's mostly landed lucky shots so far. He ducks back behind his fortress next to his fourth wife while a woman emerges from behind another one at two o'clock. Blonde hair, pale skin, and a smile I've seen from behind the counter as she peddled sweets, but that customer service grin is notably absent now from Aurora, the owner of the Sugar Plum Bakery. Her dark eyes scan the field like a robot, narrowing in on a man across the park, who's running over the snowy white grounds. She fires ruthlessly, slamming a snowball right into his...ass.

"Got you, Lennox," she taunts, which sounds funnier in her French accent.

"No! Say it isn't so." Dramatically the man crumples to the ground, and she races over and stands above him smiling, a hunter with her kill. I recognize him as a veterinarian from the city with an online series called *The Hot Vet*, but he's originally from this town.

My focus returns to Aurora briefly and then to my teammate who's just packed another snowball.

"Her left side is her weak one. She doesn't cover it," I

whisper to Fable, who nods crisply, then sprints toward the baker, ready to act. With a quick and precise aim, she lets loose a beautiful shot straight to Aurora's left shoulder.

And damn...Fable shoots as well as she lays fake rhinestones on shirts. She knocks Aurora to the ground, but then her father pops up like he's in Whac-A-Mole.

That won't do.

I aim, tossing a snowball right into his leg. He tries to dodge it but he's not fast enough. I take him out cleanly, and he groans loudly, "Are you kidding me? No way. How could you do that to the father of the bride?"

Yup, he steals the limelight. But I got him good, and it serves him right for hurting his wife when they were together. And for hurting Fable and her sister too.

I check to the side, then dart out, grab Fable's arm, and haul her back behind the fort, providing protection from anyone left—two people specifically. *Brady and Iris.*

Fable's breathing hard, her cheeks pink from the cold and the exertion, and she looks stunning. I swipe some of her hair from her cheek, tucking it behind her ear. Snowflakes cling to her dark lashes and her cheeks are flushed with the thrill of the snowball fight. Her competitive spirit is my kryptonite. No, that's not true. *She's* my kryptonite.

But there's no time to linger on my thoughts—not when Brady sneaks out from behind his fort with mischief glinting in his eyes. Iris advances the other way. A surge of protectiveness rushes through me, and my focus sharpens. Without hesitation, I grab a handful of snow and pack it tightly into a snowball. "You get her. I'll get him," I tell Fable.

"On it."

I am not letting him win. No way. Not now.

She darts around the side, and pummels Iris with a snowball. Yes! Now it's my shot. With a swift motion, I rise up, run around the fort, and cock my arm back. I let the snowball fly toward Brady. It sails through the air with precision, hitting him square in the chest. He stumbles backward, shock etched across his face, and then he topples to the ground, whining like the icy missile hurt him.

"Ouch. That was foul play!"

"Was not," Fable shouts, popping up, clearly ready to give him a piece of her mind.

I grab her arm, hold her back. "Let him whine."

"A shot that close has got to be against the rules," Brady moans from the ground as Iris rushes over to tend to his non-wounds while Sheriff Alejandro Hardick trundles across the snowy park, approaching the whiny brat. The sheriff's a sturdy man, with a touch of Texan in his voice and a no-bullshit attitude.

"Hate to break it to you, tough guy, but that was well within the rules. Better luck next time," says Hardick, who's never suffered fools.

"Not fair," Brady pouts.

"All's fair in games and Christmas. Try to be a good sport," the sheriff admonishes then heads over to join the man who's presiding over the Evergreen Falls Annual Best in Snow Winter Games Competition. That's Dan Bumblefritz, the town's mayor who owns the North Pole Nook and Tavern on Main Street with his wife and who loves all things Christmas and competition. He has thick black hair poking out of a Santa baseball cap. They confer quickly, then Mayor Bumblefritz nods and marches across the snowy park toward us with a mischievous twinkle in his eye. "The winners of the first event in the Evergreen Falls competition are..." He stops and asks our team name. We tell him and he grabs my wrist in one hand, Fable's in the other, then thrusts our arms in the air. "The Reindeer Gamers."

From the edge of the field, Leo and Charlotte cheer. So do Doctor Lennox and Aurora, Caroline and the others too, including Bibi and Sheriff Hardick.

Brady just pouts.

Serves him right.

When Mayor Bumblefritz lets go of our wrists, Fable and I exchange victorious grins as we turn toward each other.

Fable's triumphant laughter fills the air around us, a sound that I like far too much. And I feel a little victorious, too, in a whole new way. Making her come was one thing. Winning for her is entirely another, and I want to keep doing both. But the more I bend, the more I'll break, and then what will be left of me come January? When I return to my regular life? To my business and my daughter?

For a long time, I only ever believed there was one important reason to avoid romance—it's nearly impossible to trust. But I never considered how many more reasons there are to swear off relationships. Till now. Because how does anyone live with this uncertainty? With the awfulness of wondering what's next? With these ups and downs?

If I let my heart get involved over the holidays, I'm afraid there won't be much left in the new year. Trouble is, for the first time in ages, I don't know what chess piece to move in this fake romance game.

So I simply hug her, savoring the scent of snow in her hair before I think too hard on what will happen back at the cabins once we leave.

And before I know it, it's time to go.

30

VISIONS OF BANGING MY HOT BOSS DANCE IN MY HEAD

Fable

The kitchen in the main cabin is quiet. The snow covering the foothills gleams through the windows, shimmering against the inky black sky and the mountains beyond. Everyone's retreated to their cabins for the night, so it's just Wilder and me several hours later.

Us and the twinkling lights strewn around the open-plan kitchen, flickering in purples, pinks, blues, and reds as they climb over windows, around doorframes, and along the sliding glass doors leading to the deck.

The snowball fight crew had dinner together at a cute diner on Main Street. I made sure my dad and his newest wife didn't sit near my mom—or Charlotte. I don't want my sister exposed to my father's romance toxicity during this happy time for her. Or his bloviating. I can't believe he thundered into the competition like a conquering hero.

Typical, though—the man has zero self-awareness—but I put him out of my mind.

With the space to ourselves at last, and the clock ticking close to ten-thirty, it's time to celebrate the first naughty and nice list accomplishment.

As Wilder walks past me in the kitchen, I catch the faint hint of his cedar and snow cologne, and it makes my chest ache. He reaches into the cupboard for mugs, his cashmere sweater nice and snug on his stretched arm. Does he even own anything for lounging around? Maybe he doesn't ever relax. I feel underdressed in my leggings and Renegades sweatshirt, but I can't complain about his attire since that soft gray sweater hugs his strong chest and those jeans fit his toned legs so well.

He hands me a pair of matching Santa Claus mugs, and I thank him.

Even if he doesn't lounge much, at least he's indulging in hot cocoa, and I'm glad I can give him that chance since he probably wouldn't take it otherwise. This man deserves a little treat especially after what he did for me this afternoon in the Evergreen Falls park.

That was simply hot.

After I pour the cocoa, I hand him a mug, then lift my cup high in a victory toast. Hours later, I'm still riding high on the way Wilder absolutely pummeled Brady with a snowball. Did I know that watching my protective pretend billionaire boyfriend pelt the world's douchiest ex-boyfriend with a snowball would be so satisfying?

I did not, but it was perfection.

We clink ceramic Santa heads. "You earned this thanks to this afternoon's takedown." I sip the drink and lick my lips, savoring the sweetness.

He moans in appreciation, a rumbly sound that sends a little charge through me. "Tastes good," he says in a low voice, and those words rattle my brain a little.

So simple, but so suggestive too. *Tastes good.*

I hear the echo of what he said this afternoon when he wiped the evidence of my orgasm off his lips—*You taste fucking delicious.* And I shudder all over again, but the tremble is chased with questions too—like how the hell are we going to handle sleeping in the bed we're about to share?

Are we even sharing a bed? I don't think we resolved our couch-bed issue. The only resolution we arrived at is that we both like fighting. Probably because it was foreplay. And I definitely need a distraction from my very naughty and not-at-all nice thoughts.

"Seriously? How awesome are we for that snowball fight?" I try to force my mind away from the sex at hand.

Wilder laughs. "You are shockingly ruthless."

"I will take that as a compliment. Especially coming from you."

"You're a shark, Fable Calloway. And that's the highest compliment."

I preen but then turn the praise back on him as I lean against the kitchen counter. "The way you launched a missile at Brady and knocked him down? I didn't know I needed that in my life, but I'm rating it a ten out of ten."

For a second his expression shifts, his smile disappearing. Something dark passes over his eyes. A storm cloud? A mood? I'm not sure. Maybe mentioning Brady is the wrong thing. But Wilder seemed excited to wallop him. Rather than wonder, I decide to simply ask. "It seemed like you really enjoyed it too?"

With a lift of his brow, he takes another sip, perhaps considering my question, then sets down the mug on the counter. "I'd be a liar if I said I don't enjoy besting my enemies. And he's one of them. Mostly, though, it felt really fucking good to deliver our message, as subtle as it was..." He pauses and levels me with an intense stare as he says, "That he can't fuck with you."

I shiver.

That darkness? That mood? It's his protective side rearing its head again. Wilder is a man of his word. A man who sticks to his guns. A man of pure passion. "You really like doing this to make a point?" I ask, kind of amazed.

His gaze holds mine, long and steady. The air between us is charged. Pulsing even. In the dim light of the kitchen, the world still and quiet, the mountains hugging these cabins, he says, "You have no idea how much I love delivering a message on behalf of the people I care about."

Those words thrum through my body, a declaration, an anthem.

People he cares about...I'm one of those people. He cares about me. The thought is a little electrifying. I'm not sure what to do with it, so I take another swallow of the chocolaty drink. "As much as you love hot cocoa though?" I ask, feeling a little unmoored with him now. Wobbly even.

He takes another drink from the mug as if to test it, his eyes on me the whole time. "Hard to say. This is really good cocoa."

He smiles, the easy, sexy kind. My pulse skips. I blink, trying to center myself. To figure out what's going on tonight, why everything feels hazy, shimmery. "I won't tell anyone the boss had hot cocoa in his Christmas cabins."

"You're going to have to keep all my secrets," he says.

I can't resist. Before I can think too long on it, I say, "What other secrets do you have?"

He eyes me up and down with longing in his gaze. "Lots of them, Fable. Lots of them."

He takes one more drink, then spins around and sets

the mug in the sink, his tone businesslike this time as he says, "I should go to bed."

I—not *we*.

It's like something inside him is pulling and tugging, maybe even in opposite directions. I don't think it's uncertainty. It's more like he's at war with himself. Understandable. I feel that battle too.

"Yes. I should too. Soon though. I'll, um, give you space," I add, in case he wants to get ready alone. "Since tomorrow is a big day in the competition."

That didn't come out nervous at all.

"Yes, it is."

Oh! I spin around at the sound of my sister's voice. I didn't even hear footsteps, and I feel like I've been caught doing something naughty. But you're allowed to drink hot cocoa in the kitchen at the cabin with your fake boyfriend, aren't you?

With her blonde hair falling in soft waves down her shoulders, Charlotte's standing in the doorway, wearing jammies covered in elves.

"Hey, what's up?" I ask, all cool and casual, like I'm totally not thinking about banging my hot boss since I should not be thinking about banging my hot boss, even though Charlotte probably thinks I should, and *why is my life so complicated right now?*

"I was just looking for a midnight snack," Charlotte says.

"Good evening, Charlotte," Wilder says with a nod hello, always classy. "I'll let you two have some time together."

He retreats, and I watch him go till the scent of cashmere and cologne is gone with him and I miss it.

My heart pangs a little. I was enjoying that time

with him.

I try to shake it off, these wants and wishes that have nowhere to go. I turn back to my sister—the reason I'm even here in the first place. I'm about to offer to make her a snack when she gazes at the remains of the hot cocoa on the stove. "That looks good."

"Does this count as a midnight snack?"

"If it doesn't, then I don't know what does. Besides, you've always made the best hot cocoa in the world, so... gimme." She makes grabby hands and I happily pour her some cocoa, then top off mine because why the hell not?

I nod toward the back porch. "Do you want to sit outside and look at the stars?"

She beams. "Like we did when we were kids? Let's do it."

A few minutes later we're curled up in the corner of the outdoor couch, huddled under some blankets we grabbed from the linen closet. I've turned on the outdoor heaters and the electric fireplace. It crackles softly and warms us up in the December midnight air.

We reminisce about past holidays. Our favorite Christmas decorations. Some of our best Christmas moments. Some of them involve Mom. Hardly any of them involve Dad. Maybe because both of them were toxic in their own way, which is why I always tried to look out for my sister. To protect her from their warped notions of romance—my dad's notion that it was okay to cheat and come back, marching into town, bestowing gifts to cover up his sins. My mom's belief that it's okay to just keep accepting...*less* than you deserve.

My sister, though, deserves the best and always has. "What's your favorite Christmas memory?" I ask.

Charlotte hums, seeming to give that some thought.

"Honestly, it's that you always were so determined to make it amazing. I just wanted a nice holiday that Dad didn't ruin," she admits, then lifts her face and meets mine. "You were good at that. You always made sure I had some incredible homemade gift from you. That way if he was up to his usual shenanigans, I didn't have to think about it."

I smile at the sweet side of that bittersweet memory. "It was your favorite time of year. I had to make sure you had the best Christmas."

"Maybe you were the real Santa Claus," she says with a wistful sigh. "I still have that book you made me about amazing things that happened in the year I was born. And the jigsaw puzzle that you had made from a picture of the two of us."

"I hope you didn't keep those hideous matching Christmas pajamas?" I tease. "We took silly pictures all around the neighborhood in them, everywhere from the gas station to the park." I laugh as I trip back in time. "We always had fun." *I made sure of it.*

"And if they'd have a fight you'd take me to your room and we would read or dress up or play board games," she says.

My heart aches for those little girls. "And none of that spoiled Christmas for you? Their fights?"

She shakes her head. "Even though they were sometimes arguing, you and I always had the best time, no matter what. That's why it's such a special holiday for me. That's why I want to keep that going."

"You're making a brand-new memory. You're getting married on your favorite day." My heart swells with emotions, but then a wave of guilt crashes over that organ in my chest. I'm glad she has these fond memories, but I'm still keenly aware of the secret I'm keeping from her. Just like Dad kept secrets. But this is a safe secret. A good secret.

She sets her head on my shoulder. "I almost want to speed up time but I'm still cherishing every second. I'm such a cheeseball, Fable." She lifts her face and meets my gaze, her eyes imploring. "Tell me I'm the biggest cheeseball ever."

I snort-laugh. "Like there's any question about that. You're such a cheeseball but you're my cheeseball. And I'm so happy that this wedding is everything you want."

This conversation right here assuages my worries. I know I'm doing the right thing by keeping my romantic foibles locked up tight. She doesn't need to worry about this side of me—the one that's terrible at love. So terrible she needs to fake it.

I take another sip of my hot cocoa, relishing the night air and this unexpected, sweet moment with my little sister. I'm drinking the cocoa down as she says, "And that's why I think even for a free spirit like you, this new romance seems drastic."

I spit out all the hot cocoa on the deck in a chocolate splotch. "W-w-what do you mean?"

She tilts her head like she's saying *give me a break*. "Fine, I'll admit you and Wilder are weirdly perfect for each other most of the time, so I didn't spot it at first. But then there are these moments where you two don't quite fit. And it happened so quickly—your romance." She sits up straight, stares at me with a serious gaze. "What's really going on?"

Guilt crawls up my throat. I had a sneaking suspicion earlier today that she was onto us. It's so hard to keep a secret from somebody who knows you so well. And if I don't tell her the truth now, when she's asking me point-blank, I'm making the lie worse. I don't like serving up the soft, vulnerable parts of myself—the parts that someone can hurt. But she's my sister. We love each other.

I swallow past the uncomfortable knot of emotions in my throat. Past the guilt. The shame. And that residual self-loathing over the fact that I'm even in this spot, thanks to Brady dropping his drawers for Iris after turkey time.

I didn't plan to tell Charlotte the truth this way, or even at all, but I can't lie anymore. "We're each other's plus ones. That's all," I admit with some reluctance, using the same term I used with his mom, hoping that softens the blow of my lie.

Plus one sounds nicer than *he's my fake boyfriend.* It sounds less like trickery and more like we're truly helping each other—Wilder and me.

Charlotte isn't one for dress-up words. "You mean you're playing pretend. You're fake dating?"

And let's call it what it is.

I wince, feeling a little like my insides are being carved up with my own lies. "Yes?"

She frowns. But it's not like she's mad at me. It's more like she's disappointed. "Why didn't you just tell me?"

I sigh. That's such a good question. But how do I even begin to answer it? At the time, the ruse made so much sense in my head. But now I don't know if it makes any sense at all. "I just wanted you to have the perfect wedding, and I didn't want you to worry about me," I say, hoping my excuse doesn't fall totally flat.

"But I do worry about you. You're my sister and I love you. Why are you faking it?" Legitimate concern tightens her tone.

"I really do like him," I say, meaning it. "We're having a great time together. You shouldn't worry."

With worry flickering across her pretty brown eyes, she asks, "Then why fake it? Why not date for real?"

I wince. "The billionaire and the jewelry designer?"

She shakes her head. "The woman and the man who'd both do anything for those they love—including fake a relationship." She sighs, then hits me with a tough question. "Why are you doing this for me?"

This is so hard. This is everything I didn't want to tell her. My gut churns. "I didn't want you to worry about me on your special day. I didn't want to pull any of the focus from you."

"How would you even do that?" she asks, seeming genuinely confused.

And it's time for the full truth. "I have to tell you something, and I don't want you to tell Leo. I feel like such a jackass for asking that. I know he's your groom and it's a terrible thing to say, but I don't want you to tell him what I'm about to tell you—the reason."

In no time, Charlotte puts two and two together as she hisses, "Brady."

The embarrassment hits me all over again but in a different way this time. It doesn't hurt in the gut like it did on Thanksgiving. It doesn't eat away at me like it did a week or so later when Charlotte told me Brady would be going to the shower. Now, after spending time with Wilder, I feel...rationally embarrassed. Logically ashamed. There's no sting in my heart or my stomach anymore. But it was still a shitty thing to experience, so it still hurts to woman up and say, "Brady cheated on me with Iris at Thanksgiving and I walked in on them," I explain calmly.

Charlotte is not at all calm. Red billows from her eyes. Smoke curls from her nostrils. She's a cartoon character about to blow. "I will kill him now. With a pointy candy cane. Cousin Troy probably has a duffel bag full."

"No doubt, but Brady is not worth the murder rap. Trust me."

She crosses her arms fiercely. "Leo will kill him. Now. Tonight."

"Yeah, that won't cause any problems for your wedding at all if your groom becomes the candy cane killer," I say dryly. Then I pat her hand. "See? This is the thing. I don't want to draw attention at your wedding. Please don't tell Leo. Please don't say anything. I feel terrible asking you to keep this from your fiancé, but I know they're close. They're family and I don't want to get in the way."

"But I hate Brady with the fire of a thousand, million suns burning up his underwear so he has to run down the mountain streets naked in a hailstorm."

I giggle at my sister's dastardly mind. "That is sister love right there. But I can't give Brady the satisfaction of me being the pathetic ex-girlfriend, so he can't know this is fake."

She nods crisply, like a dutiful soldier. "I understand completely. And you know what? This is war. We are going to make sure he does not win the Christmas competition."

I crack up, long and echoing against the quiet night. "It's like you can read my mind."

"I'm not your sister for nothing. That asshole can't come to my wedding and think he can possibly beat you in a competition."

I stage whisper, "That's partly why Wilder and I teamed up. To take him down."

She grins like a nefarious raccoon rubbing its paws together before it plots to topple a garbage can. "That's perfect. And you have my sister-to-sister promise. I'm not going to say a word. But I also want you to know I love you and he can really suck it because I will always look out for you." She gives me a hug and then whispers, "My number one regret now is introducing the two of you. And I get why you kept it from me. I just hope you forgive me for setting you up with him."

I laugh. "Oh, please! You could never have known he'd do that. I didn't think he would either. We can't always tell what people are capable of," I say, though already in this fake relationship with my boss, I'm dead certain he'd never pull a wrapping room move.

"Well, I once liked Brady, but now I officially hate him."

"He's really hate-able."

But the funny thing is...I don't really have very strong feelings about Brady one way or the other anymore. What I do have feelings about? Feelings I'm barely beginning to understand? They're for the man in the cashmere sweater sharing a bedroom with me.

I let go of my sister and grab a towel and water to clean up the hot chocolate. When that's done, I say goodnight to Charlotte and then head to my room, feeling a little unburdened but completely unsure what to expect when I open the door.

Will he be asleep on the couch, like a stubborn man? The floor? Or will he be in the shower?

When I turn the knob, I have the answer to whether

my boss owns anything for lounging around in. He's in a pair of gym shorts and a T-shirt, and he's stretched out on the bed, and my mouth goes dry.

31

I'M DREAMING OF A WHITE CHALET

Fable

I guess it's been decided—the sleeping arrangements. "And I was prepared for you to keep fighting with me," I blurt out.

And oops. Did I accidentally let on that I'm still thinking about the way my boss tongue-fucked me on the couch in front of the Christmas tree? But at least that was better than any of the alternatives. Like *can you please take off your shirt and show me if it's true that there's one billionaire in the world who has ripped abs?* Or, *can you stop being so stoic and let me return the favor because visions of your cock are dancing in my head?*

He sets down the paperback he's reading. "Would you like to keep fighting, Fable?"

He says it with amusement. With a little bit of flirt in his voice. Like an offer. Or maybe I'm just reading sex into everything.

Get a grip, girl. You've had sex on your mind ever since you were pretty much grinding on your boss during a practice kiss.

"No. It's fine. Couch for me, right?" I ask breathily, my head fuzzy from the too-sexy image in front of me.

In a heartbeat, he's out of bed. He prowls across the room over to me by the door, and in no time, he scoops me up in his arms and carries me to the bed, dropping me on it. I'm too shocked to think or speak. He looks down at me with fiery eyes. "In case it's not clear...you're sleeping in the bed. And I'm going to sleep right next to you, behaving like a good boss."

Hello, bossy Wilder!

I've been chastened and I'm loving it. But I also kind of want to tease him, too, so he'll talk that way to me again. "But what if I don't behave?"

He stares at me with wild eyes. Heat flickers across his green irises. He breathes out hard through tight lips. "I guess you'll find out," he says, cool and in control. He's the man in charge, and that tone sends a charge through me. One I want to feel again. One I crave.

With our gazes locked, it seems like we could break once more. We could shatter any second now and lunge at each other. He could claim my lips, pin me down, fuck me into next year. But that's so risky. Even if we were to give in, we'd still have to make it through this wedding, then we'd have to return to work as broken-up boss and employee. Ugh. The aftermath would be messy. I don't need another mess in my life.

I breathe out hard, push up on my elbows, and say innocently, "I'll be good."

He nods toward me, resolute. "You do that." Then he sits on the edge of the bed, shifting focus, concern in his eyes. "Is everything okay with Charlotte?" He's serious again. No more teasing in his voice.

"She figured it out," I say with a frown. "Please don't be mad at me."

His brow furrows. "Why would I be mad at you for that?"

I shrug, feeling more emotional than I should be. It's true—back when we were outlining the rules in his office, Wilder said that I could tell Charlotte if I wanted to. That he didn't mind. But Wilder hasn't told anyone besides his daughter. Yes, he told his mother, but I encouraged him to. I wanted him to. I'm the weak link in this situationship, the hot mess, the girl who couldn't keep a guy. And Wilder? He's so good at everything that he'd never blab about a fake romance, like I'm doing. "I know you said it was fine to tell her, but some people say things and don't mean them."

Wilder reaches for my arm, his thumb stroking my wrist. It's tender, soothing, and it threatens to melt my bones. "Know this—I mean what I say." He takes his time, perhaps weighing his words, sensing I need this reassurance. "I trust you. And I've gotten to know you. You adore your sister. You put all your focus on her. But you also don't want to lie to someone you love that much. I understand."

Words Brady never said. Not when I told him about my dream shop. He never really understood me, but I think Wilder does. "Thank you. I'm doing a terrible job keeping this a secret," I say. "But you're kind to be so supportive."

"It's easy with you," he says gently. His thumb rises higher on my forearm. Stroking lightly. Pretty sure my wrist is a brand-new erogenous zone and his thumb is lighting me up. Flames lick under my skin.

Earlier in town, I wondered if his touching was for show. For Bibi. But it's just us now, and he still can't seem to stop. I feel a little mesmerized, and my voice is feathery as I tell him the details of the conversation, finishing with, "But the good news is she really hates Brady now and wants to beat him too—ideally with a pointy candy cane —and she promises she won't tell Leo."

Wilder smiles, an *it's all good here* style one. "Good. Pointy candy cane or not, Leo doesn't need to know. He looks out for Brady and frankly, he always has. It'll be fine:" Another slide of his thumb down my wrist. Another hazy moment where I'm caught up in my boss's touch. Where maybe he's caught up in touching me.

There's no show now—just him and me and this room that's heating up even without the fireplace on.

Abruptly, he lets go of my wrist, but only so he can reach for my face and run his thumb along my jaw. I'm boneless with the tender way he's touching me. "I don't think I could be mad at you," he says, with fondness but also...some angst. Like something is eating him up inside. Weighing on him.

"Are you okay?" I ask.

"Yes." He swallows it down, and whatever that weight was, it's replaced by a delicious grin. "And we're going to have so much fun destroying him."

He sounds Machiavellian and powerful, and his confidence goes straight to my panties. I'm outrageously aroused. So much so that I leap away from him. "I need to shower."

As I hustle to the en suite bathroom, I wonder how risky

or risqué it'd be to jill off while I'm showering. What a hedonist I am. He already made me come this afternoon and I want to go again. News flash: I restrain myself. But fifteen minutes later, I return to the bed, wearing a cami and fuzzy pajama pants. Wilder's under the covers now, but he pats the pillows for me. A paperback sits next to him on the bed.

"That whole fight earlier over the couch and the bed? We're going to share and that's that, like I said earlier," I say. "But I also liked fighting with you. I mean, obviously I liked your apology. *A lot.*"

His eyes sparkle with dirty delight, but something else, too—something I can't quite name. "I loved saying I was sorry."

I shiver, wanting to say *do it again, be a dick again, apologize all you like*. But I'm a good girl, so I say, "But before the apology? When we were all..." I lift my hands, pretend I'm a cat scratching. "Going after each other? That was...kind of great."

He nods tightly, an admission. "I liked it a lot too. It's a little addictive."

So are you.

But I'm sure now what I'm hearing in his voice. Right along with the desire, there's restraint in there too. I flash back to what he said this afternoon when we arrived. *I don't want to get addicted. To practice.* I need to respect that. Wilder's thoughtful and caring, and even when he's fiery and fighting, he never hits where it hurts. His remark earlier must have been his way of saying once was a slip-up, twice was understandable since it was an apology, but a third time would be nothing but deliberate.

"It is...addictive," I say. But there's nothing to be done about this addiction to him. I slide under the covers. It's past midnight, so here goes this wild next step—sleeping next to my boss.

I try settling into the pillow. Paddling my feet under the covers. Getting comfortable. As if I can.

I'm wide awake, so I cycle back to something Wilder said in the car. Something that's safer than all these rampant sex thoughts. I stack some pillows, then sit up a little higher. "You said it was your mom's dream to go to art school?" I ask, prompting him.

He sets down his book on the nightstand and turns to me. There are a few feet of space between us. "Yes. It was."

"Did you make it happen for her?"

A pleased smile shifts his lips. "I did."

Warmth floods me. A sense of pride too. I'm proud of him for how he takes care of the people he loves. "Of course you did. I had a feeling."

"Yeah? Why's that?"

"You like making people's dreams come true, don't you? You did it for me with the paint-and-sip class. And the suite at the football game. It's your..." I don't want to say love language because that's presumptuous. I pause then finish with, "Your thing."

He seems to give that some thought as he tilts his head, looks my way. "I do like to." He pauses, then pushes forward. "What's yours?"

I go still for a long beat, feeling more vulnerable and exposed than I ever have been with him. I flash back to the day of the wedding shower at his house. I tested the waters, telling him a sliver of my hopes. Well, that's not true. I hardly admitted a thing. He guessed, asking if I had an Etsy shop as a side hustle.

And I held back, keeping parts of myself close to the vest. Out of fear. Fear he'd think I was a disloyal employee.

Fear he wouldn't want to know I had dreams beyond the Renegades. But mostly the fear of opening up and someone trouncing on my feelings.

I opened up earlier to my sister, though, and she's squarely on my side. Wilder's been my biggest supporter for the last few weeks. He's been my protector. He's been my encourager.

I don't have to hide pieces of myself from him. I'm safe with Wilder.

I take a steadying breath. "I want to open an eco-friendly jewelry store someday. In the city. Maybe even a line of them. A handful, then keep growing and bringing my designs to more and more people across the country. I want to change the industry. Make it green. Revolutionize my slice of the fashion world."

I feel so raw. So exposed. So vulnerable. Especially since he's quiet for a beat. Unreadable. He just nods, as if he's taking that in. Then he shifts closer, his eyes locking with mine, holding my gaze. "Made By Fable is a big dream."

"Yes," I say nervously, twisting my fingers under the covers. "Do you think I'm a disloyal employee?"

He shakes his head. "No. Not at all. You're one of the most talented people I've ever worked with. You should do it. I know it'll be a hit. It's an exciting possibility, and I believe in it."

Relief washes over me. Pride, too, from his certainty. His confidence. And once again, his support. "Thank you. I appreciate you saying that. Really, I do."

His lips quirk up. "So a little more than an Etsy shop, Fable?"

"Just a little," I admit, but I'm smiling, maybe even

enjoying that he's caught me in that tiny little lie that was hardly a lie.

"I knew there were bigger things in store for you. Now tell me more about it. What do you envision? What do you see? The Santa cufflinks were just the beginning."

I share more of the type of necklaces I like to make, how I source materials, where I'd want to open the first shop—in Russian Hill. "My favorite place in the city," I say.

His brow furrows. "There's a good block for shops right there on Polk."

I swat his shoulder. "Hey now! Don't go surprise me with a jewelry shop for Christmas," I tease. The man is a real estate magnate too. I need to rein him in.

He cracks up.

"I mean it. Just because I told you, you can't go out and buy me one, like it's fuzzy socks or ice cream. I mean, to you it would be."

His laughter burns off. "I wouldn't treat it like fuzzy socks." Then he holds my gaze. "Thank you for sharing that."

"Thanks for making it easy." I pause and then, not wanting to end this conversation, I say, "What's your dream?"

He smiles, rests his head against his pillow, and parks his hands behind his head. "Being the best father I can be."

My heart catches. My throat squeezes with emotions. Tears prick my eyes. "I think it already came true."

He looks to me, a softness in his mouth, a tenderness in his eyes. "I have to make it come true every day."

"And you will," I say, then settle into my pillow too.

We're quiet for a long moment.

I glance around the suite, drinking in the woodsy decor with exposed wood beams, the Douglas fir tree rising to the ceiling with its strands of colorful lights blinking on and off as we chat late into the night, then a fireplace just for us. It's not crackling tonight but maybe we'll light it tomorrow. Peaked windows offer a view of the glittering mountains. Earlier, I discovered that the bathroom is well-appointed, with a rainfall shower. The carpet is so soft your toes sink into it. The bed is out-of-this-world comfy.

"Wilder?" I whisper.

"Yes?"

"Here's one thing we won't fight about."

"What's that?"

I sweep my arm out to the side. "These are definitely chalets, not cabins."

A smile tips his lips. "You're right, Fable. They are."

32

A HOMEMADE THANK YOU

Wilder

Here's another reason we could never work out—Fable is an inveterate bed hog. She's a dragon hoarding her gold, amassing pillows and sheets and mattress square-footage. She's cocooned in the blankets, lying on her stomach in the middle of the king-size bed, leaving me with a sliver of space.

It's four-thirty in the morning and I'm trying to get a corner of the covers back so I can try and return to sleep. I tug on the red-and-white-checked duvet that she's gripping, vise-like.

Carefully, I pull on the end of the material, freeing a section of it from her greedy hands. But my lovely dragon just yanks it right into her arms again. She's stolen all the pillows too. Thrown a leg around one. Stuffed two under her head.

I try one more time, jerking the cover harder to free

it...when I jerk her right into my arms. She blinks and opens her eyes.

"Are the pirates here for the cans of soup? I don't want any hemp. Close the curtains. I can't take any more flowers after midnight."

I stifle a laugh. Correction: I stifle a laugh badly. Her eyes widen more, and she blinks off the sleep. Confusion crosses her features even in the darkness, then awareness dawns. "Oh. Sorry. I was having a weird dream."

"Were you hogging all the covers in it?"

She glances down, then up at me, inching back a little. "Oops. Guess I was."

"You're the worst bed hog I've ever seen," I tell her but I'm smiling because finally, fucking finally, I have the cure to my Fable addiction once and for all—she's a bed thief, ergo we could never work. I like my bed the way I like it—neat, organized, with just enough blanket for me. This is great. Hallelujah and joy to the world!

"I guess I am," she says, then winces. "I'll go sleep on the couch."

Fuck no. She pops up, but I set a hand on her arm, firmly pulling her back down to the mattress. *With me.* "You're not sleeping on the couch."

"But you're not sleeping at all," she says.

"I'm fine. I only woke up a few minutes ago without any covers. I told you I get hot at night anyway," I say.

She looks down at the tangle of sheets and duvet then quickly untangles them, spreading them out on top of me, patting them to my chest like she's tucking me in. "There."

"You do know this is how we started trying to share this bed? We were both under the covers. Then you, my little dragon, stole them all."

"Why are you smiling then?"

Because I can get over you at last. But I can't say that to her. Instead, I say, "Because you're adorable when you sleep."

"I'm not. I'm a monster, even alone. I wake every morning twisted up in my sheets. Sometimes my pillows are on the floor. But it's been a while since I...well, shared a bed with someone."

That's surprising, given her romantic situation with fuckface a few weeks ago. "Not with Brady?"

She shakes her head. "He never spent the night at my place. I never did at his either."

I'm rarely surprised, but now that's twice in a few seconds. "Never? Why not?"

"He said he slept better alone, and he needed to be fresh for the markets. It was fine," she says, but she sounds stoic. Like maybe it wasn't fine.

"Did you want him to? Spend the night?" I ask in a strangled voice. I'm the dragon now, seething with stupid envy over a past romance. And I know better. I shouldn't ask about another man but this feels important for some reason. Now that I've gone down this path, I'm not stopping.

She twists the covers in her hands, her expression thoughtful as the moonlight streams across her lovely face. "The thing is—I wasn't bothered as much as I should have been. I mean, a man should want to spend the night, right?" She turns toward me, tilting her head, her gaze curious.

My chest aches. A fire roars in me. "If you were mine, you'd be with me every night. If you were mine, I'd tell you how much I want you to stay over." And fuck it. The sheet stealing is adorable after all because...of course it is. "If you were mine, I'd never care that you're a bed hog."

She swallows, parts her lips, then says, "I'd try not to be a bed hog for you."

My heart clutches. So much for my efforts to erect some distance between us. All I want is to get closer to her now. To feel what it would be like if she were mine. I really should try to go back to sleep, so I motion for a pillow.

She hands one to me, then says, "What about you?"

"What about me?" I ask as I lie back on the pillow.

"Did you want your last girlfriend to spend the night? When was your last relationship? Was it Felicity?"

"The last serious one, yes," I admit.

"Why didn't it work out with her? Did she steal the sheets?"

I smile then lift a hand and stroke Fable's hair, swiping it off her cheek. My fingers tingle as I touch her soft skin. I shouldn't do this—indulge. And yet, I'm doing it, and she's...inching a little closer. I answer her with, "We were together for a few years after Mac was born. But in the end, we were better as friends. As co-parents. We didn't have that...spark. We got along almost too well."

She nods a few times, then asks, "You didn't fight, you mean?"

I picture my arguments with Fable in the last few weeks, the times she's teased me, the moments she's sparred with me, then our heated fight earlier—and the filthy, fantastic way it ended. I could fight her and fuck her every day if she were mine. "We didn't," I say.

"There hasn't been anyone else?"

"Some dates. A few that turned into a little more. A couple months here, a couple months there."

"But that was it?"

"Yes," I say, wondering where she's going.

"Do you not want that? Romance? Love? A partner?" She sounds hopeful. Looks it too.

Oh.

Well, it's obvious now that that's where she was headed, yet it's a punch in the gut. Because I don't want to lie to her. But I'm also starting to question everything I thought I knew about romance. I don't have new answers, though, so I try to opt for the truth. "It's not that I don't want it. It's that I don't know if I can trust."

Her hopeful smile falters. "Oh. Sure." Her brow furrows. "Do you—" But quickly she shakes her head, like she doesn't want to go there.

"Do I trust you?" I ask impulsively, finishing her thought.

She shrugs, then waves a hand. "It's silly. Don't answer it."

I don't know how to trust. I don't know how to trust something born from a lie. And yet, here I am trusting her with the things I tell no one—like my feelings about love. "I trust that this agreement is working out well," I say, as diplomatically as I can.

She purses her lips, then nods, like it's hard to stay tough. "It would be. If I wasn't such a bed hog."

She's trying to make light of the situation. I know she is. And I hate going back to bed on such a somber note. "And yet there's no place I'd rather be right now," I say, then run a finger through her hair one more time. I'm a selfish prick, indulging. "I'll get another blanket from the hall closet, my little dragon."

"Good idea," she says, smiling again, and I head to the closet, grab a fleece, and return.

As I walk back to bed, Fable's staring at me with wide, glassy eyes.

"What is it?"

"You're..." she begins, her words like sandpaper. "You're only wearing boxer briefs."

I let my lips curve into a sly grin. "But you knew that. I was lying there in bed with only boxer briefs on. I took off my shirt and shorts while you were gathering your gold."

"I guess I didn't really take it in when I woke up." She licks her lips. "But I'm taking it in now."

That look in her eyes. So much for my restraint earlier. So much for holding back.

Fuck it. Just fuck it all.

I reach the bed, standing at the edge of it, letting her *take it in* a little longer. "Maybe you don't want to steal all the covers then."

I let my words hang there. An invitation perhaps. A suggestion. But really, an incentive for her to share.

"I don't think I do," she says, her smile a little lusty as she lets the covers fall to her waist.

It's like she's lain bare before me even in her cami. All that creamy flesh on display. My bones are tight. My skin is hot. I kneel on the edge of the mattress, ready to climb over her and devour her sweet, lush mouth.

But right as I set a hand down by her face, she presses her palm to my bare chest. Her touch makes me suck in a breath. "You said you were sorry earlier. Let me say thank you," she says.

My brow knits. "What...what do you mean?"

She nibbles on the corner of her lips as her gaze drifts down my body. "You've always said you like my gifts. My homemade gifts."

"I did. And I do," I say, wondering what she's getting at.

She blows me the faintest kiss. "Then let me say thank you for all you've done for me. A proper thank you."

And I'm connecting the dots all right. So is my cock. Still, I have to say the next thing, "You don't have to say thank you for those things."

Even though I really fucking want her to.

She slides her palm down my pecs, over my abs, her heated eyes never leaving mine. "But I want to, Wilder. I want to so, *so* much."

I could say it's the second *so* that does me in. I could say it's the bed we're sharing. I could even blame the romantic snow outside the windows. But I don't. Even though, yes, it's all of those things, but mostly it's *this*—her want.

Her words.

The plea on her lips.

I can't deny her.

I run my thumb across her top lip. "Then show me, honey. Show me how you say thank you."

In a flash, she sets both hands on my chest and pushes me down on the bed. She plays with the waistband of my boxer briefs. "Take it off, boss," she says, and my entire body crackles with electricity.

"You like calling me boss," I observe as I reach for her hand.

"I also like your orders," she says.

Well, then. "Then, *you* take them off."

Like I've given her the keys to a sports car she's been raring to drive, she tugs them down, gasping as she frees my cock.

Her lips part into the most devilish smile. "Oh, yes. I see the stockings have definitely been hung. And I'd like to say thank you for that."

I laugh, but I'm too turned on for my laughter to last long. Besides, if she wants to say thank you, I'm going all in with this game. I reach for her face, running my thumb along her jawline. "Do it, Fable. Thank me with those perfect lips."

She shivers. She fucking shivers, like this is her fevered dream when it's completely mine. I wrap a hand around the base of my aching shaft and point it toward her. "Don't make me wait," I tell her in a rough, demanding voice. "That wouldn't be very courteous, now, would it?"

A gasp falls from her pretty mouth as she slides down the bed, settling between my thighs. Then, she darts out her tongue and licks the head, and I groan so loud I'd be afraid neighbors would hear if we had any.

"Yessss, you're so fucking polite," I mutter.

"But I've barely touched you," she says, teasing me with another caress of the crown with her tongue as she licks off a drop of pre-come.

"And that's about to end. Because I want you to show me your manners," I tell her. "Take me deep right now."

She stops licking only to slide her face down the side of my dick. Holy fuck. She's rubbing my cock against her cheek, and I am shaking with lust. Her eyes float closed as she moves her face, returning her lips to my shaft, then licking down the other side. "I will...I swear, I will...It's just...so good," she murmurs.

I can't take it. Can't stand how good this feels. How sexy she is. How much I want her. I can barely handle the way I'm strung tight in every goddamn cell. The desire to take her, throw her down and eat her, then finger her, then fuck her till she comes all over my cock overwhelms me.

But.

I'd come too soon. I'm already close to the edge. I'm not sure I can last long. I fight off the urge to say *let me fuck you now, honey.* Instead, I say in my most stern voice, "If you say please, I'll fuck your throat."

She lifts her face, meets my gaze, then swirls that wicked tongue around the head one more time. "Please and thank you," she whispers against my cock. Then, she drops down, and takes me all the way into her lush mouth.

Sparks fly across my nerves. Pleasure rockets through my whole body. And Fable sucks me deep, and relentlessly, and urgently. "Yes, fucking yes," I tell her, letting go of the manners game at last. I curl a hand tighter around her head, her silky copper hair falling through my fingers. She reaches up, presses her hand tighter around mine, a signal to grip harder.

I comply as she swallows my dick once more, her hands returning to my thighs.

Her lips are stretched wide. Her head bobs up and down. I guide her along. "Yes, you're so good at that. Look at you. Taking my dick all the way."

The praise seems to spur her along. To suck faster. Relax deeper. Work my dick over and over with her intoxicating mouth. Lust barrels down my spine. My balls tighten. "Don't stop," I command. "Don't you dare fucking stop."

She goes faster with the order, then her right hand disappears...under her jammies and between her thighs. I go up in flames. "You're soaked, aren't you? Bet your fingers are so fucking wet right now. All from you sucking my dick."

On a nod, she moans. She fucking moans against my cock. And that's it. I'm done. My release crashes into me, obliterating all my senses as I come down her throat with a long, strangled groan.

My vision blurs. The world burns away. I am nothing but white-hot lust. And I don't stop moaning for a long, long time.

But I'm not so far gone that I lose sight of one very important thing. When she lets my dick fall from her mouth, I shoot her a wicked grin. "Where are my manners? I need to say I'm sorry for coming first."

I tap her hip, and in no time, she pushes off her pajamas.

"Good," I say. "Now sit on my face."

Her eyes widen like I've given her a Christmas gift. "Yes, sir."

A minute later, she's fucking my face till I can barely breathe, and I'm all too happy to be smothered in her pleasure. She comes hard, loud and beautifully, and I'm certain I'm already addicted to her.

So much that when I gently ease her off me and set her down next to me on the bed, I whisper, "Now give me one more, honey. I know you can."

She blinks woozily. "What?"

"You can do it," I say, then I stretch an arm to the nightstand and slide open the drawer.

"What are you doing?" she asks, her tone dripping with intrigue.

Well, I suppose the truth is—I gave in to all this desire for her before I even got in the car to drive up here. I just didn't admit it till now. I came prepared, after all. "I got you a toy. For Christmas," I say, then take out a brand-new bullet vibrator. With a red nose and two antlers.

Her jaw falls open in wild delight. "Is that a Rudolph the Red-Nosed Reindeer vibrator?"

"Yes. Should we see if it makes you glow?"

She tosses her head back and lets out a throaty, "Won't you guide my sleigh tonight?"

I turn it on then give her another order. "Spread those pretty thighs," I tell her.

She obeys beautifully, parting for me.

I glide it over her eager clit till she's arching, gasping, and moaning. Then, my wild, wonderful woman pushes up to her elbows and grabs my face, yanking me closer, her hungry lips devouring mine as I pick up the pace, finding just the perfect rhythm. In a few seconds, our kisses turn sloppy, and she's clawing at my hair then falling back onto the pillow as she shouts out with something much naughtier than glee.

I sigh happily. A very contented man. Even more so when Fable curls up next to me and says, "Those are the real reindeer games."

"Yes, they are," I say.

After, we straighten up, then we both return to the bed with the fleece I retrieved a little while ago at the foot of it.

This time, I don't set any new rules like *we can't do that anymore*. I don't erect any guidelines to ensure it won't happen again. I've broken them all already. So I simply slide back under the covers with her and embrace the moment.

"Turn the other way," I say. She does, then I shift closer, wrap an arm around her, and press a soft kiss to the back of her neck. She still smells faintly like strawberries and champagne from her shower earlier. I want to hold her and keep her in my arms this morning and tonight and all the nights.

Instead, I try to stay in the moment since all this practice is going to end far too soon. "It's good practice," I murmur, trying to let go of the racing thoughts of the future.

"Cuddling?"

"Yes."

"It is," she says with a sigh.

I close my eyes and breathe her in. If she were mine, I'd never want her to leave.

Later, I wake to the sun streaming through the window, Fable clutching my arm to her chest, and the two of us together under the covers.

33

HIDDEN IN PLAIN SIGHT

Fable

I'm not what you'd call a morning person, but I am a maple syrup person. Trouble is, I'm this close to missing it since I woke up late. I guess two orgasms take a lot out of a girl. Who knew? Not me.

But I also woke alone. Wilder was nowhere to be seen at nine a.m., but that didn't surprise me. He's an early riser, out conquering more worlds. (Or maybe acquiring more toys? Possibly a candy cane cock ring? Some happy holidays handcuffs? A set of ribbon restraints?)

I, however, like pillows too much so I fell back asleep. Then I finally got my butt out of bed at ten. Now I've showered and dried my hair, and my nose is leading me to the kitchen, following the homey scent.

Only I stop short several feet away, hanging back in the hallway to spy on the scene unfolding in front of me. Wilder and his daughter are at the stove, wearing aprons, their backs to me as they make pancakes.

"Can you hand me the other spatula? It's better for flipping," Mac says to her dad as she sets down a red spatula on the counter.

"But that one is the best one," he says, pointing to the red one she's relinquished.

"Nope. The black one is. It's bigger and has more surface area for ideal flippability. I'll show you." She's so much like her father that it makes my chest flutter.

She moves around him to grab the wider black spatula, then returns to the griddle, scooping up a pancake and sending it soaring, up and over.

It lands on the hot griddle with a sizzle. "See?"

He gives an approving nod. "I stand corrected." Then he chuckles. "Also, flippability? Is that a new thing?"

"It's definitely a thing," she says.

"Let me guess—it's a thing you saw online when you were watching videos on pancake making?"

"Are you saying the *only* place I learn anything new is from videos?" she retorts as she gently presses one pancake on the griddle, then does the same to another.

"I don't think I was suggesting it. Pretty sure I was simply stating the truth," he says, dryly. I love that he's a little sassy with her, just like she is with him.

"I learn a lot of things online. I learned about how to make pancakes and how to make Christmas ornaments. About how to live on a houseboat, or in a tiny house, or in a tent."

As he stirs more batter, he tilts his head, looking at her with a hint of real concern. "Does this mean you don't like our home?"

My hand flies to my chest. He's so full of dad angst at the moment, and it's adorable and unexpected. This morning, he was commanding, bossy, and outrageously hot as he wrung orgasms from me and told me to get him off. Now, he's human again, and it's a wonderful sight.

"Dad, of course I do," she says warmly, then wraps an arm around his waist. "I love where Penguin, you, and I live. I just like to see what the world is like. To check out different places."

"You're a true learner," he says.

"Just like you."

And I feel like a true snoop. I've been enjoying this sweet moment far too much. I should make my presence known.

I take a step from the hallway into the kitchen, clear my throat, and say, "Hi there."

Wilder spins around, and my chest squeezes. His apron is red with Santa hats across the bib over the words *Santa's Official Cookie Taster*. When his green eyes meet mine, they flash with filthy memories of early-morning trysts.

Mac turns her gaze toward me then waves her spatula my way. "Want some of the world's best pancakes?"

"Does Santa come down the chimney? Is hot cocoa life? Are Christmas cookies the best food ever? Yes, yes I do. I love pancakes," I say.

"Of course you do," Wilder says, the corner of his lips tipping into a grin. "You have excellent...taste."

Oh yes, his smile is full of...secrets between us. I'm pretty sure this dirty, dominating man is full of innuendo this morning, but I'd like to think he's saying I have great taste in fake boyfriends.

Because I do. Wilder Blaine is sexy as sin, including in the morning with his messy hair and fleece Henley under that apron. His stubble is thicker than usual. He probably didn't shave today, and I don't mind the beard-ier look.

I close the distance between us and head toward the cupboards. "How about I grab some plates and set the table? Or really, the counter. I don't want to get in the way though. I hear there's a big flippability debate going on," I tease, as I reach for three red plates with snowflake trim. Then, because I don't want him to think I was spying, but rather to *know* I was, I admit, "I kind of overheard you two."

Wilder arches a playful brow. "*Kind of* overheard?"

Busted.

"Fine. I definitely overheard since I listened to some of your pancake debate and also the tiny house one."

"I should show you these tiny houses. They're so cool, Fable," Mac says, enthused as she slides several golden-brown pancakes from the griddle onto a serving plate while I grab utensils. I head to the counter and set napkins, forks, and knives down.

"But houseboats are amazing too," Mac continues. "And did you know that some people have really remote cabins up in the snowy mountains and heat them with woodstoves? I'm not sure I'd want to live that far away from town."

"I don't think I would either," I admit as Mac turns around, giving me a glimpse of her apron for the first time. There's a drawing of a whisk on it, captioned, *We Whisk You a Merry Christmas*. "Nice apron."

"Thanks. I found these two here last time we visited, and I hid them for us for this year," she says, conspiratorially.

Wilder chides her, "Mac."

"What's wrong with that?" she asks.

"These cabins are available for others to rent," Wilder explains. "What if the guests needed them?"

But I'm more interested in where she hid them. "Where were they all year?"

Mac smiles impishly, then points to a cabinet. "At the bottom of the kitchen towel drawer. So really they were hidden in plain sight."

"So they weren't entirely hidden then," I say, sitting down at the counter.

"Exactly," Mac says, then pauses, clearly thinking, before she adds, "But if you think about it, a lot of things are hidden in plain sight."

Wilder meets my eyes and holds my gaze for a long moment that tugs on my heart. His eyes are softer now. More earnest. Maybe even vulnerable as he looks at me while answering her. "Yes, they are."

I can barely catch my breath as I try to process his words. Does he mean...?

No. I can't let myself think that. That's too risky. Too unlikely. Besides, he warned me that he doesn't trust easily, if at all. Best that I resist reading something into nothing.

Instead, I smile cheerily. "Truer words," I say as the smell of maple syrup fills the air, and I feel a pang of longing for a family breakfast like this.

Where did that come from? I had breakfasts like this with Mom and Charlotte growing up. Only, were they ever truly like this? Easy, carefree, fun? Weren't we always tense back then, waiting for Dad to barrel in and steal the show?

Maybe that's why my holiday pancake breakfast memories are tinged with stress. Even when we sat down at the table when we were younger, Christmas music playing, the scent of pancakes and lazy mornings filling the air, there was always some unease.

Right now, with Wilder and Mac, I don't feel anything but relaxed as they join me at the counter and we tuck in.

"When did you arrive?" I ask Mac.

"About an hour ago. We left the city really early, but that's okay because I didn't want to miss the sledding competition. It's in a couple hours. I've been practicing my sledding all year so I can win."

This I need to know. "How do you practice sledding?"

"You do it in your backyard. We have a small hill, and there's a section that doesn't have any grass on it. So I hose it down, and it makes it muddy, and that's a perfect way to practice. I worked on my sledding moves this fall, like going backward, sledding sidesaddle, and going down on my stomach," she says, then stabs a forkful of pancake and eats it before she adds, "I mastered them all."

"And my heart was beating outside my body the whole time," Wilder says warmly, but with a father's worry, too, as he ruffles her hair, then squeezes her shoulder.

That flutter? It's more like a swoon as he hugs his daughter.

She leans into him, resting her head against his chest. "I was safe, Dad. I wore a helmet."

"Doesn't matter. I always worry about you," he says.

"I worry about you too. That's why we're a good team," she says, then gestures to my pancakes. "Do you like them?"

"No," I say, then sit up straighter. "I love them."

Mac smiles. "Good." When she finishes hers, she says, "I almost forgot. I made something for you two."

I freeze with the fork midair, then ask, "You did?"

"I did," she says, then pops up and races to the adjoining living room, grabbing something from a bag next to the coffee table as I take the bite at last.

When she returns, she's holding an ornament. It's a ceramic cartoon fireplace with four stockings hanging from it. "For the tree," she says, then hands it to me with a hopeful grin that says she's eager for me to like it.

My heart melts. She's written names on the four stockings.

Dad, Mac, Penguin, and...Fable.

My throat tightens with so many unexpected emotions. My eyes are wet. I run a finger to swipe away the hint of a tear. "I love it," I say, then I hug her too.

This feels too much like the family pancake breakfast I longed for. But I'd better not get used to this warm, happy feeling too much since it'll end when the tree is thrown out.

34

AMATEUR REAL MATCHMAKER

Wilder

After we clean up, Fable turns to me, holds up the ornament, and says, "Why don't we all put it on the tree right now?"

Mac brightens but then takes a beat. "Actually...why don't you two do it and I'll take a picture?"

She gestures to the Nikon she brought that's sitting on the living room table, by the tree. Like she has something up her sleeve, since she always does.

"If you insist," I say.

Fable heads over to the living room tree that's already decorated with department-store-style decor—red and gold balls, white icicle lights, and candy canes that must've been hung by the decorators here at the—fine, okay—chalets.

Fable tests the ornament in various spots, positioning it just so, looking for the perfect branch. My heart does a funny *thud-thud* as she scrutinizes each one carefully. I don't know why I find this endearing, but I do. Maybe because she's strategic in her own way.

After she tests a few options, she declares, "This should be three-quarters of the way up."

I expect her to turn to me and ask my opinion, of which I have none, but she spins around and looks at Mac. "What do you think? Does that feel like the right spot for it?"

Mac gives a very serious nod. "That is the perfect spot. You want a special ornament to have that kind of location."

Special ornament. Yes, Mac has something up her sleeve.

Fable smiles at Mac with a twinkle in her hazel eyes. "Exactly what I was thinking too."

Mac bobs a shoulder. "We're both kind of brilliant."

Fable inclines her head Mac's way. "Kind of? I would say we *are* brilliant."

"No lies detected," Mac agrees.

My chest floods with a warmth that spreads to my bones. But it's not fatherly pride exactly. It's more... familial pride. And it feels damn good.

Oh fuck.

No. This can't happen. I can't get caught up in this homey feeling. I can't let this cozy morning take over my entire being like it's threatening to do. This is merely a fun little moment in our reindeer games. That's all.

I have to remind myself that this—the three of us hanging ornaments—isn't my new future. It's merely an item on today's agenda.

I do my best to shake off the feelings as Fable positions the ornament while Mac brings the camera to her eye. "Dad, stand a little closer," she says.

Yep. She's mistletoe-ing us again, trying to get us together. I chuckle to myself over her efforts. Still, I'll pretty much take any chance I can get to be near Fable. I slide next to her and reach for her hand, and we lift the ornament together. I cover her hand with mine.

Snap, snap, snap.

"Perfect," Mac states.

And for a moment, everything feels terribly, completely perfect.

Best to let go.

I jerk my hand away and hunt around for something to make light of the moment. Like, say, teasing Mac. "So, was that like when you engineered the mistletoe?"

Her mouth falls open. She's utterly aghast. "Dad!"

I can't help it. I crack up. Fable's clearly fighting off a grin too. "So you hung it?" Fable asks.

"He wasn't supposed to tell you," Mac says, indignant, then she shoots me a look that says she can't believe I busted her.

I hold up my hands in surrender. "I'm the worst."

"Yes, you are," Mac says.

Fable walks over to Mac. "Let me tell you something—the mistletoe was an excellent touch," she says, then she shoots me a flirty look. "I very much approved of it."

Thump, thump, thump.

Mac beams. "So it was a good party for you too?" she asks, but not in that lawyer-leading-the-witness voice. It's said in a hopeful tone.

Oh, wait.

This isn't merely Mac playing amateur matchmaker. Is she getting ideas? That this could be more than fake? I don't want to disappoint her. Yes, I brought her in on it, but I never imagined she'd want it to be real.

Like you do.

I shake that thought off too. I have to stop this train before it leaves the station. "Mac," I cut in before Fable can answer my daughter. "Why don't you get ready for the sledding competition?"

She heaves a sigh but then shrugs. "Okay."

She's out of there, racing toward the cabin she's sharing with the other kids. I scramble to take control of the day, the situation, everyone's emotions. Mostly my own. With a fortifying breath, I look to Fable and say curtly, "You don't have to go."

If I see her at the sledding competition cheering on my daughter, it might do even more dangerous things to my heart.

But she must not care about my tone since she pats my chest. "You silly man. I want to."

She spins on her heel and leaves, leaving me with these foolish holiday wishes.

We pack my car, the late morning air crisp and cold, the sun rising higher in the sky. "I can hardly wait for the competition," Mac gushes. "I'm trained and ready."

"You sure sound like you are," Fable says. "But remember, winning isn't everything. Just have fun."

I blanch. "What did you say?"

Mac scoffs. "It's not?"

As she slides into the front seat, Fable rolls her eyes and points to me. "You," she says, a playful accusation. "This is all your doing."

Mac laughs. "Just kidding, Fable. I know how to have fun. But I do want to practice. Practice is so important."

As she buckles into the backseat, Fable looks to me and whispers, "She's just like you."

My heart thunders annoyingly over how dead on Fable is with her assessment. "She is," I say softly, loving how seamlessly Fable fits in and how easily she understands my daughter and me.

Settle down. It's temporary.

Well, no shit. Of course I know that. I mean she fits in well…temporarily.

That's what I tell myself as we drive. We cruise through downtown, passing the shops on Main Street. Out of the corner of my eye, I notice the toy shop, Play All Day. I need to stop in there later for something, when I can grab a minute alone.

We arrive at the sledding hill on the outskirts of Evergreen Falls. Families and individuals are already here, setting up their sleds, laughing, and chatting. Mac excitedly points out some of her friends and cousins who have also come for the competition.

With her gear in place, Mac points to the top of the hill. "I'll get my practice runs in now," she says then takes off, joining the other kids as they zoom down the hill.

At the base, Fable and I watch and by the time Mac begins her second run, Fable's close to me, so we're shoulder to shoulder.

I close my eyes for a quick second. Then, fuck it. I reach for her hand. She's not wearing mittens right now, so our fingers slide together naturally.

Like we do this all the time. Hold hands as we…do life.

Temporarily, I remind myself.

When practice ends, Mac waves, a sign she's ready to start. She turns and heads for the top of the hill. Fable squeezes my hand harder.

I say *fuck it* once more and press a quick, chaste kiss to her chilly cheek. A soft gust of air escapes her lips.

I tear my focus away and put it right on Mac. She's ready and waiting with the other competitors, adjusting her helmet and goggles. All the participants line up, their colorful sleds ready to race down the snowy slope. Mayor Bumblefritz brings a red-and-white-striped megaphone to his mouth and shouts in a deep, booming voice, "Let the sledding competition begin!"

The sleds go zooming down the hill, snow flying in their wake. Mac's sled shoots forward, and she skillfully navigates the twists and turns. A surge of pride fills me as I watch her speed along the slope. She crosses the finish line in first place, a wide grin on her face.

As Mac hops off her sled, I rush over to congratulate her. Fable joins us, a smile on her face as she declares, "You did it! You're a rock star!"

But the part I like best is when Mac hugs Fable and says, "I'm so glad you saw it."

The trouble is, I don't think my daughter's faking. And as I look toward the two of them, I know I'm not faking anything either.

35

THE THREE LUMBERJACKS

Wilder

Sometimes people surprise you. Like, say, Brady. That evening as I'm walking along Main Street toward the town square for the caroling competition, the little troll I want to send back to the bridge he crawled out from under catches up to me.

"How's it going, big man? I crunched some numbers last night and I am ready-i-o to help you out," Brady says, grabbing the chance to schmooze while Fable is several feet ahead, walking with her friends past A Likely Story. Mac's back at the cabins playing board games with her friends and my sister's kids.

"Did you now?" I ask, amazed he can't take no for an answer.

"Sure did."

I already turned him down at the shower. I *could* turn him down again. Especially since the more time I spend with Fable and the closer we become, the less Brady matters.

But then again, this asshole toyed with the woman I adore. The woman who made me a homemade wreath, a crocheted snowman, and Santa cufflinks. The woman who cheered on my daughter in sledding. The woman who insisted on being honest with my mother. The woman who wanted to know what my dreams are.

Fuck this punk.

But if I get to know him a little better, I can learn what makes him tick, and that'll help me as we take him down in the Christmas competition. "Tell me, Brady-i-o. What do you have in mind?"

As we walk, he babbles on and on about his stock management skills and how he's aces. Okay, the man thinks he's good at everything. No surprise. He's cocky, and that means he's likely careless. When we reach the gazebo in the town square, he claps my shoulder like we're best buds. "Admit it—I'm convincing you right now?" he asks jovially.

"That's one way of putting it."

"How about if I win the caroling competition, you'll definitely grant me an audience to make a formal pitch?"

Keeping a poker face, I mull on his offer. While I won't be winning the singing competition—I can't hit a single note —I doubt he will either. I'm quite familiar with the field. I've heard Aurora from the Sugar Plum Bakery, and she has the voice of a Christmas angel. He hasn't heard the others. Once again, Brady's playing chess with the wrong guy.

"Fine," I say, confident he'll lose to Aurora and be bested by his own misplaced bravado. "You're on."

He pumps a fist. "You won't regret it, boss man!"

He's right. I won't. The goal is to take him down, and even if I'm not the one directly doing it, I'm on the right track.

He rushes ahead, catching up with Iris, whispering something in her ear that leads her to smack a kiss to his cheek. I clench my fists. The sight of the two of them pisses me off. Even if Fable's over him, I hate that she was ever hurt at all. That she felt ashamed. That he made her feel small.

All the more reason to compete hard the next couple days and prove that asshole wrong.

A few minutes later, all the competitors are gathered in front of the charming white gazebo, adorned with blue icicle lights that shimmer in the snow blanketing the ground. As I stand next to Fable, I drape an arm around her, making sure Brady knows she's with me now, only with me. Like that, I scan the crowd, sizing everyone up. I recognize most of the competitors from years past. Aurora's here. That's good. She's the race-horse I'm betting on. Fable's dad is here too, and I'd be willing to bet the man can sing. But if he can't, that's fine as well. It looks like there are a couple of new contestants as well—three burly men who resemble lumberjacks. They're all bearded and dressed in flannel and Timberland boots. If they can croon, all the better for me.

Still, I don't want to make a fool of myself in front of everyone, but especially Fable. I turn to her, reminding her of our game plan. We reviewed it earlier today. No matter the song, she'll take the lead. I've heard her sing "Happy Birthday" in the break room and it's top tier. "You're all set to be the lead singer, right?"

"Of course. But why are you so worried?"

I maintain a stoic expression. "Not worried. Just planning ahead."

"Of course you are," she says with affection.

But the truth is—I didn't tell her I can't sing for shit. Maybe she won't notice. My palms sweat a little, even though it's cold out.

Mayor Bumblefritz trots up the steps to the gazebo with his megaphone and declares, "And now, the moment you've all been waiting for. The Christmas caroling competition. We'll assign songs and supply the words on screen, karaoke-style," he says, gesturing to a TV screen set up in the gazebo, "And you'll have to simply...go!"

Fable grabs my arm, her eyes bright. "It's like improv singing!"

Which I hope is for the best since it means only one chance for Fable to hear my terrible voice. "One and done," I say.

"Maybe we'll get 'Let It Snow,'" she adds, then looks up at me. "Snow makes everything beautiful. You can have the busiest day, a million things going on, but when the snow falls, it calms the whole world down."

My heart slams against my chest. We discussed Christmas songs. But she's quoted me back to me. Everything I said. My throat goes dry. My pulse spikes. "You... remembered every word."

"I did," she says, and she sounds pleased. Like she's been wanting to share that party trick of hers with me for some time.

And I almost don't care that she'll hear my terrible voice. Because she remembered. She fucking remembered. And I'd better wipe the smile off my face. I can't let on to the whole damn town that I'm falling head over heels against my better judgment.

I clear my throat and mutter a "thanks" since I don't know what else to say. I'm speechless. Fable turns her gaze toward the crowd. Maybe she's sizing up Brady too? But when I follow her eyes, she's looking at her pack of friends —Maeve, Josie, and Everly. She waves, then makes some kind of funny face. No idea what it means, but when she turns back to me, she shrugs and says, "We have our own language of gestures."

"You can communicate through mind meld, basically," I say.

"Yes. You understand."

I smile. "I do." And I find it utterly endearing how close she is with them. But then it's like my brain stops in place. She didn't look at Brady once. Did she? She didn't check him out to see what he's up to. She doesn't seem perturbed by him. It's like she doesn't even care.

Nope. I don't want to think that yet.

Fortunately, the event begins, giving me a new focus.

I adjust the cuffs of my peacoat as a few townspeople go first, belting out "Jingle Bells," then Fable's mom and Julio hit the stage and sing a playfully off-key version of "Frosty the Snowman."

When her mom leaves the stage, she swings by and says, "I could never resist that one. It's like they know me!"

"You and Frosty are OTLs."

"Hey now," Julio says, with a smile. "Your mom's my one true love."

"Fine, fine. Mom, Frosty *and* Julio," Fable says.

Her mom gives me a little wave. "Knock 'em dead, Wilder," she says, then whispers, "and keep taking good care of my girl. I see the way you look at her."

A pang digs into my chest from the truth and the lie

twined together in her mom's observation, but I say, "I will."

A kernel of guilt wedges into my heart as we return our focus to the stage. Leo and Charlotte bound up the steps, and they duet "Santa Baby" with the groom looking like he's going to be coming down the bride's chimney tonight for sure. Aurora's up next on stage and she sends the crowd swooning with a soulful take on "Have Yourself a Merry Little Christmas."

"One of your favorites," I murmur.

Fable loops her arm tighter through mine. "I still love that song," she whispers.

"I know." I don't tell her I already have it on a playlist for her and I'm waiting for the right moment to play it.

A few more townspeople go, then Fable's father and his wife are up. "And it's 'The Christmas Song' for you," Mayor Bumblefritz says.

Fable's dad crows. "Watch out Nat King Cole. The king of Christmas croon is here."

I...cringe.

Fable winces, then hides her face briefly against my chest.

"Sorry, honey," I whisper just for her.

"Thanks," she says quietly, and I hold her tighter as her father and his wife sing about chestnuts roasting on an open fire while I contemplate whether there's any way I can arrange to have a bag of sizzling-hot chestnuts waiting on his seat at dinner to burn his ass.

When they're done, the lumberjack trio climbs the steps to the stage, forming a makeshift choir. With their deep voices and thick beards, they ooze rugged charm, then launch into a rendition of "All I Want for Christmas Is You" with such enthusiasm and gravelly gusto that it's almost impossible not to be charmed by them. *Almost.* The tallest of the crew is staring at my Christmas girlfriend from the stage.

Staring like he wants to take her home.

Like he wants to unwrap her.

Like he wants her to be his Christmas present.

That won't do.

I'd like to deliver a message to him. I slide a hand down Fable's back all the way to her fantastic ass. I squeeze. *Hard.*

She jerks her gaze to me, then waggles a finger. "You have to make Christmas cookies," she says, like I've been caught in the act.

Right. Our naughty and nice list. *Worth it. So worth it.* "Consider it done."

"I want them tomorrow."

"You'll get them," I promise.

Our moment breaks apart, though, when the wood chopping trio finishes.

Mayor Bumblefritz booms into the megaphone. "Brace yourselves, I think this competition is about to get even more interesting. I'd like to invite my darn good friend, this town's very own Sheriff Alejandro Hardick to the stage with his so very lovely teammate, Bibi Hunter-Shipman!"

Fable cheers like she's on the sidelines of a football game as my aunt and her new friend rock out to "Rockin' Around the Christmas Tree," bumping hips and doing a swing dance.

"They're too adorable," Fable says.

I have to admit, she's right.

When they're done, Mayor Bumblefritz says the words

I've been dreading. "I'd like to invite Wilder Blaine and Fable Calloway to the stage."

As we head up the steps, I groan privately, wishing I could jump ahead three minutes in time and be done.

"And your song is 'Deck the Halls,'" he adds.

I fight off a wicked smile. That ought to be easy enough for her to handle most of it while I *fa-la-la-la-la* my way flatly through the chorus.

But once Fable opens her mouth to sing the first line—"Deck the halls with boughs of holly"—my stomach drops. I can't hide behind her voice. She's so damn good that the contrast is only going to be more evident. Her singing is full of energy and sass because of course she's full of energy and sass. The best I can do is make my flat delivery seem deliberate. Like I'm deadpanning my way through the chorus all while she carries us through the season to be jolly.

When we're mercifully done, she pulls me aside behind the gazebo, out of the way. "You're human, and I like it."

My pulse speeds up, and this time it's not from nerves. "Yeah?"

"I do. You can run a football team. You can launch a fantastic hotel. You can speak Mandarin, and you can give me screaming orgasms. It's okay if you can't hit a single note."

The last thing I suspected was that my terrible singing voice would turn her a little sweeter on me. My stupid heart squeezes and a warm, heady feeling spreads through my body, and my mind too. But I remind myself that nothing is coming of this fake romance. Nothing can come of it.

Trouble is her adorable response does nothing to stem

the tide of my feelings for her. Feelings that are getting annoyingly stronger by the day. Feelings that I'll have to put out of my mind once this ends.

But...not yet.

I have a few more days here to savor this fake romance.

I drop a kiss to her cold lips and warm them up for several seconds that go to my head. I nearly ignore Mayor Bumblefritz's next words as he calls Brady and Iris to the stage then assigns them "Joy to the World."

Brady'll botch it, I'm sure. He'll bumble his way through it. Iris will probably sound like a screechy starling. When Fable breaks the kiss, I decide I'd like to watch them be eviscerated by my chess strategy.

We return to the front of the gazebo where Brady's on stage, his eyes twinkling with confidence and mischief.

Good luck.

"I've heard your carols, but you haven't heard ours," he says, then takes his phone from his pocket, sets it on the stage to presumably record himself, then reaches for Iris's hand.

Please.

But then he launches into a powerful rendition of "Joy to the World" with a voice that's richer, deeper, and smoother than I'd expected.

What the hell?

The man is like one of the three tenors, and I do regret taking his bet. Also, because...she's humming. Iris is simply humming, dropping in an occasional background *ooh* or *aah* to provide the subtlest harmony. Why didn't I think of that? I could have hummed while Fable fa-la-la-la-la'd.

But he can sing and they can strategize and once

again, the man has surprised me with what comes out of his mouth.

He's annoyingly good as he belts out the tune like he's a show-stopping Broadway star. When they finish, there's no question who's winning the caroling competition.

My fears are confirmed moments later when the mayor announces the judges committee has voted Aurora in third, Bibi and Hardick in second, and Brady and Iris in first place.

"Told you I was going to dom-i-nate," Brady shouts, pumping his annoying fist.

"You sure did, babe," Iris seconds, cheering him on. He snaps a victory selfie of the two of them.

I didn't think it was possible to hate him more, but I do. Not only did he beat me at my own game, he used his very own words from Thanksgiving—the day Fable discovered him cheating. I hate that Brady's a much more formidable competitor than I'd thought he would be. "I can't believe it," I mutter to Fable, then meet her gaze. "I won't let him win the next one."

Her smile is soft, a little placating. "You're cute when you're jealous—"

She doesn't get to finish the thought though. Leo has found me in the crowd, and he claps me on the shoulder. "Mind if I steal the best man?" he asks Fable.

"Go ahead," she says, then makes her way toward Josie and Wesley.

Leo nods to the edge of the square where a makeshift bar's set up. "My cousin has a few talents. Singing's one of them. Let me get you a scotch to make up for it."

He's the groom so I say yes, heading toward the towering ancient oak in the town square, where a bartender from the North Pole Nook mixes drinks at a red wooden cart. Leo asks for two glasses of scotch and a minute later, the man hands them to us. The warmth of the drink seeps through me, dissipating some of my irritation, but not much, since the competitiveness in me still burns. But it's not my place to rain on Leo's pre-wedding parade so I set my own feelings aside.

"Your big day is soon," I say, lifting my glass in a toast. "Have I mentioned how happy I am for you?"

His smile is wide and genuine. "Thanks. And things are going well with Fable?"

I don't quite squirm, but I come close. Even though I don't want to tell him the truth—that it's fake—neither do I want to lie. I weigh what to say, then it hits me. I don't have to lie, exactly. "They're going great."

Last night was great. That's true. This morning was great as well. The moment next to the gazebo was even greater.

"I'm happy for you then." He pauses. "Do you think this could turn into something more...?"

What a good question.

Across the snowy square, I gaze at Fable for a long beat, picturing something beyond Christmas. Maybe in some other world, I would make pancakes with her in the morning and we'd say goodnight to my daughter together in the evening. We'd venture up here for the holidays. I'd come to the opening of her first jewelry shop, and she'd cheer for her favorite team from a suite.

And we'd curl up on the couch together next Christmas Eve, turn on some music, and look at the twinkling lights of the Christmas tree.

Before I fucked her under it.

I shake off those dirty and wonderful thoughts. I'm not

equipped for that type of romance. For that type of trust. For all that uncertainty.

Except as my brain repeats those familiar refrains, I think about earlier when she remembered all the details of my favorite song. I think, too, about how she found it endearing that I can't sing. I think about the way she interacts with my daughter. And I wonder for the first time ever if I *could* live with all this terrible, horrible uncertainty of a romance that makes my heart beat like crazy from one minute to the next when I'm near her.

Could I?

I owe Leo an answer though. I can only give a vague, "It's hard to say."

It's getting hard, too, to balance the lies I tell people. Fable's mother. Bibi. Leo. But if this were real, I wouldn't have to lie anymore.

But that's a dangerous thought. Besides, it won't happen.

I try to shake it off when my attention snags on the gazebo. I do a double take.

Fable's no longer chatting with friends. Instead, one of the lumberjacks is talking with her. And he's standing far too close for my taste. That won't do. "Excuse me," I say to Leo, setting down the glass on the makeshift cart.

With the lumberjack in my crosshairs, I stride toward them. A wave of possessiveness slams into me, filling every cell. I grit my teeth. My jaw tenses. I'm a predator, ready to fight. I've never felt this way about anyone before, but whether we're real or fake, there's no way I'm letting another man come between us.

The lumberjack seems oblivious to my approach, still engrossed in his conversation with Fable. Fable's eyes sparkle with interest—but it's only polite interest. When she spots me, she gives me a weak smile that doesn't quite reach her eyes as she shakes her head at him.

I move faster. When I arrive, she pastes on a smile and says to me, "Joe was just telling me why the New York Leopards are a better football team than the Renegades, and I was schooling him. Then he wanted to discuss it over a beer."

I drape an arm around her, tugging her against my side. "My girlfriend is not available to have a beer with you. She's with me. Only with me."

The man holds up his hands. "Chill, man."

Are you kidding me? I narrow my eyes. "It's not a *chill, man* situation. It's a *she said no* situation," I say calmly and clearly as I stand my ground.

"How do you know she said no?"

The nerve. The fucking nerve. I inch closer to him, making sure there's no mistake when I say coldly, "Because I know."

He blinks, swallows, then holds up his hands again and backs off. "Sorry, dude."

When he leaves, Fable turns to me, her eyes etched with shock. "Possessive much?"

"Yes," I say, still breathing fire.

Her breath seems to catch. "I had it under control," she says, but her voice is wobbly.

"Of course you did, honey," I say, gentling my tone for her. "But so did I."

"You did," she says, breathily. She takes a beat, studying my face, seeming to weigh something up. "Like I said earlier, you're cute when you're jealous."

"Cute?"

"Like you were about Brady. But you really don't have to worry about my ex. I'm over him."

I knew that, yet I didn't know how much I needed to hear that from her till now. "Good. That's very good," I say, relieved and maybe a little elated.

She slides closer to me, runs a hand over the top button on my coat. "But I'm not over the way you like to control things," she says in a sensual tone.

"You're not over it?" I ask, picking up what she's putting down.

"Not at all." She hesitates, then her eyes flicker with avid interest. "I think I'd like to know more about what you like to control."

Fuck all the other guys. I seize the moment and cup her cheeks. "Let me take you back to the chalet and show you."

36

SHE COMES PREPARED

Wilder

I've wanted to do this for a long time.

But I don't want to rush a damn minute of my Christmas fantasy. So even though I'm dying to push her up against the wall and devour her lips the second we return to the cabin, I point to the hallway instead.

"Go to our room. Take off the sweater and jeans, strip down to just your bra and panties. And then I'm going to remind you that you're mine till the end of the year. I'm the one who takes you out for drinks. I'm the one who flirts with you. I'm the one who makes you laugh. And I kiss you and I fuck you and then make you come more times than you think you can handle."

She trembles. "How many do you think I can handle?"

I lean in close to her, catching a hint of her strawberry and champagne scent, barely brushing my lips to hers. "We'll find out soon," I say in a whisper against her sweet mouth. "But I have faith in you. You can handle a lot."

She gasps. "I think I can too."

"I had a feeling." I tip my forehead toward the hall and in my sternest voice, I say, "Now go wait for me. And that's an order."

She scurries down the hall, tugging her sweater over her head as she does. When she reaches the door she stops, tosses the garment dramatically up in the air, then catches it. She juts out a hip, striking a sexy pose, and flashing me her candy-cane-striped bra.

Her candy cane bra.

My brain scrambles, then puzzle pieces slide into place. I clear my throat. "Did you bring that with you?"

She shrugs saucily. "You're not the only one who came prepared."

She saunters into the room leaving me with that fresh new bit of intel—she packed sexy lingerie. *For me.*

Fable plays these bedroom games by my rules, but also by her own. My chest tightens, and a new emotion crawls up my throat. Something different—something not quite familiar.

Something I'm not sure I've ever felt.

I think...I'm fucking in love with her. She's obedient and fiery all at once. I drag a hand through my hair. What the fuck do I do?

But that's a problem for tomorrow.

With her in the room, I shove these dangerous thoughts into a drawer and slam it shut. I head toward the main living room and into the adjoining cabins, where Bibi will surely have brought her wrapping supplies.

I'm quiet, padding on the soft plush carpet, finding what I'm looking for right on the table in front of the couch in a little sitting room.

A large spool of red satin ribbon.

Perfect. Absolutely perfect.

I grab it as my aunt comes around the corner in her red plaid pajamas. "You're looking for ribbon to wrap presents?"

Not exactly. However, I didn't expect to see her so it takes me a beat before I say a confident, "Yes."

But in that pause, she busts me, her lips curving into a grin. "I hope you have scissors, then, and a...*fun* word to use just in case anything gets to be a little too much," she says, handing me a pair of scissors.

Are you kidding me? My aunt is giving me advice on light bondage?

"Thank you for the tip," I say evenly, trying not to give anything away, even though I probably have.

"And to think I had a dream that you were putting me on with your romance," she says. She doesn't sound strategic. She sounds...happy. "But I suppose it was wrong, as dreams sometimes are."

Actually, she sounds utterly delighted to be wrong.

I swallow, embarrassed, and maybe even ashamed. We were putting her on. Now tonight feels all too real.

The lines between real and fake are blurring far too much for me to keep track of.

My head hurts in a whole new way, and for so many reasons it's best if I leave—mostly, though, because of the woman in my bed. "Bibi, I hope you understand I have something else to do right now," I say.

Her smile is magnificent as she shoos me off with a "Go, go, go, go, go."

As I return, a new awareness hits me. Bibi's a lot like Mac. She likes my fake girlfriend far too much. She likes the possibility of a real romance.

I can't believe I didn't see this coming. When the holidays end, I'll be disappointing both of them.

But for tonight I'm going to wrap up Fable like the present she is.

I go to the room.

All thoughts of this ending fall from my head when I see her spread out on the sleigh bed, arms above her head, copper hair fanned out on the white pillows, creamy skin on display, and a very naughty smile coasting across her pretty lips.

And...all those red-and-white stripes on her body.

I drink in the scene.

My fake girlfriend brought sexy lingerie for me. She also turned on the lights to the Christmas tree and flicked on the fireplace. It's crackling. She's set the scene and all that's left is the playlist I made. I take out my phone and hit start. Tinashe fills the room.

Then, I advance toward the woman of my fucking dreams.

37

ONLY A BOW

Fable

Never have I ever worn a big, red decorative satin bow and nothing else. Until tonight.

I'm all wrapped up on the sleigh bed, a surprisingly soft ribbon traveling around my back and tied in a big, looping bow under my breasts, boosting them up. My hands rest right under them, crossed together. I can wiggle my fingers, but I can't move them since Wilder's tied my wrists together using long ends of the big bow. The material's thick so it doesn't dig into my flesh.

My breath comes fast and he hasn't even touched me. Well, besides to wrap me up. His fingers trailed across my skin the whole time, making me shiver every second. Translation: I'm so ready for him.

He stares wantonly down at me, then licks his lips. "Safe word. We need a safe word."

I give it some thought, but one comes quickly. I arch my hips slightly as I say, "Rudolph."

"Perfect." He tips his forehead to the nightstand. "There are scissors there just in case."

I'm not worried I'll need them, but I'm glad he's prepared. He's prepared for everything.

Wilder slides off the bed, standing at the foot of it, staring at me and looking hot as fuck. He's wearing jeans and a cashmere sweater, and he's so sexy I can barely stand it. Tall, powerful, deliberate.

Everything about him is purposeful. Every move he makes is intentional.

This is a man who knows what he wants, and I've never felt so desired as when he stares at me.

He is the opposite of...everything I've experienced.

I never felt this way with Brady. I never felt this way with anyone I've ever dated. I've never felt this kind of fiery gaze. This kind of need. This kind of desire from a man.

A cover list of sexy Christmas tunes plays from his phone as he shakes his head in admiration as he seems to eat me with his eyes. "This," he begins in a smoky drawl as he regards me, "this is what I asked Santa for."

A shudder runs down my body. "Me naked on a sleigh bed?"

"Yes. Because I want to unwrap you like the fucking gift you are."

A wave of heat crashes over me from those words. Wilder doesn't dirty talk like he's reading routine filthy lines fed to him from AI. Everything he utters feels like it's just for me. "I can't wait," I say.

"But first I'm going to remind you that you're my gift. My present. *Mine*," he says, as he tugs off his cashmere sweater, revealing a white T-shirt that shows off his muscles and toned chest.

I shiver from the possession in his tone. So single-minded. So certain. "How are you going to remind me?" My voice is feathery. I feel like I've been on edge all night, and I don't think that's going to end as he yanks off the shirt next, tosses it to the floor and climbs back onto the bed, shirtless and glorious.

His skin is toned and tan, and the tattoos on his forearms are on display—abstract designs that I keep meaning to ask about. But I haven't yet. Right now, he doesn't look like he wants to talk. He looks like he wants to do something else entirely with his mouth.

Because I'm learning something private about my boss.

He *really* likes to eat.

He slides his hands along my ankles, up my calves, and to my thighs as he spreads me open. "But I'm not going to unwrap my gift just yet." His gaze is molten, his words gravelly. "I just want to...taste it."

I moan and he hasn't even touched my pussy. But I'm ludicrously wet for him.

He spreads my legs as wide as he possibly can, humming approvingly. "What a pretty pink gift. And I like my presents wet." He rubs his trim stubble against the inside of my thigh, and I gasp. "And glistening." He blows a stream of air against my eager clit. "And very, very horny."

"You've got your wish," I say, aching for him.

"Yes, I really have," he says, like he's mesmerized with me. On a growl, he buries his face between my legs and French kisses my pussy. The relief is instant and electric. Delicious heat spreads inside me as I throw back my head against the pillow.

My hands are bound at my chest so I can't grab his

hair, but I can arch my hips. And I do, shamelessly begging him with my body.

He laps me up, his tongue stroking up and down and flicking delirious circles around my clit. I groan and writhe—it's just so good. Then he flattens his tongue and gives a long, thorough lick before he thrusts his tongue inside me. It's like a circuit breaker fries inside my head and pleasure pops everywhere.

"Please, please, please, please, please," I chant.

He stops, looks up innocently. "Please what?"

"Give me more than I can handle," I beg, breathless with lust.

He returns to my thighs, murmuring, "Gladly." Then he devours me till I come so hard my vision blurs and my brain goes offline.

A minute later, when I open my eyes and blink off the haze of pleasure, Wilder's rising to his knees. He wipes his hand across his very satisfied mouth, then wastes no time dropping that same hand between my thighs and gently stroking me.

I flinch, since I'm still sensitive from the orgasm.

But he's determined. "How about another?" he says, slowly building me back up, taking his time with long, tantalizing brushes of his talented fingers. "Think of it as *my* gift too."

"My multiple orgasms are your gift?"

His grin is wolfish. "They really fucking are, Fable."

"It is Christmastime, I suppose," I say playfully.

He takes my *yes* and slides two fingers inside me. In no time, I'm grinding down on him, fucking his hand as he plays me once more and sends me over the cliff a few minutes later.

I'm desperately trying to catch my breath when he

eases out his fingers and climbs over me. Bracing his palms on either side of my body, he gazes down with the most unguarded look in his eyes. "God, you're so fucking beautiful," he says in a rasp, then he crushes his lips to mine in a hot, passionate kiss that feels different from the ones that have come before.

As he consumes my mouth, I try to pinpoint the difference. To figure out what's changed. But it's hard since my brain is all neon. I'm not thinking in words. I'm thinking in brilliant colors. In wild sensations. Everything feels more intense with him. Everything feels like we mean it. Like we've pushed past that practice phase. Like we're taking all the things we truly want. And I want everything that Wilder wants to give me.

When he breaks the kiss, I look up at him. His lips are bruised from kissing me, and his eyes are wild. But they're also...soft. Filled with raw desire, but also some tenderness that makes me feel like every word he said tonight is so true.

I don't normally let down my guard. I don't like to show the softer parts of myself for fear someone could hurt me like Brady did. Like other guys I've dated have done before. But right here, in bed, I feel safe with Wilder —safe with him and with my desires. I hardly care about the reasons we started our fake romance. I only care about these very real feelings right here, right now. "Do you want to unwrap me...and do whatever you want to me?" I ask, my gaze drifting down to the big bow, knocked a little out of place but still wrapped tight enough under my tits.

He growls. "I really fucking do." His tone is raw and earnest. Then he runs a hand along my face, a reverent gesture. "Thank you for trusting me."

It's only a bow, I want to say.

But it's not only a bow. It's letting someone in, and that's not my strong suit. But tonight I've gotten a little bit better at it. "I do trust you, but I want you naked too. Now, why don't you strip for me. I would do it myself," I say, then wiggle my fingers, "but I'm all tied up."

"Don't you dare unwrap my gift," he warns in a commanding tone.

He hops off the bed and takes his sweet time flicking open the button on his jeans, then unzipping them and pushing them down.

When he gets down to his boxer briefs, my tongue darts out, and it doesn't go unnoticed by Wilder.

"You like that, don't you?" he asks.

"Yes. Your dick is a fucking present," I say, then feeling daring, I add, "Tastes like a present too."

His breath hisses. "Your beautiful filthy mouth...It looks so pretty with my cock in it." He pushes his boxers down, his thick, hard cock springing free and pointing my way. "But you don't get to suck it tonight."

"What do I get?"

"What you need," he says with authority.

I shudder. I need him to fuck me so badly. And I don't want to keep that thought to myself. Here in bed with him, I can speak the truth of my heart. "I want you to fuck me so badly," I say, and I can't believe I've said that, but it feels so good.

His eyes squeeze shut for a second like this is hard for him. Like he has to collect himself. When he opens them, he says, "You have no idea how much I want you."

But one look at his cock, leaking at the tip, and I think I do know how much. He crawls between my legs, his hard dick bobbing. He takes his time tugging on one end of the ribbon to undo the bindings on my wrist. When the fabric falls to the bed, he reaches under my breasts and starts to free them too, unknotting the bow. "I have wanted to unwrap you for so long," he says, his tone a shade of desperation.

"Since we started this?" I ask impulsively. Because I have to know. I can't leave that confession untouched.

He swallows, pauses, and I'm pretty sure he's about to say yes. Instead, he says, "Well before that."

Then he shuts up and finishes unwrapping the red satin ribbon, leaving me with that admission. My friends were right. He's had it bad for me for a while. But how long? Since before Brady?

The thought makes my breath catch. My mind whirls with this new information. My body aches with this fresh want. When he's freed my hands, I sit up and rope my arms around his neck, pulling him close. We're tangled up together, kissing so deeply it feels like we could last well beyond the holidays.

I don't know what to make of that thought so I focus on the physical, on the way the kiss turns into a white-hot ache right between my thighs. I break the kiss, panting, "Fuck me now."

He grips my chin roughly. "You don't give the orders. I do."

I grin wickedly, arousal gathering between my thighs. I'm so turned on I can feel wetness sliding down the inside of my thigh. "Then order me around."

"Get on your hands and knees."

I comply, and I wait for him to line up behind me. But first, he grabs the ribbon, and...

Oh.

When he moves behind me, he adjusts my legs, and ties up...my ankles, each one separately, leaving just enough ribbon in between so they're a foot apart. "Down onto your elbows," he commands.

I sink down, craning my neck to watch him the whole time as he grabs a condom, slides it on, and notches the head of his cock against me. His jaw tightens, like he's at war with himself, then he seems to lose the battle. "I've wanted you for so fucking long," he says then shoves his cock into me and fills me all the way.

I cry out with pleasure.

"Wanted to fuck you when it's snowing. Wanted to kiss you by the fireplace. Wanted to taste you," he says, and I'm overwhelmed by the pleasure and the admission.

"Don't stop. Please don't stop," I say.

He eases in then out, his hands gripping the flesh of my ass as he finds a rhythm that matches the flickering of the lights on the Christmas tree. With a passion that mirrors the sultry tone of the music. With a lust that's stronger than the crackling fire.

We smash all our fake romance guidelines that we set long ago. We throw out the dating handbook. We move together like we *are* together. He covers my back, grabs my chin, turns my face, and kisses me as he fucks me.

It's hot and deep and burns to the center of my soul. I want to spread my legs, but the ribbon's keeping them in place, so it's like I can't escape the sensations, the building of the orgasm I have no control over.

He hits a spot deep inside me over and over again. I'm close, so close, and I don't want to lose it, so I tell him urgently, "Use your fingers."

"I'll accept that order." He slides a hand between my thighs and strokes my clit as he fucks me deep and hard into the snowy night.

In seconds, I'm clawing at the sheets, shaking, and then falling apart beneath him.

I expect him to follow me there but he doesn't.

As the aftershocks ripple through me, he eases out, unties me, and flips me over in seconds. He pushes my knees up to my chest and settles between my legs, looking down at me like a man unleashed. Like a man who thinks I'm his.

He fucks me like I am his.

And he feels like mine as his body jerks, shakes, then stills before he collapses on me with a smoky, soulful, "You."

I don't know what will happen tomorrow. I don't know what will happen when we leave these cabins. But for now and the next few days, I think I like this filthy Christmas magic.

I like it more than Christmas revenge.

* * *

Later, when we're cleaned up and sliding under the covers, I say, "It really doesn't matter that you can't sing."

"Why is that?"

"Because you fuck like a rock star."

* * *

In the morning as sunlight streams through the window, I expect Wilder to be off buying a new hotel or striking a clean-energy deal on a Sunday morning.

What I don't expect is him to grab his ringing phone from the nightstand, while grabbing his clothes, and answering, "What's wrong, Victor?"

A chill sweeps over me. That's his dad's friend.

38

SOME KIND OF METAPHOR

Wilder

Victor's name on the screen alone sends a flash of fear through me, so I brace myself for bad news as I snick the door shut.

"Hey," I say as I yank on jeans and shoes, then jerk the phone away from my head to pull on my sweater, nearly getting my arm stuck in the neck. "What's going on?"

"Just wanted to check in," he says in his diplomatic way as I beeline to the living room.

"Thanks. I'm okay." When I reach the sliding glass door, I jerk it open and head onto the deck, then move past small talk to get to the heart of the matter. "What's going on with Dad?"

"Just wondering if you've heard from him?" Victor asks as I pace across the deck in the cold of the Evergreen Falls morning. It's chilly since it's late December, but this was never going to be a warm and fuzzy call anyway.

"No. I haven't heard from him," I answer, but I'm

always ready for bad news when it comes to my father. To hear he hurt himself. He lost stomach-dropping amounts of money. He's in jail. He's dead. "I take it this means you haven't?"

"It's been a few days. But last night I got word from my friend Diane Diamond over at Desert Springs Casino that he got caught counting cards."

I groan, dragging a hand through my hair. "Are you kidding me? He's cheating now?"

Victor sighs, long and resigned. "If you believe what they say."

He's a nice friend. That's kind of him, to not crucify him without evidence. That's friendly of him, to hedge his bets. But I believe what they say. It's exactly what Dad would do. "Let's assume it's true for now. What does this mean exactly?"

I should know since I got started in the hotel business in Vegas. After I invested well in some startups, I had enough capital to bulldoze some of the shitty, rundown hotels in Vegas and build big, beautiful ones. I got my start by razing the kind of places where my dad plays cards. I'm sure there's a metaphor there. A childhood wound I'm trying to heal from. Right now, though, I just want to know what the fuck is going on.

"It means he's not welcome at Desert Springs anymore," Victor says. "And you know how people talk."

"Yes, I do." Casino managers will tell other casino managers, and that'll make it harder and harder for him to play. Which means he'll probably become even more desperate. Which means who the hell knows what he'll do to get his fix? "Give me a shout if you hear from him. I can try him as well. Maybe he'll pick up if I call."

"That'd be good. Why don't you give it a shot?"

"I can do that," I say. At least it's something. "I'll call his apartment complex and see if he's at his place."

"Let me know what you find out."

"Count on it."

The second I hang up, I try my dad. He doesn't answer. I send him a text. I make a couple quick calls to people I know in Vegas. People who might know him or know where he is. The manager of the apartment complex. The woman who lives next door. Nobody's seen him, but I ask for them to let me know as soon as they do.

A sick feeling twists in my gut, but then a voice slithers in my ear, saying, *"He's fine. He's done this in the past. He always does this."*

I've been down this road before. My father's pulled this disappearing act many times. Usually he goes someplace else, like Reno. He'll resurface there, lose a ton of money, and then call me and ask me to pay it off. And what will I do?

Pay it off.

I stare at the mountains in the distance, the cold air seeping deep into my bones. He's the problem I can't solve.

I slump onto the outdoor couch and stare at the stark outlines of the peaks, wishing I had their certainty and, when it comes to my dad, their strength.

I stare off into the distance long enough for the door to slide open and Fable to pad across the deck in a pair of the fuzzy socks I gave her. They're adorable. A fleece blanket is wrapped around her. Her hair is still morning messy but her eyes are bright and filled with concern. "Hey, you," she says.

"Hey," I say, my tone flat.

"You okay?"

"Yes. Of course. Absolutely."

She gives me a soft but admonishing smile. "A triple denial?"

Saw right through me. I meet her gaze, hold up my hands, and shrug. "What can you do?"

She glances down toward the couch cushion. "Want company?"

With her, the answer is always yes. "I do," I say quietly, not even trying to hide how badly I want her presence.

She sits next to me, tucks her feet under her, then says, "That was your dad's friend."

There's something so refreshing about the fact that she's direct. She's cut straight to the heart of the matter. "Yes," I reply.

"The one who calls to give you a heads-up about what's going on?"

She remembers everything, from why I like snow to what kind of man my father is. With some embarrassment over my dad's ways, I look up, meet her soft gaze, then pause. Am I doing this? Telling her the full truth? Telling anyone? But my chest is tight, tighter than it's been before. Maybe telling her will help loosen some of the tension I carry around with me.

So I tell her everything Victor shared, ending with, "And I wish I knew what to do."

But as soon as I say that, I hate how weak it makes me sound. How helpless. Like I don't know how to do my job. Like I can't run a business. How hard can it really be to find a lowlife gambler?

I don't give her a chance to respond. I've got to be able to figure this out. "But maybe there's something I can do. I can make some more calls. I need to bail him out. It's just smart."

Fable shoots me a doubtful look. "Is it though?"

How can she possibly understand? Sure, her father is a showboating jackass, but at least he's not an addict. Besides, she's the one who said, *Sometimes, we aren't always ready to do the hard thing. So we have to do something easier first*. This is just easier. "I have the money. It's ridiculous not to pay it. It's selfish not to pay it. What is the point of working this hard if not to spend it on my family?"

"Wilder, is that what you want to do?" It's asked thoughtfully, with consideration and care.

But what I want to do is irrelevant. I've never been able to do what I want with him. Paying it off is what I have to do. It's what I'm supposed to do. It's the right fucking thing. Doesn't she get this? "I'll try to help him," I say, but that falls flat even to my ears. He has to help himself. I know this but still the knot of tension cranks even higher. "I'll just pay it off. And then we'll move on."

She takes a beat, like she's being careful with her words. "Do you think paying it off is going to solve it?"

But I'm barely listening to her. "Actually, I can take care of everything right now. I don't know why I didn't do this beforehand." Except maybe I'm turning soft. Like I was last night when Brady played me better by having Iris hum along. I can't keep missing opportunities because I'm distracted. "Why don't I call Desert Springs and pay off whatever he owes them? I'm sure he owes them something."

I grab my phone and immediately start googling the phone number for Desert Springs Casino. I'm about to hit call when Fable's hand comes down on mine. She's not gentle. She's firm and crystal clear as she says, "Look at me."

I'm not used to people talking to me that way. It catches my attention and I look up. "What? Why?"

She looks me straight in the eyes. "You don't have to fix it. I'm sorry it's happening. But you might not be able to solve it, and you also don't *have* to solve it."

She's so calm, but I'm like a washing machine on a vigorous spin cycle that shakes the entire house.

"But I do," I insist because that knot in my chest is getting tighter.

"Don't you see what you're doing? You keep bailing him out," she says, her words cutting me to the core.

"He's my dad," I say.

"I know, and I'm just looking out for you."

"You don't get it," I bite out.

She inches away from me on the couch but she doesn't back down. "Just because it's not my experience doesn't mean I don't understand it. You've told me about it. And I understand people. What I'm trying to say is if you feel you need to go look for him, that's fine. If you want to leave here and go to Vegas to find him, I get that. But I don't think you should pay off his debt."

She's quiet for a long moment, perhaps to let me stew on that last comment. But I'm actually stuck on what she said right before.

"You wouldn't object if I wanted to go?" I ask so I'm clear.

"If that's what you needed to do, I'd stand by you. If you wanted me to go with you, I would. If you needed to be alone to deal with it, I'd understand."

This is hypothetical, I tell myself. This is all hypothetical.

But no one has ever said anything like that to me

before. No one has ever offered something that selfless. Something so focused on...family.

My heart softens even more for her. Every time I'm with Fable, I fail miserably to get over her. I fail horribly at moving on. I fail awfully at forgetting how much I adore her.

And I don't know what to do with failure. But relationships always seem to go wrong. And somehow, some way, this one is going to as well. I know it even as I say, "I'm not going to leave. And I'm not going to that casino. And I'm not going to bail him out either."

At least not today.

"Good. I'm proud of you," she says.

The knot in me loosens a little bit.

I lift my arm, inviting her close. She slides in, snuggling against me. I whisper in her ear, "I can't believe you're up and out here, given how you hate mornings."

"I had a feeling you needed me."

I kiss the top of her head. "I did."

Far too much.

39

FLYING FIGGY PUDDING

Fable

"Seven-layer bars?"

From behind her black-and-white glasses, Josie's big blue eyes pop as she gawks at the tray that I bring my friends that afternoon. Wilder made them with Mac a little while ago since he owed them to me. But he also said it took his mind off his dad, and I was glad he had a distraction.

"Your man actually made seven-layer bars?" Josie asks again, even though the evidence is right here in the living room that connects our cabins.

Maeve darts out a grabby hand. "Who cares if he actually made them? I want one. They look delicious." She promptly stuffs it in her face and rolls her eyes in pleasure. "Oh my god, the man can bake. Wait. Can he fuck too?"

Sparks shimmy down my body. But I glance around,

making sure nobody is nearby. I nod a big, exaggerated yes. "It's like a whole new land of fucking with him. Last night, he tied me up with a red satin bow so that I looked like a Christmas present."

Maeve's hazel eyes flicker. "That's a very specific kink, and I am here for it."

"And I was there for it too," I say. "He's kind of like a borderline pleasure Dom. He's a little obsessed with giving me multiple orgasms."

"I'm still not hearing the problem," Josie deadpans as she walks me farther into the living room.

"He can bake, he's a good dad, and he fucks like a god," Everly says, counting off on her fingers. "Did I get that right, Fable?"

Tingles rush over my skin because actually, that's not all the man can do. "Oh, there's more. He's a great listener. He's thoughtful. He's smart. He can change a battery in a smoke detector. And he spoils me rotten. I mean, he booked us that private class and the dinner and the hotel room, and he treated my sister and me to a Christmas shopping spree, and he booked us all that private suite at the football game."

Everly grabs a bar from the coffee table where I've placed the tray and breaks off a corner, popping it in her mouth, then moans like a cooking show star. "Do not let go of him when the holidays are over."

That's not really an option though. I sigh. "We already agreed to an end date. It was always going to have one."

Josie pats the couch in front of the Christmas tree. "Sit," she orders and I comply. She gives me the Very Serious Look. "Can we discuss the elephant in the room?"

"I thought we were discussing the elephant in the room," I say, glancing at the tray of baked goods. "That the billionaire could actually bake? Incidentally, he baked those as punishment for squeezing my ass. It's a game we play," I say, and I'm giddy as I tell them about our list. "It was his idea to keep us on the up and up with this romance. If we do anything that's over the top and might make it obvious it's fake, we have this naughty and nice list we reference. And we get and give punishments, but fun punishments like cookies and massages."

Maeve blinks several times. "Ma'am, excuse me. We need all the details. We should all do this list. But first I have to know—did you purposely do something over the top so that he would bake for you?"

"No, he did something over the top," I explain.

"He squeezed your ass and you got cookies? It sounds like a win-win for you," Maeve adds, then crosses her legs with a certain panache.

Josie clears her throat to get our attention again. "Which only bolsters my point. The real elephant in the room is that this romance doesn't look fake."

The room turns silent. All eyes look my way. The weight of that statement hangs in the afternoon air.

I flash back on last night, and the things he said in bed. The way I felt then, but also at the caroling competition. Payback was the farthest thing on my mind. Then I picture this morning with him on the deck. He was so frustrated, so hurt by his father, and he obviously felt so helpless. Wilder was entirely stubborn—but then, he let me in. He accepted my support and my comfort, and it was a joy to be able to give him that. I hope he hears from his father soon.

I twist my fingers together and acknowledge Josie's elephant. "It doesn't *feel* fake anymore either," I admit.

That's the first time I've voiced it out loud. "And I don't know what to do about it."

Maeve seems to give my dilemma some thought before she says, "You have feelings for him. Big, mushy real ones that make you feel like anything is possible?"

Me? I don't like opening up. It makes me feel like my mother when I was growing up, as she opened the door for my father again and again. It makes me feel like someone could walk out and then return and do it one more time. Still, these big, frothy feelings for Wilder are getting harder to ignore. "I do. But we work together. I don't know what it would be like when we return to the office in the new year."

"You already cleared it with HR," Everly points out. "That's a big hurdle you don't have to worry about. The whole office believes you're together, so you're off to a great start." She flicks some errant blonde strands of hair off her cheek, then adds, "And I work with Max and it's a lot of fun."

But before it became fun, she faced a host of challenges with her very forbidden workplace romance. That's what happens when you fall for the goalie on the hockey team while you've been assigned to fix his bad reputation.

"Yes, and that's good. And I'm so glad you and Max figured everything out. But what if we tried something for real and it all went wrong?" I ask, picturing how uncomfortable it'd be seeing him at the office. It's one thing to return to the office after the holidays with our scripted breakup—it's entirely another to try a real romance and then have to endure a real breakup. "He's still the boss. I'd still have to see him."

"But why can't it last?" Everly challenges me.

I sweep out my arms and gesture to the lovely tree in

the corner of the room, decorated with red bows and silver garlands and snow globes, to the windows showing off snow-capped peaks in the distance, to the tray in front of us, loaded with sugary treats. "Because this isn't real. Right now is the honeymoon phase. It's Christmastime. Everything is wonderful. Wilder and I are throwing snowballs and singing, and we have a Christmas-tree-decorating competition in a few hours, and I'm eating seven-layer bars with my best friends, and last night I was tied up with red satin, and I don't give a fuck about Brady anymore. But I'm not a fool. I know what this is—I'm playing pretend with my boss." My throat catches, and I take a moment before I fight off a frown and add, "What happens when it's real life?"

That's what worries me. Even if this fake romance is starting to feel real, even if I couldn't give a flying figgy pudding about my ex, what happens when Wilder and I take this romance out of Evergreen Falls? What happens when there is no more Christmas magic?

"Also, I don't think he wants it to work out," I add, thinking back to our conversation early yesterday morning. *It's not that I don't want it. It's that I don't know if I can trust.* I don't want to break his private confidences, so I won't share what he said or why he said it. But carefully, I add, "He has some trust issues."

Everly scoffs. "So did Max."

That's true. Her guy had some hurdles to get over and she did too. "Yes, and I'm so glad he worked through them. But not everyone can. Or wants to," I say, swallowing roughly, already sad over a future real breakup.

The room is quiet for a long beat. Then Josie meets my eyes and asks gently, "Fable, the only question that matters is...do you want it to work out?"

I've been mulling that over a lot more lately. "Part of me does. But that seems foolish. Eventually you have to throw out the Christmas tree, and it dies on the side of the road."

The sound of the cabin door opening catches my attention, and from the other room I can just make out the sounds of laughter.

Maeve shrugs happily as she reaches for another seven-layer bar, "If you get a fake tree you don't have to throw it out. They last."

I chew on that point, and my seven-layer bar as Max and Wesley stride into the living room, arguing over whose sledding skills are more elite.

"Did you two have your own impromptu sledding competition?" Everly asks, with an amused grin as she looks at Max.

The big, bearded goalie shoots her a look. "Have you met me? Of course we did," he says, sinking down next to her on the couch and tugging her onto his lap. "And of course I won."

Wesley rolls his eyes as he drops into a chair, snuggling close with Josie. "Max, you seem to have a misunderstanding of what the finish line is. It was the thing I crossed first," he says then reaches for a seven-layer bar and takes a bite. "Damn, these are good."

"Do you two want to have a bake-off?" Josie suggests. "If you want to flex those competition skills in the kitchen, I think we'd all be grateful."

Max lifts a finger. "I'm in."

"Me too," Wesley says, and soon the conversation shifts from my fake romance to their real lives.

As I watch the two couples, I think about the ways they've let each other in, the changes people make for each other, the ways we bend and grow, and the things we're willing to do to get out of our comfort zones when we fall in love.

But is that what's happening to me? And if it is, would Wilder be willing to meet me on the other side of Christmas?

40

THE THREE OF US

Fable

I'm not the most competitive person in general, but when it comes to my home turf—design—I don't come to play.

I come to win.

Later that afternoon in the town square, I call Wilder and Mac into a huddle next to a spruce tree. We're dressed for speed—fleece pullovers, jeans, and snow boots. Even though Mac has been competing in the kid's division for other events, the Christmas-tree-decorating competition allows teams to pull in younger members too.

"Here's the plan. We're going to execute a Retro X with two running backs," I say, giving a football-esque play name to my plans. "Mac and me."

I tell them the rest of my approach for this supermarket sweep-style Christmas-tree-decorating competition. Each team has thirty minutes to decorate a tree right here in the town square. You can use the first five minutes of that to scoop up ornaments from various boxes in the middle of the square. They've been gathered from donations over the years. Volunteers wait next to the boxes to open them when the timed contest begins.

After I review the strategy, I finish with, "It all comes down to how you line everything up on the tree."

"Got it," Mac says with a crisp nod, her game face on.

I break the huddle as we wait for the starting whistle. The sun is dipping low on the horizon so we'll finish after sunset, then turn on the trees.

Wilder turns to me, approval in his eyes. "You're like a quarterback."

"I like football, and I like strategy," I say, owning it.

"Hot," he whispers.

I laugh, glad he's not stressing over his dad. Glad he took my advice. Maybe this is what it would be like if we were a real couple—helping each other, supporting each other.

Is he thinking that too? I hope so, but he turns his attention to Mac, who's staring at the boxes in the center of the square like she has X-ray vision.

"Are visions of Christmas trees dancing in your head?" he asks her.

"I'm just trying to psych out the competition," she says, then nods subtly to Brady and Iris in the corner who are jogging in place by a Douglas fir, like jogging will help them decorate faster. "Especially that guy. He's kind of a jerk."

More than kind of. But I'm curious why she's labeled him. "Why do you say that?"

"Because he doesn't like cats. He said so at the shower when he ran into Penguin in the hallway after he used the bathroom."

Wilder scoffs. "That settles it. Reason enough to beat him."

"I don't trust people who don't like animals," Mac adds, crossing her arms.

"One hundred percent reasonable approach to life," I say as Mayor Bumblefritz strides into the square with his megaphone at his side.

He smiles grandly as he weaves through the boxes full of mismatched ornaments.

I think back to when Wilder and I began this fake romance in his office for the sake of his aunt. She asked me pointedly if I was good at Christmas tree decorating. When I'd told her I knew my way around a string of lights, she'd said, *"Then I hope you beat that Brady character in the competition."*

I don't care about Brady anymore, but I do care about Wilder's aunt so this one is for Bibi. I want to win for her. Because the Evergreen Falls Annual Best in Snow Winter Games Competition matters to her. They're her Olympics. They're her big game. I'm going to do my best for her since she's been so good to me.

Maybe that'll make up for the guilt I feel about lying to her—even though when I look at the handsome, brilliant man by my side, nothing feels fake anymore.

I also want to do my best for another person. For this fabulous young woman Wilder's raising. I look at Mac, my heart filling with warmth for her spirit, her mind, and her feisty attitude that I admire.

I could get lost in these warm and fuzzy feelings, though, so I'm glad Mayor Bumblefritz is climbing up the steps to the gazebo now. We take our places by our designated trees. A crowd has gathered around the square to watch the competition.

The mayor brings that candy cane megaphone to his mouth. "Ladies and gentlemen, boys and girls, humans of all ages! You'll have thirty minutes to decorate your tree. You'll each need to grab what you want from these boxes of ornaments. No new ornaments were purchased for the games. These have all been donated so they're getting a second chance in our contest as they do every year." He takes a beat. "There's no telling what kind of festive magic you'll create with these. The Christmas spirit is all about making the most with what you have, wouldn't you agree?"

There is a collective murmur of *yes* from the contestants as we eagerly wait for him to announce the theme. He takes a weighty beat. "The theme this year is open to each individual team's interpretation." Another pause. "And it's...*home for the holidays*. Let the tree-decorating competition begin!"

I can't take a moment to process this theme because we're going to have to figure it out on the fly as we sift through what each box holds. The volunteers open the cardboard flaps and Mac and I take off running. Wilder's behind us holding a red bag that we'll fill with the ornaments.

I kneel at the first box, scanning the goodies. I don't see a random collection of ornaments, but a puzzle waiting to be solved. My mind begins to race, envisioning the perfect arrangement of colors, shapes, styles—the perfect design for *home for the holidays*.

"Grab the reindeer," I say, pointing to a wooden ornament in the corner of the box. Mac grabs it, then points to a red wooden sleigh. I snatch that up. She smiles at me, nodding and understanding, knowing instantly that we're going for a homey vibe. I spy a wooden nutcracker. "That one too."

"Got it," she says, darting out a hand.

We race to the next box as Wilder holds open the bag. "What'll it be, ladies?"

I scan the treasures so fast, then dole out instructions. We grab a wooden Santa, an elf, then a sled.

We're off in no time to the next box when an idea strikes. I motion for Mac to come closer, then whisper. "Let's do old meets new," I say. "That's kind of the point of home for the holidays?"

Her eyes brighten. "Yes! I love it. We'll get baubles and sparkly things and mix them with the old fashioned ones."

"It's like you can read my mind," I say.

"That sounds perfect," Wilder says, watching us with so much affection, it nearly breaks my heart. I almost want to stop right here, right now, and say to him, "What if this was real? Do you feel it too?"

But the clock is ticking and this girl wants to win. For others.

Mac is off and running so I shut down distractions. We're faster than the other contestants, racing with our collection. At the final box I spot something red and shiny at the bottom. I grab it before anyone else can then dash to the spruce in the corner of the square.

After Wilder adds lights, Mac and I move like clockwork to create a vintage-meets-modern style. We hang our ornaments in diagonal rows that crisscross along the branches of the tree.

When we're finishing, Wilder flicks on the twinkling lights. "I do love Christmas lights," he says with a little innuendo that I pick up on.

"Me too," I say, my stomach flipping from the way he looks at me with eyes that hold secrets. Perhaps also from the piece de resistance. I grab the red ribbon I found at the bottom of the last box of ornaments.

"I'll take care of that," Wilder says with authority.

"Yes, you will," I reply.

With the same skill he used when he tied me up in one, he fastens the ribbon in front of the tree into a lovely looping bow.

We step back, the three of us, regarding it.

"You did it, Fable. It looks like home for the holidays," Mac says, patting my arm proudly.

My heart glows with affection for this girl as I squeeze her shoulder. "No, *we* did it."

"We sure did," she says.

Wilder stands next to her too, his arm wrapped around her, his hand touching mine on her shoulder.

This feels all too real too. All too possible. And entirely too wonderful.

It can't last. It just can't.

Except, what if it can?

"Let me take a picture of the tree," Mac says as she fishes her cell phone from her pocket and snaps a shot of it, then looks to her dad then me with hope in her green eyes. "I want another one. Of the three of us."

The three of us.

Those words lodge in my head and in my heart as Mac calls over Bibi.

In front of the tree, Wilder wraps one arm around me, the other around his daughter then lets out a soft, unguarded murmur.

Like he's imagining all new things too. Like, the three of us.

My heart catches in my throat.

This is merely holiday magic, I try to tell myself. This is the cocoon of Christmas. The sparkle of falling snow making everything feel possible. But even so, everything *is* starting to feel possible.

Except...me liking eggnog. When the owner of the North Pole Nook wheels a red cart into the square with a chalkboard sign for eggnog, I cringe a little. But Mac wheels around to Wilder. "I love eggnog. Can I get some, Dad?"

He adopts a straight face. "Just one cup."

"Thanks," she says and rushes off to the cart, lining up right behind Charlotte to snag a cup of the holiday treat. The cart must catch Iris's attention, too, since she and Brady trot over from their tree and line up right behind Mac.

I turn to Wilder and shrug. "She's pretty much perfect in every other way."

"It's her only flaw."

We take a moment to survey the other Christmas trees as the judges wander around checking each one, but something catches my attention at the eggnog stand once more. I jerk my gaze back over to the commotion.

The bride-to-be is clasping a hand over her mouth, like she's shocked as she looks down at Brady, who's kneeling on the snow. Looks like he was tying his boot. Only now, his head is covered in eggnog. "I'm so sorry," my sister says loudly, holding an empty cup, like she's so terribly contrite for her clumsiness.

I fight off a smile as I tug Wilder's hand and we rush over to get a better look at the scene.

"I'm so very sorry," she says again but I don't detect an apologetic note in her voice.

"It's fine," Brady mutters, but there's a hitch in his voice. Poor guy. He always did love his hair.

Wilder peers down at my ex. "Same, Brady. But good thing you and Iris are really, really good at cleaning up eggnog messes."

Brady gulps, his eyes widening. *Oh shit* seems to flash in them.

Charlotte lifts her chin at her groom's cousin, shooting death stares at him. "I bet you are." She walks off to join the groom, who I suspect is none the wiser that his bride just delivered some unexpected payback for me.

A second later, Mac joins us empty-handed. "I lost my appetite for eggnog."

"Perfect," I mouth to Wilder.

And so is the end of this afternoon, since a little later the three of us win and come together in a group hug.

The theme of the tree-decorating competition sticks with me later that evening when we're back in our cabin. Wilder's lounging on the couch, listening to a podcast, while I gather up the red and green glitter dick T-shirts I brought so I can head to Charlotte's cabin for a little bachelorette party. All of my best friends are here, and I'm lucky like that—to be surrounded by people who make me feel like I'm home.

An idea starts to form as I drop the shirts in a bag, but my focus turns elsewhere when Wilder sits ramrod straight and stares at his phone, then me. He whispers cautiously, "It's a text. From my dad."

"What did he say?" I ask desperately as Wilder hits stop on the podcast.

His eyes are sad, but his lips curve up slightly. "He says he's sorry to worry me. And that he's okay." He pauses, then adds, "And that's all."

"Maybe it's enough?" I sit down with him on the couch, setting a hand on his shoulder.

"Maybe."

I don't know if Wilder feels reassured from the text, but he covers my hand with his and says, "Thank you."

"Anytime," I say, meaning it in a whole new way, hoping to find the courage to tell him sometime soon how I feel.

I glance at the time. I should go and meet my friends, but the idea is crystallizing. Today, I felt like I was home for the holidays, but what about people like his father, whether it's from their own doing or not, who don't have this warm, cozy embrace of family and home at this time of year? What about children and families who don't have all...*this*? Chalets and lights, seven-layer bars and movie evenings? Those who are fighting just to keep the lights on rather than to decorate with them?

"Wilder?" I begin.

"Yes?"

"What if we make some time tomorrow to wrap presents for kids who don't have them? To buy and to wrap," I clarify.

His smile is warm. "Let's do that. I'll find a local organization and set something up."

That's so very him to jump right in.

* * *

Wilder joins Mac and her friends and cousins along with his sister for a movie while Charlotte and I catch up with our girlfriends. We wear the glitter dick T-shirts, pour champagne, and indulge in the most fantastic charcuterie board that Josie has put together. It's low-key by bachelorette party standards but that's what Charlotte wanted—just some time with friends before her big day in two more nights.

We toast several times and when it's my turn I lift my flute high. "To the eggnog spiller. She is the queen!"

Everyone clinks and says, "Long may she reign!"

Charlotte's eyes fill with pride and happiness. "I swear it was an accident."

Josie nods, exaggerated. "Say that in court. You nailed it."

"I will," Charlotte says, then lifts a glass my way. "A toast to my sister who means the world to me. And who's helped make this holiday into the best Christmas ever."

That's what I've always wanted for her. I pull her into a hug, grateful I told her the truth the first night here, and grateful, too, for all these new Christmas memories that we're making.

The party winds down around eleven, and I return to the honeymoon cabin, looking around at the fireplace, the twinkling tree, and the sleigh bed. It's just me in this quiet suite. Wilder's not here, but a text on my phone says he's having a scotch out on the deck with Leo and will be back soon.

Perfect timing, since I just thought of a special gift for him.

I know my way around a string of lights after all.

41

THAT SPECIAL SOMEONE

Wilder

It's never a bad time hanging out with Leo and enjoying a glass of scotch as the stars wink on and off in the inky night sky. You can see forever here in Evergreen Falls, far away from the city. But when the telltale signs of snow—a pinkish-orange tint to the night—burn brighter, I start to wonder if Fable is back in the room and if the bachelorette party has ended. The answer comes when Leo looks at his phone then turns to me with a grin. "I've been summoned."

And that answers that. "Then you should go." I glance at the empty tumblers. "I'll take them in."

With a quick thanks, he's practically off and running.

I take the glasses, bring them inside and leave them in the sink, then head down the hall, the day playing on a loop in my head, from the tense morning phone call that threw me for a loop, to making seven-layer bars with my daughter, to decorating a tree with Fable and Mac in an afternoon that was lovelier than any afternoon had a right to be.

That afternoon is making me rethink if I might be wrong. If something that started with a lie could actually turn into something good.

Even in spite of all the evidence I've seen. Even in spite of my mother's happiness without romance. Of my father's self-destructive ways. Of my own track record that has sent me here today. I'm nearly forty, and I'm not sure if I've ever been in love.

Except...I think I might be now. The way my heart thunders around Fable scares the hell out of me, but I also can't stay away from her. When I reach the door, I stop then spin around and return to the kitchen. My Fable likes to have fun in bed. She likes to play. And she loves mint so I swing open the refrigerator door and grab a fresh canister of peppermint whipped cream. When I've returned to the suite I rap once on the door. Sultry music plays, its own telltale sign.

"Come in," she calls out.

When I swing it open, I hiss out a breath. She's spread out on the bed like the most gorgeous gift. "Merry fucking Christmas to me," I say awed at the sight.

She smiles, the kind that says she's pulled this off. She fucking did. "I thought we could have our own Christmas-tree-decorating contest. Do I look like a tree?"

"The sexiest tree I've ever seen," I say as my gaze travels up and down my naughty Christmas elf. She's wrapped a string of Christmas lights around her shoulders, across her breasts, over her stomach, and then around her hips. Red, purple, pink, green, and blue lights flash on and off against her pale flesh in the soft lighting of the room. Outside, snow is falling.

Inside, I am.

I advance toward her, mesmerized by the soft haze of lights dancing on her skin. Lucky lights. "Do you know that the pinks and the purples and the blues reflect on your skin?"

Fable glances down at the light show on the canvas of her body. "I do like to find new ways to use things," she says, reminding me of something else I adore about her—her mind, the way she sees the world, and how she creates new ways of using things.

"Your mind is a beautifully filthy and creative place, and I fucking love it," I say and I'm one step closer to uttering words I can't take back. Words I'm not sure I should say. But words that pound in my head and heart.

When I reach her, though, I swallow those emotions and focus on the practical—her pleasure. I set the peppermint whipped cream canister on the foot of the bed and run my hands from her ankles up to her knees.

She arches her hips ever so subtly as she glances at the canister. "I see you're into Christmas kink too, Mr. Blaine."

Those two words—*Mr. Blaine*—crank me up. Maybe I do enjoy power games...or perhaps I simply enjoy everything with her. "I'm into *you*." That's a small start, and her eyes brighten at those two words. Then I add, "You like mint and I like to give you everything you want."

"You're very good at it," she says as I draw circles with my thumb along the outside of her knee.

"What exactly are your plans for that mint?"

I gaze at the sensual light show playing on her body. "Who knows anymore? Your lights trump my mint," I say, running one hand farther up her thigh.

She gasps, then shudders.

My god, it's such an unparalleled thrill to watch her

reaction. To witness her getting turned on as she's wrapped up in lights. With each move I make she parts her legs a little wider.

"You're an overachiever, Mr. Blaine. Pretty sure we could do both," she says.

That's clear. She wants the mint and what Fable wants she gets—because I like to give it to her. "We can do everything," I say.

For a long time. For well past the holidays. Do you want that too?

But I don't ask that yet. That's far too vulnerable. And besides, she's shifting gears quickly, nodding to the big arched window with a view of the mountains—a view that's starting to turn white. "It's snowing."

I glance at the windows, but even the view of falling snow—one of my favorite sights in the world—has nothing on her. "It is," I say, touching her thighs, then running a finger along a pink light that's perilously close to her perfect pussy.

"The first time we went to dinner, I'm betting you were already imagining fucking me while it snowed."

A laugh bursts from me. "Am I that transparent?"

She bobs a naked shoulder, a pleased smile curving her lips. "Maybe."

"Guilty as charged then," I say, dropping my face to kiss her thighs. What did I ever do to deserve even a brief romance with this naughty angel? She ignites something carnal in me. Something greedy. My voice comes out in a low rumble as I rise up and reach for the end of the strand of lights resting on her hips. "Fable, I need to take these lights off you. I need to kiss every inch of your skin. I need to make you come countless times. Because this"—I nod toward the window and the white flakes floating down—"is a fantasy, but *you* are my real fantasy."

Her breath seems to come faster. "Take them off right now."

In seconds, I unwrap her, and once she's free of the lights, she throws her arms around me and whispers, "You've become mine too."

There's a vulnerability in her eyes that I'm not sure I deserve, but one I still desperately want. I can't let her be the only one to say the hard thing, though, so I cup her cheek. "I meant everything I said last night right here in this bed. I have wanted you for so long. For more than a year. You've been front and center in my mind. I've been thinking of you, and craving you, and wanting you. You've been like a dream I didn't think I could ever catch."

Her breath halts, then comes in a soft stutter. "You're not dreaming," she says, her fingers playing with the ends of my hair. "You're awake and I'm all real. All yours, Wilder."

My chest is so hot. My skin is like the surface of Mercury, but it's because my heart is on fire. I can't take it anymore. I claim her mouth in a deep and passionate kiss. I pour all my feelings into it—all the emotions that I'm terrified to say, but I'm even more terrified of not saying them soon.

And *soon* I will.

When I break the kiss, she tugs at my shirt.

I take the hint and strip it off, then grab a big towel from the en suite. "Lie down on this," I say as I return to the bed, then move the towel under her.

I settle into my favorite place—between her legs. "This afternoon you showed off your tree-decorating skills. Now I'll show off mine."

Her lips part in naughty delight. "Will you now?"

"Yes, even though I already have an advantage. My tree is the sexiest tree ever." I take the canister from the foot of the bed and point it toward the hollow of her throat, spraying a dollop of cream there. She shudders. I dip my face and lick it off with a throaty groan.

She gasps softly. I kiss her throat once more, making sure I get every last drop.

I spray some whipped cream on her tits, a generous dollop for each nipple. Pulling back, I take a good, long look at the gorgeous woman naked before me. "You are the perfect holiday treat," I say.

She gives me a saucy smile. "Better taste me and make sure."

"Quality control and all," I say dryly.

I flick my tongue across her gorgeous breasts, licking the treat off her, savoring every single taste till she's moaning, "That feels so good."

"And I'm not even close to being done."

"I never think you are, Wilder. Never. You're insatiable," she says.

I raise my face and look her straight in the eyes I love. "You make me insatiable."

Then I decorate her stomach with swirls and lines all the way down to her belly button, and I take my sweet time licking it all off. When I'm done, I climb over her and gaze down at the redheaded beauty who's become the center of my world. Who makes my heart thunder and my mind spark. And who makes my soul feel settled. "What did I ever do to deserve you?"

It's not quite saying *I've fallen in love with you* but it's close. So close.

"Everything," she answers decisively, then her gaze strays to the Christmas tree in the room.

As it flashes on and off, I don't know why this didn't occur to me sooner, but I'm glad it's occurred to me now. "Do you know what good girls get for Christmas?"

"What do they get?"

"They get fucked under the tree."

The look in her eyes is wild anticipation, and I have half a mind to carry her off the bed and sit her down under the tree right now, but first things first. In the en suite, I grab another towel and wipe the remnants of the whipped cream off her.

When that's done, she gathers the fleece blanket from the bed and spreads it underneath the tree, then lies down on her side, giving me the sexiest *come hither* look ever. "Mr. Blaine, why don't you tell Santa I've been very, very good?"

If there has ever been a better gift for anyone on earth than this woman lying naked, waiting for me, I won't believe it. "Ohh, he knows. He already told me to give you multiple orgasms tonight."

"He must have read my Christmas list."

Heat floods every damn cell in my body, and I give her a long, lingering look as I grab a condom. "I did, honey. I did."

I snag some extra pillows from the bed then join her on the floor, positioning the pillows under her back so it's comfy for my woman.

I take a beat to stare at the beauty in front of me, here for me, opening up for me in every way. I want to deserve her. I want to earn her. Most of all, I don't want to hurt her by saying something too soon that I can't back up. But I think I can try with her. I think I can toss out all my old beliefs and embrace new ones.

But I need to be sure I won't fail.

First, though, I need to fuck her good. I line up my hips flush against her and sink inside. My brain scrambles, my nerves firing with incandescent pleasure.

She's tight and hot and all mine. And when she whispers my name in a shuddery breath, I nearly say *fuck I love you*.

I grit my teeth and swallow down the dangerous words.

Then she's quiet, and I am too as I ease out, then slide back in, letting her feel every inch of me.

Her breath catches, and her eyes go a little glossy. "It's so good with you, Wilder. Everything's so good with you." It sounds like a confession, like she's on the verge of something. Of falling too? Could she be? That would be too wonderful. I can barely let myself entertain the possibility that all these feelings could be returned the same way.

But I have a job to do—making her come—and I won't fail at this one either. "Wrap your legs tight around me. I need to fuck you deep. Need to take you hard. Need to show you how much you mean to me."

She complies, hooking her ankles around my ass, and then demands, "Show me."

I fuck her slow, and deep, and passionately. I kiss her as I swivel my hips. I whisper sweet everythings as I thrust. I tell her she's beautiful, incredible, absolutely amazing as I touch her.

I'm *almost* saying it. Almost, but not quite.

Still, I want her to feel it—the strength of this connection between us. I want her to believe it can last well beyond the holidays. Right now, I want her to lose control for me. I rise up on my knees, slide my hand between her thighs, and play with her clit till she's coming hard and fast then begging for another one.

All too happy to oblige, I hook her ankles over my shoulders so she can barely move. Her arms loop around my neck and her wild eyes say she's holding on tight. In no time, I find a rhythm that has her moaning and begging.

Our bodies slide together. Her fingers tangle in my hair. Her eyes hold mine with such intensity and desire that words nearly burst from me. I can hardly believe that in a few short nights I've done the thing I swore I wouldn't do. I've fallen completely in love with her, with no hope for coming out.

Pleasure seizes my body, and I'm lost.

"Give it to me," she urges and she's taking all the control, arching up, rocking against me, dragging her nails down my back and squeezing my ass.

I'm desperate to give her another, but my own climax has seized control of me. I'm shaking and shuddering, but then she's crying out too. Like my pleasure has sent her over the edge again.

The world goes offline and I'm not sure I want to come back to it.

Not here, under the Christmas tree, as if the rest of the world has gone to sleep, and it's only us.

A little later we're in bed, under the covers, her fuzzy socks on as she rubs her feet against my leg. Snow falls gently beyond the cool glass of the window.

"Remember that first dinner?" she asks, her voice fond

as she reminisces about an event that was only a few weeks ago.

"Of course," I say. I remember everything about her.

"I can still hear what you said about snow when you look out the window," she says.

"Tell me. Tell me what I said." I remember it too, but I want to hear the words crossing her lips.

She turns to face me. "It's romantic. When you look out the window and you see the flakes falling and everything goes hush, it makes you want to spend the day, and the night, with...that special someone." Her voice catches on those last three words, and her mouth is soft.

My heart is beating so fast, so loud. She has to hear it.

"I feel it," she adds in a bare whisper.

My brave woman takes the first step.

I cup her cheek, look her in the eyes, and say, "There's nothing fake about us."

42

THE CLEVEREST WINGWOMAN

Wilder

The thing about kids is they rarely outgrow the desire to make snow angels. So I'm up and at 'em at eight in the morning thanks to a text from Mac that consisted mostly of emojis of snowflakes, angels, and prayer hands.

Spy code, she's called it.

But I was able to decipher it, so here I am behind the porch of the cabin, lying in the soft blanket of fallen snow on the ground. I'm waving my arms and legs back and forth right next to my daughter when the tromp of boots catches my attention.

I turn to the sound. It's Fable's cousin Troy trudging closer to us, wearing black jeans and a black hoodie. No coat because of course he doesn't get cold. He's licking a candy cane.

"Hey," he grunts, stopping when he reaches us, his tone flat. He's the king of monotone.

"Good morning," I say, then push up to my elbows in the snow angel mold I'm in.

Troy wastes no time. "If you wanted to date a girl, would you take her to see the new horror retrospective at the local movie house or invite her over to listen to a true crime podcast about unsolved murders?"

This feels like a set-up. Still, as Mac watches our exchange with avid eyes, I ask, "Is this hypothetical or about someone in particular?"

"No. I met a girl at the tree thing yesterday. She told me she has a black tree with ornaments of fictional serial killers on it, so naturally, I want to ask her out."

"Naturally," I say.

Mac pops up. "Troy! It's obvious. Ask her which she prefers. Also, do it now!" She gestures like she's shooing him off.

"Really?"

"Yes. She might be leaving town really soon."

He licks the pointy end of the candy, then nods. "If you say so."

"I do. Go," Mac says.

He trudges off and frankly, the answer's obvious for me too. If Troy can do it, I can. I stand, dusting the snow off my ass and legs and back. "Mac, I need to do something."

Her eyes are inquisitive. "Is it…ask out Fable on a real date? Because I'd highly recommend taking her to the pottery-making workshop at the Art Center For You in the city and then dinner at her favorite restaurant, which incidentally is Happy Cow in Hayes Valley. I'd be happy to arrange a res. Or if you want to go for the extravagant thing, you could suggest a private rooftop dinner, then a helicopter tour of the city. That would be fab for your first real date."

I roll my eyes, but I can't stop my smile. "I take back what I said about you going to law school. You clearly need to go into theater and become a director. Or go into sports and become a head coach. Or enter politics and become a chief strategist."

"Those are all excellent ideas, Dad. But for now, I'll be the chief strategist for you," she says, then stage whispers, "Now go. Make your fake romance real!"

I can't believe my daughter is my wingwoman. But really, there's no one better. As I head up the steps with Mac beside me, I ask, "When did you start planning that?"

"Planning what?" she asks innocently.

"Planning how to make everything real," I add.

She gives a cheeky smile. "Chief strategists never tell."

As I stride across the deck, I spot Fable in the kitchen, pouring coffee. She's wearing jeans and a soft red sweater, her hair piled on her head in a beautifully messy bun. I absolutely should have asked her out last night. But I was too caught up in the snow, in the moment, in the words. Now I need to act. If my own daughter engineered an entire set-up with Fable's candy-cane-licking cousin just to make a point, then, well, I need to make a point.

I slide open the door, Mac right behind me. My daughter snags a front-row seat on the living room couch while I make my way to the woman I adore, wrap my arms around her from behind, and say, "What are you doing on New Year's Eve?"

Mac and I are slated to see her mother's concert the next day, and I'd like to invite Fable to that, too, a family event. But first things first—a date.

Setting down the mug on the counter, Fable turns in my arms. "Is that a trick question?"

"Um, no." My brow furrows. I am perplexed. I've asked out women before. I don't usually get this response.

"The answer," Fable says, "is that on New Year's Eve I'm going to be in bed at ten-thirty, reading and then falling asleep."

And I fall even harder. She's so delightfully blunt. But I can be direct too. "Then when I take you out that night, I better get you home before ten-thirty."

She arches a brow. "Presumptuous."

"Yes," I say. "I can work with your schedule. I'd like to take you out for a rooftop dinner and a helicopter tour of the city. Or a pottery-making class and dinner at Happy Cow. Go out with me. On a real date. On New Year's Eve."

Her eyes say yes before her lips do. "Yes."

Mac pumps a fist. "Did it!"

"It seems we have a little matchmaker," I murmur.

"We do, and I choose...*both* dates," Fable says, then lifts her coffee and downs some.

"I'll give you both," I say.

A knock on the door keeps me from basking in these plans. I check my watch. The car I arranged to pick up my mother at the airport is about due, and when I head to the door and open it, my timing proves accurate. She's here—dark wavy hair, clever eyes, and arms open wide. "Merry Christmas, kiddo!"

"Grandma!" Mac pops up from the couch, rushing over to greet my mom.

It's another group hug and when we pull apart, Mom walks inside, takes off her coat and scarf, and smiles. "You must be Fable? So good to meet you."

Fable crosses the living room to give her a hug. "Good

to meet you, Elizabeth. Would you like some coffee or tea?"

Mom doesn't hesitate. "Coffee, please. I've been in London too long, and the tea tastes like muddy water." She tilts her head, crinkles her brow. "Though, I suppose some might say coffee tastes like mud."

Fable smiles. "That's the Libra in you."

Mom's eyes light up. "You remembered." Then she looks Fable up and down. "And you? Wait. Don't tell me." Mom blows out a thoughtful breath, then declares, "Leo."

"How did you know?"

Mom nods toward me. "Wilder told me. He texted after you arrived. Told me a little bit about you. All good things." Mom leans in to whisper in Fable's ear, but not so low I can't hear. "He seems quite taken with you."

Fable meets my gaze with a hopeful one of her own. "The feeling is mutual. In fact, we're having a real date in San Francisco after Christmas."

"And I set it up," Mac puts in.

Mom ruffles Mac's hair. "Of course you did." She looks at Fable, then me, then smiles smugly. "I hate to say I told you so, Wilder. But I told you so."

"And you were right," I say.

"Yes, I was."

A little later, we check the agenda for Evergreen Falls Annual Best in Snow Winter Games Competition. Since the last event is the gingerbread house-making tonight, we'll have plenty of time for a family shopping trip. As promised, I found a local group organizing a community toy drive with nearby charities. I spoke to the organizer, and she emailed me a list of top requested type of gifts this season. We'll pick up some items from the list, then visit the community center where volunteers are gathered to collect and wrap donations for the drive.

I show Mom to her cabin next to Mac's, where she can set down her bags before we tackle our shopping. We're about to head out when Mom stops in her tracks on the soft carpet. "I can't believe I almost forgot. I need to say hello to my sister."

I wince. "Good catch." If we're going to Bibi's now, I should invite her to join us. My aunt's position as head of charitable contributions at Blaine Enterprises is more than a job. It's part and parcel of who she is. She'll want to come with us.

At Bibi's cabin, it's a hugfest, and when the sisters finish bestowing endless compliments on how fabulous the other one looks, I ask Bibi if she'd like to join us.

"Of course I would, but I have to be back in time for my date," she says with a mischievous grin, then adds, "Before the gingerbread house-making competition."

"Who's the date with?" Fable asks, then answers her own question. "The sheriff."

Bibi's smile is Mona Lisa levels of pleased. "However did you know?"

Fable shrugs easily. "You have a definite vibe going on with him. Did you also need Mac to—" Fable blinks and, possibly realizing she was veering into a faux pas, she quickly reroutes. "Did you also need Mac to...take pics of you two?"

But I suspect she was about to ask, "Do you need Mac to set you up?" It's a good thing she didn't because my aunt, of course, believes we've been together for a few weeks. No need for Mac to set us up today. Just as there's no need to reveal our hand now.

Bibi shakes her head. "Maybe if we have another date. Just like the two of you."

Fable's shoulders relax, looking relieved. But the guilt over lying to my aunt sits heavy in my chest.

But it's not fake anymore. Does anyone need to know that it once was?

I think not. Best to wait till after the wedding. Besides, there's no need to expose ourselves. Explaining will mean the eggnog story will come out, which will cause major awkwardness in the wedding party. No one needs that. Time to dismiss the guilt and move forward. We load into the car and go.

43

JUST A LITTLE HOLIDAY PAYBACK

Fable

My first thought as we head down the freshly shoveled sidewalks of Main Street is *I wish Charlotte were here*. This is exactly what I wanted for her when we were growing up—this kind of family moment during the holidays.

But I know she's having a lovely time with friends doing her final wedding prep this afternoon. So I snap a couple pictures of downtown Evergreen Falls to share with her, then put my phone away.

Freshly fallen snow lines the edges of the sidewalks. The scent of gingerbread from the nearby Sugar Plum Bakery floats past us. A bell tinkles as I walk into Play All Day with the man I'm dating, his smart-as-a-whip daughter, his mother, and his aunt.

And I couldn't be happier.

Plus, this toy store rocks. It's a veritable wonderland, with everything from plush animals to board games, wooden puzzles, and dollhouses lining the shelves. Mac surprises absolutely no one by heading for the board game and puzzles section. The woman behind the counter calls out in a voice like a duchess. "Let me know if I can help you with anything."

"We will," Mac answers.

"Games and puzzles were on the list of top-request types of gifts from the organization. I bet she's going to pick out a thousand-piece jigsaw puzzle," Bibi declares.

"My prediction is Settlers of Catan," Wilder's mother says.

I smile, knowing they're both close but no cigar.

Her father shakes his head. "That kid is getting chess. She'll want everyone to learn it," he says confidently, and yep, he's right. At the end of the row, Mac stretches up on tiptoe to grab a chessboard from a shelf, and her dad calls out, "Do you think that's the game kids want for Christmas?"

Mac shoots him a look like, *How can you even ask*? "Chess is for everyone. But so is Settlers of Catan and these puzzles and Monopoly." She tugs those off the shelves too, stacking them high in her arms. "I also highly recommend we get Exploding Kittens, Clue, and Cat Crimes. Also, Would You Rather. For kids, of course."

Wilder quickly strides to the end of the aisle, taking some of the boxes.

At an endcap of intricately crafted dollhouses, complete with miniature cardboard milk cartons on tiny wooden tables in Lilliputian kitchens, Bibi fails to stifle a laugh and turns to her sister. "Every day. This is what your granddaughter is like every day."

It's said with such obvious affection, but when Wilder's mom smiles there's a hint of sadness in her eyes. "I miss this," she says softly.

And my heart, my squishy, soft heart is officially a marshmallow as I witness the wistful interaction from a few feet away.

Emotions swim up my throat, twisted up with nostalgia and the wish that I had this when I was younger. But there's also gratitude that I can have it in new ways as an adult. I'm lucky that my sister and I stayed close through all the years. Now, she's getting her dream wedding tomorrow and we're finally having a holiday free of the kind of drama and the toxicity that plagued our home when we were growing up.

I look down the aisle at Mac, focused, precise, and also happy as she grabs gifts. She's wise beyond her years, and yet her parents allow her to be exactly eleven. They don't expect anything more from her than to be her age.

We pass the dollhouse endcap and join them, then help to carry some of the games to the counter when Mac notices a nearby display of wooden toys. "Not everyone likes games. Some kids like toys. Those were on the requested list too," she says in that confident, take-charge tone. "We need to get those too."

"Don't forget the artsy kids," Elizabeth puts in, then shoots me a knowing look. "Right, Fable?"

I feel like a can of soda shook up, fizzy, and warm. I smile back at her. "Artsy gals have to stick together."

"Don't I know it."

His mother and I head to the art supply section, picking out crafts and paintbrushes, chalk and sketch pads, and pen sets that would have made my younger self squeal if I'd opened these under the tree. Come to think of it I'd probably squeal now.

Bibi sweeps over to us, adjusting the pom-pom on her

simple red-and-white Santa cap. "Don't forget some kids just like to get up to all kinds of mischief."

"Some things never change," her sister says, "and I know exactly what to get for people like you."

We pick Lego sets and construction toys, science kits for making volcanoes, as well as soccer balls, basketballs, and even kites to help burn off energy. All from the list.

We're nearly done when Wilder points to a section with globes of all kinds—from historical to raised relief, some with topographic maps and others that light up. "We can't forget a globe. The topographic one is fascinating."

Mac rolls her eyes. "Dad, I assure you kids don't want globes for Christmas."

"I did. Besides, it's just an extra gift. Why not, right?" He's so earnest and straightforward and clearly thinks it's a great gift. And maybe it is. We are all snowflakes, I suppose. No two are alike.

Before we're done, the counter is stacked high with gifts that we'll wrap and donate.

Wilder runs his gaze over the stacks like he's doing a quick calculation, then turns to us, and shrugs. "We got everything on the list. What if we gave a little more? A little extra? It's Christmas after all?"

This man. "Go for it," I say, beaming.

He turns again to the woman behind the counter, who's dressed in a snowman sweater with the name tag Maryam over the top hat. "Would it be possible if I bought three of everything you have in the store to donate to a local organization for the holiday? I would be happy to pay for delivery, too, Maryam."

Her jaw falls to the carpeted floor, which is printed with a map of the world. "Are you serious?"

"Yes." There's no joking in his tone. No argument

either. This is a man putting his money where his mouth is.

"Yes, of course," the woman says. The two of them work out the details of immediate delivery to the donation center. Then, she brings her hand to her chest. "I don't even know what to say."

"How about *where's your credit card?*"

She laughs then says, "Where's your credit card?"

He slaps down his card and buys out half the store. As they're chatting about the final details, Wilder pulls the woman aside and says something I don't hear.

When they're done, we load some of the toys into his car. The store will deliver the rest this afternoon to the donation center.

The five of us head over there and start wrapping.

* * *

Finished wrapping a toy train in the community center basement, Bibi checks the big clock on the wall and frowns apologetically. "I hate to do this, but I need to go."

"Don't apologize," I say. "Dates are very important."

Wilder flashes me a knowing grin then presses a kiss to my cheek. "They sure are." No need for the naughty and nice list to make sure we stay on message. We *are* on message.

We send Bibi on her way and wrap board games and craft kits for another hour, then it's Mac's turn to frown. "I have to go. I'm a gingerbread aficionado, and the kids' event starts soon. I need to decorate the gingerbread house I made."

Her grandmother tilts her head, seeming bemused. "You know the word aficionado? Wait. Of course you do.

You use it?" But then she holds up a hand. "Don't even answer me. Of course you use it. You are your father's daughter."

Wilder turns to his mother. "I believe you are a gingerbread aficionado, as well. Do you want to take her back?"

"I do. It'll be a good chance for us to catch up some more."

"And you can hang out with me while we decorate," Mac says. "I enlisted Cousin Troy as my partner because I think he is secretly, weirdly creative."

"I think you're right," I agree.

They head off for the competition, leaving Wilder and me in the basement with several volunteers, a mountain of gifts, rolls of wrapping paper, tape, and bows. For a moment, I stare at the gifts on the table, a little daunted by the towering pile. "We'd better work quickly. The gingerbread house-making competition is the last event, and then the awards ceremony is tonight. We've got about two hours before we have to go."

I baked the gingerbread yesterday, but we'll need to decorate it in the Sugar Plum Bakery, which is hosting the contest. But as I stare at the generous heap of toys and games and puzzles, I'm unsure if we can pull this off.

"We can do it all," Wilder promises as he wraps a crafting kit, folding a corner of red reindeer printed paper. "And I think we can hang onto first place too."

Since we won the snowball competition and the tree-decorating one, we're still in the lead, despite our middling finish in caroling. "I think we can too."

Though it's irksome that Brady and Iris are clinging to third place thanks to their epic performance in the caroling competition. And Iris can probably make a damn good gingerbread house since she's a chef. But I won't let that bother me. I can't.

"All we have to do is place well in this last event," Wilder says as he reaches for another gift and methodically wraps a square of mistletoe paper around a set of paintbrushes. "That should keep him out of first place." Then he shoots me a soft smile. "Even though I don't want to win just to beat him. Ask me why I want to win."

"Fine. I'll bite. Why do you want to win?"

He scans the basement, then lowers his voice. "Because it turns you on when my team wins. I've noticed that after football games, your cheeks are pink and your chest is flushed."

Anything is foreplay for this man.

"That's true," I say, then he steals a kiss that sends shivers all the way to my toes as if he's proving his point.

But we have more work to do, and I focus on that. Only it seems the more we wrap, the more we have to wrap. The stack of presents is multiplying. Which is great because it's all going to a good cause. Still, I don't know how we'll get through it all.

As evening nears, I shake out my wrists, which are sore from all the gift wrapping. Wilder stops and rubs them for a minute, and then we return to the pile on the table, tackling the soccer balls next.

"I guess wrapping takes a long time when you buy half a store," I say with a wry smile.

"Good wrapping is always worth it," he says with a naughty gleam in his eyes as he perfectly ties a green satin bow on a box.

"Now I really want to go," I say.

The problem is by the time the clock strikes six, there are still easily one hundred presents left to wrap.

I glance around at the hard-working volunteers wrapping gifts for kids who might not otherwise have them. "If we're going, we should go," I say softly, but the words don't match my tone. I don't want to leave.

Wilder simply says, "Or we could stay."

And I fall a little harder for him.

"I would really like that," I say, grateful. I love that he's giving up the contest for this.

"There's just one thing I need to do." He already sounds satisfied, but he takes his phone from his pocket and dials a number. "Brady-i-o," he says, then pauses. I tilt my head, wondering why the hell he's calling my ex. "Actually, no, I don't want to hear your formal pitch tomorrow. Or the next day. Or any day. I don't work with cheaters. And I definitely don't work with people who hurt my girlfriend. I'd say good luck with your stockbroker business, but I wouldn't mean it, so I won't."

My lips form a wide O as he hangs up with a powerful stab of his finger against the screen.

"That was hot." I stretch across the table and throw my arms around him, whispering in his ear, "You are going to get fucked so good tonight."

"No, Fable. You are."

Chills rush down my spine. "True, true," I say, then send a text to my sister so she won't worry about our whereabouts.

We spend an hour or more wrapping gifts and missing the Christmas gingerbread contest, hardly even caring about the competition.

Sometimes other things are more important.

* * *

Eventually, we finish and say goodbye. We've worked long into the night, and we get to the town square right as the awards ceremony is about to begin. Everyone is assembled by the gazebo, clutching hot cocoa and chatting while the lights of the trees we decorated yesterday flash on and off.

Wilder and I stride across the snowy town square, where Brady is chatting with Mayor Bumblefritz. When Brady spots me, an evil grin spreads across his face, and something like payback sparks in his eyes.

I gulp, suddenly afraid. My pulse spikes with worry.

Brady darts a hand toward the mayor, snatches his candy cane megaphone, and bounds to the gazebo, pointing it our way as he brings it to his stupid mouth. "You've finally arrived! Will you pretend you're happy to see me win, Wilder Blaine? Like you've been pretending everything else? Like, oh, say, your little romance with Fable that's actually one hundred percent, certified fake. And guess what, big man?" He stops to let out a victorious cackle. "No one likes a liar at Christmastime."

44

KANGAROO COURT

Wilder

Make no mistake, I *can* bluff. Have done it plenty of times in business, in countless negotiations.

The second those nasty words fly from Brady's mouth, I'm ready to deny them and armed with the truth. The evidence too. Fable's hand in mine, our upcoming date, our very real and very true romance.

But there's my friend's wedding, and I don't want to pull attention from the bride and groom, so I call out in a calm, clear voice, "Enough, Brady. Your cousin's getting married tomorrow. Let's talk privately."

Brady's fired up and he points like an accuser in a kangaroo court. "You are not a man of your word," he shouts into his megaphone, letting the whole damn town know.

The mayor clears his throat and climbs the steps, his hands splayed in front of him as if he's trying to cool this hothead down. "Now, this is best handled privately, young man."

The sheriff's heading up the stairs too. "We don't air our problems in the town square," Hardick admonishes.

"But maybe you should," Brady says to him, holding the megaphone above his head, playing keep-away as he moves farther from the pair and speaks into the megaphone again. "Because I competed here in these games in this beloved town. Because I was invited. By *that man*." He points at me. "At Thanksgiving. He offered me a chance to pitch him on my business as a stockbroker, my small business, *if* I won the caroling competition in this lovely town. And I worked hard. So hard. I sang. I practiced. I worked, like all of you hard-working people." The lies roll off his tongue. Next to me, Fable covers her mouth, clearly mortified at the traffic wreck of her ex on stage. Brady addresses the gathered crowd again, who can't stop rubbernecking. Why would they? It's a show, and half the crowd has their phones out, recording it.

"But it was all a trick. Because he said today, he wouldn't give me that chance I fought for. Why? Because Wilder Blaine likes to trick people. All of us regular people. And ask yourself—if he'd lie to me, if he'd invent a girlfriend during Christmastime, for Rudolph's sake, how might he be tricking all of you?"

I'd like to rush the stage and tackle the fucker. But that won't get me anywhere but thrown into jail. I squeeze Fable's hand tighter. "I'm sorry," I whisper to her. Then louder, to everyone, I say, "Nothing is fake. I assure you. It's all real with Fable." Then to Brady, I try once more. "Let's discuss this like gentlemen in—"

"No. We'll discuss it here. How about we have a

competition? A new contest in the Evergreen Falls games. We can let everyone decide if you're a liar!"

Holy shit. Someone is unhinged.

Nearby, Aurora stares at the stage, like she's unable to look away. The man who runs the North Pole Nook is caught in the tractor beam of Brady's rant. The three lumberjacks wince, their collective expressions saying *better you than me*. A few feet away, my best friend stands next his bride-to-be, studying me like he hardly knows me.

Aww shit. Did I mess up by not telling him, after all? Should I have shared the truth about the fake romance and his cousin?

Meanwhile, Fable's dad is munching on a box of popcorn, popping kernels in his mouth and muttering delightedly, "This day just got better."

Fable's eyes flood with regret. She looks so miserable, and this is my fault. But I can't let Brady ruin this day, this season, this wedding tomorrow. So I won't stoop to his level. I won't tell the town he had his dick sucked at my aunt's house on Thanksgiving. I won't ruin Leo's relationship with a family member, even a jackass.

I try again with reason. "Brady, I appreciate that you're frustrated, but Fable and I are together." I lift our joined hands like that proves a point. "We're here together. We've been together for a while, and we'll be together after this."

Fable shouts angrily at her ex, "We have a date for New Year's Eve, and he has more manners in his right toe than you will ever have, and he treats me like I matter and like he cares, and he doesn't—"

"That date?" Brady's eyes flicker with vengeful delight as he cuts her off with his megaphone. "Let's talk about that date."

My hackles rise. What the hell? "I don't think that's necessary. Let's stop this now and discuss it privately."

"Nope," he says, popping the word. "Let's discuss your dates *here.* Why are you faking it? Because I won the singing competition fair and square?"

My god, he's as myopic as he is detestable. "This is not a public matter."

"Brady, that's enough," Leo calls out, his tone crisp and firm. He's clearly done with these shenanigans.

The sheriff looks ready to drag Brady off stage. "Put down your megaphone. No weapons in the town square."

"Fine," Brady says, like a petulant little child. "I'll put it down because I have this."

From his back pocket, he grabs his phone and what looks like a mini speaker, and dramatically swipes a finger across the screen. "I had a feeling about you two. I took an educated guess. Just like I do with stocks every day. And I was right." He hits play and my daughter's voice booms through the speaker. "Is it...ask out Fable on a real date?"

I go cold. That's what Mac said to me earlier when we were making snow angels. In a second, the ice in me changes to fire. Red clouds billow from my eyes. This asshole was snooping on us? He lurked behind my cabins and recorded my *private* conversation *with my daughter*?

He skips the part where Mac suggests the various options for dates then cuts to Mac saying, "That would be fab for your first real date." Then, to Mac saying, "Now go. Make your fake romance real!"

That's enough. With a wildfire in my veins, I march to the stage and rip his phone out of his hand then hit stop. "She's a child," I bite out. "You should be ashamed of yourself."

I take his phone and walk off the stage, swiping fast

and methodically, deleting his files, his recordings, and then uninstalling every single app and sending them to the trash. I don't have his password, so I can't do a factory reset. But this is enough. He loves his phone, and I hate him.

In the minute or so that took, the town square has exploded into chaos. Charlotte wraps an arm around a worried Fable. Leo marches toward me like he can't believe I've hid this from him. He asks me point blank, "Is this true?"

Before I can answer *no, not really, maybe a little*, Aunt Bibi beelines for me, cuts off Leo, and asks in a terribly hurt voice, "Did you really do that?"

But I can't lie anymore. I nod, I did do it. I did it simply to make my very easy life easier. What a weak reason. What a terrible plan. What a horrible idea.

Fable's mother and Julio scurry over to Charlotte. Leo doesn't bother waiting for me. He spins to face his bride and shoots her an accusing stare.

Charlotte winces and says, "I swore I wouldn't tell."

Leo drags a hand through his hair angrily. Townspeople are whispering, with Aurora saying, "Is the wedding still on?" And Lennox asking, "What happens next?" And the North Pole Nook bartender saying, "Do they still need all the champagne?"

This is all my fault. But I ignore them all. Fable has peeled away from her sister and is rushing over to me, setting a hand on my arm—a hand I hardly deserve. "Go to your daughter," she urges, and my heart pounds in fear.

I really fucked up by bringing my daughter into this.

At the edge of the square Mac's standing with my mother, who's holding her close in her arms. My tough daughter. My chief strategist. A lawyer in the making. But not tonight. When I reach her, a lone tear has slipped down one cheek. "I'm so sorry, Dad."

My heart sinks to the ground. I've hurt...everyone.

I pull her into my arms, comforting her, saying, "You've done nothing wrong."

As I hold her close, I spot Bibi across the square. Her arms are crossed, her gaze is fierce, and she's staring at Fable. I can make out the shape of the words coming out of her mouth, "I'm awfully disappointed."

Of course she is.

This was bound to happen.

It started with a lie. It can't end in true love.

45

AS REAL AS SANTA

Wilder

I'm back at the cabins, trying to forget everything for a minute as I say goodnight to Mac, who's sturdy again.

"I'm fine, Dad. I swear. It was just a moment when I wasn't tough like you," she reassures me as she yawns and heads into her bedroom.

My gut sinks. "Have I taught you to be tough all the time?" I ask, my voice wooden.

She shrugs. "Well, you're the toughest person I know. Nothing hurts you."

Ouch.

That hurts more than it should because it's probably true. I've been stoic and reserved. But then again, where did being vulnerable get me? Oh, just my daughter being mocked in public by a jackass, my best friend arguing with his bride-to-be, and the whole town thinking I'm a liar.

Because I am.

But I haven't even dealt with the Bibi aftermath. I tell Mac I love her, and when I leave her room, I head for my aunt's cabin. I need to deal with that sooner rather than later. My mother's in the kitchen, busying herself by cleaning the counters. Bibi's waiting for me on the couch, tapping her toe, her chin held high.

"Why did you lie?" she asks straight out as I cross the living room to apologize for my sins under the lights of the Christmas tree. "And don't lie now, *wild child*."

There's nothing tough in her voice. She's hurt, and I have to give her the courtesy of the truth. "I didn't want to be set up," I admit with a helpless shrug.

"Then just say that," she says crisply.

"I tried to tell you," I point out.

She arches a doubtful brow. "How hard did you try, Wilder? How hard did you ask not to be set up? As hard as you tried to run a billion-dollar business? Were you as committed to that as you were to lying? Were you as devoted to telling me the truth as you were to beating Brady in the competition?"

Triple ouch. "Fair enough," I admit.

"You didn't have to resort to this," she says tightly, taking the high road.

"You're right. I thought I did. I'm sorry."

"Bibi, cut him some slack," my mom says gently from the kitchen. "He really likes her."

Bibi snaps her gaze to her sister. "Did you know about this all along, Elizabeth? And you went along with the ruse?"

My mother looks over her shoulder, then says truthfully, "I've known for a few days."

Bibi draws a sharp breath and holds up a stop-sign hand my way. "You played me for a fool. I expected more of you."

Then she walks off, away from her sister and me.

I drag a hand down my face. Everything is a shit show.

I trudge through the kitchen. "I should go...talk to Fable," I say to my mom.

"Yes, you should, kiddo," Mom says with a smile.

I see nothing to smile about. I knew this was a bad idea from the start, but I did it anyway and hurt nearly everyone. This is what happens when you lie. I'm just like my father after all.

With heavy feet and a heavier heart, I enter the shared living room, then trudge down the long hallway to our cabin, where I find Fable in our honeymoon suite, curled up on the couch, clutching her phone like she's waiting for something. She tears her gaze away from the screen and turns to me, a flash of worry in her beautiful eyes.

More questions pummel me from that look alone.

What would happen if I let this go on? And sure, it's been easy to play boyfriend and girlfriend while we're living together during the holidays, but how would Fable fit into my real life? Where would she wind up? Sucked deeper into this mess at work?

Fable's trying to achieve her dreams. To open her jewelry shops, not to get caught up in a complicated romance that started from a lie.

If I let this continue, how could it possibly go anywhere good? Love never does. Bibi's husband died, Mom's romance sputtered out so badly she's happier alone, my father can't break his addiction, and I somehow stupidly thought a fake relationship was a good idea. Clearly, I'm not cut out for romance.

It's not that I don't trust Fable. I don't trust myself with her heart.

Because trust is as real as Santa Claus.

46

IT'S ME. I'M THE PROBLEM

Fable

Don't you dare let on this hurts.

It doesn't hurt.

You're fine.

So fine that the second the door snicks shut, I erase the sad face I know I'm working right now. I'm the bold one, the fun one, the one who keeps her act together. I did it for my sister growing up, and dammit, I'll do it now. I can't take a chance ruining her wedding with my drama.

I'm on edge, waiting to hear from her. In the chaos of the town square, she told me she needed to talk to Leo, who was hurt that she'd kept this from him, and that she'd text me when they sorted it out.

I've been glued to my phone, but she hasn't messaged yet.

Wilder comes in, I try to hide my surprise at his appearance. I've never seen him like this. Broken down.

Exhausted. Like he's reached a dead-end maze and can't figure out how to turn around.

But first things first. "How is Mac doing?"

"She's fine. She was embarrassed and felt terrible. But she was over it pretty quickly." He blows out a heavy breath. "Bibi, not so much." He waves a hand like he's psyching himself up. "But I'll figure it out. I'll sort it out. I'll..."

He trails off like he's run out of steam.

The man who bought out half a store, the man who invented a naughty and nice list so that we could ace this, the man who developed a plan so we could be the best fake daters. The man who figured out all my wants and needs before I even told him.

Right now, he's got nothing. He's a car sputtering into the driveway with no gas left in the tank.

It breaks my heart into ragged pieces. "You don't look okay though," I say gently.

He drags a hand over his stubble, shaking his head, his green eyes brimming with frustration. He's a man who's mad at himself. "I've been better," he says.

He's deadpan as he delivers the understatement of the century, but it still shreds me. This is when he should feel the best he's ever felt. Instead, everything has turned upside down thanks to my own bad decisions. I knew it was best not to let him—or anyone—see the truth of my feelings. The depth of them.

Romance has never worked out for me. Whenever you let someone see who you really are, they can walk all over you. Wilder might not be like my father or my ex, but look where my first big chance at love landed me—a fake romance that went tits up.

What happened at the gazebo an hour ago is proof that I'm terrible at choosing.

Not that Wilder is a bad choice.

I'm the bad choice.

Me.

I'm the problem.

"Wilder?" I ask carefully. Stripping the emotions from my voice ought to be easy. I've done it plenty of times before. But it's hard now because everything I felt for him was so real.

But it was just a honeymoon, only a holiday romance.

"Yes?" he asks, his voice flat.

"We should..." It's hard to say the next words. It's like a door shuts on the sentence as it's forming—*we should stop.*

I started this, and I need to finish it. I made the mistake, and I need to unmake it. I did a stupid, foolish thing for a stupid, foolish reason. I wanted to prove to my ex that I was over him. What a petty, unimportant reason.

In my quest to prove to Brady that he couldn't hurt me, I hurt Wilder, Mac, Bibi, my sister's groom, many others, and...myself.

Brady went and ruined everything because that's who he is. And I am who I am—a woman who doesn't have a clue how to have a healthy relationship.

I force myself to look at Wilder. His eyes are filled with regret, and I know what he came here to do. I don't want to be hurt all over again, so I have to beat him to the punch.

"Fable, do you—"

I cut him off with, "Maybe we should cool things."

He furrows his brow, but the confusion lasts only a second then he breathes out a noticeable sigh of relief. In his *agenda item* tone, he says coolly, "That would be for the best."

Of course he agrees. He came here to break up with me. And I can't let him think I'm truly hurt. "It was always supposed to wind up like this, anyway," I say, forcing a cheery tone. We're just moving up the deadline on what we'd always planned to do.

He nods tightly, like he understands me completely. "Right. Yes. It was. This is just...this is...I'm sorry." He scratches his head. "I've been saying that a lot today. I thought I had a handle on things. I thought I had everything together." He sighs, seeming resigned to this fate. "I was wrong."

A tsunami of emotions slams into me, threatening to yank me under. But I won't let the feelings drown me. I am the dam that holds them back. Chin up, I say, "We had a plan. We should stick to it. Tomorrow we can stand at the wedding as best man and maid of honor, and it'll be fine."

Except that little issue of Brady.

One thing I've learned from our faux romance is that I can't fake my way through problems. Jerks are a part of life, and I have to face them head-on. I have to face my own hurt, my own shame, and my own feelings about how I should be treated.

I have to stop hiding.

This is the beginning of me really trying to change.

And that should start by me doing what I came to Evergreen Falls to do—stand up for my sister—not protect myself. "I really should go check on Charlotte," I say, pointing to the door, but then my gaze strays to the bed. What happens later when we both want to sleep?

My gut churns with a whole new worry.

Will we do the bed/couch dance again? But like

always, Wilder reads me instantly. "I'll sleep on the couch," he says, like it's an order.

I don't have any fight left in me. It will be beyond awkward to have him sleeping on the couch ten feet away, but sometimes life is awkward and you have to live with the discomfort. "Sure, that's fine. I'll get you a blanket."

I get up to grab one, but he's faster. Then he says, "I'll be in the living room on *that couch*."

Oh.

Looks like I got that wrong too.

He grabs some clothes and toiletries, then leaves. The second the door shuts, I am not fine at all. I cry giant, messy, sloppy tears. But they're silent. Because I don't want anyone to hear me.

47

MAN BABY TANTRUMS

Fable

There's a knock on my door a few minutes later. I sit up, grab a tissue to swipe at my eyes, and croak a wobbly, "Yes?" as hope bangs its drum in my chest.

He's back.

He misses me.

He doesn't want to stop anything. He wants to start everything.

"It's us," Josie says. "And we have something for you."

My heart sinks, but not for long. I need my friends badly, maybe more than I need Wilder right now. "I hope it's a time machine so I can go back to three weeks ago and undo my dumb decisions."

"The second-best thing," Maeve says cheerily through the wood. "It's wine and cheese."

I sniffle. "That'll do."

I drag my sorry ass up and open the door. The parade of besties marches in—Maeve, Everly, and Josie are dressed in their Christmas jammies, carrying box wine, mugs, and a charcuterie board covered in cheese, olives, and crackers. Everly carries a canvas bag on her arm.

They sit cross-legged on the floor in front of the Christmas tree, and I join them. "I'm such a freaking mess," I blurt out. There's no point pretending I'm fine. I texted them earlier in the day to tell them about our New Year's Eve date. But they would have found out at the Great Town Square megaphoning anyway.

Josie gives me a sympathetic smile. "You're not a mess. But tonight was definitely a disaster, and I'm really sorry that happened."

Everly rubs my arm, the ends of her ponytail swinging as she moves. "Do you want to talk about it? How are you feeling?"

My instinct says *don't talk about it*. But I'm so tired of holding everything in. I'm so exhausted by my own fears and tired of pretending I'm okay all the time. As Maeve pours a glass of wine, I waste no time saying, "I'm not fine. We went from...falling to...we're not going to date after all." My voice breaks.

The soft blue lights from the tree flicker across Maeve's face, and she shakes her head like there's water in her ears. "You're not going to date at all? Why not? What's the point of that? I thought you had real feelings. Sure, they were complicated since you work together, but then it seemed like you uncomplicated it by just...embracing all these feelings."

"Then it got complicated all over again. See exhibit A. Tonight."

Everly peers at me with those thoughtful big brown eyes. "Because you have an ex who's an agent of chaos. A lot of people do," she points out matter-of-factly. "Like

Max does. Sometimes they stir things up. Remember last month?"

I flash back to earlier in the hockey season when her boyfriend's famous ex showed up out of the blue and nearly ruined an event. His pop-star ex is not exactly like Brady, but she's cut from the same narcissistic cloth.

That event became a hot mess, too, so her point has been made, I suppose.

"You're right. But the whole thing tonight forced me to look at myself, and that's what I'm trying to do."

"Right, but why is the answer—don't date?"

My throat hitches. "Once Wilder came to see me a little while ago, it was clear in his face, in his eyes. I knew he was going to end it anyway. I couldn't take it. I didn't want to get fooled again," I say, serving up my shame and my insecurities. "It was bad enough when it happened with Brady, a guy I only sort of liked. I can't imagine how much worse it would feel with somebody I—"

I stop before I say the words—*fell in love with*.

But Josie tips her chin my way. "It's okay. You can say it. We're all friends here."

"Say what?" I ask, pretending I don't know what she means.

Maeve nudges my arm.

Everly pats me on the knee. "Say it."

But it's so hard to voice those words. I keep my mouth shut.

Maeve doesn't though. "It's so obvious that you're a dream come true to him. Why don't you let your own dream come true?"

Way to see inside my soul. "How do you know this is a dream of mine?" I counter.

"Because I know you," she says. "Because you love

deeply. You love your sister deeply. You love us deeply. You feel everything. I've seen the way you look at him, but you're so afraid the things that scare you have become more powerful than love."

Her words ring through my head and slither into my heart. They stare at me pointedly like a cat refusing to budge. "But how do I get past them? Aren't you ever scared?"

Josie smiles softly. "Of course I am. But I try to face it now."

"You know *I* am," Everly seconds. "But life is sweeter when you can move past your fears." And it's true she's been there, done that.

Maeve smiles sympathetically. "I am too. All the time, every day. I've been scared every day since my parents died when I went to college. I've been scared since my mom told me to follow my dreams. I've been scared that I'll never be able to achieve them." Her eyes shining, she adds, "But you just have to keep trying."

Josie gives her a side-arm hug and then turns her gaze to me. "Love hurts, but so does letting it go."

"Do you really want to let him go?" Everly presses. "Because I don't think you do."

Who needs therapy with friends like this? I flop back onto the carpet. "Why did you come here? To make me cry and feel everything? I hate feelings so much. So very, very much."

They join me, flat on their backs, too, which there's space enough to do because this really is a chalet, not a cabin.

"If you're not ready to do the hard thing, have a piece of cheese until you are," Josie offers.

That's not a bad idea. "Okay," I say as I sit up to take a bite of a smoky Gouda.

As I eat, Josie adds, "It's like you sometimes say to us—*sometimes we aren't ready to do the hard thing, so we have to do something easier first*."

I side-eye her. "You tricked me. You're quoting me back to me."

She smiles. "I am."

I heave a sigh then give in, doing the easiest thing first. "Fine. You're right. I fell in love with him."

They erupt into cheers.

I roll my eyes. "Stop, stop."

"The first step is saying it," Josie goads.

"The second step is doing something about it," Everly adds.

"The third step is banging," Maeve finishes.

I laugh, but then sigh. Nothing is fixed, and there's no evidence it will be. I don't know how Wilder truly feels or what he's willing to risk.

"I'll think about what you said. See how I feel in the morning. How's that?"

Everly smiles, then pats the canvas bag she brought. "Fair enough, but in that case, we have to wait till morning to show you what's in the bag."

No fair. "I want it now."

"Not until you admit you're going to try. Not simply consider it," she says, holding the bag tight.

I huff but relent. "I'll try."

Josie nods toward the bag. "Show her."

Everly reaches into it and dramatically extracts a crushed red-and-white cardboard box for a store-bought gingerbread house. "Brady's not the only one who can look around and snoop. We can too. And we found this in his cabin after he threw his big man-baby tantrum on the gazebo stage. Somehow, it wound up on social under that hashtag—manbabytantrums. Which happens to be the best hashtag ever," she says.

I can't help it—I grin.

"It is."

"And," Everly continues, "the rules for the gingerbread competition were quite clear. You have to make the houses yourself."

I smile devilishly. "And what are you going to do with this discovery?"

Josie lifts her chin proudly. "We already brought this to the judges. We'll see what happens tomorrow."

I say goodnight, then get ready for bed alone for the first time since I've been here. While I do, I think about the Girlfriends' Guide to Getting Your Man Back.

Step one—saying it. Step two—doing it. Step three—coming back together.

And I'm pretty sure I want all those things more than I want to stay here, stuck.

I'm ready to do the hard thing.

I'm ready to fight for my man.

48

A PERFECT PAIRING

Wilder

After a half hour of pacing the grounds outside in the dark, crunching through the snow on hills by my cabins like a fucking caricature of a lonely billionaire (cue the violins), I'm fed up with myself more than I'd thought possible. I miss Fable horribly, but I don't know what the hell to do about it.

I don't have a spreadsheet to figure out this ache or a deal memo to stop these pangs of longing. There's no business plan to navigate safely to the other side of these damn vexing emotions that have no place to go.

All I know is this—I've messed up spectacularly, and I need to go back to square one.

Fix one thing at a time.

I stop pacing, draw a deep breath of crisp winter air, and let it fill me with the first answer.

I'll start with my friend. Maybe because that's the easiest, but sometimes that's how you have to begin.

I return to the main living room, march down the hall to Leo and Charlotte's cabin, and lift my fist to bang on the door. Before I knock, though, I call out, "Look, I fucked up. I should have told you. But don't fight with your bride because of—"

The door swings open, and a disheveled Leo appears, tugging on a sweatshirt, hair a mess, a cocky grin on his face. "What were you saying?"

I blink, taking a beat to process the obvious. "I thought...you and Charlotte were..."

The corner of his lips quirks up. "Fighting?"

"Yeah, you seemed pissed earlier," I say.

He shrugs. "I was for a minute. But then she explained that some shit went down with her sister and my cousin, and that was all she needed to say."

Oh. My brow furrows. "It was?"

A voice calls out from beyond the door, "Yes, it was!" Charlotte adds, "We're all good. I mean, we're great. Really great. *Oh* so very great."

"Clearly." I breathe my first real sigh of relief. "I thought I messed things up for you two."

Leo scoffs. "Impossible." He calls over his shoulder, "Be back in a bit, sweetheart."

"Don't take too long," Charlotte warns in a sensual tone that hints at another round of makeup sex.

"I won't." He shuts the door, claps my shoulder, and nods down the hall. "Deck and scotch?"

"A perfect pairing for tonight."

A few minutes later, we're parked on the outdoor couch under the stars, the electric fireplace on, drinks poured. Leo holds up a glass. I don't feel much like toasting, but the way I feel isn't important, so I clink back and say, "To your wedding tomorrow."

He shakes me off. "You don't need to toast my wedding tomorrow. It's going to be great. We'll toast to you telling me the truth." My nice, happy-go-lucky, charming, green-flag best friend who's kind to everyone shoots me a stern look. "What really happened with my cousin?"

I pause, debating how much truth to tell him, pinch the bridge of my nose, then say *fuck it*. Half-truths won't fix this mess. Avoiding the real story because it might cause awkwardness in the wedding party won't help anyone. "I didn't want to tell you. He's your cousin and a groomsman. You looked out for him growing up. He's family."

But Leo just beckons with his fingers. "Serve it up."

Gladly. Fucking gladly. "At my Thanksgiving dinner, he hooked up with the caterer at Aunt Bibi's house, sneaking off with her to the wrapping room, where Fable found them right while Brady was singing 'Joy to the World' while Iris hummed along with her mouth full."

Leo freezes for a second, then the glass falls from his hand.

Our hustle to clean up shards of glass on the deck feels like a fitting metaphor for tonight.

49

NO TRESPASSING

Wilder

It's not my place to say *let's kick him out.* But it is my absolute pleasure to agree when Leo declares, "Let's kick him out."

I drop the last dustpan full of glass shards into a sturdy paper bag, then put it in the outdoor garbage bin, saying, "More than happy to." Tossing out that fucker might be one of the best Christmas presents ever. It's also the next thing I need to fix in the long list of mistakes I've made.

"Yes, but we need a plan." Leo strokes his chin in the universal signal for *I'm devising a brilliant scheme.*

But brilliant schemes are right in my wheelhouse. The perfect strategy has come to me fully formed.

I explain it to Leo, and his eyes light up. "Let's do it now."

First, I make a few phone calls, arrange a handful of details, and enlist some troops. As I do, Charlotte calls Leo and tells him she forgives him for being late. She also has juicy new info about the gingerbread competition.

When Leo shares it with me, I'm not surprised. But I will enjoy the hell out of this extra ammo.

As soon as everything and everyone is in place, my best friend and I head directly to Brady's cabin on the outskirts of the resort I own.

The operative words—*I own.*

The clock nears eleven. Leo raps loudly on the outer door and I stand to the side, out of view. Rustling sounds come from inside the cabin, then the trudge of tired feet. Brady swings open the door in the middle of a yawn.

"Hey, cuz." Leo's upbeat tone gives nothing away. "Got a minute to chat about the big day tomorrow?"

The yawn deepens. "Any chance this could wait till the morning? I'm tired and Iris is asleep."

I roll my eyes. What a lazy jerk.

Leo flashes him a smile as he shakes his head. "Groomsman business. Needs to happen right now."

"You sure, man?"

"Positive."

"All right," Brady says, like he's so put out. "It's just been a rough night for me, you know?"

He has no idea how much rougher it's about to get.

"Thanks," Leo says and crosses the doorway.

My turn. I move from beside the door, stepping in front of the beady-eyed asshole. Brady's wearing a bathrobe, boxer shorts, and a T-shirt advertising a podcast on how to get rich fast. Prick.

"It's your least favorite person," I say as his eyes bug out, brimming with fear. "Which is entirely mutual."

"W-what the hell are you doing here?" Aww, it's cute

that he's scared, but then he adds in a mean voice, "After you ruined my phone."

He cares nothing about people. Only things, money, and himself.

I step inside, closing the distance between us. "Fuck you and your phone. You ruined the entire Christmas competition." I advance on him through the foyer as he backs deeper into the cabin. "Ever heard of respect? Decency? How about manners? You lurked around *my grounds* and recorded a private conversation with *my daughter*. You cheated in the gingerbread competition with a store-bought gingerbread house. You begged me for an audience to pitch your portfolio management, and when I turned you down—which businesses do all the time, so get used to it, Brady-i-o—you chose to get even with a public shaming."

He backs into the couch, nearly tumbling onto it, and grabs the arm to steady himself.

"That's not how you handle a *no* in business," I continue. "Learn a little grace, maybe a little humility. Learn how to handle failure. You think you're a smart businessman?"

I pause, giving the jackass a chance to answer. He manages a shaky, "Y-yes."

"Wrong," I bite out. "You're nothing but a lying, cheating scum. And you know how I know that?"

I wait again.

Brady swallows and maybe for a split second a shred of guilt crosses his eyes. "How do you know?"

"Because I know how you treated the woman I love in my aunt's wrapping room at Thanksgiving."

"Fable was *my* girlfriend then," he says, digging an even bigger hole, then falls onto the couch like a turtle.

Shaking his head in disgust, Leo strides to his cousin. "Do you even hear the words that come out of your mouth?"

I answer for Brady. "I don't think he does." Then I turn my full fury back to the prick. "I love Fable. I love her in ways you could never imagine. I love her because she's smart, and daring, and kind, and big-hearted. She cares deeply for people, and she keeps me on my toes, and you could never appreciate her because you can't appreciate anything but yourself. You don't have a clue what a complete and utter dumpster fire you are. But let me enlighten you. Cheating on your girlfriend is not okay. Lying to her is not okay. Treating her like she's anything other than the center of the universe is not okay." I take a breath, a very satisfied one, then turn to Leo. "You want to tell him what else isn't okay?"

A hint of sadness flashes across my friend's eyes. My heart stops. Will he go soft? But Leo is a good man who doesn't suffer fools, and a few seconds later, he speaks in a calm, centered voice. "What's not okay is walking by my side as a groomsman at my wedding after what you did tonight and what you did on Thanksgiving. You cheated on my bride's sister, and you did it seconds before I proposed. You're out of the wedding party."

Brady sputters, then his lower lip quivers. "But Cousin Leo—"

"And since Wilder owns this resort, guess what else you're not in?"

His eyes turn watery. "What else?"

He's crying. He's fucking crying. Holy shit. This is the best thing ever. Wait, no, *this is*. I puff out my chest and say, "You're not staying here at my cabins—fuck it—my chalets a minute longer."

He gulps as tears streak down his cheeks. "Where am I supposed to go?"

"That's a really good question, Brady. You might have won a few battles, but I'm going to win this strategy game because I've arranged your escort out of town."

Right on cue, the sheriff pulls into the driveway, cuts the engine, and climbs out of the patrol car. He's not alone. Mayor Bumblefritz exits the passenger side, keeping one arm tucked behind his back. They both stride up the stone path to the door and into the cabin foyer, accompanied by a gust of crisp air.

Sheriff Hardick clears his throat, hooks his thumbs into his pants pockets, then rocks back on his heels. "Every year, we host a friendly holiday competition in the spirit of sportsmanship and gentle-humanly behavior. And you ruined it with your petulant, whiny, bratty antics tonight. So it will be my absolute pleasure to escort you out of this town and leave you at the county limits."

Brady gulps. "On the side of the road? What do I do then?"

The mayor whips out his megaphone from behind his back and booms, "We don't give a shit."

I turn back to Brady and smile. "As the owner of this resort and someone who grew up, in fact, *a regular guy*," I say, sketching air quotes, "it gives me great pleasure to say get the hell off my property. You've got one minute to get your things."

Exactly one gratifying minute of frantic scrambling later, Brady and a very tired Iris scurry out of the cabin in their bathrobes, with their clothes poking out of their duffel bags.

But before he can dart down the stairs, I grab Brady by the neck of his bathrobe and yank him toward me. "If you ever talk to the woman I love again, bother her, or contact her in any way, shape, or form, you'll have me to answer to. And remember—I started as just a regular guy, and I know how to play every single game. Now get the fuck out of town."

"Yes, sir," he says, and with his tail tucked between his legs, he runs to the sheriff's vehicle for a ride out of town.

"And don't come back," I call out helpfully.

"Don't you worry about that, Mr. Blaine," Sheriff Hardick says as he tips his cowboy hat my way. Then he turns to Brady and Iris and adds, "In case that wasn't clear, you're not welcome at Evergreen Falls. We like everyone except for cheating little cheaters who cheat in our Christmas competition."

They peel off, and that's one more thing fixed.

Leo turns back to me, then nods toward my cabin. "Maybe it's time for you to deal with that whole *the woman I love* thing."

Huh. I did say that in the heat of the moment. More than once in fact. And I felt it all deep in my bones, and into the far corners of my soul.

Trouble is, when I reach my cabin, the light's off in the honeymoon suite.

50

ONE LITTLE THING

Wilder

Fable's likely asleep. My woman loves her shut-eye.

My woman.

She still feels like mine even though she's not. Even though I let her go—another foolish move.

As I return to the main cabin, my heart pounds mercilessly in her direction and my attention strays down the hall to the suite we shared. Two hours ago, she said she wanted to stop this thing between us. Just because I'm madly, deeply, painfully, terribly, incredibly in love with her doesn't mean that's going to change.

Unless you tell her you love her.

Does she even want to hear it, though? Do I trust myself to get it right? Those questions chase me.

When I left the suite, I started out with the aim of fixing the mess I made of Christmas. I've left something unfinished, and I need to set that right.

Bibi.

She's a night owl, usually. I reach her cabin and tap gently on the door to her sitting room. I barely touch the wood, and the door falls open.

"And then he said, *I'll be there right away*," Bibi is telling my mom as the two of them relax on the couch. I've come in mid-conversation and they haven't heard me yet.

"I wish I could have seen the looks on all their faces," Mom says warmly.

"Me too. But he'll tell me tomorrow, I'm sure. Or... maybe late tonight."

Well, Bibi seems in a better mood. Maybe I should leave. Talking to me is likely to ruin it.

I don't want to ruin this nice moment between sisters who haven't seen each other in a while. I came this close to ruining things for Charlotte.

Or did I? Leo and Charlotte made up nearly immediately.

And that's exactly what I need to do with my aunt.

Stop turning the other way. Stop avoiding the hard thing. Stop pretending.

I clear my throat. "Hello, Mom. Hello, Bibi. Do you have a minute, Bibi?"

My aunt turns her face an inch, her expression hardening. Gone is the sweet Bibi who was chatting with her sister. "Of course," she says, giving me a chance because she's gracious.

I head over to her, taking a seat on the couch.

"I'm going to excuse myself for a moment," Mom says.

Once she's gone, I attempt a better apology than the one I offered earlier tonight. "You're right. I'm sorry. I should have said something to you in the first place."

"You should have," she says stiffly. "I would have

understood. I'm a Pisces, after all. Don't forget we're understanding and compassionate."

"You are."

But I also know she's not going to forgive me that quickly through signs of the Zodiac.

Her smile disappears. "What you did was hurtful. You put on a show for me. You pretended for me simply because I was trying to set you up. That hurt my feelings. Also, it kind of seems like it was a bad plan, wild child."

"Well, yeah." I gesture in the general direction of the town square. "It didn't really work out."

"That's not what I mean. It was a bad plan because you've always said you didn't believe in love." She pauses, then adds, "But look what you did."

"What did I do?"

She thumps me on the side of the head. "You went out and fell in love."

That four-letter word terrifies me still, but less than it did earlier tonight. "Was it that obvious?"

"As obvious as the hideous gingerbread house that fool made. I don't know how they missed that it was pre-bought, but I'm glad they've found out. But enough about the Christmas competition. At first, I had my doubts about you and Fable, but the second you arrived here, it was clear that you were mad about the woman. And honestly, I suppose it's okay you *faked it* because I got to watch a very, very fun show for the last few days." Her stony face disappears, and a devilish, up-to-no-good smile arrives in its place. "I got to see you fall in love for the first time." She pats my knee. "Whatever are we going to do about your little love situationship?"

I laugh. "Never change, Bibi."

She leans back and calls to my mother, "Elizabeth, you don't want to miss this."

When my mother returns, Bibi pats a couch cushion for her sister. "We need to help him get his woman back."

"We sure do," Mom agrees. But then she shoots me a serious stare and says, "Are you ready?"

I arch a brow. "What do you mean?"

Mom lets out a big breath. "What I mean is your whole life you've been so afraid of turning out like your father. You fear you'll be the same, so you work hard to be different," she says, nailing my daily motivations for, oh, say, all my adult life. "You've remade yourself as his opposite in every way. You think if you do that, you can avoid hurting, but you forgot one important detail."

I take that on the chin because I deserve it. I need it. And because it's true. But I need to do something about it, so I ask without guile, "What's that?"

She holds my gaze with warm eyes that know me. "You think you can't trust love, but really, all you need is to trust yourself and believe you can handle love." She takes the beat. "I believe in you. You're not him."

I let those words soak in. Maybe they're the words I've always needed to hear.

Still, there's that little problem of what to say to Fable. Fear is the issue there too. That's what's held me back. Not the belief that love is a lie, but the fear that love might be true. If it is, someone can hurt me.

"You might be right," I tell Mom. "But a little while ago she said she thought we should stop dating. And isn't tonight evidence that I would just make a big mess of it if we continue?"

Bibi tuts. "Wilder, Wilder, Wilder. Love is messy. Deal

with it. Now, set an alarm and be ready to tell her when she wakes up that you were a dumbass tonight."

I sit with her comment for a while, and soon, I'm nodding. "I think you're both right."

"We are," they say in unison.

I thank them and head to the couch with my name on it tonight, strip out of my jeans and shirt, and pull the fleece blanket over me, ready to fix one more thing in the morning.

* * *

When I wake with the sun shining on Christmas Eve morning, I fold up the blanket, brush my teeth in the guest bathroom, and change into fresh clothes.

I return to the main living room, ready to check on Fable. But out front, a cab pulls up to the cabin, and a familiar figure steps out onto the snowy sidewalk.

My father.

51

EXTRAORDINARY LOVE

Wilder

Dread crawls up my body. It wraps its cold arms around my throat. I stare at what feels like a mirage, but it's all too real.

Why is he here?

Whatever the reason, it can't be good. I stand at the door, holding it open for him, my chest crawling with worry but also something like relief.

He's alive.

It's a fear that has never stopped chasing me. But I suppose that's part of loving an addict—worry is never truly far away. With his head hanging low and an embarrassed hint of a smile shifting his lips, he heads along the snow-covered stone path and up the steps, and stands in front of me.

"Hey, son," he says brightly. Like I was anticipating his arrival on the day before Christmas. Like he's the last guest we've been waiting for.

"Hi," I say plainly, unsure where we're going.

"Merry Christmas," he says.

"Merry Christmas?"

Dad shifts his duffel from one hand to the other.

"How did you get here?"

"I took a plane. You know, they're those things that have wings and jet engines?"

But I'm not in the mood for making light. "What are you doing here?"

"I came to wish you a happy holiday," he says.

That's a lie. I'm tired of his lies. I'm tired of the chokehold addiction has on him. And I'm exhausted by the chokehold it has on me. I sweep an arm toward the empty cabin, and he goes in.

Once the door is shut, I cut to the chase. "What's going on with Desert Springs Casino? Are you in trouble? Do you owe them money?"

He winces as he kicks off his boots. "It kind of seems that way," he says with maybe a tinge of embarrassment, possibly a morsel of regret.

"You were card-counting, Dad. What the hell?"

He meets my gaze with sad eyes. "They say I was card-counting."

"Were you?" I ask point-blank.

He shrugs. An admission.

I shake my head. "What is going on? Why are you here? You don't just show up randomly unannounced."

He sighs, and this one is full of a clear emotion—regret. "I'm in a pinch," he says, embarrassed, but also borderline begging.

Of course that's why he's here. "What happened exactly?"

He waves a hand airily like he can dismiss the

specifics. "You know how it goes. But I could make it back in a game. I could hit the tables at the casinos here in the mountains. I know I could."

My heart sinks, heavy and leaden. That's the true reason he hightailed it out of town, catching a red-eye. He's here not only to convince me to pay off his debt but to snag money for a new score.

I tear my gaze away from him, staring at the window that looks over the deck and out onto the nearby mountains. My heart hurts. My throat aches. My head pounds.

This is all so familiar.

I try to sort through what to do next when what Fable said the other morning echoes in my head. *You don't have to solve it.*

I've always solved his gambling problems. I've always enabled him. I've always fixed it.

And if I don't stop, I'm going to wind up just like him. Maybe not an addict. Maybe not penniless. But loveless all the same.

That won't do.

It's time to do things differently. "Why don't you sit down on the couch and I'll make a pot of coffee for us?"

"Thank you," he says, and his voice sounds genuine. Maybe it's just for the coffee, but at least that's a start.

* * *

A few minutes later, we're sitting on the couch by the Christmas tree as the sun rises higher in the morning sky, the white snowfall from the other night sparkling and bright.

I hand him a steaming cup, still chewing on what to say exactly. As I gather my thoughts, I glance at the ornament my daughter made—a ceramic cartoon fireplace with four stockings hanging from it with names on them.

Dad, Mac, Penguin, and...Fable.

The three of us plus a cat. That's what I want. I don't want to be loveless. I don't want to be tough all the time. I don't want to be the guy who believes love is a lie.

I want a family. I want togetherness. I want to come back here year after year with the love of my life.

But I won't be able to get to Fable unless I take care of this roadblock in my heart.

Sometimes you have to do the easier thing first, but eventually you have to do the hard thing.

Like now.

And I finally know what to do because of the love of Fable, my daughter, my mom, and Bibi. All the women in my life are extraordinary, and they love extraordinarily too.

It's time for me to live up to their example.

I look my dad square in the eye, and I say, "You know what I'd like for Christmas?"

His brow furrows in confusion. He didn't come here to give me a gift. "What's that?"

"I'd like for you to go to rehab."

He flinches. "But what about the debt? What about the money I owe Desert Springs? That's going to be haunting me. I've got to take care of that first," he says, desperate for another hit, another game, another gamble.

They say an addict needs to want to change. I'm not sure he does. But maybe the change will come if he no longer has a safety net.

"I'm not going to pay your debt."

"But you have the money," he says, his voice pitching up.

"I do, and I'm going to use that money to send you to rehab. I'm going to find a great facility for you. A program where you can check in for a month or so and get real help day in and day out. Someplace where you can get help so that next year I can actually invite you to Christmas and you can see your granddaughter and show us all your one-year chip." I stop when my throat clogs with emotion. *Deep breath.* "I'll handle all of that. I'll take care of all of that. I'll set it up."

His jaw ticks, and he seems to fight off a traitorous tear. "But what about the money I owe?"

I hear Fable's voice again, asking me if paying it off is going to solve anything.

I don't have to solve it either. But perhaps I can help in a new way. A better way. A way that matters. "I am going to call Desert Springs, and I'm going to ask for a grace period. I'm going to arrange a payment plan for you so that you have plenty of time to get yourself together and then to pay it off. When you get out of rehab, I'm going to get you a job with my company. Maybe you'll be a ticket taker at the Renegades. Maybe you'll be an usher. Maybe you'll restock the vending machines at one of my hotels. Or maybe you'll find your own job. But you're going to get a job and pay it off yourself. I'm not covering for you anymore." I pause and collect myself. "And it's not because of the money. It's because I love you. And I want you to get well."

He swallows, his throat working as more tears fall down his face. For a few seconds, he seems at war with himself. Like he wants to run to the door and hit the tables. He probably does. But, finally, with a shrug of resignation, he simply says, "Okay."

It's enough. Because it's a new start.

He heads to Brady's former cabin to take a shower, and I stand at the counter with my phone, searching for the closest and best rehab facilities for gambling addiction.

The soft pad of fuzzy socks registers, and seconds later, the smell of strawberries and champagne floats past me. My whole soul calms down, and a voice in my ear says, "I heard the end of that. I'm so proud of you."

I don't waste another second. I turn around, cup her cheeks, and say, "I love you."

That was terrifying but it was wonderful too. I suppose both things can be true at once. Love can hurt you, and love can heal you.

Before she can answer, I say it again, "I love you so much, Fable. I should have said it last night. I should have said it the night before. I should have said it every second we've been here because I was falling in love with you when we walked through that door. And I've fallen harder and faster every second I've spent with you. I love you," I say again, unable to stop. "I love you so much. You are extraordinary, and I want to love you that way too. I want you to be mine for real, for today, for tomorrow, for New Year's Eve, for all the days."

I wait for her answer.

52

MY TOO MUCH

Fable

"You beat me to it! That's not fair." But it's hard to be mad. Not when I'm overjoyed and bursting with big, scary, incredible feelings.

"Did I now?" he asks, wrapping his arms around my waist.

"You did. And we'll have to fight about it," I say, and I don't try to hide the happiness that floods my cells.

"I would love to fight with you."

"You've got it because I love you, Wilder Blaine," I say, making myself vulnerable at last, but he's worth it. He's so worth it. "I love you so much, and I came out here this morning determined to find you and to tell you I was ridiculous for saying we should stop. I was so scared of telling you how I felt for real. And I thought you wanted to end things, and I didn't want you to hurt me, so I chose the coward's way out," I admit, finally serving up all my fears.

"I never want to hurt you, honey. I'm sorry I did," he says, gripping me tighter, holding me closer.

I shake my head. "It was my fault. I wasn't honest about my feelings."

"I wasn't either. It was my fault," he says, adamant.

And I laugh. "Are we fighting about whose fault it is?"

"Well, you *are* my favorite sparring partner," he says, grinning now.

"And you're mine." But I'm not done opening up. There's so much more to tell him. "But it took me a while to say how I felt. I was so terrified that romance would never work out and I hate being vulnerable, and I somehow thought keeping all my feelings locked up would be safer. Then when everything blew up, I just shut down," I say, and there's no stopping the train of my emotions now. It's hurtling down the tracks. "And I was so lonely without you last night, and I was so up in my feelings. But now I want to be up in my feelings *with you* because I am so in love with you." I loop my arms tighter around his neck. "Real love, big love, true love. The kind that lasts well beyond all this holiday magic."

He gathers me even closer in his arms. "Good. Because that's what you're getting with me. You're getting this year round."

I could squeal. I could scream in happiness. He is too much. But he is *my* too much. I drop my mouth to his and kiss him hard, clasping his face, stroking his stubble.

Our kiss feels like coming home for the holidays. It feels like extravagant romance. And like true love, which sums up this man.

Only, I can't rely simply on touch to communicate. I need to use words. More words. I break the kiss. "For so long I thought that if I let someone in they'd hurt me.

That's what I saw growing up. That people walk all over you when you let them in." I draw a deep, comforting breath of him—the fading scent of snow and cedar. "But you proved the opposite. You showed me from the start what it's like to be treated..." I pause, wanting to make sure the next thing doesn't sound cocky, but instead self-assured. "The way I deserve."

His smile is warm as he strokes my face. "You deserve the best, Fable."

"And you give your best. All the time." I play with the ends of his hair. "It took me a while to believe it was real. And not just you being your very excellent self."

"I'm not always excellent," he says.

Please. I shoot him a doubtful look. "Want to fight me on that?"

His smile is smug. "I'll win. With my tongue."

I like the sound of that, but I won't let him distract me. "But I thought you were just being great at fake dating. Like when you said we'll be the best fake daters ever."

He laughs softly, and there's a new note in it—a calm, a relaxation, a joy I've only ever seen with Wilder when he's with his daughter. "Want me to let you in on a little secret?" he asks.

"Of course I do."

He tilts his head, gazes at me like I'm precious. "I've had a crush on you for a very long time. When I told you I'd wanted you for more than a year, I meant it. I've been a little obsessed with you," he says, then rolls his eyes. "That's a lie. A lot obsessed. And when I finally had you, you were more incredible than I'd even imagined. And I'd imagined a lot."

My heart goes up in flames. I feel like confetti and champagne. "You really did?"

"I really did."

This man is above and beyond. He is extraordinary in so many ways, including one very important one. I set a hand on his heart. "I'm so proud of you and what you did with your father this morning. That took real guts. Real courage. I want you to know I'm behind you every step of the way."

With a relieved sigh, he gently presses his forehead against mine, then pulls back and says, "When I was talking to him earlier, I thought of you. What you said to me the other morning. That gave me the courage to tell him I wanted him to go to rehab. So I think we make a pretty good team."

My heart swells with hope. "Is he staying for Christmas and then going?"

Wilder shakes his head. "No. I found a program. It's nearby. I'll take him shortly."

My eyes widen. "You already arranged for it?"

But as soon as those words come out, they sound ridiculous. This is Wilder. He arranges things immediately.

"Yes," he answers.

"Do you want me to go with you?"

"I would love that."

And that's how I meet his father—on the way to rehab. We take him to a facility a half hour away, drop him off, and wish him the happiest of holidays. And a second chance.

* * *

When we return to the cabin and head up the steps

together, Wilder shoots me a filthy look, then says, "About that fight."

"Fight me," I taunt.

He scoops me up, tosses me over his shoulder, and carries me down the hall with long, purposeful strides. He kicks open the door to our suite and drops me on the bed. "Now, if my memory serves, you didn't think I'd win this disagreement."

A shudder runs down my body as my very possessive, very generous, very hungry, and very real boyfriend strips off my clothes, spreads my thighs, and says, "I didn't have breakfast. I think I'll eat you instead."

I gasp, then I moan from the feel of his tongue, soft and determined. His mouth covers me, and he sucks and kisses, caressing me. I grab his hair, tug him closer, and rock against him.

He groans, then scoops his hands under my ass, burying his face between my thighs. It doesn't take long at all. Soon, very soon, I'm singing "O Come, All Ye Faithful," and I am feeling very joyful and triumphant.

But I'm also in a giving kind of mood so when I come down from my high, I sit up and then beckon him closer with my fingers. "Strip. It's the only way to get off the naughty list."

"I don't want to get off the naughty list," he says.

"Funny thing. Neither do I."

"Good. Then sit on my dick so I can make you come again."

"But it's my turn to make you come," I point out.

He shoots me a look. "Don't make me prove you wrong."

I smile back, my body aching for him. "Prove it."

My man proves me so very wrong.

And everything with us feels completely right.

53

ALL MY HOLIDATES

Fable

There's no way I'm *not* ruining my makeup during this wedding. Just look at my sister. She's stunning in a tea-length white dress with silver beads on the bodice and a faux-fur bolero jacket.

A tiny tiara is perched on her blonde head and her makeup is sparkly. She holds her bouquet of green succulents from Kiss My Tulips and lets out an excited breath.

That evening, we're standing in an anteroom in a red converted barn on the edge of the property. It's a perfect venue for events and weddings with all this space, a view of the mountains, and plenty of heaters. We've dubbed this room, out of view, *the bridal suite*. "Are you ready?" I ask, but I know the answer.

"So ready," she says, then smiles. "And I'm so glad you worked it out with the best man."

I wave a hand, not wanting to steal her thunder. "It's your wedding day."

With her free hand, she reaches for mine, squeezes it. "And I want you to be happy too. And you are. So there."

I give her a careful hug that's loaded with feeling. "I love you."

"And I love you."

"Let's get you married."

She nods, and as the music begins, I leave the bridal suite and enter the barn that's a winter wonderland, bathed in the warm glow of white lights. The scent of pine wafts through the air from the nearby trees. I walk down the aisle, passing rows of friends and family, unable to tear my gaze from the best man.

Tuxes were made for Wilder Blaine, and he's pure, powerful, handsome perfection in his black tailored tux and bow tie. His green eyes. His wry smile. His faint dusting of stubble.

When I reach the front of the barn where the justice of the peace waits, I take a stand across from Wilder and he looks me up and down in my red dress and mouths, "*Beautiful.*"

The wedding march begins, and all eyes shift to the bride. My sister walks down the aisle, with both of our parents giving her away. It's a compromise, because sometimes that's what you do with family.

I swallow down tears of joy. She's not only having the Christmas Eve wedding of her dreams but she's marrying the man who adores her. A man she loves madly too.

It's everything I could have wanted for her.

When she reaches us and hands me her bouquet, a sense of calm washes over me. That might have something to do with the snow that's falling just beyond the barn entrance and over the hills and through the woods.

I sneak a glance at Wilder and mouth, "*Snow.*"

"My favorite," he mouths back.

Then I turn my focus to the bride and groom as they promise to love and cherish each other, and I swear when Wilder looks at me, I can see forever in his eyes.

It doesn't scare me anymore.

* * *

Later that night after the *I dos* and the dinner and the first dance, the best man pulls me onto the dance floor when "Silver Bells" begins. As the music fills the rafters, I glance around. Bibi's dancing with the sheriff, laughing and probably teasing him. He gazes at her like she's hung the moon. It's not "Blue Christmas," the song she danced to with her husband, but it's a new song for a new memory —a new Christmas to treasure.

They also won Evergreen Falls Annual Best in Snow Winter Games Competition. Once Brady was disqualified, Bibi and her new beau were next in line. The prize? A medal in the shape of a candy cane. Oh, also, a weekend-stay at a certain resort. Bibi said she's looking forward to that, and she's also working on picking her favorite charity for the donation Wilder promised he'd make on behalf of the winner.

Mom's on the dance floor too, swaying with Julio to the music. Max and Everly dance together, and Josie and Wesley too. Maeve came to the wedding solo, but her good friend Asher popped by at the last minute as her plus one. He's a hockey player too, and they're dancing in the corner, and he seems enrapt in whatever she's saying. But then, he always seems enrapt in Maeve.

When we swing past them, I catch the tail end of their conversation.

"So there's this player auction coming up soon, and I can't believe I've been roped into it," he tells her.

"Yes, I know how much you hate it," she says dryly.

"It's the worst when everyone bids on me."

"It'll be so rough when you go for the most money."

"That's not what I'm saying," he says, but he sounds too amused by Maeve.

We dance on, and the rest of their conversation fades into the night.

As for me, I'm caught up in this man who's wearing the Santa cufflinks I made him. As I glance at them, I catch a view of the abstract ink peeking out on his wrists. I've never asked. "What's your ink for?"

He smiles. "Various things."

"Tell me," I demand.

He pulls up the cuffs and shows me a swirling black line. "This is for trust," he says, somewhat solemn. "I got it after college."

"Your dream," I say.

He meets my eyes. "Now my reality."

My heart jumps. "Yes, it is our reality."

He points to another. "This is for family," he says, "I had it done for my mother."

"That's lovely."

And there's still one more—a tiny black cat. "This is for my daughter."

"I love that," I say. "It's so very Mac."

He glances toward his girl, who's giggling with the table of cousins and friends, pointing to the cake table, eager to dig in, I'm sure. "It is." He sighs contentedly. "She really cares for you. She wanted us to be together."

"She knows best."

"She does. She's happy," he says, proudly.

I know that. We told her earlier together that we'd worked it out and she'd pumped a fist and said, "Yes. Can we all do Christmas tomorrow together then?"

We gave her the only answer—*yes*.

I turn my focus back to Wilder as he studies my face. "I'll need to get one for you."

My heart skips ten beats. "You will?"

"Yes."

That's all he says.

A simple yes.

This man. This life. This love. It's so very real. I kiss him chastely, then savor the feel of dancing in his arms as I take in the winter scene. Friends, family, music, snow, and no one here I need to prove a damn thing to.

When I look back at the man in my arms, I say, "You're my favorite holidate."

"I'll be your favorite date every day of the year."

* * *

"Wake up, wake up, wake up! I need to see if my secret door is here."

I groan at the sound of Mac banging on the door. Of course she knows there's no portal, but of course she still pretends to believe a little in magic. As I glance at her father, rustling awake next to me, I suppose I do too.

"We'll be out in fifteen," I call.

"Excellent. I'll make cocoa," she says.

Fifteen minutes later, we're freshened up, teeth brushed, and dressed in our Christmas jammies. We head down the hall and settle onto the couch in front of the tree, where three cups of cocoa await.

I take a sip, and it's perfect.

Wilder—no surprise—has plenty of gifts for Mac under the tree from him, including a new instant camera and that Pegasus series with the sprayed edges.

But he starts with one from both of us and hands it to his daughter.

She rips it open, and her eyes spark with excitement. "A chessboard! Yes. And I want to beat you with this one, Dad," she declares.

"We'll see about that," he teases

She beelines for me and gives me a hug. "And thank you. You can learn to play too. And really, you should. I need lots of opponents so I can become the best."

"Deal," I say, then I point to the gift I picked out yesterday when I sneaked off to shop for Wilder. "Can you hand that one to your dad?"

Under the tree, Mac grabs a round gift and eyes it suspiciously as she carries it to her father.

Wilder rips it open and tosses his head back in laughter as he spins the globe. "It's the one I was looking at in the toy store," he says, seeming too delighted for words as he runs his fingers over the topographic maps.

I am too. "I thought you might like it."

"I love it," he says, then kisses me on the cheek. He picks up a small gift for me in a rectangular box.

I'm giddy as I open it since his gifts are always good. Not because of the cost, but because of the thought behind them. I tear off the silver paper and find a dove gray box. I open it, fold down the tissue paper and gasp. It's a beautiful silver chain with a tiny snow globe charm.

"I had it made for you," he says, hopeful.

It's a tiny replica of Evergreen Falls, with a snowy Main Street scene. "I had it made at Play All Day and put on a chain I'd bought from...well, I ordered it online from Made By Fable."

"You did?" I gasp, but then it hits me. Of course he did. There was an order I received the other week for a single, recycled silver chain. And he added the snow globe. "It's perfect," I say, thrilled with the care he put into it.

"I know you wanted the Golden Gate Bridge, but I thought I'd start with—"

"Stop it! I love it!" I cry, touched by his gesture. "It's the place where we fell in love."

"Let me put it on you."

I turn around and hold up my red hair. He positions the necklace just so, clasping it, then running a finger along my neck. When I let my hair fall, I catch Mac smiling our way, like a Cheshire cat.

"I was right," she says proudly.

"You were," Wilder and I say together.

Together—like how we'll spend the rest of our days and our holidays. And on New Year's Eve, he takes me to that private rooftop dinner and helicopter ride above the city.

A real date, planned by our matchmaker.

EPILOGUE: A NEW SIDE HUSTLE

Fable

The bell above the door to Made By Fable jingles and I say goodnight to the last customer as she leaves the shop a few days before Christmas. Then I flip the sign to closed and turn around. I take a moment to savor the scene, as I've been doing for the last few months since I opened my first shop in Russian Hill on Polk Street, like I'd envisioned. I wanted to do it on my own, and I was able to with enough money saved up to start my first eco boutique. I didn't need a cent from my billionaire boyfriend and I'm proud of that. He gives me so much and it was important I open this shop on my own.

Everything I carry here is recycled and I'm still a little amazed I've pulled this off. But dreams have a way of coming true if you work hard for them. My grand opening in September was a hit, and it's been a busy few months. I stepped down from running merch at the Renegades to focus on the shop and, well, on my fantasy football team.

News flash: I'm winning again.

Tomorrow morning, we're heading to Evergreen Falls for the holidays, so I finish up, then drive home.

It once was Wilder's home but it's become ours. I live with him and Mac now—our little happy family. In the morning, the three of us head up to the little snowy town together.

* * *

A couple days later, we toast to Charlotte and Leo winning the Christmas games on their first anniversary.

On Christmas morning, we're in the main living room in front of the tall tree, opening gifts with Mac, Bibi, and Elizabeth, who moved from London to San Francisco to be closer to family. Wilder's dad is here too and he has his one-year chip. That's the best gift of all.

When the tree is empty and wrapping paper is strewn everywhere, Wilder says, "I have one more thing."

Then my boyfriend gets down on one knee and flips open a sapphire blue velvet box.

I gasp, my heart swelling as he says, "Fable Calloway, you're the woman of my dreams, my favorite date, my one and only. I adore you, and I want to keep treating you like the center of the world because you're the center of my world. Will you marry me?"

Tears well in my eyes—happy ones. "I love you so much. I can't wait to be your wife."

He kisses me and when he breaks the kiss, he slides a brilliant, four-carat diamond solitaire on my finger. As he puts it on, I catch a glimpse of his new ink for me on his forearm. The word *real*.

I gaze at my ring, then kiss the man who's going to be my husband.

We spend the day sledding, and eating, and hosting an impromptu snowball fight, and when everyone's gone to bed, Wilder turns on the tree in the room in our honeymoon suite. As if surprised, he points to a brand-new gift sitting under the tree.

A small, wrapped box.

I already have the kind of gift that comes in a small box so I have no idea what it could be.

"Looks like Santa brought you something else," he says, amused as he picks it up and brings it to me on the couch.

I'm wildly curious. "What is it?"

"Find out."

With excitement pinging in my veins, I tear off the paper and open the red box. Inside there's a piece of paper with the words Deal Memo across the top.

Then, I read the terms.

And my jaw drops. I can't breathe. My hand flies to my mouth. I can't speak for a minute, or many more, until finally I croak out, "You didn't."

He grins, clearly pleased. "I did."

"Wilder," I whisper. "You can't give me your football team."

He's bossy as he says, "I can."

"But why?"

"You once asked me not to buy you a jewelry shop in Russian Hill. And I didn't. You opened it entirely on your own." He pauses, a sly smile forming on his lips. "But I needed to find a workaround in case you want to expand Made By Fable. Open more stores. Take it international.

So I'm giving you this. You can use it to grow Made By Fable. Or you can use it for fun and run a football team. Or you can use it just so you have the best suite in the house to watch games from." Then, like this is no big deal, he adds, "I'm busy with my hotels and green energy businesses. Really, you'd be helping me. Think of it as a side hustle."

"This is my side hustle? Running a football team?"

"Yes. You can do it," he says, steady and certain, believing in me. He's always believed in me.

I take a moment to absorb the scope of this. The magnitude of it. The extravagance. Then, I throw my arms around him and say, "Want to be the owner's date at the next football game?"

"I'd love to."

And I kiss the most generous man in the world, who's mine. All mine.

Binge these couples' spicy romances! All available to download now in KU!

Josie and Wesley's roommates-to-lovers, he-falls-first, teammate's little sister romance: The Boyfriend Goal

Max and Everly's enemies-to-lovers, player and the publicist, forbidden romance: The Romance Line

Rachel and Carter's friends-to-lovers, fake dating sports romance: Plays Well With Others

Maeve and Asher's best friends-to-lovers marriage of convenience romance is **coming in early 2025** in The Proposal Play

For more Fable and Wilder, click here for an extended epilogue or scan the QR code!

Bonus Scene My Favorite Holidate

Turn the page for more fun!

BE A LOVELY

Want to be the first to know of sales, new releases, special deals and giveaways? Sign up for my newsletter today!

Want to be part of a fun, feel-good place to talk about books and romance, and get sneak peeks of covers and advance copies of my books? Be a Lovely!

ACKNOWLEDGMENTS

Thank you to Kayti, Sandra, KP and Editor Lauren for their invaluable contributions during the entire process! Thank you to Kim, Lo, and Rae for helping me fine tune details. Thank you to Rosemary for her refinements! Special shoutout to Rae for tips on bow tying and whipped cream!

I am deeply grateful to my author friends— Corinne, Laura, AL, Natasha, Lili, Laurelin, CD, K, Helena, and Nadia, among others.

Thank you to my family for understanding when I'm lost in the world I'm writing.

Thank you to Samantha Brentmoor and Jason Clarke for your tremendous narration.

Most of all, I am so amazingly grateful to you — the readers — for picking this up! I hope you love Wilder and Fable like I do!

CONTACT

I love hearing from readers! You can find me on TikTok at LaurenBlakelyBooks, Instagram at LaurenBlakelyBooks, Facebook at LaurenBlakelyBooks, or online at Lauren-Blakely.com. You can also email me at laurenblakely books@gmail.com

Made in the USA
Columbia, SC
23 November 2024

47391507R00272